Donnie's appetite had deserted him, but his thirst became unbearable. He went into the kitchen to find a huge glass, and was in the process of filling it with ice and water from the refrigerator's dispenser when he detected the faint temptation of Angelique's perfume. Sure enough, there she was behind him, holding two glasses and waiting for her turn at the water.

He looked at her and could feel his face heating up, although for the life of him he couldn't understand why. He gulped the water rapidly and would have filled the glass again, had Angelique not spoken.

"Adonis, you don't look too happy," she said frankly. "It's not good luck to start the New Year with a bad disposition, you know."

Donnie rolled the cold glass between his palms, trying to cool off the burst of warmth that had encompassed him. He eyed her warily as she set down her two glasses on the cupboard.

"It's not good luck? Well, I sure don't want to have any bad luck." he mumbled. He looked at the water glass in his hand as though it were a relic from an alien civilization. He'd seen one of these before, he just couldn't remember what it was for. Angelique seemd to know, however, as she took it from his hand and set it on the cupboard with the ones she'd just discarded.

"I don't want you to have any bad luck either, Adonis," she said as she came closer to him. "I want you to have a happy New Year." Taking hold of the front of his cashmere sweater, she gently pulled him down to her level and kissed him softly and sweetly.

A Merry LITTLE Christmas

MELANIE SCHUSTER

ARABESQUE

BET BOOKS

BET Publications, LLC
http://www.bet.com
http://www.arabesquebooks.com

ARABESQUE BOOKS are published by

BET Publications, LLC
c/o BET BOOKS
One BET Plaza
1900 W Place NE
Washington, DC 20018-1211

All Kensington Titles, Imprints, and Distributed Lines are available at special quantity discounts for bulk purchases for sales promotions, premiums, fund-raising, and educational or institutional use. Special book excerpts or customized printings can also be created to fit specific needs. For details, write or phone the office of the Kensington special sales manager: Kensington Publishing Corp., 850 Third Avenue, New York, NY 10022, attn: Special Sales Department, Phone: 1-800-221-2647.

BET Books is a trademark of Black Entertainment Television, Inc. ARABESQUE, the ARABESQUE logo, and the BET BOOKS logo are trademarks and registered trademarks.

First Printing: October 2004
10 9 8 7 6 5 4 3 2 1

Printed in the United States of America

Dedication

This is dedicated to Yolanda Jones, a true heroine for our times. Without question, you are the most courageous woman I've ever known. May God continue to bless you.

In memory of Helen Antecki,
a great reader, a great lady, and
a true romantic.

In honor of Ms. NeAsia Symone Hopkins.
Welcome to the world.

Acknowledgments

Thank you to Demetria Lucas, my very patient and creative editor. Your support is invaluable to me.

To Wayne Jordan, a very sincere thanks for my beautiful Web site.

Thank a million to the Women Who Know, a very special group of friends, especially Janice Sims, Brenda Woodbury, Leslie Cannon, Gwen Osborne and Dera Williams. Everyone should be blessed to have friends who make them laugh, make them think, give them support and possess the collective wisdom of the universe!

Thanks also to Betty Dowdell for being a thorough reader and keeping me honest. You see I got them a plane! Thanks for your support.

A special thank you to Craig Mohland—he knows why.

A very special thanks to Dr. Derek Tesoro and the lovely staff of Valley Foot and Ankle for the excellent care and for going the extra mile. Thank you really isn't enough.

And thank you to Toni Colton and Kim Gamet for the medical information.

To Clayton Smith: here's hoping that you'll be home to stay.

To Anthony Howard, a true man of style and substance.

And as always, a very, very special thank you to Jamil, whose support and encouragement can't be measured. Every woman should have someone as wonderful as you in her life. Thank you for always knowing what to say and always being there for me.

Prologue

Angelique Deveraux drove slowly through the familiar streets of her parents' neighborhood in Atlanta. She drove like a little old lady because she was only truly comfortable in her own car, a Saab. But she was very familiar with the area; she knew it like the back of her hand and it felt safe. And she was also taking her own sweet time because she didn't want to go back to her mother's house just yet. Everything there was warm and wonderful with the sounds and smells of Christmas, and Angelique had never felt less like celebrating. She'd have felt awkward in any case—as she was the proverbial black sheep of the Deveraux clan—but the fact that she'd been living in Detroit for six months made her feel even more like a stranger in her own family.

In a family full of tall, beautifully mannered, brilliant sons with magnificent wives, Angelique was the only female and the oddball—the "mean" Deveraux with the nasty temper and few redeeming social graces, and, of course, no husband or children. Her exploits were the stuff of community legend: she'd been known as a holy terror since kindergarten. Being extremely beautiful served only to make her reputation worse; people practically rubbed their hands in glee when recounting the latest scandal in which Angelique was center stage. It didn't matter whether the story had any basis in fact—any juicy tidbit that included her name whipped through Atlanta and its suburbs like a flash flood. There was no way Angelique could have lived down her reputation, even if she'd wanted to. And that was one of the most confounding things about her, at least to those who knew her best. She never attempted to deny any accusation or give her side of any story. When confronted, which wasn't often since most people feared her fiery temper, all she would do is drawl, "So what else would you expect from me?"

The seasonably warm Atlanta weather was bothersome to Angelique. She had gotten accustomed to the cool, brisk weather of Michigan and actually longed for it. Somehow it had felt more Christmasy in Michigan with the periodic snow showers and the cold, windy nights. Now she was home in seventy-degree weather, trying and failing to summon up a shred of Christmas joy. When did it stop being fun and start feeling like a horrid, gaudy farce? She sighed deeply and was about to turn into the long drive of her mother and step-father's home when she noticed a figure some yards past the drive.

There at the foot of the next driveway was Bobby Foster. Bobby, who had Down syndrome, was the adult child of the neighbors. He was wearing a magnificently mismatched outfit of Christmas pajamas and a padded jacket that was buttoned wrong. He also had on a shiny hat that looked like a remnant from a birthday party and he was blissfully leading an imaginary parade with masterful strokes of his makeshift baton, a wooden spoon. Angelique stared at the improbable picture and her throat immediately started to hurt from the huge lump that formed in it. She stopped the car and covered her mouth with her hands, trying to stop the onslaught of hot tears she felt coming.

She was gorgeous, wealthy, spoiled beyond reason and in excellent health, but with all her heart she wished for the carefree joy Bobby had in such abundance. *Snap out of it, cow. Try to think of someone other than yourself for a change,* she chastised herself.

She got out of the car and waved at Bobby. "That's a sporty outfit, kiddo, but I think you should be inside, don't you?"

Bobby's face lit up and he ran over to give her a hug. "Hello, Angel! Come home with me," he said happily. "We have cookies, I helped make them. And you can see what Santa brought me."

"I'd love to, but only if you let me give you a ride," she replied, hugging his soft, sweet body once more. They got into the car and she rolled the car up the driveway to his house, listening to his happy chatter all the way.

At least one of us still believes in Christmas.

Part One

Chapter One

"I still don't like the idea of you being so far away, Angelique. Isn't it time for you to come home permanently?" The voice, full of concern, belonged to Lillian Mercier Deveraux Williams. The expression on her face was also deeply marked by worry. She was sitting in the living room belonging to Angelique's brother Clay while various Deveraux children and a very happy golden Labrador named Patrick were racing around, making the customary noises associated with holiday gatherings.

Angelique was busy clearing the room of any discarded wrappings, toys or anything else that didn't belong there, but upon hearing the genuine longing in her mother's voice, stopped what she was doing. Walking to where her mother was seated in a big art-deco–style armchair, she leaned over and kissed her on the cheek, then sank gracefully onto the matching ottoman.

"Mama, I originally went to Detroit to help A.J. with his documentaries, but I love living there, I really do. It's an exciting place to be. There are so many cultures there, it's amazing. So many different kinds of people and lifestyles and the architecture and the different neighborhoods—it's just so fascinating!" Angelique took one of her mother's hands and squeezed it gently. "And there's actually a lot of interest in my work, too, Mama. The African-American museum is talking to me about having an exhibition, can you imagine? I'm not just a photographer's assistant anymore, I'm a real photographer, hard as that is to believe," she added in satisfaction.

"Well, of course you are, Angel! A.J. knew you had talent from the very beginning, that's why he was so glad to be working with you." The new voice was that of Angelique's newest sister-in-law, Vera Clark Deveraux. She had wandered into the room and curled up on one of the two big leather sofas that faced each other in front of the huge fireplace wall. She was as beautiful as the day she and Marcus Deveraux had met, but she had an extra radiance that came from her recently announced pregnancy. Angelique smiled broadly at Vera before replying.

"Vera, that's very sweet of you, but we both know that isn't quite true. A.J. recognized the importance of his *paycheck* and when he was saddled with me he just made the best of it, that's all. I'd been through every other department at the Deveraux Group, and making me A.J.'s assistant was just one more attempt to find me something to do. Now that's what really happened, my dear sister." Angelique was laughing but no one else joined in.

Vera rubbed her still-small tummy and yawned. "Angel, that sounds dangerously close to you trying to disparage my dear friend, and as I've told you before, I ain't having it. A.J. really did recognize your talent very early on and he loved working with you. Believe me, he'd have thrown you out on your F-stop if he hadn't," she said firmly. "So what if it took you a while to find your forte? You found it, and that's all that matters. Every time I look at those pictures you took for Christmas, I start bawling. They're the most fabulous things I've ever seen."

Angelique blushed with pleasure and mumbled her thanks. She still wasn't comfortable with praise over her work. She had taken pictures of each brother's family and of her mother and stepfather as a Christmas present. The background was off-white and everyone was dressed in casual off-white clothing. Each portrait was a singular work of art, but they were posed in such a way that if all the photographs were displayed together, as they were at her mother's house, it would look like a giant portrait of the whole family. The only person missing was Angelique—something her mother had pointed out.

"Angel, baby, this is a beautiful set, but it's not complete without you. Anyone would think you weren't a member of the family," she'd said indignantly. And she brought the subject up again as soon as Vera mentioned the fantastic pictures.

"Mama, I promise, as soon as I get back to Detroit I'll get A.J. to take a picture of me. I swear I will. Now, see, there's another reason for me to go back to Detroit. You want your set complete, right? Well, this is the only way it will happen. And besides, it's not like I'm all alone up there," she said persuasively. "I've got the best roommate in the world since Paris is still doing her internship at Cochran Communications. I'm never lonely because Renee and Andrew have me over all the time, and Paris and I even go up to Saginaw and see Vera's parents. Mrs. Clark cooks as good as you do, Mama, and she always makes us a feast. I'm doing just fine, I really am," she said, leaning affectionately against her mother. "And you know A.J. would never let anything happen to me."

Lillian made a little noise of grudging assent. She knew her only daughter was perfectly safe in Detroit. Her oldest son, Clay, was married to Benita Cochran, whose family owned Cochran Communications. Benita's family consisted of five brothers, all of whom lived in Detroit and treated Angeique like family. And as for A.J., whose real name was Alan Jandrewski, there was no question that he would protect Angelique to the death. A.J. had been born and raised in the Polish enclave of Detroit known as Hamtramck, son of a Polish steelworker father and an African-American nurse mother. Discovering that he had cancer had been the impetus for

A.J.'s decision to leave fashion photography; upon his recovery, he'd decided to start making documentaries, and took Angelique with him to Michigan to assist with the first one. To everyone's surprise, she took to her new environment like a baby duck to a pond of fresh spring water and decided to stay.

It was ironic that Angelique would find success outside the family business, the Deveraux Group. They owned and operated magazines, weekly and daily newspapers and a cable network, yet Angelique's artistic success had come on her own. Lillian shook her head and sighed. She still wasn't thrilled that her only daughter had so completely left the nest. She opened her mouth to express this thought when the entrance of more relatives to the living room interrupted her.

First to join them was Benita Cochran Deveraux, still radiant after five children. She and her beloved husband, Clay, absolutely thrived on children—both seemed to get more energy after a new arrival. They had a son and two sets of twins; the older twins were rambunctious boys and the younger were two adorable baby girls. Bennie, as Benita was known, agreed with Angelique that she was a welcome guest in any Cochran home. "Lillian, I know you worry about her being so far away, but she's in good hands in Detroit. She's well loved, don't you worry," Bennie said warmly.

Angelique laughed at this last remark from her dearly loved sister-in-law. "Bennie, not all the Cochrans love me, as you well know. Adonis would just as soon drop me in the Detroit River as look at me, and you know it."

Bennie joined in the laughter. It was true, her youngest brother, Adonis, commonly called Donnie, had a volatile history with Angelique. "Oh, you just get to him because you don't fall all over him like most women do. Besides, Daddy is crazy about you and so are the kids," she said confidently, referring to her many nieces and nephews. "Donnie will just have to get over it, that's all."

Marcus, the youngest Deveraux son, joined the group, carrying little Anastasia Angelique Deveraux, his first child and pride and joy. Angelique brightened and rose to take the baby from her brother. "Let me hold her. I don't get to see her that often and we need to bond together."

He handed her over and sat down with Vera, wrapping his arms around her. "How's my bride doing? Is there anything I can do for you, baby?"

"I'm fine, Marcus. All I need is you." Vera smiled. Marcus was always a doting husband, but when his wife was pregnant he went overboard with affection and joy.

The relative quiet of the living room was shattered anew when Ceylon Simmons Deveraux entered with Lillian's husband, Bill "Bump" Williams. After being Ceylon's mentor in the music business for years, Bump had found out that the two were actually father and daughter—something that once had caused Angelique a great deal of jealousy. That was all in the past now.

"There's my girls! Seems to me somebody owes me some sugar," Bump declared as he held his arms out to Angelique and Anastasia. She and the baby each gave Bump sloppy kisses of greeting and enjoyed as he pretended to wipe off their kisses with big swipes of his hands. Angelique nuzzled her niece on her baby-sweet neck and whispered, "Let's get out of here, Stasia. We need some quiet time."

They ended up sitting in Bennie's airy sunroom off her big, well-appointed kitchen, admiring the lush poinsettias and small Christmas tree that brightened the area. Angelique stretched out on the loveseat with little Anastasia on her lap, while Aretha, Bennie's big, black, longhaired cat, posed regally on the windowsill behind the loveseat. Angelique was being a doting aunt and simply drinking in the child's beauty, while the baby was coaxing Aretha down from her perch.

"Weefa, Weefa, come here," she crooned softly. When the stately cat didn't move, Stasia turned her big eyes to her aunt.

"Angel, make Weefa come down," she demanded.

Angelique smiled at the little girl and ran a finger along her incredibly soft skin. "No, sweetie-pie, let's leave Aretha alone. She needs some peace and quiet, too." She cuddled her niece close to her bosom and was rewarded when the child nestled to her shoulder and gave a big yawn. Aretha seemed grateful, too, as she reached out a paw and patted Angelique on the cheek before curling up to go to sleep. Angelique might have also drifted off to sleep, but her cousin Paris Deveraux joined them in the sunroom. Paris had just come back to Atlanta from Lafayette, Louisiana, where she'd spent the holiday with her family. She and Angelique were heading back to Detroit the next day. Paris smiled at the adorable picture they made.

"Aww, you look so pretty!" she exclaimed. "You look just like a Christmas card," she added as she took a seat in a comfortable overstuffed armchair. "I was wondering where you sneaked off to; now I see you just kidnapped your namesake. God, the two of you look so much alike, it's amazing. You would think she was your baby instead of your niece."

Angelique looked down at her little treasure and had to agree that there was a startling resemblance. They both had café au lait complexions, thick, shiny black hair and thick eyebrows and lashes so long they looked false. They also had deep dimples and even shared a tiny beauty mark near the corner of their full, pouty lips. The resemblance was all they shared, as far as Angelique was concerned. There was no way she would ever let this precious little girl turn out like she had. *You're never, ever going to be anything like me, my sweetie. Never in a billion years.* But she didn't say it out loud, knowing how strongly Paris would react. Instead she asked Paris the question that had been on her mind ever since she'd come home to Atlanta for the holidays.

"Paris, remember when Christmas was like the most wonderful thing in the entire world? Remember when it was the most exciting, the happiest time of the entire year? Does it still feel like that to you?"

Paris was slightly taken aback by the utter sincerity with which Angelique spoke. She sighed a little before answering. "Yes, of course I do. I remember when Christmas meant something entirely different than it does now. When the stores didn't start decorating the day after Halloween, when everything was holy and magical at the same time and it was really a season of miracles. And when we still believed in Santa Claus. Of course I remember. No, it's not quite that way anymore. But it still feels nice; you've got to admit that, cousin. Being at home with your family, with all the babies and the excitement, doesn't that makes up for some of it?"

Angelique took her time about answering, rubbing her cheek against her niece's soft, curly hair before speaking. "I don't know, Paris. I don't exactly know when the feeling got away from me, but I just feel kinda numb. I don't feel happy, I don't feel sad, I'm just here, going through the motions," she said softly. "I'm glad to be home and see the family, especially all the kids. I had a lot of fun buying Christmas gifts for them and going to church, but it's just not the same. I just feel empty, Paris, and I don't know why."

Now it was Paris's turn to pause before answering. She had a very good idea of why Angelique was feeling so strange and an equally good idea of what would cure her of her holiday malaise, but now was not the time to bring it up.

Angelique roused Paris from her thoughts. "Can you take the baby for a second so I can get up? She needs to be put down for a real nap and I need to go play with the other kids—I really miss them when I'm away," she admitted.

Forgetting her decision to keep her mouth shut, Paris rose from her chair and took the sleeping child from Angelique, who stood up and held her arms out for the baby. Looking at the charming picture they made, Paris said softly, "You're gonna be a great mommy one day, Angel."

Angelique's response was instant and emphatic. "No, I won't, because I'm never having children. Never! The day I have a baby is the day I start believing in Santa Claus again!"

Anyone else would have been startled at the passion in Angelique's voice, but Paris was more than used to her mercurial cousin. She nodded absently as she followed the young woman and the sleeping baby out of the sunroom. If Paris was reading the signs correctly, there were a great many surprises coming for Angelique in the next few months. Maybe not a baby, but a lot of new things were definitely on the way. There had already been so many changes in her life, she seemed like a different person—something only those very close to her recognized. And since Paris was as close as a sister, she could read the signs better than anyone. *Yes, my dear cousin, next Christmas is going to be very, very different for you. You'll believe in a lot more than Santa Claus, I guarantee it.*

Angelique wasn't the only person suffering from holiday angst. Back in Detroit, Adonis Cochran was sitting in the breakfast room of his brother Andrew's house, looking glum. He'd been moody and withdrawn for most of the holiday, something most unlike him. He was usually even-tempered and extremely pleasant, with a disposition that matched his good looks. All the Cochran men were handsome, well over six feet tall with caramel skin, black wavy hair and beautiful dark eyes with long lashes and thick eyebrows. And even with this bounty of male beauty, Adonis Bennett Cochran was considered to be the best looking of the sons. The sculptured quality of his features lent him an air of distinction that was often embarrassing to him, especially since he was stuck with the name "Adonis." He despised the name and answered only to Donnie.

Andrew's wife, Renee, was in the adjoining kitchen, cooking dinner, and took pity on Donnie. She appeared in the doorway of the breakfast room with a look of concern on her face.

"Donnie, honey, I just hate seeing you like this. Isn't there anything I can do to cheer you up?" she asked.

He grimaced, but had the grace to look ashamed of himself. He shook his head and rose from the table. Walking over to Renee, he embraced her. "Nope, there's not a thing you can do, unless you can talk Aneesah into changing her mind," he said morosely. "I still can't believe she turned me down flat," he added, letting go of Renee and walking over to the huge refrigerator. He opened the door and stared into it as though something new and appetizing had materialized since his last inspection fifteen minutes before.

Renee tasted the contents in her big stockpot and added a bit more basil to the fragrant spaghetti sauce she was making for dinner. She'd heard quite a bit about Donnie's proposal several times during the past few days and thought now was the time to offer some sisterly advice.

"Come and sit down while I make the garlic bread. And stop poking in the refrigerator, we'll be eating in about thirty minutes," she reminded him.

Donnie turned away from the refrigerator with the same hangdog expression and nothing in his hands. He sat down at the tall work island across from Renee and slumped onto the butcher-block top, bracing his head with one hand while he watched her mix pressed garlic, oregano and basil into a bowl of softened butter. His mood had been the same since a few days before Christmas, when his college sweetheart, Aneesah Shabazz, turned down his proposal of marriage. He was about to bemoan his fate again when Renee surprised him by making a few points.

"Honey, let's talk about this. I know you and Aneesah were quite close for a long time, but your relationship basically ended when she went to graduate school in California. You became friends, not boyfriend and girlfriend, remember? And after she got both those master's degrees and her Ph.D., she decided to move back to Michigan, but it wasn't like she was moving back just to be with you. Now, I know you two have been dating again, but frankly, I was surprised when you announced you were going to propose to her. And I think she was just as surprised when you presented her with that ring. Well, actually I *know* she was, since she turned you down. I know it hurt your feelings, sweetie, but the thing is," she paused as she gave the now-fragrant garlic butter a final stir, "I don't think it really broke your heart." Giving him a loving look, she began to spread the butter on the big loaves of dense Italian bread she'd sliced earlier.

Donnie made a halfhearted attempt to steal a piece of the bread and was rebuffed. He continued to look glum for a moment and then spoke.

"Now you sound like Aneesah," he admitted. "It was kind of a shock to her, I guess, because she looked pretty stunned when I whipped out the ring. Maybe I should have waited a while, given her a chance to get used to us being together again. Maybe I should have waited for her to get more settled into her new job, I don't know. I just didn't see the point in waiting around forever, Renee. It's time that I was married, that I started a family."

"Everybody's married except me and Adam," he continued. "And who knows when or if Adam will ever tie the knot." He scratched the nape of his neck and brooded about the fact that he and Adam, his older brother, were the only two Cochrans still single.

Renee finished with the loaves of bread and wrapped them neatly in foil to prepare them for the oven. "Getting married because your siblings are married doesn't sound like a reason to propose, Donnie. There's got to be more to it than that," she said gently.

Donnie nodded in agreement, but defended his position. "Look, Renee, I feel like I'm *ready* to get married. As far as business is concerned, things couldn't be going better. The stations are thriving; the merger with the Deveraux Group is paying off beautifully. I'm working on some more creative outlets for Cochran Communications that look really promising. But my life can't be all about business. I want what you and Andrew have, what Bennie and Clay have, what everyone around me seems to have in abundance. I want a real home and a real family with a loving wife and kids and I want it before I'm ninety. I don't think that's asking too much, do you?"

Renee regarded her brother-in-law with amazement.

"Donnie, I've never heard you talk like this before. You've been so busy dating all those beautiful ladies of yours, it never occurred to me that you were thinking seriously about matrimony. Or did you just start thinking about it when Aneesah moved back to Detroit?"

Donnie looked reflective for a moment, then acknowledged that he really wasn't sure. "All I know is Aneesah is the kind of woman I want to marry. She's brilliant, educated, accomplished and beautiful," he said, ticking off the points on his fingers. "And she's the right size, which you know is a non-negotiable requirement," he added with a laugh.

Renee made a sound of reproach but Donnie was unrepentant. He had a weakness for big, beautiful women and he made no secret of the fact that a full-figured woman was the only kind who could catch his eye. He'd never been known to date anyone who wore less than a size eighteen, and Aneesah, who was five-nine and curvy, more than fulfilled his wishes in that respect. But, as Renee was glad to inform him, those attributes weren't enough on which to build a lasting future.

"Well, I see you've given this some thought," she said ironically. "However, checking off a laundry list isn't exactly the way to begin a relationship, much less a marriage. Just because you feel like you're compatible with someone doesn't mean the two of you are destined to be together. There has to be something more, you know."

Donnie scowled and opened the refrigerator again. He was about to defend his impulsive behavior when the back door opened and a horde of little girls poured in. It wasn't a true horde—merely his four nieces—followed by their father, his oldest brother, Andrew. After shouting greetings to their mother, the little girls made a beeline for their uncle, who soon found himself in a tangle of arms, legs, cold cheeks, and wet kisses. Donnie, who was quite adept at removing coats and hats and scarves, made himself useful by getting his nieces out of their outdoor gear. They had been visiting relatives with their father and were quite animated as they told him about their day.

"We saw Granddaddy and Grandmommy, Uncle Donnie. And we saw our cousins, too," reported little Andie. Andie was short for Andrea, and she was a mirror image of her mother, with velvety chocolate skin and big golden eyes. The triplets, Benita, Ceylon and Stephanie, whose chatter was punctuated by the barks of Renee's little dogs, Patti and Chaka, made additional comments. Donnie was buried under a pile of little girls, all talking and hugging for all they were worth. He adored his nieces and reveled in their attention, but tonight their presence only served to underscore the unsettled feeling he'd been battling. He could see into the kitchen from his vantage point in the breakfast room and what he saw didn't help his mood one bit. Even after several years of marriage, Andrew and Renee were in the warm, fragrant kitchen kissing and flirting like teenagers. Their love surrounded them like a halo of light, shining so brightly that only a fool could have missed the fact that they were totally in love with each other. Their closeness only underscored his odd mood, and he was more than glad when Renee announced it was time to wash up for dinner.

Renee's excellent meal helped restore Donnie's usual good spirits. Like all the Cochran men, he loved to eat and, luckily for him, all his brothers had married fine cooks who never minded an extra person at the table. His stepmother, Martha, was of the same school and it was perfectly possible for Donnie to have a home-cooked meal every night of the week if he so chose. He tried not to overstay his welcome in any one place, but he thoroughly enjoyed dining with his family members—like this evening. His nieces were being taught nice manners by their parents and it was a pleasure to share a meal with them. By the time the table was cleared and everyone had been served dessert, he was so mellow, nothing could have disturbed his mood. Nothing except for an innocent remark by little Andie.

"Guess what, Uncle Donnie? Auntie Angel is coming back tomorrow. Isn't that good?"

Donnie tried not to let his dismay show on his face, but it was difficult, to say the least. Andrew, who could easily read his brother's mind, immediately picked up on the remark.

"That really *is* good news, sweetie. We sure will be glad to see her, won't we?" he asked innocently.

Donnie's face went through several contortions in an effort to maintain a neutral expression. He knew what Andrew was up to and he wasn't falling for it this time. He looked at the sweet little faces of his nieces, waiting for his answer, and gamely managed a smile. "Yeah, that's great. Auntie Paris and Auntie Angel are coming back tomorrow. That's really nice," he said with a clenched jaw.

Refusing to let Andrew get the best of him, he looked across the table at his tormentor. "I guess I'll go pick them up from the airport," he said, the glint in his eyes at odds with the helpful statement.

"Oh, that's not necessary," Renee said absently as she dabbed at little Stephanie's mouth. "I talked to Angelique last night and A.J. is going to pick them up. It's all taken care of."

If someone had offered him a large sum of money, Adonis couldn't have explained why he suddenly felt left out. No one was a bigger pain than Angelique and there was no one he wanted to avoid more. So why was he suddenly feeling weird about not picking her up from the airport? Why was he even thinking about her at all? What he needed to be doing was going home and taking his dogs out for a run and trying to rid his mind of clutter. And after clearing the dishes and loading the dishwasher for Renee, that's exactly what he did.

Chapter Two

As happy as she had been to see her family, Angelique admitted to herself that she was relieved to be back home. And yes, she did consider Detroit to be home now. She and Paris emerged from the Deveraux Group's private jet at Detroit Metro Airport to find Alan Jandrewski waiting for them. A.J. was not only Angelique's mentor and inspiration, he was one of her closest friends. Her face lit up when she saw A.J.'s tall, lean body walking toward them. She ran to him and threw her arms around his neck for the big hug she knew awaited her.

"Welcome home, Angel. How was your holiday?" he asked after a long, satisfying embrace.

"It was wonderful, how was yours? Did your mom make chitlin pierogies?" she teased.

A.J. laughed along with Angelique as Paris caught up with the two of them. A.J. often made jokes about how his African-American heritage blended with his Polish-American heritage in strange and wonderful ways.

"No, she didn't put chitlins in the pierogies this time, but I'll bet we were the only ones in the neighborhood with Czarina soup and collard greens in the same meal," he said cheerfully.

Paris didn't completely get the joke. "Now, what are pierogies again?" she asked.

"They're these little dumplings that have a filling in them, either meat or potato or cheese, and they're really good," Angelique answered before A.J. could respond. "And Czarina soup is made with duck blood. It's delicious."

While Paris tried to stifle her reaction to the soup description, Angelique hugged A.J. again. "Did your parents like their present?" she asked shyly.

A.J. smiled down at Angelique and put an arm around her shoulders. Kissing her on the cheek, he assured her they had loved the photograph she'd given them. It was a shot she had taken of A.J. the summer before when they were in Africa. It seemed to sum up everything there was to know about him: in the shot, he was leaning against the mud-spattered jeep that had been their transportation through the remote villages they'd visited. He'd been wearing a ratty T-shirt, baggy khaki shorts and hiking boots, and, as always, had an expensive camera around his neck and a light meter in his hand. Angelique had captured the rakish essence of him with the radiant smile that showed off his perfect white teeth, the cleft in his chin, the golden warmth of his skin and the genuine happiness in his dark, long-lashed eyes. Even after the surgery to remove the tumor that had invaded his brain, and the grueling radiation and chemotherapy that had followed, A.J. was an incredibly handsome man.

After the usual delay in getting the myriad suitcases and bags into A.J.'s Range Rover, the trio was at last on their way to the duplex Paris and Angelique shared. It was near Indian Village, one of several big brick houses owned by Andrew and Renee. Before his marriage to Renee, buying and remodeling older houses had been Andrew's chief hobby; now he kept them for investments. After his marriage, his main occupation—other than his medical practice in reconstructive surgery—was doting on his wife and children. The house Paris and Angelique now occupied had been Andrew's last residence before marrying Renee. It was typical of the houses of that era, with hardwood floors, ornate woodwork and large, beautifully proportioned rooms. The baby grand piano that was once the center of the living room was gone now, but the rooms were still attractive and welcoming to the eye.

Angelique was the one in charge of decorating; she had a flair for combining colors and finding unusual objects that made the rooms lively and inviting. She had chosen a warm color palette, with a golden apricot glaze on the heavy plaster walls. The deco-style sofa, which she'd found at a resale shop, was an unusual shade of citron with bright pillows in hot pink, red and orange. The tall windows had bamboo blinds and colorful curtains made of Indian bedspreads from Pier 1 Imports, one of her favorite stores. The coffee table and the end tables were authentic Danish modern, circa the 1960s, and had come from the Salvation Army. After a long weekend with both women working very hard, they now looked brand-new, gleaming with polish. There also was a beautiful shelving unit that housed Paris's colorful collection of ceramic water pitchers and teapots in fanciful shapes.

The armchairs came from IKEA, and the cushions were covered in geometric prints that echoed the colors of the throw pillows. The big rug in the middle of the room also combined the warm colors in stripes; the rug was typical Angelique—she'd found colorful, handmade cotton rag rugs at Target and sewn them together by hand to yield a big, bright accent that pulled the room together beautifully. Anyone who came into the room would think a professional had decorated it, but it was just Angelique's creativity at work. Although, as A.J. frequently reminded her, she *was* an artist and a professional. Further evidence of this was present in the big, happy abstract painting over the fireplace, and the photographs displayed; all were Angelique's work.

The total effect was charming as well as relaxing, as attested to by Paris and A.J., who lounged comfortably while

Angelique hauled bags and suitcases upstairs. On one of her forays through the living room, A.J. grabbed her arm and pulled her down on the sofa beside him.

"Can you chill for a minute?" he said playfully. "You've been racing around here like a madwoman. Those suitcases aren't going anywhere; sit a while and talk to us."

Paris eyed her active cousin with a smile. "Please make her be still for a minute, A.J.! She has way too much energy—that's why she never gains a pound."

"And she's compulsively neat, besides. The whole time we were traveling, our tent always looked like a Martha Stewart layout." A.J. gave Angelique a one-armed hug and grabbed her hand to prevent her from hitting him with a throw pillow.

"I'm not compulsive," she defended herself. "But I have to be organized, you know that. And it was really nice being home and seeing all my babies again. How was your Christmas?" she asked, deftly switching the focus of the conversation.

They chatted for a while and made plans for dinner and salsa dancing later in the week, and then both women walked A.J. to the door. After he left, Paris turned around and leaned on the heavy oak door. Heaving a deep, theatrical sigh, she closed her eyes and moaned.

"Dang, dang, *dang* that man is fine! I mean he is *phoine!*" She gave the word the "sistah girl" pronunciation. "Girl, are you sure you two are just friends? Don't you want to just tear his clothes off and have your way with him?" When she realized her cousin wasn't hanging around for the inquisition, she followed her into the kitchen. Finding Angelique in the process of getting out cleaning materials for the microscopic amount of dust that had accumulated while they were away, she repeated the question, this time demanding an answer.

Angelique laughed the way she always did when Paris brought up the subject. "Paris, A.J. is my friend. He's like a brother to me and, no, we don't secretly have the hots for each other. I used to have a crush on him a long time ago, but he's been so good to me, and taught me so much, that the crush just went its own way. I do love him, I love him a lot, but I'm not *in* love with him," she said honestly. "He really is good-looking, I'll grant you that. But believe it or not, as handsome as he is on the outside, the inside is ten times as beautiful."

She looked pensive for a moment, and then issued a soft sigh of her own. "Besides, he thinks he's too old for me. Just because he's forty, he thinks I'm too young!"

Paris's matchmaking instincts, never far from the surface, surged to the fore. "So it's an age thing," she mused, twirling a strand of her thick hair around her finger. "Well, all we have to do is show him that age is nothing but a number and you'll be on your way."

Angelique held up her hand and pointed a spray bottle of Windex at her dearly loved cousin. "Paris, don't even think about it," she said evenly. "A.J. is my best friend and nothing else. I don't want to change that; we're both very happy with our relationship the way it is, thank you very much. And if you're so geeked up about matching folks up, why don't you do something about your own crush?" The pink flush on Paris's cheeks let Angelique know she'd made her point. With a mischievous smile, Angelique sauntered off to dust and polish the living room furniture.

Once the heat in her face had subsided, Paris followed her into the living room. She sat down in one of the armchairs and curled up her legs. "Um, what do you mean, my 'crush'? What makes you think I have a crush on someone?" she asked in what she hoped was a nonchalant manner.

"Paris, please. Does the name Titus Argonne ring any bells with you? You and I both know you have a thing for the man, not that I blame you. But do you do anything about it, like try to talk to him? No, you jump and run like a scared rabbit every time you see him, don't you?"

This time the flush surged up Paris's neck like a wildfire and she turned as bright as one of the pillows. It was true: she was mightily attracted to Titus Argonne, a friend of Angelique's brother Martin. She'd met him on several occasions and for some reason her ability to speak deserted her whenever he was around.

"Okay, okay, you win. You're right, I have no right getting all up in your business when I can't handle my own," she admitted. "I have no idea why I get so tongue-tied around that man, but so help me, I turn into a stammering nitwit every time he's in the room."

Angelique gave a final buffing to the coffee table and replaced the decorative object that adorned it. "Well, we're just going to have to work on that, aren't we? You'd like him even more if you ever talked to him—he's very smart, he has a good personality and he's a good conversationalist. He's not boring at all and he's not a lech, either. You'd probably make a nice couple," she finished.

Paris brightened considerably when Angelique finished speaking. "Well, now, that sounds pretty promising, actually. I think I'll put him on my list of New Year's resolutions," she said thoughtfully. Paris had an ingrained habit of making a list of resolutions each January. "In fact, let's both resolve that we're going to have real boyfriends in the New Year. Tall, handsome and rich, if possible. Let's put our order in now, there's only a few more days left in this year."

Angelique gathered up the cleaning supplies and headed for the dining room to divest it of dust. "You make all the resolutions you want, sweetie, but leave me out of it. A boyfriend is the last thing I need or want in this life. No, thank you. But if you fix us something to eat, I'll unpack for you. No resolution needed. How's that?"

Paris was so taken aback by her cousin's emphatic rejection of a man in her life, she simply nodded. Slowly rising to her feet, she made a silent vow to find out why Angelique was so opposed to being part of a couple. *Everybody needs somebody, cuz, and that includes you.*

The last person Donnie expected or hoped to see was inexplicably standing at his brother's door. Donnie was nursing his still-hurt feelings over Aneesah's rejection at his brother Adam's loft when the chimes that substituted for a doorbell rang. Telling Adam that he would get the door, Donnie crossed the vast open area that served as a living room and looked out the peephole of the huge double door. *Aww, dang, what's she doing here?* was Donnie's first thought. He opened the door a crack and said in a high-pitched voice, "My daddy said go away, I can't have any company."

Angelique burst out laughing and replied, "Well, it's a good thing I'm not here to see you, isn't it? Open the door, Adonis, I'm in a hurry."

By now Jordan and Pippen, Donnie's golden Labradors who accompanied him almost everywhere, had detected Angelique's presence and were barking frantically for her to gain access. Sighing in defeat, he finally opened the door.

Angelique ignored him and turned all her attention to the two pretty dogs leaping around her in joy. It galled Donnie to no end that his dogs, his pets and companions, found this irritating woman irresistible. It made him think back to the first time they had encountered her. Back when she'd first moved to Detroit, she was staying in the garage apartment behind Andrew and Renee's house while she secured a more permanent place for herself and Paris. The apartment was known as the Outhouse and served as a guest cottage from time to time. It was a rainy evening in late spring and Donnie had left the dogs on the back porch of the house as their feet were good and muddy from running through every puddle they could find. Renee had no sooner reminded him that their feet needed to be cleaned when a loud shriek sounded from the back.

He had dashed into the kitchen and pulled open the back door to find Angelique with big muddy footprints all over her chic raincoat. Her chic *parchment-colored* raincoat, which showed off the mud really well. He braced himself for the screaming and epithets that were sure to follow, and was totally stunned by what was taking place. Instead of pitching a side-door fit, Angelique was kneeling down and giggling like a little girl as Jordan and Pippen gave her wet sloppy kisses and generally showed her the kind of affection they normally gave only their master. And the love affair continued to this day; as usual, the two dogs were all over her with yelps of happiness. He took a moment to give her a good once-over while she was ignoring him.

Despite not being his type at all, she was darned cute. No, not cute, *beautiful,* in the fresh, natural way of Halle Berry. Her hair was a lot longer than it used to be; it came nearly to her shoulders in a blunt-cut style. Her bangs, which made a lot of women look silly, looked adorable on her pretty face. She was too short, only about five-seven, and way too skinny; she was as slender as a ballerina. But still, there was something sexy and appealing about her, even though he didn't like her one bit. She was wearing a classic navy pea coat, impeccably pressed jeans and a red turtleneck sweater—and managed to look like she had just strolled off a runway. Even after the dogs had jumped and slobbered all over her, she didn't have a speck of their golden hair anywhere. For some reason, this small observation contributed to his irritation and it came out in his question to her.

"What are you doing here?" he asked without a hint of warmth. Before he could register his quick shame at being so abrupt, she responded.

"Hello, Adonis. Happy holidays to you, too. I'm delivering something to Adam from Benita, if that's all right with you," she said evenly.

Just then, Adam emerged from the work area of the loft with a welcoming smile on his face. "Hello, Angel! Benita told me she'd loaded you down with stuff—thanks for bringing it by. Come on in and get warm, my brother has apparently forgotten his manners entirely," he said with a sidelong look at his sibling.

Angelique took the hand Adam offered and entered the big loft. In her other hand was a big, colorful shopping bag that she handed to him. "Here you go. And this is for you, too," she said as she stood on tiptoe to give Adam a big kiss on the cheek. "Bennie said to make sure to give you a kiss from her and the babies."

Adam smiled wickedly and returned the kiss with enjoyment. While Donnie might be considered the most handsome of the Cochran men, it was usually conceded that Adam was the sexiest. He was broad-shouldered, well muscled and wore his wavy hair long in a thick braid down his back. With his piercing eyes and thick, glossy mustache, he was pretty irresistible. And charming as well—when he chose to be, as he did now. "You really are an angel, Angelique. Thanks for taking the time to bring this over. Come sit down and let me fix you some tea or some hot chocolate or something," he coaxed, pulling her farther into the big open space that led into a restaurant-quality kitchen.

"Oh, I can't stay," she demurred, "I have to go by your dad's house, and the twins . . . umm, did you say hot chocolate?" A thick, rich cup of hot cocoa was a weakness of hers and the longing on her face made it plain that she wanted some.

Adam sensed her desire and gleefully divested her of her jacket. Tossing it at Donnie, he ordered him to hang it up. "Now you come with me, cutie, and I'm going to make you the best cup of *chocolat* you ever consumed in your life."

The two of them went off to the kitchen, leaving Donnie standing in the entrance area with Angelique's jacket in his hand and a vacant look on his face. Like an automaton, he drew the thick wool garment to his nose and inhaled deeply. The rich essence of her fragrance cut through him like a knife. His entire body reacted quickly and passionately to this stimulus, much to his dismay. For some unknown reason, he felt a stirring in parts of his body that should have known better and he didn't like it one bit. After taking one more forbidden whiff of the coat, he hung it neatly in the closet and then scowled at the slight tremor that surged through him. Wasn't anything going to cooperate with him? Glaring at the zipper in the front of his pants, he whispered, "Cut that out. We don't like her, remember?"

Praying that his body wouldn't continue to betray him, he

went into the kitchen to see what witchery Angelique was up to now. Sure enough, she sat on a stool at the long work counter with Jordan and Pippen lolling at her feet and Adam making a huge show of concocting some kind of hot-chocolate confection from scratch. None of this should have bothered Donnie in the least, but for some reason it was eating him up. That little woman had gotten under his skin from the first moment they'd met, and things showed no signs of improving. The most annoying part of the whole situation was that she seemed to be completely unaware of him. He could have been one of the pots Adam had hanging from the ceiling, for all the attention she paid him. Something was definitely wrong with this scenario, and he was going to fix it and quick. He wasn't much for New Year's resolutions, but he was making one this year. Angelique was a thorn and he was getting her getting out of his side and soon.

Donnie would have been stunned to know that he was causing Angelique as much discomfort as he was suffering. Despite her appearance of nonchalance, she was more than aware of Donnie, and this awareness made her feel unsettled and uneasy more often than she liked. She tried not to think about him at all, but since her brother Clay was married to his sister Bennie, it wasn't as if she could ignore his existence altogether. Besides the marriage and babies that bound the families together, the Cochrans and the Deverauxes were now in business together.

With the merger of the companies, the two clans were inextricably tied to each other for all time. It was inevitable that she and Donnie would meet regularly. And try as she might to act with total indifference, it was difficult. Adonis Bennett Cochran was not a man who could be overlooked. For one thing, he was tall, more than six-six, yet the height alone wasn't what did it—all of Angelique's brothers were extremely blessed in the height department, too. He was also physically blessed, like her handsome brothers, even a sightless person would have recognized the fact that he had exceptional looks.

Angelique pulled into her home's shared driveway. She'd been listening to one of her many audio books as she drove, but had been daydreaming more than listening. Ever since encountering Donnie at his brother's loft, she'd been thinking about him. She tried to tell herself he just reminded her of her brothers: tall, handsome and charming. But even more than that, he was very smart and savvy when it came to business. He was recognized as a genius in broadcasting and had taken his family's string of small urban radio stations and parlayed them into a network that now spanned the country. And he'd added television stations, as well. Brilliant, bold and innovative—those were the words usually used to describe him, and that was why he reminded her of her brothers. But the things causing her mind to go into overdrive were the characteristics that didn't excite a brotherly reaction in the least.

As she got out of the car and took a deep lungful of the cold, crisp evening air, she had to smile when she thought about Donnie's legendary charm—although *charming* was a relative term, since Donnie was a perfect gentleman to everyone but her. He was extremely kind and perfectly mannered to all he encountered, but rubbed her the wrong way and had since the first day they met. They fought and argued and generally treated each other with the gentility reserved for known terrorists. It was bad enough when she lived in Atlanta and only saw him a couple times a year; now that she was on his turf, they seemed to trip over each other. She reached the back door and used her key to open it, finding the kitchen warm and bright with the smells of dinner all around her. She closed her eyes and sniffed as she took off her coat. Paris, bless her heart, was making dinner, and whatever it was would be divine. She walked through the house to hang up her coat in the closet, calling Paris as she did so.

"Hey, girl, I'm home! What are you cooking? It smells wonderful."

Paris ran lightly down the stairs and dashed into the kitchen to give the pot a stir. "Thanks for the compliment, cos, but I can't take credit for this, it's your recipe. I made that white-bean chili everyone loves so much, and some jalapeño corn-bread muffins and fruit salad. Very filling, full of fiber, and low-fat," she said.

Paris was, like all the Deverauxes, tall and good-looking, but she was very conscious of everything she ate. She'd battled a weight problem all her life and had managed, in the past few years, to lose weight through careful eating and lots of exercise. Her friend Aidan Sinclair, who lived in Atlanta and also worked for TDG—as the Deveraux Group was commonly known—liked to take credit for her transformation as he'd forced her to diet and work out with him. Regardless of who was responsible, there was no denying that Paris was a changed person. She was five-ten and fair-skinned with long, wavy black hair she no longer kept in a ponytail twenty-four–seven, but wore in a becomingly layered style. Her figure was still bountiful, but she was a firm size sixteen instead of a fluffy size twenty, and she now wore trim, fitted clothes instead of the baggy things she once used to camouflage her figure faults. Tonight she was wearing a comfortable-looking outfit of cotton cashmere in a pretty coral color. The knit pants fit properly and the scoop-necked top showed off her collar-bone as well as the dramatic line of her shoulders.

Paris turned off the burner under the chili and said they could eat in five minutes if Angelique would set the table. "Where've you been all afternoon? I thought about calling you on your cell phone, but I figured you were busy with A.J. or something," she said.

Angelique sighed as she dried her hands on a paper towel. Turning to the cupboard, she got down the colorful Fiestaware that had been a housewarming gift from Vera and Marcus. "I was delivering those packages for Bennie. I went to see Renee and Andrew, and Andre and Alan, and Mr. C and Miss Martha," she recited. "Mr. C" was how she referred to Big Bennie Cochran, the patriarch of the family and father to Benita and her brothers. Miss Martha was his wife, the woman he'd married so many years after his first wife, the mother of his children, had passed away.

Working quickly, Angelique set two places with plates, soup bowls, bread plates, water goblets and silverware and turned back to the cupboard to get footed dessert dishes for the fruit salad. Casually she added, "I also went to Adam's loft, and he had company. Adonis was there."

Paris stopped in the middle of serving the piping-hot chili. "Uh-oh. Did y'all get into it?" she asked with a smile.

Angelique finished the table settings with big, soft cotton napkins and took a pitcher of Crystal Light peach-flavored iced tea out of the refrigerator; both she and Paris were addicted to the beverage. Taking a seat, she shook her head no. "Actually, he was pretty well behaved today."

The two women reached out and took each other's hands and said grace, as was their habit. Then Angelique placed her napkin in her lap and daintily dug into the aromatic and very tasty chili. Paris followed suit, but she couldn't leave well enough alone. She had to go there again, just to satisfy her curiosity.

"You know, y'all don't fight nearly as much as you used to. What happened? Did you declare a truce or something?"

Angelique took her time answering as she had just taken a mouthful of a flavorful muffin. "Mmm, that's delicious! A truce? No, I don't think we declared a truce, exactly, but ever since he took me to the dentist, it's been awfully hard to be mean to him. He was too nice to me that day," she said reflectively.

Paris smiled broadly. "So does that mean you won't call him Spongebob anymore?"

"Oh, no, girl. As long as he calls me Evilene, he's gonna be SpongeBob SquarePants. But that doesn't negate the fact that he was really nice to me when I needed him."

Paris thought back to that fateful day and had to agree that Donnie has come through like a champ. Angelique was never one to complain about physical ailments—in fact, she was something of a Spartan when it came to matters of health. She was rarely ill, and when she did get a touch of something, she'd soldier on until it was over. However, what had started as a mild headache had worked its way into horrifying proportions that left Angelique almost delirious with pain. In her usual fashion, she hadn't mentioned the pain to anyone, just tried her best to cope with it. Paris finally found her curled up on her bed, sobbing like a child. This alone alarmed Paris, as she'd never seen her cousin in tears before, but the fact that her right cheek was also swollen to three times its normal size was terrifying.

Angelique obviously had an infection or abscess of some kind and needed immediate attention, so Paris had called the first person she could think of, Renee, and luckily Donnie answered the phone. Almost before she'd hung up the phone, he was at their place. He had a good friend who was an endodontist and was able to work Angelique in as an emergency. The only problem was that Angelique was terrified of dentists and refused to go.

To Paris's utter amazement and permanent gratitude, Donnie had taken Angelique onto his lap like one of his nieces and held her tightly, assuring her that his friend wouldn't hurt her, and would take her pain away. "Evie, sweetheart, I can look at you and see how much pain you're in. That cute little face is all swollen and I know you must feel like crap. C'mon, Evie, let's go make it better, okay?" After those soothing words, Angelique did indeed let him take her to the endodontist, and Donnie even stayed with her during the whole process. Paris suspected that he'd held her hand the entire time. After that incident Angelique and Donnie just didn't seem to argue as much, not even when he called her Evie, a diminutive of Evilene, the name he'd called her for years when he wanted to push her buttons.

Paris observed her cousin while she slowly sipped her iced tea. Carefully setting her glass down, she decided to wade in with both feet. "So, have you ever thought about dating Donnie? I think he'd be fun to go out with," she said innocently.

Only a slight redness along her cheekbones betrayed the emotions Angelique was feeling. With admirable restraint, she merely said, "No. Not my type, actually."

Paris opened her mouth to probe further, but a slight tightening of Angelique's jaw told her this was dangerous ground. Just then the phone rang, and with a look of pure relief Angelique dashed to answer it. Paris sighed and speared another chunk of pineapple from the remains of her fruit salad. *Okay, "not my type,"* she thought. *Whatever you say, cuz. Whatever you say.* Then she laughed, knowing that if Aidan were present, he'd give her a good whack on the back of her head and warn her not to do what she was thinking about doing. Not that it would have stopped her. Not in the least.

Chapter Three

While preparing to make dinner in his well-equipped kitchen, Adam was taking great pleasure in raking his younger brother over the coals. He was amused at Donnie's current angst and to some small degree he sympathized with it, but wasn't about to let him get away with his behavior.

"Adonis, what is wrong with you? Why were you so rude to Angelique? You were acting like she turned you down instead of Aneesah. What's your problem?" he asked bluntly.

Donnie frowned at Adam and took another swallow from his bottle of mineral water. "Okay, look—I admit I was less than cordial to Evilene, but that's how we communicate. It's just how we get down," he mumbled.

Adam shook his head as he assembled ingredients on the counter. "Don't you think it's a little childish, Donnie? I can't believe my brother talks to a woman like that," he said disapprovingly.

"Aww, man, Evie doesn't trip over it, why does it bother you? She likes to play and she can take it. She can also dish it out," he said with a short laugh. His mind automatically drifted back to another incident that had occurred shortly after she came to Detroit. Donnie hadn't liked the idea of Angelique staying in the Outhouse and made his position plain. Even now he felt a little warmth in his face when he recalled the things he'd said.

Angelique had been playing with his nieces in another part of the house while he'd been venting to Renee. "I just think you're asking for trouble having her here, Renee. Let her stay in a hotel or something—you don't need her underfoot. And you don't need to be waiting hand and foot on the little princess, either."

Renee had been busy folding laundry and barely looked up from her task. "Donnie, I don't know why you're behaving like this. Angelique may have been a handful at one time, but she's turned into a very nice young woman, which you might realize if you'd stop to take a look. Besides, she's wonderful with the girls; they adore her. And for your information, she's a big help to me."

Donnie cringed now as he remembered his next words. Even after months had passed, he was still embarrassed by what he'd said. "That just goes to show you, children don't know any better. That woman is a waste of skin. There isn't one redeemable feature about her, Renee." No sooner had he finished speaking than there was a soft gasp behind him. He'd turned to find Angelique standing there with a stricken look on her face, and felt himself shrivel up inside as he watched her cover her mouth with a slender hand. Before he could say a word, she had dashed out the back door, leaving him alone with Renee, who was glaring at him as though he were the worst scum on earth,

He'd immediately taken off after Angelique to apologize, when he suddenly had the breath knocked out of him—Angelique had leaped on his back and grabbed his ears to use as reins.

"A waste of skin, huh? I got your waste of skin right here, you overgrown tree! You thought I was out here crying, didn't you? Well, I got news for you, buddy, I don't shed tears, I *cause* them!" And to Donnie's utter amazement, they ended up wrestling like children and chasing each other around the backyard to the consternation of Renee and the delight of his nieces, who thought it was some sort of game.

Donnie laughed out loud at the memory. That was one of the things he had to admire about Angelique: she was tough and more than capable of taking care of herself, and also had a surprising sense of humor. They had actually started having a little fun with their adversarial relationship after that. And he had apologized for the incident all the same—an apology she accepted with no comment.

Adam looked over his shoulder at his brother, who was lost in thought. "I still think you need to watch how you talk to Angelique. You wouldn't like it if someone talked to Benita like that," he pointed out.

Donnie's thick eyebrows drew together at the mention of his sister's name; his protective instincts leaped to the fore immediately. Donnie was, like all Cochran men, territorial and almost paternalistic when it came to taking care of those they cared about. "Well, of course I wouldn't put up with that. Nobody better talk to my sister like that, even if they call themselves playing. I ain't having that," he growled, then became silent for a moment, contemplating what Adam had said. It was true, Angelique was someone's sister, too, and it was probably time he remembered that. Besides, he wouldn't have wanted anything bad to happen to her.

"I understand what you're saying, but believe me, Adam, she gets me as good as I get her. I admit it, I used to like to get her going by calling her Evilene, but she just turned the tables on me and started calling me SpongeBob. And she doesn't just *call* me SpongeBob—I have a SpongeBob bumper sticker on my Jag that I certainly didn't authorize, not to mention about a thousand SpongeBob toys she gives to the kids to give to me. She told them how much their Uncle Donnie loves that stupid cartoon, and bless their little hearts, they believed her. She actually sent a singing, dancing SpongeBob telegram to the office one day. That was real jolly," he said with a laugh. "And on top of everything else, she manages to put a SpongeBob sticker on me every time we're within twenty feet of each other. As a matter of fact, check me out," he said, jumping to his feet.

He turned around slowly and heard Adam's shout of laughter. There was indeed a small sticker, bearing the guilelessly smiling cartoon character, stuck discreetly on his left shoulder.

"She's good, man. Really good," said Adam in a voice of admiration. "Maybe you should think about getting with her since you both share the same warped sense of humor."

Donnie reached for the sticker, then looked at his brother as though he'd lost his mind. Then, surveying the array of ingredients on the long counter, he asked what Adam was preparing; Adam liked to cook, but generally didn't go for elaborate meals, and this one looked like it required everything but the kitchen sink.

"Alicia's coming over and she's making paella. If you behave yourself she might let you stay," Adam replied. Alicia Fuentes was Adam's business partner and best friend. They were both architects who not only designed new buildings, but had a passion for reclaiming neglected and abandoned structures. They had been friends since college and enjoyed an exceptionally close personal, as well as a working, relationship.

"So, Adam, when are you going to admit that Alicia is the only woman in the world for you? When are y'all gonna take it to the next level?" Donnie drawled.

Adam stroked his thick mustache with a forefinger and fixed his brother with an icy stare. He was an extremely private person when it came to his love life and he didn't appreciate inquisition, even from a family member. "You're my brother and I love you. I may even like you, but Alicia is not a topic for discussion now or ever. Got it?"

Donnie was saved from answering by three short chimes, which meant Alicia was at the door; they didn't have to answer it, as she had her own key, just like Adam had a key to her place. In seconds a tall, shapely woman carrying two shopping bags joined the two men. Donnie took her coat while Adam divested her of the bags. "Hi, Donnie!" she said cheerfully. "Are you staying for dinner?" She accompanied the words with a brief kiss on his cheek.

"Yes, if I'm invited. I love anything you cook, Alicia, you know that." Between Alicia's African-American mother and Cuban father, Alicia had a grasp of cooking that rivaled that of a Cordon Bleu trained chef. While watching Alicia wash her hands and Adam empty the shopping bags, Donnie remembered that Angelique hadn't given him a gift from his sister; she had told him she'd planned to drop it off at his house, but, since he was being snippy, he could instead pick it up at the open house she and Paris were having the day after New Year's.

Alicia looked up to find him with a dazed look on his face, and playfully snapped a dish towel at him. "Hey, you. If you eat, you work. Put on the Buena Vista Social Club CD and an apron. How are you at scrubbing mussels?"

Soon the lilting sounds of Cuban music filled the loft and the three of them were busy putting the savory paella together. All thoughts of spurned engagements and feisty little women from Atlanta vanished and Donnie once again felt like himself. Unfortunately, the effect didn't last very long.

Paris and Angelique observed New Year's Eve very differently than most people; they had evolved a unique way of celebrating over the past few years. Neither one of them liked the idea of going out trying desperately to have a good time, so when Paris moved to Atlanta, she and Angelique began going to church to pray in the New Year with a quiet family worship service, and then spent the evening with family, usually at Bennie and Clay's home. The next day would be an open house at Lillian and Bump's house where everyone wandered in and out and the men congregated in front of the big-screen television for a football orgy. This year would mark their first New Year's in Detroit, but their plans were about the same.

"Paris, are you about ready? We need to leave early so we can get a seat," Angelique called out. She was ready to go, sitting in the kitchen watching CNN on the small television mounted under the cupboards. She was dressed exquisitely as always, and warmly, too, in a simple black skirt that buttoned all the way down one side, a pair of low-heeled black boots and a cashmere sweater in a luscious shade of raspberry pink that made her toffee skin glow. She wore a simple gold chain with a big pearl dangling from it, and matching pearl studs in her ears.

The only jewelry on her hands was a dainty gold ring with a small pearl, bordered by two tiny peridots, which were her birthstone. She also wore two slender bangle bracelets, a silver one on one wrist and a gold one on the other. The ring had been given to her as a child and she always wore it on special occasions; she never took the bracelets off. Her nails were short and neatly shaped with a clear polish as their only adornment; Angelique used her hands too much to fuss with elaborate manicures. Now her fingers anxiously stroked the soft leather of the cashmere-lined kid gloves that lay on the table with her scarf, gloves and purse. "Paris, what are you doing?" she called in exasperation.

It was ironic the way their roles had reversed over the years. A few years ago Paris would have been cooling her heels while Angelique took her own sweet time to make sure every hair was in place and her makeup was perfect. Paris would have had her customary quick shower, thrown on one of her oversize outfits, pulled her hair into a ponytail and been ready to go while Angelique primped. It had never bothered Angelique one bit to keep people waiting, as she liked making an entrance too much to worry about being on time. But now it actually meant something to her to be on time. A.J. had taught her the importance of being reliable in business, and that meant always being prompt. Being prompt meant you took your job seriously and you respected the people with whom you were working. And it meant you respected yourself as well.

Paris appeared in the kitchen with an apology on her lips. "Sorry it took so long. Let's go!" In short order the two women were on their way to the A.M.E. church they attended with the Cochrans. The midnight watch service was spiritually moving and uplifting, and also shorter than the one that took place on Sunday mornings. Afterward everyone went over to Andre's house for a midnight buffet and a quiet family celebration. Andre and his twin brother, Alan, usually hosted the New Year's festivities. There would be a traditional New Year's dinner at Alan's the next day, with the usual attention to the various bowl games.

Even Donnie was less grumpy after the religious service; at least he was until he caught a glimpse of Angelique. She was talking to his father and stepmother and looked good enough to eat. And, he noticed for the first time, she had more booty than he realized—he actually cocked his head to one side and was staring at her high, tight derriere in the slim-fitting black skirt like he'd never seen a fanny before. Fortunately, only Adam caught him doing so. He had materialized next to Donnie and seemed vastly amused at the look in Donnie's eyes.

"Stop staring, bro, you're beginning to drool," Adam said slyly.

Busted. There wasn't anything Donnie could say when he'd obviously been caught doing exactly what Adam said he was doing. He narrowed his eyes at his brother and slunk off to the buffet table, but it wasn't an escape because Angelique was there, busily filling two plates with food.

He watched her in silence for about two seconds, then commented on her gargantuan appetite.

"This is for Miss Martha and Mr. C," Angelique said, without looking at him. "Older people don't like to mess around with buffets, you should know that." She managed to take the two plates of food with napkins and utensils to where his father and stepmother waited, all without looking at him one time.

Suddenly Donnie's appetite deserted him, while his thirst became unbearable. He went into the kitchen to find a huge glass, and was in the process of filling it with ice and water from the refrigerator's dispenser when he detected the faint temptation of Angelique's perfume. Sure enough, there she was behind him, holding two glasses and waiting for her turn at the water. And this time she was looking right at him.

He looked at her and could feel his face heating up, although for the life of him he couldn't understand why. He gulped the water rapidly and would have filled the glass again, had Angelique not spoken.

"Adonis, you don't look too happy," she said frankly. "It's not good luck to start the New Year with a bad disposition, you know."

Donnie rolled the cold glass between his palms, trying to cool off the burst of warmth that had encompassed him. He eyed her warily as she set down her two glasses on the cupboard.

"It's not good luck? Well, I sure don't want to have any bad luck," he mumbled. He looked at the water glass in his hand as though it were a relic from an alien civilization. He'd seen one of these before, he just couldn't remember what it was for. Angelique seemed to know, however, as she took it from his hand and set it on the cupboard with the ones she'd just discarded.

"I don't want you to have any bad luck either, Adonis," she said as she came closer to him. "I want you to have a happy New Year." And taking hold of the front of his cashmere sweater, she gently pulled him down to her level and kissed him softly and sweetly.

The new year dawned bright and cold. There was no snow to speak of, but in Michigan, you never knew about the weather. Angelique lived in hope that there would be a big snow, and soon. She found that the cold weather of her new home suited her and she was anxious for a huge snowfall; she'd never had the chance to really play in the snow. While Paris was relaxing in the living room, Angelique was in her bedroom, rearranging her already fastidiously organized closet. She'd also taken everything out of her dresser drawers and put in new scented liners, dusted and polished all the furniture and put clean linens on the bed. She'd also done a couple of loads of laundry. Angelique didn't believe in starting a new year with dirty clothes in the house.

Finally, she stood in the middle of her bedroom and surveyed her surroundings. Everything was sparkling clean, the way she liked it. The rest of the house was immaculate as always, and everything was ready for the open house the next day. She walked over to the window and looked out; maybe a long walk would do her some good, blow some of the cobwebs away. She was in the same pensive pose when Paris's voice came though her doorway.

"My goodness, woman, you're like a machine! Come work some of that magic in my room, you know it needs it," Paris said cheerfully.

Angelique followed Paris into her sunny bedroom and quickly hung up the few garments arrayed on the bed and the small slipper chair. Paris guiltily gathered up the magazines spread across the bed and put them on the small desk that sat in front of the large window in lieu of a dressing table. "These are like homework for me," she confessed. "I read all of TDG's publications and everybody else's, too, just to stay current with the industry. Once my internship here is over I'll be just about ready to assume a permanent position in Atlanta, and, I have to tell you, I'm not quite sure what I want to do. My bachelor's degree is in journalism but that MBA in leadership is pulling me in another direction," she continued as she rearranged the items on her desktop.

While Paris was talking, Angelique had stripped the bed, dispatched the linens to the hallway and fetched clean sheets from the linen closet. She was almost finished making the bed when she suddenly whirled around and looked at her cousin.

"Paris, I did something really stupid," she said slowly. When Paris turned around to face her, she blurted it out in a rush. "I kissed Adonis last night."

Instead of looking shocked, Paris immediately smiled with glee. "Girl, why are you wasting time with those stupid sheets? Tell me everything! Was it good? Did you like it? Did *he* like it? Where was it?"

Angelique spread the blanket and duvet over the bed and then flopped across it with a huge sigh. Paris sat down on the end of the bed and crossed her legs Indian style. She reached over and shook Angelique's arm as she launched her inquisition again.

"Angel, don't lay there like you're dead—you'd better tell me something! When did he kiss you and what was it like?"

Angelique moaned slightly and rolled over on her back before sitting up to face her. "*I* kissed *him,* Paris," she said wearily. "Yes, I did. We were in the kitchen. He was drinking water and I was getting some ice water for Miss Martha and Mr. C and I have no idea, just no idea what made me do it."

Angelique's eyes went soft and dreamy as she recalled the events of the night before. "He was just standing there looking grumpy and mad like he usually does when he's around me. And all of a sudden he started drinking that water and his Adam's apple was moving up and down and his neck looked really sexy. . . ." Her voice trailed off for a moment, and then she finished in a rush. "I just reached up and grabbed the front of his sweater and yanked him down and kissed him. Just pounced on him. Can you believe I did that?"

Paris made no attempt to hide her amusement. "Yeah, I can believe it! Why not? He's tall and handsome and sexy, why not kiss him?"

"Paris, Adonis and I don't even like each other! Yes, he's cute, but I've never been the type to just walk around kissing

cute guys for no reason. I have no idea what came over me."
She moaned. "He was just standing there looking lost and all
of a sudden I'm all over him like a cheap suit. I can't even
begin to tell you how embarrassed I am about this. I'm never
going to live this down."

"Oh, come on, now, it wasn't that bad," Paris said brac-
ingly. "It was New Year's Eve, a traditional time for kissing.
How did he act when you were doing all this smooching?
Did he push you away or gag or run out of the room or something?"

Angelique's eyes got dreamy again when she remembered the kiss. "No, he didn't do any of those things," she
said softly. "He was a little surprised at first, I think, but then
he started kissing me back and it was wonderful. He's a great
kisser, Paris. He's a *wonderful* kisser. He has the softest lips
and his mouth was still cold from the ice water but it was hot
at the same time and he just . . . well, let's just say it was a
great way to start the New Year," she said with a soft sigh of
contentment.

*So that's why brotherman was staring at you the rest of
the night,* Paris thought. *I knew something was up.* "So
what's next? What's your plan?" Paris asked with a sly smile.

"My *plan?* I have no plan other than trying to avoid him
for the next few months until he forgets all about last night.
I'm telling you, Paris, it may have been a harmless gesture
that kind of backfired but he's going to hold this over my
head forever. I still can't believe I did that." She sighed, rubbing her hand across her forehead. "If I had to lose my itty-
bitty mind last night, why on earth did I lose it with him?
Why?" Again, she moaned dramatically as she once more
threw herself face down on the bed.

This time Paris did give a short burst of laughter, but she
also gave Angelique a comforting pat on the back. "C'mon,
girl, it's not that bad. Let's get ready to go—you know everybody is expecting us at Alan's. You'll feel better once you've
faced him and see it's not as bad as you think."

Angelique rolled over and looked at Paris as though she'd lost her mind. "Are you crazy? I'm not going anywhere near that open house! In fact, I'm not going near any of the Cochrans until Easter, at least! Adonis Bennett Cochran is the last person on earth I want to see."

Chapter Four

Donnie's reaction to events of the previous evening was slightly different from Angelique's. He had risen early the next day and taken Jordan and Pippen out for a run, a much longer run than usual, and they were now lolling in front of his fireplace, dead to the world. Donnie would have joined them in slumber, but his mind was in overdrive. After what had happened between him and Angelique the night before, he had a lot to think about. Some details were hazy, such as the moments right before the kiss, but one thing was certain: Angelique had kissed him. An unexpected, unsolicited and completely delightful kiss, at that.

He was stretched out on his long, comfortable leather sofa with his eyes closed, and anyone observing him would have thought him asleep. On the contrary, he was thinking about the moment Angelique had pulled him down to her level so she could touch her lips to his. It was something he wasn't going to forget, not ever. The heady fragrance of her perfume wrapped around him like the warm moisture of a steam bath and the softness of her lips sent a sensation through him that was like nothing he'd ever experienced. He felt her start to pull away from him and he took over, tightening his arms around her slender form so that the delightful warmth of her, the taste of her wouldn't be lost to him.

A soft sound of surprise had made her moist, tasty lips part just enough for his ravening tongue to seek hers out. When he deepened the kiss, he did so hungrily, like a starving man given his first meal in weeks. He completely lost himself in the hot sensations Angelique generated in his body. As she slid her arms around his neck and strained on her toes to get closer to him, he held her even tighter and slid his questing hands down to cup her behind, squeezing it gently but firmly. She might have started the kiss, but he was controlling it now, kissing her passionately over and over, and tasting the sweetness of her mouth while she did the same to him. He could still hear the arousing little sounds of pleasure she made as her enticingly firm breasts pressed against his chest. Only the fact that other people were entering the room made him stop kissing her. Left to his desires, they'd still be locked together in a passionate embrace, but it wouldn't have stopped at kissing.

On his couch, his stomach muscles tightened and other parts of his body reacted almost as strongly as they had last night. A convulsive shudder passed over him, and he welcomed the abrupt sound of his doorbell. Jumping up from the couch, he adjusted his jeans—he was wearing an ancient Howard University sweatshirt that mercifully covered his now-hard member. He glared at the offending instrument and instructed his body to behave. "I told you before, we don't like her. Go back to sleep," he said sternly before opening the door. Oddly enough, the sight of his visitor made his body become dormant immediately.

It was Aneesah Shabazz, wearing a red coat and a big smile. Before he could figure out how he was supposed to react, Aneesah walked right past him into the foyer, saying, "Happy New Year," while she did so. She removed her coat and held it out to Donnie, who was just staring at her while she made herself at home.

"Happy New Year, doggies. Don't get up on my account,"

she said dryly. Jordan and Pippen never moved from their places on the hearth, merely thumping their tails wearily in acknowledgement. Aneesah, meanwhile, had sat down on the couch and was holding out a cake tin to Donnie.

"Here you go. These are some tea cakes my mother made. I was going to tell you I baked them but you know what a lie that would be!" Aneesah laughed uproariously at the thought; she was known for her dislike of cooking in any way, shape or form. As Donnie still hadn't said a word, Aneesah snapped her fingers a couple of times to get his attention. "You know, you might want to offer me some coffee or tea or something. It's customary when you have a visitor, especially on a holiday," she said pointedly.

Donnie finally rallied enough to accept the tin and sit down in one of the large leather club chairs that flanked the sofa. "Sorry. My mind was elsewhere, I guess. Happy New Year to you, too. You look wonderful, by the way," he added. And she really did, in a slim-fitting pair of gray slacks with a crisp white shirt topped by a black merino jersey V-neck sweater. Her short coif was perfect as always—what could be seen of it under her jaunty red beret—and her smooth brown face was devoid of makeup, also as always, her deeply set long-lashed eyes sparkled with intelligence.

"I wish I could say the same to you, Donnie, but you look kinda bad. You look like you haven't had a good night's sleep in a while. And you look like your housekeeper is on vacation," she said pointedly as she looked at the newspapers, gym shoes and other clutter around the large living room.

Donnie sprawled out in the chair and nodded absently. "Yeah, Mrs. Montez is away for the holidays. I wanted her to know how much I missed her while she was gone, so I haven't picked up anything," he said absently. "And no, I didn't sleep too well last night, now that you mention it."

Aneesah stopped smiling and looked contrite. "I'm not to blame for that, am I? That's one of the reasons I stopped by, to make sure you and I are okay. We've been close for so long, I don't want anything to happen to our friendship.

Even though we're not destined for marriage," she said quietly.

Donnie blew out a loud, dramatic breath before answering. "If I said I was pining away for you, dying for the love of you, would it make any difference? Would you change your mind?" he asked with hope in his voice.

It was Aneesah's turn to sigh. "No, Donnie, it wouldn't make a bit of difference. You and I had a lot of fun when we were younger. You were one of the best boyfriends I've ever had, no question about it. But I'm not ready to get married. You might think *you're* ready, but I'm not so sure about that," she said firmly. "And I know for a fact that we don't have the deep, passionate, abiding love you need to make a marriage work. We like each other, we even love each other like brother and sister, but we're not 'in love.' You need to be really deeply in love for a marriage to be about anything and you of all people know that. Look at your brothers and your sister, for example. They all married for love, real true love, and look how happy they are." She shook her head in exasperation. "And where is that tea, friend? I want one of those tea cakes."

Donnie didn't respond for a moment while he pried open the tin of homemade cookies. A burst of a delectable vanilla fragrance wafted out and he smiled for the first time as he looked at the fat, lightly golden pastries. His stomach rumbled and he suddenly realized he hadn't eaten that day. He stood up and bowed slightly.

"It seems I've forgotten my manners entirely. Come with me, my dear, and let me remedy that," he said with a gesture toward the kitchen.

Angelique was sorting photographs when her phone rang. It was A.J., who immediately put a smile on her face.

"I'm coming over, so come open the door. My mother says it's good luck for a man to be the first person to cross your threshold on New Year's Day. Am I your first visitor?"

"Yes, you are," Angelique answered with a smile. "I can't think of anyone I'd rather see. Hurry up and get here!"

Paris was sprawled across her bed, talking to one of her best friends. "Aidan, I'm telling you, all the signs are there. When they're around each other, the sparks constantly fly. They pick at each other, they have horrible little pet names for each other and they're always staring at each other. They circle around each other like two starving animals fighting for the same piece of meat," she told him.

Aidan made the customary sound of the long-suffering on the other end of the line. "Oh, well, that settles it. They're stalking each other like strays fighting over carrion; it must be true love," he said sardonically. "You're back to your Martha May matchmaker tricks, aren't you? I've warned you about that, haven't I? Why won't you listen to me?"

Paris sat up straight to play her trump card. "Aidan, you don't understand! She kissed him on New Year's Eve! She doesn't even know why she did it, she just grabbed him and laid one on him and he kissed her back. Now that's definitely a sign."

Aidan was silent for a moment, and then replied. "Hmm. Unplanned kisses with no explanation, huh? Well, there may be more to this than they know. But that doesn't mean you need to get involved. Just leave it alone and let nature take its course. You need to worry more about your love life or lack thereof, Martha May."

"A lot you know, Aidan. For your information, I *have* been dating. I've been seeing three different guys, thank you very much, and having a great time," she said smugly.

"Yes, but none of them work that ol' heart of yours like the detective man, now, do they? By the way, I saw Mr. Titus Argonne last week," Aidan said carelessly. "He was walking through the complex with your cousin Martin."

Paris was silent for all of ten seconds before bombarding Aidan with questions. No matter how much she tried to deny it, Titus Argonne was like an itch she couldn't scratch. She was so intent on Aidan's answers, she didn't hear the doorbell ring.

Angelique threw open the front door to admit A.J. She smiled happily when she saw his handsome golden face and immediately threw her arms around him for one of his fantastic hugs. He obliged by giving her a bone-crushing embrace that lifted her off the floor. "Happy New Year, baby, you look beautiful," he said honestly as he set her down. She did look adorable in carpenter's jeans; a thick, cream-colored turtleneck sweater; heavy woolen socks; and no shoes.

Angelique waved aside the compliment the way she did all comments about her appearance. "Come on in and make yourself at home. Did you go out last night?" she asked.

"Naw, it's too crazy out there and I'm too lazy," he replied. "I went to midnight mass with the family and then we sat around and played euchre and pinochle all night."

A.J. had a close relationship with his family, closer still since his run-in with cancer.

He took off his coat and hung it in the in the foyer closet like someone who felt completely at home, which he did whenever he was with Angelique. Following her into the dining room, he looked at the pictures she had spread out on the dining room table. "Angel, these are magnificent. You truly have a gift for this," he said admiringly as he looked over the black and white prints.

Angelique laughed self-consciously at his praise. "A.J., you seem to forget that you're the one who taught me how to take pictures. Well, you and Clay, that is. So, in a way, you're just taking credit for your own talent," she pointed out.

A.J. groaned, then swatted her on the butt. "Haven't I told you about that? Learn to accept a compliment, little girl, because you're going to get more and more of them."

He ignored the exaggerated "ouch" Angelique gave and easily ducked the punch she threw at him, then he did something her brothers had done to her for years—placed one large hand in the middle of her forehead and held her at arm's length while she vainly tried to get at him. As he avoided her windmilling arms, he continued to study the artwork scattered on the table.

"Are you sorting these out for the museum showing?" he asked.

Angelique immediately stopped trying to hit him and stood still. "Yes, I am. I still can't believe someone is that interested in my work," she said quietly. "I don't think I'm ready for all this."

A.J. pulled her into his arms for another fierce hug. "Listen, Angel, don't ever doubt your skill with the camera. Ever. I'm going to go over every picture with you and help you catalog them into an exhibit. Clay and I may have taught you the craft of photography, but the art is in you. It's all you, Angel. When do you meet with the folks from the museum?"

Angelique didn't answer him for a moment—she was too happy to be held in his long arms. She really did love him; A.J. was an indispensable part of her life. "I meet with them in a couple of weeks. Actually, it's not a them, it's a her. She was just hired not too long ago. I think she moved back here from California or someplace."

A.J.'s face lit up with interest. He knew some people at the museum and was always interested in what went on there. "Oh, yeah? What's her name?"

Angelique immediately consulted the neat leather notebook that was like a second brain to her. She laboriously scanned her precise block print and pointed at a name she had written phonetically to remind her of the pronunciation. "Umm, she has an unusual name. It's Aneesah. Aneesah Shabazz. That's pretty, isn't it?"

A.J. agreed that it was a stylish name indeed. He stuck his head into the kitchen and asked where the food was. "Aren't you guys cooking today?" he asked wistfully. Eating was one of his favorite things to do, especially on holidays.

Angelique immediately looked so woeful that A.J. asked what was going on.

"We were supposed to go to an open house today but I can't go now. I'm hiding from Adonis Cochran because I kissed him on New Year's Eve," she confessed.

A.J. tried without success not to look amused. "So are you a bad kisser or something? Why do you have to hide from the man?"

"Because we hate each other, A.J., you know that. And because I kissed him and I have no idea why. And for your information, I'm a very good kisser. I think I am," she amended. She gave him a good imitation of a sultry look and offered to show him her technique.

"No, thanks, I'll take your word for it! Tell you what, take me to the open house and pretend like I'm your date. We'll stuff our faces and get out of there fast and then go down to the beach and shoot some film before sunset. Hurry up, get dressed," he demanded. "I'm hungry!"

Angelique dashed up the stairs to change clothes and get Paris off the phone. Suddenly she was looking forward to the afternoon.

Aneesah finished sipping her cup of tea while she watched Donnie across the kitchen table. He returned her look of concern with a carefully bland look of his own.

"Okay, what's on your mind, Aneesah? I can hear those wheels turning from here," he said.

Aneesah shrugged as she got up to put her cup and saucer in the sink. Washing her hands carefully, she patted them dry with a paper towel from the dispenser on the counter and then turned to face Donnie. "I don't want you to think that I took your proposal lightly," she said softly. "I was honored, Donnie, I really was. But I care about you too much to wander into something that's going to end in disaster. I respect you too much and I value your friendship too much."

Donnie nodded briefly and continued to look at Aneesah,

admiring her beauty. "I'm not going to say I don't understand what you're saying, because I do. I've always viewed marriage as something sacred, something to be taken very seriously. My family gets married and stays married; you know that. But I have to be honest with you and tell you that I've been giving more and more thought to the idea of being married. I want that commitment, that partnership, that love and companionship that makes marriage so wonderful. And you're the kind of woman I want to be married to, Aneesah. I can't lie to you about that."

Aneesah stared at him for a few seconds and then crossed the room to take her seat again. "The 'kind' of woman you want you marry?" she repeated in a dangerously quiet voice.

"Yes," Donnie said confidently. "You're tall, full-figured, smart, educated, you have class, style and ambition. You'd make a perfect wife for me and we'd have some big healthy babies, too." He sat back and smiled with satisfaction until he got a better look at Aneesah's face, which was wearing an expression of total incredulity. He could see that he'd wandered into a minefield, but, like most men, had no idea how he'd gotten there or how to get out. He then resorted to the universal and ancient male plea for enlightenment.

"*What?*"

Aneesah had the universal female response to the one-syllable word drawn out to several times its normal length by the floundering man across the table. She puffed up her cheeks and blew out a long and forbearing breath, then crossed her arms over her ample and tempting bosom.

"Adonis Cochran, you need to quit! Here I am feeling bad for turning you down and you had no more love for me than the man in the moon!" she said indignantly. "You look around and decide it's time for you to have a wife and you whip out your PalmPilot to make a grocery list. And when you decide that I have more of the items on my shelves than anybody else, you decide to do your shopping at my store, is that it? Well, I have news for you, Adonis, you don't go shopping for a wife off a list of attributes, or what you *think* are attributes," she said hotly. "You're an intellectual snob, you know that? I never would have thought it possible, but you are! As long as somebody has a few degrees and some 'back,' you're right in there. You should be ashamed of yourself. That's not how you go about deciding on a life mate, you idiot!"

By now Aneesah was so steamed, she'd risen from the table and was pacing back and forth and gesturing with her long, graceful hands. Donnie had dropped his head down to the table and was groaning aloud as he listened to her recite his many shortcomings. How had his life become so very unmanageable in such a short period of time?

"Are you listening to me?" Aneesah asked sharply. "This wouldn't be a good time to fall asleep, I assure you."

Donnie sat upright immediately. "I'm listening, Aneesah, I'm listening! But I think you're overreacting a little—" His words were cut off by Aneesah's prompt response.

"I'm not overreacting, you're *under*reacting! Who in the world makes a checklist and then tries to pick out a mate on that basis? Where in the world did you get that nutty idea?" she railed at him.

Donnie, gamely trying to gain points, actually had an answer for her. "British royalty," he said triumphantly. "They do it all the time."

Unfortunately, his words seemed to push yet another button in Aneesah. "Oh, great! This is your model for a happy marriage, an all but defunct political system that has nothing whatsoever to do with how you live your daily life? Or maybe you think you're some kind of king, is that it?"

His face blazing with heat, Donnie was torn between trying to argue more and trying not to laugh. Aneesah was really worked up now, and she was really beautiful when she was angry.

"Donnie, love is something that catches you unaware, it's not something you just go out and pick up when it's convenient for you. Marriage is hard work. It's tough being around the same person day after day in good times and bad. It's hard enough when you love that person to death. But when you just up and decide someone is a good candidate for matrimony and it's time you were hitched, you're committing romantic suicide.

"For a marriage to work, you need to have passion, excitement, desire and romance. Someone needs to be able to take your breath away with a kiss, to surprise you with love every day. And you can't sit there and say that the person has to be this tall, this wide, have this degree or that many IQ points. Real love doesn't work that way." Aneesah paused for a moment and put her hand on her hip. "You dodo, I thought you had more sense than this. My whole Christmas was ruined because I thought I'd really hurt you. And when I think of how much you spent on that stupid ring . . . ooh! Come walk me to the door. I'm about to leave in a rage because now I'm mad at you, Adonis."

Donnie watch her big, shapely bottom move as she whirled around to leave the room and decided that having two feet in his mouth was plenty; he probably needed to shut up right about now. He got up from the table and hastened to get Aneesah's coat.

"How long are you planning to stay mad at me?" he asked politely.

Aneesah looked at his handsome, unshaved face, his rumpled jeans and cruddy sweatshirt, and made the sound sistahs the world over make when disgusted. "*Mmm*-hmm! At least the rest of today and maybe part of tomorrow, that's for sure. I may allow you to take me to dinner at Southern Fires later in the week to make up for it. But you have to swear that you're going to think about what I said," she said as she slipped into her coat. "Don't just sit around watching football today—really think about what I said. Love is too precious and marriage is too important to play around with."

Donnie hugged her tightly and promised her. "Aneesah, you're right, and I was wrong. Although I still believe in my heart that you'd make a beautiful wife for me or any man, I promise that when I get married it will be to the right person for the right reasons. I swear," he said solemnly, ending the hug and holding up a hand like a scout reciting his pledge.

"The words are nice, but that's the wrong hand," Aneesah said wearily.

Chapter Five

No one was happier than Donnie to have the holidays over and the normal work year start in earnest. He'd had quite enough of parties, rich food and endless gatherings, and was ready to go back to work and get back in his right mind. Even though he was back on a normal kilter as far as his feelings about marriage and Aneesah's refusal of his proposal, there were some strange things afoot in his world. He knew that whatever remained of his mental turmoil would be erased once he plunged back into work. The strange things all centered on the woman he called Evilene, but he was sure it was leftover holiday angst.

There was the New Year's Day incident, for example. After his heartfelt chat with Aneesah, he really did think about what she'd said to him, and after a long shower and a much-needed shave, he'd hauled himself over to Alan's house for the traditional open house. He was ready to relax and kick back with the rest of the family, and was even anticipating seeing Angelique again while the memory of that spectacular kiss was still fresh in his mind. He'd have been less than human if he hadn't admitted to a certain amount of curiosity about how they would react upon seeing each other. Within minutes of his entrance he had a very different perspective on the situation: there was Angelique and there was that A.J. with his arm around her.

Oh, so it's like that, is it? Okay, cool, if that's how you are, Evilene. Donnie let this and other savage thoughts disrupt his enjoyment of what usually was a relaxing day with his family. He'd given a lot of thought to how he would act when he saw her again, but it hadn't once occurred to him that Angelique would bring a date to the open house. He'd always suspected that this A.J. had a more-than-brotherly interest in Angelique and now he was sure of it. A.J. was hanging on to her like she was his personal property, and she was acting like she enjoyed the treatment, smiling up at the man for all she was worth. Donnie hadn't really noticed those deep dimples before, but now it was all he could see. Her long, thick eyelashes, her pretty, juicy lips turned up in a constant smile and her amazing dimples begging for the tip of his tongue to sample their sweetness—the entire package drove him crazy.

Donnie was so twisted at the sight of Angelique and A.J. that he ignored her presence completely for the short time they were there. He had just gotten Faye, his sister-in-law, to fix him a plate of fried turkey, black-eyed peas, greens, cornbread and yams when he looked up and the objects of his disdain had vanished, not to be seen again the rest of the day. With considerable effort he concentrated on watching football with his brothers and playing with his nieces and nephews. He made it a point, however, not to attend the open house Paris and Angelique were hosting the next day. He wouldn't have admitted it to a living soul but he was really angry with Angelique. She had no right to kiss him like that if she was involved with some other man. And to bring that man into his family's home . . . well, that was just too much. The less he saw of the sneaky little wench, the better.

His desire to see less of Angelique was complicated by the fact that she had a studio in the Cochran building. Cochran Communications, under Donnie's leadership, had moved from its original home on Jefferson Avenue to a new location in downtown Detroit that was closer to the heart of the city. Detroit was enjoying a resurgence of vitality and energy and Cochran Communications was right in the middle of it all. The new building was one that had been renovated by Adam and Alicia and preserved the elegant architecture of the auto-baron age combined with a sleek modern interior. Located near the Greektown Casinos, the new Ford Field indoor arena where the Detroit Lions played football and the beautiful Comerica Park, home to the Detroit Tigers, the Cochran building was home not only to Cochran Communications, but several other businesses.

Angelique had leased office space there and it hadn't fazed Donnie one way or another, but that was before the kiss. Now it was pretty much a moot point since Donnie was in and out of the office so much that he'd never see her. At least that was the plan until his first day back at work.

There on his desk was a huge, obnoxious SpongeBob SquarePants gift bag. Donnie hung up his coat while eying the bag with suspicion. His secretary thought Angelique was sweet and would have delivered the package to his office without hesitation. He approached the parcel warily, and found a more conventional bag with a gift tag that indicated it was from Benita. He smiled and reached for the inside bag eagerly, then remembered why it was necessary for him to get the gift in this way. He was supposed to get the package at Angelique's open house and he hadn't gone. And now he had the package and no need to encounter that evil little woman again for a good long time. Life just couldn't get any better.

Angelique was so busy after the end of the holidays, she barely had time to remember there was an Adonis Cochran in the world, which was just fine with her. At that moment she was in her studio in the Cochran building, matting the photographs she would bring to her presentation at the African-American museum. The bright winter sun streamed through the windows and her precise, careful movements occupied all her attention, keeping her thoughts at bay. To think about him meant that she remembered that kiss and that was something she really didn't want to do.

That kiss . . . it was so sweet, so sensual that the mere memory of it took her breath away and put her right back into a place where she could still taste his lips, still feel his strong arms locked around her, still feel the wild and unfamiliar longing that only he could assuage. The tender memory was always followed by the recollection of his behavior the very next day, when he had ignored her completely. That was also something she'd like to forget. Suddenly, despite her efforts to concentrate on her work, her mind drifted. With a sound of disgust, she stopped what she was doing and propped her head in one hand, the past few days coming back to her with unerring clarity.

She, Paris, and A.J. had all gone over to Alan's house and she'd even brought a huge bowl of shrimp salad to contribute to the meal. It was her mother's recipe and Lillian's shrimp salad was welcome wherever it went—it was that spectacular. The real reason she'd brought the salad, however, was because Donnie loved it. He'd had it on several occasions when he was visiting Bennie and Clay in Atlanta and always raved about it, so she'd taken the shrimp salad out of the refrigerator without hesitation, even though it was for her party the next day.

After A.J. and Paris convinced her to go to the party, she decided to cast caution to the wind and see if there was something more to the spontaneous kiss than either she or Donnie realized. Dressed in the beautiful lapis-blue cashmere sweater Paris had given her for Christmas, Angelique really thought she was looking her best. She had on midnight-navy velvet jeans and sleek ankle boots, and a sheer misting of her favorite fragrance, Youth Dew by Estée Lauder. She was ready to face Donnie, whatever the outcome. Yes, she'd made herself vulnerable to him and even a target for his ridicule by giving him that kiss, but now she was ready for the consequences.

Angelique suddenly sat up straight with fire in her eyes. She picked up a matting tool and stared at it, then put it back down. She couldn't trust herself to cut anything in her present mood. There was no point in trying to avoid it—the memory was too galling to go away.

After greeting all the Cochrans and introducing A.J. to anyone who didn't know him, Angelique had really begun enjoying herself despite the little thrills chasing around in her stomach in anticipation of seeing Donnie. Tina, Alan Cochran's wife, had just said something to Angelique about the possibility of her showing at the museum and Angelique had confirmed the information. A.J. had put a brotherly arm around her and was praising her work when Donnie finally walked in and everything went wrong.

Donnie looked as handsome as ever in another gorgeous sweater, this one a soft blue gray that warmed his already rich skin tone and made it more appealing. He was wearing jeans and some good-looking black shoes that laced up and looked very Italian, although they were probably Doc Martens. His smooth face was freshly shaved and he smelled wonderful. Angelique's mouth had become dry and her hands had gotten damp and itchy—she couldn't have said anything if she'd wanted to. As it turned out, she didn't have to say a word; Donnie had ignored her completely. He didn't look at her, he didn't greet her in any way and he had acted as though she didn't exist. A hard, cold weight formed in her stomach and the rest of the time went by in a blur. Luckily, A.J. was serious about shooting some film and they left rather quickly. They drove to Metro Beach and took some shots of the setting sun over the bleak winter shore.

Angelique jerked out of her reverie, suddenly reminded that the film would be ready that day. They'd been shooting in color and she didn't like to do her own color processing. She'd developed a good relationship with a small lab that wasn't too far from the building, and they were always willing to expedite her orders. She glanced at her watch and saw it was almost time for lunch, so she decided to go pick up the order, reasoning that a brisk walk in the cold air would do her some good anyway. Abandoning all pretense of work, she quickly put everything away and went down to the main lobby. As she waved at the concierge and turned quickly to the big brass doors that led to the street, she ran smack into what seemed to be a wall made of wool.

The wall was actually a tall, good-looking man who seemed rather pleased at the collision. "I guess I was in the right place at the right time," he said. "I didn't hurt you, did I?"

Angelique looked up into a broad, smiling face and had to smile herself: the man was adorable. It was a strange adjective to use about a big, handsome, obviously well-off man, but there was no other word that fit him so well. He was about six-two and a big teddy bear of a man, with that Gerald Levert kind of sex appeal. His skin was a rich, warm brown and his full, chiseled lips were surrounded by an impeccably groomed mustache and beard. His eyes were kind and merry with thick eyebrows and long, straight lashes.

"I'm fine, thank you. I think I should be apologizing to you," she said nicely.

"I wouldn't hear of it. Here, let me help you with your coat," he said gallantly, holding out his hands for the garment.

Angelique promptly gave it to him and allowed him to assist her. He waited while she shifted her purse and gloves from one hand to the other, then made sure the coat was on her shoulders properly. "No hat today?" he asked.

Still smiling, Angelique shook her head no.

"Now, that's not good. You lose most of your body heat through your head and your feet," he chided gently.

"You're not wearing one either," Angelique said with a raised eyebrow.

"Aww, baby, now, look at me. I'm a walking furnace," he

said with a chuckle. "Besides, I don't want to mess up my hair." He gave his hair a pat with an exaggerated flutter of his amazing eyelashes.

He did have a pretty head of hair, thick and black and perfectly trimmed. Angelique thanked him again for his chivalry and promised she would get a hat.

"I have to run now. Take care of yourself," she said as they each gave a brief wave good-bye. Suddenly the cold winter day was warmer and more cheerful, all because of a chance encounter.

"Mr. Cochran, Dr. Alexander is here."

"Thanks, Margaret, I'll be right there." Donnie smiled broadly as he went to the door of his office. It was his habit to personally receive all visitors; Benita had taught him this courtesy when she was head of Cochran Communications. This time he was combining business with pleasure, as Dr. Warren Alexander was one of his oldest friends. The doctor had been interviewed on the talk-radio station owned by Cochran and the two men had arranged to have lunch afterward. Donnie met his friend in the reception area of the executive floor and took him back to his spacious private office, where the two men began chatting.

"So how're you doing, man?" There was real concern in Warren's voice, as he knew the story of Donnie's proposal and the less than stellar results.

Donnie shrugged and spread out his hands in a gesture of acceptance. He and Warren were both seated on the long Ultrasuede sofa that graced his window-lined work space. "I'm doing okay. Better than okay, actually. I had a long talk with Aneesah and she made a lot of sense. I think I was more in love with the idea of a partnership than I was with her," he admitted. "Although, I don't agree with her that I'm an intellectual snob."

"An intellectual *what?*" Warren asked with a raised brow. Donnie related the entire conversation to Warren, who took advantage of his old-friend status to laugh in Donnie's face. "Yeah, well, she's right, my brother. You do have some fairly rigid standards when it comes to dating. If a woman isn't superlative in all ways, from size to height to intellect to credentials, you aren't interested. You do make up a list and go shopping in the woman store, Cochran."

"Okay, maybe I do. But I like what I like, how can you fault me for that? I grew up with amazing women all around me, Warren. Benita practically raised me—I really don't remember my mother at all—and look at her: she's an incredible woman, probably the most incredible woman I've ever known. Beautiful, brilliant, kind, compassionate and talented. There's nothing she can't do, Warren," Donnie said. "She ran this company from the time she was about fifteen, practically, as well as kept everything running at home and raised us after Mom died. My aunt Ruth, she resigned her commission in the army to help raise us; she's another outstanding woman. My sisters-in-law, Tina and Faye—check them out. Tina is a circuit court judge and Faye is a college president. Adam's partner, Alicia, is considered to be one of the leading architects in the country, Warren. Not the city or the state—she gets national recognition, man. So why shouldn't I have high expectations for the woman in my life? I've had nothing but brilliant examples of womanhood around me all my life."

"Okay, you make a good point. But can we continue this over lunch? You can't maintain a physique like this one unless you feed it regularly," he remarked, giving his barrel chest a rub. "I can shoot holes in your argument quite nicely over a big Greek salad and a gyro."

Donnie agreed that lunch was in order. While he was getting his topcoat out of the closet, Warren stood up and stretched. "I gotta ask you, though, how do you manage to get all these fine women in one place? Every time I come in this building I see one beautiful face after another. One of them ran smack into me when I was walking across the lobby—now *she* was a knockout!"

Donnie put on his coat and picked up his leather gloves in anticipation of the harsh cold. "Nothing changes, Warren—you were on your way to this serious interview about neurolinguistics and the latest advances in the field, and you're trying to pick up women in the lobby."

"Not true, Cochran. I was so busy thinking about the interview that I didn't try to pick her up, but I wish I'd gotten her name or number or something. She was gorgeous, friendly, smelled like a million bucks and had dimples you could swim in. Just beautiful." He sighed.

"Warren, I think you need to start getting out more, you're sounding desperate, man. She couldn't have looked all that good."

"You're just jaded, my friend. You're so caught up in finding Superwoman that you don't know how to appreciate God's bounty when you witness it. Beauty like that is a gift in itself, Cochran."

The two men continued to banter as they descended in the brass-fixtured elevator to the marble-floored lobby. The doors opened and Warren's eyes lit up.

"Cochran, get ready to eat your words. There's the beauty right there. And this time, I'm getting a name," he said gleefully.

Donnie's head dropped and he stifled a groan. "Don't bother to get it, I can give it to you. Her name is Angelique and she's more trouble than you want to deal with, now or ever."

Chapter Six

Warren ignored Donnie's words and approached Angelique, who was exchanging a few words with Fanchon, the attractive, friendly concierge. "We meet again," he said with a smile.

Angelique turned to face him and her charming smile again allowed him a glimpse of her dimples. "So it would seem," she replied. "Have you rescued any more maidens who weren't watching where they were going?"

"Not in the last hour or so. I must be overdue." He laughed. "By the way, I'm Warren Alexander."

Angelique extended her right hand to shake his. "I'm Angelique Deveraux. It's very nice to meet you, Warren."

By now, Donnie had joined the twosome and was looking less than thrilled. Warren turned to Donnie and said, "I understand you know this man, so he can vouch for me. I'm God-fearing, clean, wholesome and healthy and I would consider it a true pleasure if you would accompany us to lunch." He bowed slightly.

Angelique hadn't retrieved her hand; it was still enveloped in his warm, strong grasp. She smiled again—there was something truly sweet about this big guy. "As nice as that invitation was, I'm going to have to say no," she said softly. "I was just out for lunch and I have to get back to my studio. I have some appointments this afternoon."

Warren sighed deeply. "I can't leave here without knowing I'm going to see you again. I just can't do it. Do you like art?"

Angelique's interest showed on her face at once. "Why, yes I do. Very much, in fact."

"Would you consider going to a gallery with me? There's going to be a showing at a small gallery and I think you might enjoy it," he said persuasively.

"I'd love to go, thank you for asking me," she said, giving him another glimpse of those amazing dimples. "If you give me my hand back, I'll give you a number where you can reach me."

Instead of looking embarrassed, Warren smiled. "I was hoping you wouldn't notice that I hadn't let you go. But since you did . . ." He lowered his head and kissed the fingers he was still holding.

Angelique giggled like a schoolgirl and promptly went into her purse to extract a card case. Taking one out, she handed him her business card and told him he could reach her on her cell number. "It was a pleasure meeting you, Warren. I'm looking forward to hearing from you. And I'm looking forward to the showing."

With a last brilliant smile, she turned, leaving Warren and Donnie staring after her slender figure as she walked away. Warren gave a low whistle as he watched her sexy walk. "Cochran, now *that's* what I call a woman. You see how things just work themselves out? I was in the right place at the right time and I may have just met my dream girl," he said gleefully.

"Oh, no, you haven't, Warren. What you just met was your worst nightmare."

The two men faced each other across the table while waiting for their lunch orders. They had opted to eat in a small diner near the office known for good food, large portions and swift service. Warren looked amused, while Donnie's face had a look of intensity that to Warren seemed all out of proportion with the situation. His words to his friend reflected this. "Well, now, Cochran, I met a nice young woman and asked her to go to an art gallery with me. You're acting like I'm selling arms to Al-Qaeda or something. What's the problem?"

Donnie took out his frustration on the ice in his glass of water, crunching it noisily and violently before answering. He was also buying time, because he wasn't sure why he'd reacted so strongly to the scene in the lobby. Warren standing there, dripping his legendary charm all over the place, and Angelique acting like a debutante at a social irritated him mightily. He shook his head before speaking.

"Warren, if you knew Evilene like I knew her, you wouldn't be asking me that question. You know how she is; you've heard me talk about her before. She's Bennie's sister-in-law, the little piece of work I've been telling you about. The woman is evil, I'm telling you. She's nothing but trouble."

Warren raised his brows at the passion in Donnie's voice. "So that's the woman you call Evilene. You never told me she was that *fine,* Cochran!"

Donnie ignored the heat that gathered in his face. "Yeah, well, if you think she's fine, good for you. But it's like I've been telling you, Warren, she's mean as a black snake. She's hot-tempered, she's spoiled rotten, she's . . . Man, if you were to look up the phrase 'high-maintenance' in a dictionary, there'd be a picture of her sharpening her claws."

Warren laughed out loud at that one. "Aww, come on, Cochran! So you two don't get along—that doesn't put her on America's Most Wanted list, does it? There's lots of people I don't get along with, and some of them are female. Take my cousin Charice, for example. We can't be in the same room for ten minutes without getting into it about something and we're both adults, both physicians, both had home training and we can't stand the sight of each other. So

Angelique's high-spirited and a little spoiled. If I was that good-looking, I'd probably be spoiled, too." Warren stopped talking because the waitress had arrived with their food.

He said a quick grace, and then took a mouthful of the piping-hot gyro that had been placed before him. After chewing it thoroughly with a look of total enjoyment, he resumed his interrogation of Donnie.

"I've never known you to be this bent out of shape about anybody, Cochran, especially not a woman. Why do you let her get to you like this?"

Donnie stared morosely at the Reuben sandwich that lay before him. For some reason he seemed to have lost his appetite, even though the food looked delicious. "Because she's not only a spoiled little princess, she's a player," he said finally. "She's dating this other guy but that didn't stop her from making a date with you, now, did it?" He picked up half his sandwich and took a huge bite. "And it didn't stop her from kissing me on New Year's Eve, either."

Warren finished the bite he was consuming before picking up his glass of iced tea. He looked long and hard at his old friend, then pointed out that this disclosure put a new spin on the situation. "Well, now, seems to me like there's a little more interest on your part than you're letting on, my brother. Do I detect a little bit of jealousy in there somewhere? Could it be that you're more involved with Miss Angelique than you're willing to admit?"

Donnie sputtered and almost choked on his Boston Cooler. "Man, what are you trying to do, kill me? Jealous? Of Evilene? Me? Not now, not *ever* will I be jealous of anything she does and anyone she does it with. It's not like that, Warren, not at all. I just know her for the deceitful little wench she is and I'm telling you as a friend to stay away from her."

Warren calmly finished eating while watching Donnie compose himself with some degree of success. "Look, Cochran, it's not that serious. She was a pretty lady and she seemed to have a good sense of humor. I'm not trying to get busy with her—yet," he added, just to rile Donnie. "But there really is a charity event for the college of medicine this week. It's at that new gallery—should be fun. A major exhibit, an auction, good food and wine—you can come along and chaperone, if you think she's that bad. And she might surprise you; she might be nicer than you think. Sometimes you just need to see someone in a different light in order to appreciate them fully."

Donnie's skepticism was plain but he refrained from answering because his mouth was full. Warren waited until Donnie had picked up his drink again and said in a voice of total innocence, "She must be one great kisser, Cochran."

After another choking spell, Donnie gave him an answer that was both profane and hilarious, if Warren's loud laughter was any indication.

Paris looked Angelique over carefully before letting her go downstairs to wait for Warren. Angelique turned around and struck a sultry pose. "Well? Will I do?" she drawled.

She was wearing a simple long-sleeved dress made of merino jersey. The hem was midcalf and, in deference to the cold January night, she wore sexy black boots with high heels. The dress had a deep surplice neckline that stopped just short of showing any cleavage, but looked exquisitely sexy all the same, due to the close fit of the supple knit, as well as the vibrant red color. Her hair was done in a soft French twist with careless tendrils along her nape and surrounding her face. Her only jewelry was a pair of big gold hoop earrings. She looked exciting, fresh and utterly lovely with the soft scent of her signature fragrance surrounding her and a red lipstick that matched the dress.

"Girl, you look wonderful. As Aidan would say, I have three words for you: Fab U Lous! You're gonna knock that Warren off his feet, I promise you!"

Angelique made a face as she pulled a big, warm wool scarf in a beautiful paisley print out of her drawer. Taking it

and her small leather bag, she turned to Paris. "I'm not trying to turn anybody's head," she said earnestly. "He was just
so nice and pleasant, I couldn't say no. And I'll be honest
with you, the fact that Adonis was standing there looking
like somebody's warden made me say yes, too. He hasn't
spoken a word to me since New Year's Eve and he had the
nerve to look at me like I was trying to pick his friend's
pocket! Believe me, Warren could have been a lot less attractive and I would've still said yes. But he was so *nice*,"
she said with a little sigh. "Wait till you meet him, you'll see
what I mean."

About forty-five minutes later, Angelique was still smiling over the look on Paris's face when she met Warren
Alexander. Warren had arrived promptly, smelling divine
and looking like the cover of a Gerald Levert CD in a beautifully made charcoal-gray cashmere coat. He was also
wearing a crew-neck cream sweater with black pleated
slacks and a three-quarter-length jacket that looked custom
tailored. He'd presented Angelique with a dozen deep-red
tulips that matched her dress, and after the introductions
Paris had taken the flowers into the kitchen to put in a vase.
When Angelique followed her to let her know what time she
planned on coming back, all Paris could do was nod and
wave weakly. "He's too pretty, girl. *Way* too pretty. Dang."

Warren was indeed handsome, but he was also funny and
warm and an entertaining person to be with. To her delight,
she ran into A.J. at the showing and happily introduced him
to Warren as her dearest friend. The two men looked each
other over swiftly but thoroughly as they shook hands.
Angelique was having a ball walking around, looking at the
pieces on display. Warren, it turned out, knew quite a bit
about art and was a wonderful person to chat with as they
strolled around. There was only one thing that kept the
evening from being perfect and that was the presence of
Donnie, looming around like a vengeful wraith. He seemed
to be watching her every move as though he truly believed
she was going to try to take Warren's Rolex or pocket his

wallet or something. Even when he was talking to other people, she could feel his eyes following her. She was idly contemplating revenge at a later date when she became aware that someone else was staring at her, too.

This time it was a woman, a very attractive woman, petite in stature with a very pretty head of hair worn in a tousled bob. She was wearing a long leather skirt, low-heeled boots and a beautiful cream angora sweater with a huge cowl neck worn off the shoulder. Every time Angelique looked up, the woman's eyes were on her, and it suddenly occurred to her that she wasn't the target of the woman's scrutiny—it was Warren who had her eye.

After the auction started, Angelique lost track of the lady, but Donnie was never far away. To her intense irritation, he had latched on to her and Warren and seemed determined to be a part of their date. Even after they left the gallery and went to an afterglow at a fashionable restaurant, Donnie was still there.

They were all seated at a nicely secluded table; Warren was the most comfortable of the group. He was being charming and attentive without being grabby and Angelique was really enjoying herself, or she could have if that lanky, overgrown Adonis would find himself something to do. Surely he had a woman of his own to torture. Despite her efforts to be a perfect lady, there was something about the way he was staring down her throat that made her want to scream. He looked handsome as always, in a midnight-navy suit that had a nice casual look to it with the gray band-collared shirt he wore as well. Every so often he'd be close enough for her to catch the expensive fragrance she always associated with him, which for some reason increased her irritation. After his terse greeting back at the gallery, he hadn't said another word to her, but he stared all night. She had reached the limit of her endurance and was about to get vocal with him when the mysterious woman from the gallery stopped at their table.

In a low, sexy voice with the slightest hint of an accent, she greeted them. "Hello, everyone. Pardon the interruption, but I wanted to say hello to Warren. I haven't seen him in such a long time," she said sweetly.

Warren gave a deep, genuine smile and stood up to give the woman a brief social hug. "Hello, Lisette, it really has been a long time. Everyone, this is Lisette Francois. Lisette, this is Angelique Deveraux and Donnie Cochran," he said graciously.

Lisette nodded and smiled at everyone at the table. "So nice to meet you all. I don't want to keep you from your friends, Warren. It was nice to see you again." She was about to leave when Angelique spoke up.

"Are you here alone? Would you like to join us?" she asked warmly.

Lisette stared at her for a moment and seemed to sense her sincerity. "Well, thank you, I'd love to if no one minds," she replied.

In no time most of the people at the table were chatting away like old friends. The one exception was Donnie, who was uncharacteristically quiet. He would speak when spoken to, but for the most part, he was watching Angelique as though he expected her to levitate out of her seat or something. It had been a most trying evening altogether for Donnie, starting with the gallery.

He'd managed to get there before Warren and Angelique and from his position could see Warren helping her take her long black topcoat off. She also removed a brilliant paisley stole and handed it to Warren, a move that caused Donnie pain. He'd never seen her with her hair up, nor was he expecting what seemed to him to be a plunging neckline. There was no denying it: she looked wonderful. Beautiful, sexy, and happy. How one evil little woman could look so delicious and be so mean was beyond him.

He loitered around and watched with great interest as the couple encountered A.J., who was there with a date. To his astonishment, Angelique not only didn't seem upset, but she and A.J. had exchanged pecks on the cheek like siblings and introduced their dates to each other. *Okay, so maybe she's not really dating the guy.* That didn't change the fact that she had played him on New Year's Eve, however.

The auction turned out to be a complete waste of his time, although it gave him an additional opportunity to check the couple out. Warren was being the perfect gentleman, it seemed; whatever he was doing had Angelique smiling for all she was worth and looking even more radiant

Just to be on the safe side, he decided to trail along to the afterglow, not caring a bit that he was probably making a jackass out of himself. He managed to maintain a modicum of dignity by being at least sociable enough to speak to people he knew, to look like his normal affable and charming self to everyone except Warren and Angelique. But when he wasn't exchanging greetings and smiling at old friends and business acquaintances, his eyes were glued to them. In his entire life he'd never lost control like this and he had no idea why he'd done it tonight. Other than the fact that his little Evilene was the most captivating woman in the room, he had no reason to behave like this, none whatsoever.

Get a grip, get a grip! What's wrong with you, man, you act like you've never seen her before in your life! Donnie berated himself and tried to regain some ground in the maturity department, but it seemed to be impossible. Being seated across from her and Warren was driving him crazy. The whole idea behind him coming was to make sure she didn't make a fool out of Warren, but every time her amazing lips turned up in a smile, he was the one who made a fool out of himself.

He was about to cut his losses and leave when a pretty woman who looked vaguely familiar stopped at their table. After he and Warren both stood up to acknowledge the lady and Warren had made the introductions, Donnie was about to bid everyone good evening when Angelique invited the woman to sit with them, something he would never have expected from her—never in a million years. Yet the two of them were chattering away like old friends. This evening was getting stranger and stranger. . . . He was jolted from his deep thoughts when the women decided to visit the ladies' room, causing the two men to rise from their seats.

As the ladies left on their pilgrimage of sisterhood, Warren signaled the server for another round of drinks. Then he turned to Donnie with his thick brows knit together in total puzzlement. "Do you care to tell me why in the world you're acting like her bodyguard? Why are you hanging around here with your cheeks full of wind? If you want her so bad, why don't you ask her out, man, instead of trying to block my play?"

Donnie took a deep breath and looked Warren full in the face. "You're the doctor, Warren, isn't it obvious that I've lost my freakin' mind? I told you that woman was dangerous. Now do you believe me?"

Warren looked at the despair on his friend's face and burst out laughing. "Oh, man, Cochran, you have to know that I'm gonna be dogging you about this for years to come. You know this, right? I'm coming over this weekend, so knock the dust off the pool table and get some Coronas in the house. I'm going to enjoy this, man, I really am," he said with an evil grin.

Donnie tried to change the subject because he knew Warren could keep up this kind of trash talk all night if necessary. "So, Warren, who's the lady who just had to say hello to you? She's kinda fine, where've you been keeping her?"

Warren got quiet for a moment. "Lisette's family owns Le Coeur de la Maison, the place that was decorating the house when Tracy and I were getting married. As a matter of fact, Lisette was there when the engagement was called off, sort of."

Donnie regretted bringing it up—he knew how devastated Warren had been over the breakup of his engagement. Surprisingly, though, Warren's overcast expression cleared rapidly. "It was nice running into Lisette, though. She's a sweet lady and very, very talented. You should see some of her work; she's an amazing designer. I wish I'd had her finish the house, maybe it wouldn't look like such a barn," he said reflectively.

"That's something you should think about. Look, I've exceeded my limit for idiotic behavior for one night. I'm going to leave now. Thanks for not punching my lights out," he said ruefully.

"Hey, you may as well wait until the ladies come back. You know how they are when they make that trip. What in the world do you suppose they do in the so-called powder room anyway?"

Donnie gave a short, harsh laugh. "They talk about *us*, what do you think they do?"

Angelique and Lisette both washed their hands slowly, looking at each other's reflections in the ornate mirrors over the sinks. That they liked what they saw was obvious, as they both smiled at the same time. Angelique was drying her hands on a paper towel when she asked the question that would make her and Lisette friends for life.

"You really care about Warren, don't you?" she asked quietly.

Not even the faintest hint of blush touched Lisette's almond-toned cheeks. She nodded her head slowly and admitted it was true. "I'm in love with him. I've been in love with him since the first time I laid eyes on him and he has no idea. Just none."

It was Angelique's turn to nod. "I saw you watching him at the gallery. I just met him a few days ago. He's a friend of that gloomy man who's sitting at the table with us."

Lisette smiled gently. "The one that *you* have feelings for?" Seeing Angelique's face turn red, she grabbed her hand. "Ahh, don't tell me you don't care for him! As he does you, I wasn't the only one staring tonight," she said with a smile.

"Oh, no, you're wrong about this. We can't stand each other, really we can't!" Angelique protested.

Lisette raised an eyebrow and tilted her head slightly. Angelique took a deep breath and blew it out in a sigh. "Oh, it's complicated. Really complicated," she said glumly. "Listen,

I've only lived here about six months and I don't know that many people other than my cousin Paris—would you like to go out for lunch or brunch this weekend? You'll like Paris, too, she's a lot of fun."

Lisette's eyes grew warm with appreciation. "I would love to! And maybe between the two of us we can make some things less complicated with these men, hmmm?"

Chapter Seven

The next couple of weeks brought a lot of changes into several lives, especially Angelique's. She and Paris and Lisette all hit it off beautifully, and spent time together eating out, going to movies and just talking. Angelique was convinced that Lisette and Warren belonged together and was taking a page from Paris's book of matchmaking hints to make it happen. Lisette wasn't as easily convinced.

One frigid Saturday afternoon found the three women at Angelique and Paris's house doing one of their favorite things. A huge bowl of popcorn was in the middle of the table, flanked by a box of tissues and a pitcher of Crystal Light peach tea, all the needed accompaniments for a chick-flick marathon. After watching a classic black and white in which the heroine sacrificed her love to save the hero pain, Angelique turned to Lisette and told her she had to do something about Warren.

"Okay, Lisette, enough is enough. You've got to let Warren know how you feel. You've just *got* to. Look at that woman, how miserable she was! And he was miserable, too. All she had to do was speak up and let him know she loved him and she could have saved them both a lot of grief," she said sternly.

Lisette laughed bitterly. "If only it were that easy." She sighed. "I can't ever tell Warren how I feel about him because . . ." Her voice trailed off and she lowered her head and pinched the bridge of her nose. When she looked up, Angelique was alarmed to see tears gathering in her long eyelashes. Lisette wiped them away with her forefinger and rallied on. "Because I was the one who caused his engagement to be called off," she said quietly.

Paris almost dropped her glass of tea. With huge, rounded eyes, she stared at Lisette, who nodded unhappily. "It's true, I did it." She sighed again. As always when she was emotional, a slight French intonation crept into her speech. She was bilingual and it showed in moments of stress or turmoil; she was Afro-French, her mother from Senegal and her father from France.

Angelique immediately turned off the DVD and faced Lisette. She and Lisette were on opposite ends of the couch and Paris was on the floor by the coffee table. Paris poured her another glass of tea and Angelique handed her the box of tissues. "Okay, Lisette, this is obviously a story you need to get off your chest. Tell us what happened. And you have to know that we don't think you could have done anything evil, it's just not possible," Angelique said comfortingly.

"Well, as you know, my family owns Le Coeur de la Maison and we do interior design for any and everybody. I don't like to use the word 'celebrity' but we have a lot of prominent people who use our services. That's how I met Warren," she said, a soft look coming into her eyes. "He came into Maison one day and said he was meeting his fiancée there, that he had bought a new house and it needed everything done to it. He was so captivating, I didn't tell him he had to have an appointment. We're so busy, you know, we have to schedule our clientele. But he was so . . . *mmm!*" Lisette sighed and looked lost in thought for a moment until Paris reached over and jiggled her foot.

"Okay, we got that, he was fine as wine and you were smitten. What about the fiancée?" she demanded.

At once, Lisette's pretty face became tight and drawn. *"Zut alors,* what a cow! She was a dreadful, dreadful woman! Just awful! She was beautiful, yes, but a horrible personality. She was a *beauty queen,"* Lisette spat in the same tone she would have used to say the woman did animal testing or something equally cruel.

Angelique nodded knowingly. "One of those women who thought she was all that because she was cute? I know the type."

Lisette shook her head earnestly. "No, she really *was* a beauty queen. Miss Tracy Lovejoy." She sniffed. "She was a runner-up in the Miss America contest. Or Miss Universe or Miss World or Miss Stuck Up Hateful Cow, I don't remember which one. But she did everything but wear a tiara and a cape into the salon, believe me. She wanted everyone to know that she was the queen of the universe and the rest of us were her slaves.

"She tried to be sweet when she was with Warren, of course, but when he wasn't around, *mon dieu,* what a horror." Lisette shuddered. "You probably don't know this, but Warren is quite wealthy. His family has boatloads of money and he has money of his own from his income and investments. How do I know this? Oh, little miss runner-up, of course. She and her coven of friends and her greedy sisters, they made sure that everyone with whom they came in contact knew that Warren Alexander was filthy rich, and believe me, they were determined to spend every penny. And those friends of hers, they were horrible." She gave another exaggerated shudder. "They traveled together like a pack of lady dogs, if you know what I mean."

Lisette stopped and drank deeply from the glass of iced tea, then held out the glass for more. "All she wanted was money, money, money. He bought her a ring that made the Hope Diamond look like a pinkie ring," she said indignantly. She was so fired up by now, the word *"hope"* sounded like *"ope."*

"So what did you do, exactly? I mean, you knew she was

just out to get her mitts on Warren's money and I can see how angry that made you, but what did you do?" Paris scooted closer to the sofa in her eagerness to hear more.

Lisette gave a short laugh. "You can tell I'm angry because I start to sound like Pepé Le Pew, I know. It is a family curse. We all sound like cartoons when we get wound up," she said on a hiccup. "Well, this is what really made me furious. She always acted like I wasn't there, you know? She talked over my head or behind my back, but she never gave me any respect as a trained professional. I got used to that in a way, but I was always amazed at what she would say; it was like she didn't care who heard her, she was so sure of Warren that she could just . . . ooh!" The fire returned to Lisette's voice and her eyes snapped with anger.

"When I was showing her these exquisite dining room chairs, she started laughing like a hyena and said Warren was so fat, he would break the chairs." Lisette's face got red with indignation as she recalled the scene. "A big, handsome, *kind* man like Warren and she called him fat. Fat! Warren is a prince, a *king,* he is a beautiful, big man, and this wench, this hoochie calls him fat! And her little coven, all the ugly witches were laughing with her. *Merde!* I couldn't take it anymore. I wanted him to know what he was in for with that witch and I fixed it so that he would find out.

"How did I do it? I told her there was a very special bedroom at DuMouchelle Gallery, the most expensive set ever made. Of course she said she must have it, so I arranged to personally pick up her and her fellow witches and take her there to see it. I didn't want her car to be anywhere near the premises, you see. Then I called Warren and told him I had found an exquisite set of bedroom furniture I knew his darling fiancée would love, and wouldn't he like to surprise her with it, and of course he agreed and I set a time for him to meet me at DuMouchelle."

Paris and Angelique looked at each other and then at Lisette, who was sitting back on the sofa with a satisfied look on her face. "Oh, yes, you guessed it. I took those women to look at the bedroom set, which was magnificent, by the way, and I got them talking about it because I knew that the matter of his weight would come up. I left them there and went to meet him at the door and took him back to where all the vicious talk was going on, and sure enough, all you could hear was the fiancée going on about how much it cost and how much money he had and how he'd *better* buy it for her because that's all the fat boy was good for." Lisette's face fell and she dropped her head into her hands. "She said the only reason she ever gave him the time of day was because he was so rich she'd never have to work again and that's all she wanted from him. She said she had plenty of men on the side to take care of her sex needs. She really said that!

"Oh, it was horrible, it was worse than horrible. The look on Warren's face . . . I'll never forget it, never. It was terribly painful to see him so hurt. But I couldn't let him marry that woman; she would have destroyed him. She would have eaten him alive, I know it in my heart. But not a day has gone by that I don't feel terribly ashamed for what I did," she said sadly.

There was an awkward moment of silence that ended when Angelique spoke up. "Well, you need to get over it, toots. I'd have done something much worse if I saw someone I cared for about to walk into a scorpion's nest. He should be down on his knees kissing your feet to thank you for getting him out of that mess," she said succinctly.

Paris had to agree. "I know you feel terrible about witnessing his pain, but what else could you have done, Lisette? Knowing what you knew, how could you have let him marry that woman?"

Lisette availed herself of the tissues Angelique had thoughtfully provided. "I could have written him an anonymous note, or told his parents or something." She sniffed. "His parents are wonderful, I met them a couple of times and they are so sweet, just lovely." She noisily blew her nose.

Angelique groaned. "Girl, have you learned nothing from

these movies?" she asked indignantly, pointing to the pile of DVDs on the coffee table. "Men don't listen when they're in love, or *think* they're in love. You can't tell them anything. He wouldn't have paid any attention to a note, especially one with no name on it. And if he's really far gone in the infatuation department, he's for sure not going to listen to Mama and Daddy. He would've eloped with her before he broke up with her."

Angelique leaned over and grabbed the hand that hadn't been involved in the nose-blowing and squeezed it. "You did the best you could. And it worked. He might have had some moments of heartache, but it's better than having years and years of real pain from being married to someone who doesn't love you and only wants to take advantage of you. You did the right thing, Lisette. Now, go wash your face and let's figure out how we're gonna rope this big bronco for you," she said.

Despite her tears, Lisette had to laugh.

The basement of Donnie's house had been cleverly converted into a game room, complete with pool table, arcade games, a wet bar and a huge plasma TV mounted on the wall. Warren carefully chalked his cue as he surveyed the pool table. Donnie was dividing his time between watching the basketball game on TV and watching what Warren was doing at the pool table. He wasn't particularly worried about Warren beating him; his friend could have had a fine career as a pool hustler if medicine hadn't appealed to him more. He knew Warren would beat him, the way he almost always did.

There was something on Donnie's mind, however, but he didn't want to bring it up. Luckily, Warren brought it up for him.

"So, Cochran, what do you think about Lisette?" he asked in an overly casual tone.

Donnie turned his full attention to the pool table then,

preparing to take his shot. He wasn't surprised by the question at all, since the two men had seen Lisette and Angelique a few times since the art auction. Apparently, Lisette had made quite an impression on the doctor.

After making several successful shots in a row, Donnie finally gave Warren an answer. "What do I think about her? She seems to be talented, successful, smart and personable. And she's very, very pretty. She may be half French, but the booty came directly from the homeland," he said with admiration.

"Watch your mouth, man." The words were spoken without heat, but Donnie knew Warren was quite serious.

"So I take it you're a little interested in Miss Lisette Francois," Donnie said. "And you know I meant no disrespect to her, it was just an observation. For a little bitty woman, she's put together quite nicely. Dang, that makes me sound like a hound, doesn't it?"

"That's because you are a hound, Cochran," Warren said with a wink. "Anyway, I told you she was the designer we hired to put the house together, right? And I'm sure I also told you that she was kind of instrumental in me finding out what my ex-fiancée was all about." The game forgotten, Warren went over to the bar and sat on a tall stool while helping himself to a Corona. "Tracy was a first-class actress, I'll give her that. And it's not because she looks so cute in that Farmer Jack commercial," he said with a wicked smile.

Tracy's dreams of stardom had evaporated after their aborted engagement when it became apparent to those that mattered that her talents were fairly limited outside of some spectacular measurements. She now did local commercials once in a while, like the one for the Farmer Jack grocery chain, to supplement her income from selling furniture on commission at Art Van.

"She always acted like the sweetest thing in the world, so feminine and adorable. If I hadn't walked up on her and her girls in that gallery dogging me like I was the biggest geek in the world, I would've actually tied the knot with that heifer.

Lisette saved my life, man." He took a deep draught from the bottle and stared at it reflectively. "I always had the feeling that she did it on purpose, you know? Like she set the whole thing up to head me off at the pass. I always wanted to thank her for that, but I didn't know how."

Donnie made a few more passes with his cue stick and replaced it in the rack. Joining his friend at the bar, he also took a beer. "So why don't you tell her now? It's never too late," he said.

Warren shook his head and went around the bar to get a glass of ice water from the small refrigerator. "No way. If you could've heard the things Tracy was saying about me, calling me a fat chump, saying I'd break the bed down with my big butt, just generally clowning me . . ." he said glumly. "It's not the kind of thing you want to think about, especially when someone as beautiful as Lisette heard the whole thing. I need a woman who's going to love me and respect me for *me,* not someone who feels sorry for me. And that's what was happening there, Cochran. She obviously felt pity for me and she didn't want to see my dumb butt get cleaned out by a gold digger. So, she intervened."

After draining the glass of water, he put it in the small sink behind the bar. "I still want to thank her in some way," he said thoughtfully. "And I must agree with you, Cochran, she sure is fine. And she's as sweet as can be, too. We're going to the Auto Show next week, you should come."

Donnie looked puzzled. "You're going on a date? You were just acting like you didn't want to ask her out," he said.

"No, I meant we're all going, me and my harem, Paris, Angelique, Lisette and who knows who else. My sister might come, too. Angelique called me and asked if I would come with and I said sure. They're all cute and they're all fun. You need to come, too, so I won't look like Dr. Pimpenstein with all those pretty women." He gave a deep belly laugh and pointed his index finger at Donnie. "It'll also give you an opportunity to keep an eye on Angel since that's all you want to do. 'Cause if you think I'm scared of Lisette, it's nothing compared to you. That little woman has you turned out and you just won't admit it," Warren gloated.

Donnie gave Warren a look of disgust. "Throw me another lime, they're in the refrigerator. And give me another Corona. If you're gonna start with the snaps, I need to be well lubricated," he growled.

But what he was really wondering was when Warren had crossed over into the place where he could call Angelique by the pet name only family and very close friends called her. What was that hot, nasty feeling? Surely it wasn't jealousy, not over Evilene. A sudden spasm in his stomach made him change his mind. "Never mind the Corona, doc. Is there a Vernor's in there?"

Warren gave him another evil grin. Vernor's ginger ale was the Michigan remedy for all ills from upset stomach to flu to headaches, but as far as he knew, it wouldn't cure budding passion. He kept this to himself and merely passed the green and gold can across the counter. "Drink up, Cochran," was all he said.

"So it's settled. We'll have a big Super Bowl party here and invite Warren and make sure you guys get some quality time," Paris said happily. She was in her element when she was mating up likely couples.

Angelique was curled up on the end of the sofa and her face was bright with excitement. "This'll be perfect. We'll make a lot of food and invite some fun people, and before everyone gets here, we'll make sure you have a moment or two alone with Warren," she said. "Make sure you wear something kinda sexy—oh, never mind, you could come in a sack and you'd still look good." She laughed.

Lisette also laughed a little, but out of embarrassment. "Oh, please. That's enough about me and Warren, when are we going to do something about you two?" she asked archly.

Paris held up her hand. "I'm not looking for a serious entanglement. I'm going to be finishing up my internship here and heading back to Atlanta for the rest of my management training. My cousins love me to death, but that doesn't mean they don't want their money's worth. I have too much on my plate to get serious with anybody right now. I'm having fun with my friends, that's all I need."

Lisette then glanced at Angelique, who was studying her fingernails. "Okay, that sounds like a legitimate reason for a fabulous woman like you to remain casual about your relationships. But that doesn't excuse your sweet cousin, who is obviously intrigued by Mr. Cochran," Lisette said mischievously.

Paris had to put her two cents in and cosign Lisette's statement. "Well, Angel, she does have a point," she said cheerily. "I rather think there's some mutual interest there, don't you, Lisette?"

"Yes, I absolutely do, Paris. I think we might have the makings of a wonderful couple here," she said with a smile. "What do *you* think, Angel?"

To their surprise, Angelique slumped back against the throw pillows without saying a word. When she spoke, it was with an air of finality that was most unlike her. "I can admit that Adonis Cochran is not repulsive in any way. He's very attractive, very smart, he has nice manners most of the time and he's not boring. He at least has a sense of humor." She sat up and pulled her hair behind her ears, looking at the two women observing her every move with great interest. "But I'm not crazy, and there is no way he would ever be interested in me as a girlfriend. I'm not his type," she said quietly.

"Not his type? You're every man's type! You're pretty and funny. . . ." Lisette's words died off as Angelique held up her hand to silence her.

"Honey, 'pretty' is not going to get the job done. I'm sure Paris hasn't told you this, but I'm dumber than a box of rocks, Lisette. I almost didn't graduate from high school and I couldn't even finish a two-year program at a community college. I have dyslexia. I can barely read. A man like Adonis

Cochran wouldn't be caught dead with a nitwit like me," she said in a dead voice. "I'm going to make some more popcorn." Without another word, she got up and took the big bowl into the kitchen, leaving Lisette staring at Paris in disbelief.

Paris looked so sad and distant, Lisette didn't dare ask her any questions. Paris, however, began to explain.

"Angelique is not stupid—it's obvious that she's very intelligent. But she's never been able to accept that. Like most dyslexics, she's actually very bright, very creative and extremely talented. Her mind just processes information differently than other people. She does an amazing job of coping with it, though, and she has a very severe form of dyslexia. And whatever you do, please don't start rattling off a list of famous people who've overcome dyslexia, it drives her crazy.

"She's had a hard time all of her life because of the way she learns. Like a lot of dyslexics, it wasn't diagnosed for some time. By the time they figured out what was wrong, she was in middle school and was so traumatized by school in general that she had all kinds of behavioral problems. She ended up having to go to boarding school, and it was supposed to help her, but it almost killed her. For her it was like being sent into exile. It was like the ultimate punishment, being away from her family. I don't think Aunt Lillian realizes to this day what it did to Angel to be sent away. But her family really thought it was for the best. They just didn't know what else to do," Paris said softly.

Angelique reappeared, bearing a heaping bowl of fragrant popcorn and a fresh pitcher of iced tea. "They didn't know what else to do because I had driven them all crazy," she said flatly. "Don't sugarcoat it, Paris, I was hell on wheels and you know it."

She put down the refreshments and resumed her seat on the couch, curling her feet up under her. "Lisette, I was the worst child in the entire five-county area that makes up metropolitan Atlanta. I was possibly the worst child in the state of Georgia. If I live to be a thousand I can't undo all the damage I did to my family, so don't let Paris kid you that I was some poor sad little child. I was a *bad* little child, that's what I was."

With studied nonchalance, Angelique helped herself to more popcorn. She met Lisette's inquiring gaze and gave her a wry smile. "When I was little, I wanted to go to school so badly I could taste it. My brothers were the smartest, handsomest, sweetest men on earth and I wanted to be smart like them. They knew *everything* as far as I was concerned. When my father died it was kind of a surreal experience for me because I was young. He traveled so much, so I was much closer to my big brothers than I was to him; well, I knew them better than my father, if that makes sense." Suddenly she gave a huge, genuine smile.

"I used to call Clay and Martin and Malcolm my daddies. If someone messed with me, it was, 'I'm gonna tell my daddies!' " She laughed at the memory. "Even Marcus was more like an uncle than a brother. We're very close in age but he was always so grown-up, he seemed a lot older. He never hung out with guys his age, he hung out with Clay and the twins. All he wanted to do was be grown, like them. And I wanted to be like them too, in a sense. They were brilliant and they could do anything. I thought they all hung the moon and it shone just because they wanted it to."

She stopped and took a long swallow of tea, then sighed. "Then I started school and it was not pretty," she said ruefully. "I was okay at first, in kindergarten and first grade, but as I went on it was just really hard for me to keep up. I tried and tried but I always got bad grades. It was so confusing for me. Everybody else could do the work, but nine times out of ten, I'd be screwing something up. And I would be trying so hard to do it right, to get good grades. The frustration was just unbearable.

"I stayed mad all the time. I was the most hostile, the meanest, the angriest child you ever met. And I was pretty cute when I was little, so that made it worse. For some reason people have all kinds of expectations for you if you look a certain way. If you're cute you're supposed to be this way, if you're ugly you're supposed to be that way—you know how people are. It didn't take very long to get labeled a dummy. 'She's a pretty little thing but she sure is stupid. Lillian better hope that child marries money 'cause she is definitely slow.'" Angelique perfectly imitated a gossipy-sounding older woman. "I was just *mean,* Lisette. I was like a wild animal at times. Paris, you remember Lonnie Brown? He still crosses the street when he sees me coming." Angelique gave a short laugh.

The ringing telephone put an end to the conversation. Angelique was heard to verify that, yes, she knew how to take a relay call, and she excused herself and left the room with the cordless phone.

Lisette looked at Paris and her confusion and sympathy was all over her face. Paris sighed as she rose from the floor and came to sit on the sofa in the spot Angelique had vacated.

"That relay call is from her friend Mateo. He's hearing-impaired, so this call will take a while. The operator has to relay the information from Angel to Matt and from Matt back to Angel. But we need to talk fast. Look, there's a lot more to the situation than Angel is telling you. She makes it seem like she was just this terrible person but it's not true.

"That Lonnie Brown she mentioned? The first summer I visited Angel and her family in Atlanta, this Lonnie creature was making fun of me because I was fat. Angel never said a word; she just picked up a rock and decked him. Coldcocked the evil little troll," she said with a shake of her head. "But then she wouldn't explain why she'd done it. She got in so much trouble! She was on punishment and missed trips to the zoo, to Six Flags—she missed out on so much that summer because she refused to say why she'd done it, and she told *me* not to tell either, because she didn't want me to get in trouble. I finally broke down and told, though. Of course she shouldn't have hit him with a rock, but that's how she is:

mess with somebody she loves and it's *on,* baby. Angel will walk over fire for her family and her friends."

Lisette finally managed to speak. "My goodness, I had no idea. She thinks she's not very bright and yet she's one of the most resilient, clever people I've ever met," she said with wonder in her voice. "When she used the word 'complicated,' she wasn't kidding, was she?"

Paris put her hand on Lisette's arm. "Lisette, I hope you don't start treating her any differently. Aside from me, you're the only girlfriend she has. She has four sisters-in-law and she loves them like her sisters, and she's close to Renee Cochran, who is Donnie's sister-in-law. But friends are different—you know how special it is to have a real friend," Paris said earnestly. "Angel has two friends from that boarding school and she's talking to one of them on the phone. The other one is a woman named Nicole; they were all tight in school and they're still friends. But friendship is something that has been in very short supply for her. Women used to pretend to be her friend so they could push up on those fine brothers of hers. That was devastating to her, although she pretends like it didn't bother her. She tries to be tough, but trust me, she's not as hard as she would have you believe."

"You don't have to explain that to me, Paris, I can see that she's not tough at all, at least not in that way. But in other ways, she's quite something, she really is."

Angelique came bouncing back into the room with a big smile. "Guess what? Mateo and Nicole are coming to Detroit next month, how cool is that? Lisette, these are the coolest people in the world. We all went to the rich dummy academy together and we were best friends." She laughed at Lisette's expression.

"Oh, that's what we called it, the rich dummy school. It was an 'exclusive boarding school for creative students who needed academic challenges not available in a traditional classroom setting.' In other words, it was for wealthy problem children whose families had run out of options, like my family did. Anyway, they're coming here and you get to meet them!"

Changing the subject swiftly, she asked what the menu would be for the Super Bowl party; standing in front of the coffee table, she tapped her finger against her lower lip.

"We don't have long to get this arranged and it can't look thrown together if we're going to make it successful," she reminded the two women. She looked at Lisette and smiled. "You and Warren deserve this; it's your turn for some extra happiness."

Lisette surprised Angelique when she got up from the sofa and gave her a fierce hug. *It's your turn, too, Angel. It will be your turn,* she thought.

Chapter Eight

The day of the Super Bowl party dawned bright and clear although it was quite cold. Angelique surveyed the backyard with mixed emotions. There was enough snow out there to qualify as winter, but not nearly enough for Angelique. "When are we going to get some real snow?" she asked no one in particular. "I thought y'all kept snow up to your kneecaps all winter long."

This made Lisette laugh. "Sorry to disappoint you, sweetie, but I've lived here almost my whole life and you just never know about the weather here. I'm perfectly happy with the snow we have; we don't need any more, if you ask me. But like they say, if you don't like the weather in Michigan, just wait five minutes, it'll change."

The two women were in the kitchen surveying the already prepared food and anything else that still needed to be put together. The refrigerator held a huge pot of gumbo, which only needed to have the rice made and shrimp added during the last part of reheating. There was also another variation of Lillian's shrimp salad, this one made like a traditional potato salad with the addition of cooked shrimp. The vegetables were all washed and cut up for a big pretty tray of crudités; there was cut-up fresh fruit for those who didn't indulge in rich desserts and there would be cheesecake and homemade ice cream sandwiches for those who did. Angelique had also procured some wonderful breads and rolls, with a huge platter of sliced roast beef and smoked turkey for sandwiches. Now they were trying to figure out if anything was missing.

"Let's see, pickles, olives, three kinds of mustard, two kinds of mayonnaise, hot pepper rings . . . oh, I know what— lettuce! We need lettuce and sliced tomatoes for the sandwiches," Angelique said. Paris entered the kitchen in time to hear her last words.

"I got you covered, kid. I sliced up some tomatoes early this morning and I washed and wrapped two heads of romaine lettuce," she said.

Lisette had made two huge cheesecakes, one with a raspberry swirl and one praline, but she was also about to make her special dip for the fruit. "It's so easy it's ridiculous but it tastes very complex and rich. All you do is take some sour cream and stir brown sugar into it until it's all blended. People think you slaved over it and it's so easy, a child can do it," she said with a grin.

"I hope you can do it fast because it looks like Donnie and Warren just arrived," Paris said dryly.

"Why on earth are they here so early? Why can't men ever do what they're supposed to do when they're supposed to do it?" Angelique asked with obvious irritation.

"Because then they'd be women," Paris answered. "Okay, we'll have to regroup. I'm going to disappear upstairs to take a shower and get dressed, and, Angel, you're going to have to drag Donnie off somewhere on a fake errand. Go get some ice or some wine or something. Ready?" She looked at both women before opening the back door, which led into the kitchen.

There stood Warren and Donnie with an alarming-looking apparatus and a big box. Warren gave them a winning smile and informed the ladies that they were going to deep-fry a turkey as their contribution to the dinner. "It marinated all night, plus I injected it with my special mixture and it's going to melt in your mouth," he promised them.

In short order the patio had been cleared of snow, the deep-fryer had been set up and all was ready for the undertaking that would begin as soon as the oil was hot. In the meantime, Angelique had to take matters into her own hands. She turned to Donnie with a big fake smile and asked where the dogs were. Donnie looked surprised for a second, and then replied that they were at home. It would never have occurred to him to bring Jordan and Pippen to Evilene's lair.

"Well, we have to go get them," she said gaily. "They love a party and they're very well behaved. And we need some more ice," she said hurriedly. "I'll meet you at the car, let me get my coat." She stared meaningfully at Lisette as she skittered out of the now-crowded kitchen to fetch her coat from the hall.

Paris immediately jumped up and said she had to go get dressed. "I went to TaeBo this morning and I have to get clean and cute. See you later," she said as she also left the room.

Warren and Donnie looked at each other and shrugged. "I guess we'll be back soon. If I'm not back in an hour, put out an APB on me," Donnie said as he went out the back door.

Lisette was saved from having to say anything as Angelique called her from the living room. She went to see what her friend wanted and was touched to see Angelique fluffing her shiny black hair and taking a last look in the small mirror in the entry hall. "Okay, I'm going to keep him gone for a least an hour," she instructed Lisette. "So you better go for it." She looked down at her outfit and mumbled, "Do I look okay?"

She was wearing jeans that fit perfectly, accentuating her long legs, and had on a pretty turtleneck with horizontal stripes in bright colors, plus her low-heeled ankle boots, nicely polished as always. Angelique had a fetish for keeping her footwear like new. She was wearing her usual Youth

Dew and a smaller pair of gold hoop earrings. Lisette assured her that she looked adorable. Angelique smiled at her friend as buttoned up her pea coat and put on a knit cap and the long knitted scarf that matched the sweater.

"You look beautiful as well," Angelique replied. "Now, go get busy, we're on a schedule here!" With a wink she dashed out the front door and ran lightly down the steps to Donnie's car. He was waiting next to the passenger side and gallantly held the door open for her, making sure she was seated before closing it behind her. In seconds, he had come around to the driver's side and seated himself, fastening the seat belt and checking the traffic before expertly backing the car down the driveway.

The car was filled with music as the thrilling voice of Will Downing poured from the stereo system, and the air was full of the utterly masculine odor that was part Donnie, part his expensive aftershave. Suddenly, Angelique found it a bit hard to breathe. She sat up a little straighter and reminded herself to stay calm. Something was overwhelming her; it was like being in a fragrant steam bath at a luxury spa, only a lot more sensual. Before she could figure out why she was so caught up in a simple car ride, Donnie reached over and took her hand, the left hand that wasn't yet wearing a glove.

"So you've finally got me where you want me. Now what?" he asked in a low, sexy drawl.

Lisette went back into the kitchen, hoping she looked more composed than she felt. She looked perfectly lovely in black straight-leg jeans and a green sweater that buttoned up the front with tiny, enticing mother-of-pearl buttons. Her wavy hair was shiny and soft and she was wearing small, black opal studs in her ears. A soft, beguiling fragrance trailed her as she went to rejoin Warren. She appeared serene and composed, but at the moment she was anything but. Warren was leaning against the kitchen counter as if awaiting instructions. Smiling, she offered to hang up his leather jacket. "Why don't you make yourself comfortable?" she invited. "Would you like to watch television in the living room?"

Before she could chastise herself for inviting him to go into another room and leave her behind, Warren took the lead. "No, I don't want to watch television," he said with a smile. "What I want to do is watch you. There's nothing on television that can compare to you."

Lisette knew she was blushing—she could feel the heat along her cheekbones. She went to Warren and held out her hands for his jacket. "That's the sweetest thing anyone's ever said to me," she said softly. "Now, why don't you go sit down and I'll make you a cup of coffee or something."

Warren shook his head. "I'll hang this up, I know where the closet is. And why don't you sit down and I'll make something for you, honey. I can tell you ladies have been working all day. Allow me to do something for you, Lisette."

The smile she gave him was as warm as summer. She did as she was bid and sat down at the wooden table in the sunny window-lined eating area of the big kitchen. In a few minutes Warren had returned to the kitchen and washed his hands at the sink, singing softly as he did so.

"You have a nice voice," Lisette told him.

"Glee club. Glee club and years of singing in the church choir," Warren said casually. With a minimum of effort, he located the coffee and the filters and soon the rich aroma of coffee filled the room. He and Lisette chatted easily while the coffee brewed and he located two big cups with matching saucers. He worked quickly and efficiently, heating milk and taking a bottle of chocolate syrup out of the refrigerator. He brightened upon finding a container of heavy cream and took it out, too.

Lisette watched in fascination. "What are you making, Warren?"

"I'm making you a cup of café mocha, honey. It's going to be so good, you'll want it every day, so be careful you don't get addicted," he said with a comically raised eyebrow. He looked in a drawer and found a small whisk, which he used to whip a small amount of the cream. Finally everything was ready and he prepared two cups of a mocha mixture that smelled absolutely heavenly. He topped off each cup with a swirl of cream, asking Lisette if he'd put too much on hers.

"There's no such thing as too much whipped cream. I adore it," she confessed.

Warren smiled as he scooped up a dollop from the small bowl in his hand. He held his finger out and Lisette licked the cream off delicately with a little sound of pleasure. Warren put the finger in his mouth as if to savor the taste of her tongue. He looked incredibly sexy doing it and Lisette suddenly felt light-headed.

She lowered her gaze and picked up her cup with unsteady hands. "Thank you so much, this was very sweet of you," she murmured.

Warren looked at the adorable picture she made in the bright sunlight and he moved his chair closer to hers and sat down. He took a small drink of the mocha and made an expression of approval. "I haven't lost my touch," he said with a half smile. Then his face got serious and he looked directly at Lisette, examining each aspect of her beauty, noting her fine features, her soft skin, her full lips and her bright, alert eyes, which were fastened on his face. Abruptly he asked her what fragrance she was wearing.

"It's called Lumiere," she replied.

He nodded absently. "I've never smelled that on anyone else. And now I don't want to smell it on anyone but you. It's perfect for you, soft and feminine just like you," he said, still looking into her eyes. He could have stared at her for the rest of the day and been perfectly content, but he knew he was making her uncomfortable. "I'm trying to memorize your face. I want to learn everything about the way you look, so that when I'm not with you can I remember you accurately and get excited about the next time I'll see you."

Lisette's hands started shaking again and she set her cup down rather abruptly. "That was very beautiful. It was . . . poetic," she said shyly.

Warren smiled and took her small delicate hand in his. "Don't be shy with me, Lisette. I hope you know I would never hurt you or disrespect you in any way," he said solemnly.

Lisette looked at him with equal seriousness. "I know that, Warren. I trust you," she said simply.

They continued to sit that way, with her tiny hand resting in Warren's big, capable one. Lisette was smiling and she looked perfectly happy. Warren began rubbing the back of her hand with his thumb, slowly tracing a circle on her soft skin. "I need to ask you something, honey. I know we don't know each other well, but I want to remedy that. I want to get to know you and I want you to know me. What I want," he said in a soft voice so unlike his normal booming tone that Lisette had to strain to hear him, "is to spend some time with you." He looked at her hand and brought it to his mouth, caressing it with his lips until she sighed. "That's not completely accurate, Lisette. I don't want to 'spend some time' with you; I want to date you, if you think we suit each other. I want . . ."

Lisette finally squeezed his hand to silence him. "Yes, Warren, I think that's a brilliant idea. I think we will suit each other nicely." She smiled and reached across the table to stroke his cheek with her free hand. "And I think you should kiss me."

Warren's handsome face broke into a wide smile. His eyes lit up with passion and pure happiness. "Your wish is my command, Lisette."

He stood up and held out his other hand to her. She rose and came around to his side of the table. He pulled her into his arms and they held one another for a long, delirious moment before their lips found each other. They opened their mouths to taste the sweetness that awaited them, their coffee-flavored tongues mating and dancing over each other in an awakening of passion so satisfying it was almost like pain. When they finally pulled away from each other, Warren was alarmed to see tears in Lisette's long lashes.

"What's wrong, honey? Didn't you like it?" he whispered.

Lisette smiled at the concern in his voice. She rubbed her face against his big broad chest like a sleepy kitten and looked up at him with yearning and surrender. "I loved it," she confessed. "And I want some more, please."

"Well, then, more is what we'll have," he replied before bending to her lips again.

After Angelique got over her initial shock at Donnie's remark, she realized he was just playing with words, teasing her. She regained her equanimity and told him they needed extra ice for the party. "And maybe some wine or beer or something," she added. Donnie drove around until he found a Merchant of Vino, a big market that specialized in spirits and gourmet foods. He parked the car and they went inside in a companionable silence. Donnie asked her what kind of wine she wanted and she confessed that she wasn't much of a drinker. "It all tastes the same to me, especially champagne. What do you think would be good?" She looked up at him with a smile.

Donnie almost stumbled as he looked down into her face. She looked adorable, as always. The bright red hat she wore made her toffee skin glow, and her clear lip gloss made her mouth look edible. Her fragrance had the usual effect on him and her happy mood made him want to do something really crazy. Instead he found a cart and tried to act as though her presence at his side wasn't affecting him in the way it was. He selected a few bottles of Mondavi Chardonnay and a few bottles of a great merlot from Australia called Black Opal. Placing them in the cart, he looked down at Angelique, whose hand was resting next to his on the cart. "Now what? Can you think of anything else we need?"

Angelique bit her lower lip very gently as she thought. The simple gesture brought that old lovin' feeling back to a body part Donnie would prefer remained inert. She suddenly stopped biting her lip and ran her tongue across it, ending in the corner where the cute little beauty mark resided. She did it so quickly and naturally, Donnie knew it was unintentional, but it was like something had reached inside him and gave him a good squeeze. Luckily for him, Angelique spoke and it seemed to break the spell.

"Do you think we need more beer? We have a case, I think, but is that enough?" Again she turned her face up to Donnie, so sweetly and naturally that for a moment it felt like they were a couple. He cleared his throat and gruffly replied to her question.

"I think that's plenty. If the guys want some more they can go get it. Maybe some pop for the kids, but that's about it."

"Oh, we have fruit juice for the kids—too much soda is bad for their teeth. That's the leading cause of tooth decay; I'll bet you didn't know that, did you? Oh, look," she said as she darted off down the aisle.

Donnie looked at her as she was exclaiming over something in the gourmet section. The mention of teeth made him think about the time he'd taken her to the endodontist, something he hadn't thought about in a long time. She'd been in so much pain that day and so frightened that it hurt him to look at her. The memory of that afternoon was permanently etched in his brain. He'd had to hold her like a child to convince her to let him take her in, and once they were there, the thought of him leaving her side was out of the question. He had to stifle a chuckle as he recalled the fact that no one on the office staff dared tell him to sit in the waiting area.

He'd pulled a stool up next to the chair where she was being treated and held her hand the entire time. Anytime she made so much as a whimper, he'd glared at his friend John Taylor, the endodontist who'd been kind enough to take her in as an emergency. Afterward, he'd apologized to John, who waved it away like it was nothing. "Don't worry about it, Donnie. I'm the same way with my wife. You should've seen me in the delivery room when we had our last kid. I'm pretty sure I'm permanently banned from the hospital," he'd told him.

Angelique rejoined Donnie before his reverie got any weirder. She showed off her prize, a big jar of marinated artichoke hearts, something she and Paris both adored. He led the way to the checkout where he took out a platinum card to pay for everything. They left the store in a few minutes and drove to his house to get the dogs. "You know, we really don't have to get them," he said.

"Yes, we do! I haven't seen them in such a long time, and I'm sure they don't like being home alone. Besides," she glanced at the dashboard's digital clock, "I can't go home yet."

That caught Donnie's interest. "What are you up to, Evie? Why are you running me all over town and trying not to go back to your own home, hmm?"

Angelique gave him a smile that was both sheepish and defiant at the same time. "I'm, umm, well, *we're* matchmaking, if you must know. Paris and I are both doing this, so I guess we have to share the blame. Lisette is crazy about Warren and we're trying to give them some time alone," she said. "I think he likes her, too, at least it looks like that to me. What do you think?"

By now they'd reached Donnie's bungalow and he brought the Jaguar to a stop in the driveway by the rear entrance. He turned off the ignition and turned to look at her. "I think it's about time somebody busted a move. Warren is crazy about her, too. How much longer do we have to be gone?"

"About a half hour or so. Do you mind?" she asked with a shy smile.

"Not at all, this is just what Warren needs." He swung his long legs out of the car and went around to the passenger side to let Angelique out. Even though the drive had been neatly shoveled and there were no icy patches, he held her arm until they got to the back door. He opened the door and apologized for going in first. "Excuse my manners—I just don't like the idea of you getting set on by my beasts," he said.

Angelique smiled to herself at his thoughtfulness. In a few minutes they were greeted by the happy, dancing Labradors, who were thrilled with her unexpected visit. Donnie calmed them down after she petted and praised them. "Go lay down. Go," he said sternly and they went to their big pillows in his laundry room, albeit with great reluctance. Then Donnie turned to Angelique and asked if she'd like to see his house.

"Yes, I would," she said thoughtfully. "I've never seen your house, Adonis."

He looked surprised for a moment, and then thought about it. "I guess you haven't. I've never invited you over here before, I wonder why?" he mumbled, more to himself than to Angelique. "Okay, Angel, you're now going to get the grand tour. Come with me."

He took her hand and led her through the kitchen, the dining room, the living room and the three bedrooms. One of the bedrooms was completely unfurnished, one was set up like an office and one was apparently Donnie's bedroom, judging from the mammoth unmade bed. Like her very tall brothers, Cochran men had a need for a huge bed. There was a bathroom with a big claw-foot tub, and a powder room he deemed unworthy of a visit. They talked about the house as they toured it. It was a typical Arts and Crafts–styled bungalow typical of Detroit in the 1930s. There were hardwood floors throughout and big fireplaces in the master bedroom and the living room. It was nicely furnished in a masculine manner, but it lacked a real personality, although Angelique prudently kept this thought to herself.

They ended up in the basement game room, with Angelique wandering around and admiring the arcade games. Donnie, meanwhile, was admiring her. She walked over to the bar and sat on one of the tall stools. Playfully, she patted her hand on the counter and called, "Bartender!"

Donnie walked slowly across the room and stood behind her stool, leaning in so that he pressed against her back. Their eyes met in the big mirror behind the bar. "Are you thirsty? I can fix you something to drink, if you like," he said in a husky voice. Still staring into his reflected eyes, she shook her head no. Donnie pressed even closer and wrapped one arm around her. "Are you sure you don't want anything?" he asked, his warm breath bathing her cheek.

She whispered, "No, I don't want anything," and Donnie nodded absently, removing her red hat and stroking her silky hair while he kept his other arm locked around her. "Well, I want something, Angel. Something only you can give me," he whispered.

Instead of tensing up, Angelique felt her body melt against Donnie's and she leaned back into him. "What do you want?" she whispered.

He let her go long enough to turn her around on the bar stool and pull her into his embrace. "I want this," he murmured as he brought his mouth down on hers. He kissed her softly at first. Once, twice, three times their lips touched each other, and then his tongue traced the same path hers had followed earlier. He painted her lips with the moisture from his mouth, softly and thoroughly learning the curves of her soft lips. Then they began kissing in earnest, harder and wilder as they reveled in the taste of each other, the feel of each other. Kissing her mouth wasn't enough; Donnie pulled her from the stool and held her as close to him as their coats would allow. He kissed her temple, her cheek, her neck, and moaned as her warm scent drove him crazy. Kissing his way back up to her lips, he parted them slightly with his hot tongue and initiated the intimate contact again, the sweet, tender explosion satisfying him like nothing ever had.

They might have gone on kissing for hours, if it hadn't been for the insistent noise of a cell phone. Angelique finally recognized the persistent buzzing as her own phone, which she snatched out of her pocket with a look of extreme irritation. "What is it?" she snapped into the little phone.

Paris answered with her usual good humor. "Just letting you know the coast is clear—looks like the mission was accomplished. I think we have some lovebirds over here," she said cheerfully. After a monosyllabic grunt from Angelique, Paris's nimble mind put two and two together. "Ah-*ha! You* two been gettin' busy, haven't you? And it was good, too! Ooh, wait till I get you home!"

All Angelique could do was stare wordlessly into Donnie's sexy eyes. *Now what have I gotten myself into? And do I even want to get out?* Before she could answer her own question, Donnie pulled her back into his arms and his lips put an end to any more thoughts.

Chapter Nine

Days after the Super Bowl soiree, the attendees were still talking about what a good time it was. The food, the company and the general atmosphere of fun made it a day to remember. The guest list was varied and included some of Paris's coworkers at Cochran Communications, a few neighbors and those members of the Cochran family who could make it. Renee and Andrew were in Renee's hometown of Cleveland that weekend for her parents' anniversary and couldn't attend; Alan and Andre Cochran had already made plans with their fraternity brothers for Super Bowl Sunday and were also absent. But Adam was there with Alicia, as was the patriarch of the family, Big Bennie Cochran, along with his bride, Martha. And, of course, A.J. attended with one of his female friends.

The evening was a complete success in all ways, especially the matchmaking part. Warren and Lisette appeared well on their way to bliss—something Paris continued to talk about, to Angelique's chagrin. "Chagrin" because Paris would start talking about the couple who belonged together, Warren and Lisette, and end up interrogating Angelique about Donnie. No matter how many times Angelique changed the subject, issued outright denials or threatened Paris's life, the end result was the same. She was being treated to it again this very morning while Paris was having a late cup of coffee in Angelique's studio on the first floor of the Cochran building. Paris had come back to the building from a business meeting and dropped in to see her cousin before heading upstairs. And, once again, the normal conversation led right into what Angelique thought of as Paris's Fantasy Land.

"Angel, I don't know how you do it, but this is the greatest coffee in the world. You make the best coffee I've ever tasted," Paris said appreciatively. She watched Angelique at work and they talked about this and that, until—like the homing pigeon she was beginning to emulate—Paris went right back to the topic Angelique wanted to avoid more than anything.

"So, Angel, when are you going to admit that something happened between you and Donnie? I could see the way you two were looking at each other all afternoon; something happened and you and I both know it. Y'all came back here looking like two sixteen-year-olds on your first date and you were all moony-eyed the rest of the day. Lisette didn't notice because she and Warren were doing the same thing, but *I* certainly saw it. Even Willis asked me if you two were an item," she added slyly.

That gave Angelique pause and she narrowed her eyes at Paris. Willis Gaffney was a friend and occasional date of Paris's—an advertising account executive who did business with Cochran Communications. "I certainly hope you told him there was nothing between us," she snapped.

"Actually, you'd better be glad he thinks there's something going on. He was just about to make a move on you that night and Donnie put an immediate stop to that." Paris chuckled. "All he did was look at him, but I think it made poor Willis's heart stop. That's when he asked me if you two were a couple."

Angelique dropped her head into her hands and gave a muffled shriek. "What did you tell him? You didn't tell him we're dating, did you?"

Paris enjoyed her cousin's discomfort for a few seconds, and then showed her mercy. "No, I didn't. All I said was, 'What do *you* think?' and let him draw his own conclusions. He's not going to say anything to anybody about it because Donnie scared him half to death with one look. I was pretty impressed, actually. Nobody's ever looked at anybody like that on my behalf," she reflected. Arching a neatly shaped brow, she gave Angelique a wicked grin and said, "Which brings me back to my original question: what's going on with you and Donnie? You know how nosy I am, put me out of my misery."

Lifting her head up, Angelique shot a mean look at Paris, which didn't scare her one bit. "I'd like to put you out of your misery, all right. Permanently. For the last time, there is nothing, I repeat, *nothing,* going on between me and Adonis Bennett Cochran," she said with a grimace.

Just then the buzzer sounded. Angelique had a reception area as well as a big office and workroom. Because she did not employ a receptionist, she had the buzzer installed for security. Paris glanced at her watch and said she would get the door on her way out. "I need to be getting back to work anyway." She left Angelique in the big main room and went to the reception area to find out who was calling.

When Paris didn't return immediately, Angelique's curiosity made her go to the reception area to see what became of her. "Paris, who was that at the . . ." Her voice faded away as she looked into the amused eyes of Donnie.

Paris also looked quite entertained as she waved at her cousin, then left, saying, "See you later, Angel. Have a good trip, Donnie." Angelique made a mental note to do something really bad to Paris at her earliest convenience. In the meantime, she concentrated on looking composed. "Hello, Adonis. What can I do for you today?" she asked politely.

Donnie was looking better than any man had a right to at that hour of the morning—at any hour of the day, as a matter of fact; the man was ridiculously handsome. He was wearing a beautifully cut, tan cashmere topcoat over a charcoal-gray suit no doubt custom-tailored to accommodate his height. His leather gloves were in one hand and his over-the-shoulder briefcase was sitting by the door. While she took in every detail of his appearance, Donnie was looking around her studio with great interest. Angelique cleared her throat and repeated her question. "What is it that I can do for you?" she said more sharply than she intended.

"I'm here because I wanted to see you. I haven't seen you since the party, and I never told you thank you for your hospitality. It was a good time. My dad is still talking about that gumbo," he said with a smile as he shoved his gloves into this coat pocket.

"Even though I'm the one who made it?" she said with a slight grin.

Donnie dropped his head for a moment, then looked up with a plea in his eyes. "You're not going to let me live that down, are you? It was a mistake, I admit it."

At the party, when the buffet had been laid out and people started eating the wonderful repast, Donnie had looked at Paris and said, "Girl, you put your *foot* in this gumbo. This is the best I've ever had."

Paris had smiled and said, "Well, thanks, Donnie, but I didn't make that. Angelique is the real cook, I just kind of putter around."

Remembering the scene, Angelique gave him a grudging look of amusement. "Hard as it is to believe, I can do a few things, Adonis."

Now it was his turn to smile. "You know something? I never liked my name. Never could stand it, it was just too affected for me. But I like the way it sounds when you say it. I know you use my name to irritate me, but it sounds really sexy coming from your mouth."

Angelique's eyes widened and she took a step backward, even though they weren't standing close. She was still in the entrance to the reception area and he was in the middle of the room. Donnie could sense her nervousness and he wanted to put her at ease as soon as possible, though that might be difficult, given what he'd come to say. It was his turn to check her out and he liked what he saw, very, very much.

"You're looking very stylish today. Beautiful, in fact," Donnie said appreciatively. He enjoyed the faint pinkness that spread along her cheekbones at his compliment, but he meant every word—Angelique looked like a high-fashion model. She was dressed in a stunning black outfit: a pair of slacks with a kimono-styled jacket over a white tunic with an asymmetrical, mandarin-styled collar. She looked *courant* and avant-garde, yet professional. Her hair was once again worn in a updo, but this time it was sleekly styled off her face and had two abalone chopsticks stuck though it. She smelled differently, though, and Donnie tried to place the scent. "You have on a new perfume today, what is it?" he asked.

Angelique was so surprised by the question that she answered him without hesitation. "Cashmere Mist."

Donnie filed that information away for future reference. "I like it. It's as nice as the other one you wear."

"I'm so glad you approve," she said snidely. "I live for that, you know."

He liked the look of her studio; it was done in calming neutral colors and had a clean, minimalist effect, due to the lack of doodads. The walls were done in eggshell and the taupe furniture consisted of a long sofa and two chairs. Aside from a coffee table with magazines, a simple but elegant floor lamp and two ficus trees, there was nothing in the room except a few photographs on the walls, all in black and white. The space looked sophisticated and artistic.

"This is a nice place, Angel. But it doesn't look like you," Donnie said honestly. "It's too cold, too impersonal. I don't know you as well as I should, but I can tell you that this room isn't anything like you."

Angelique blinked and then shook herself quickly. She crossed her arms as if she was chilly and needed the warmth. "I don't know what you're talking about, Adonis. This room is exactly like me. Cold and impersonal, that's me all over," she said hotly, as she returned to the main work space. To her displeasure, Donnie followed her.

This room was neat as a pin, but it was much more colorful, with some color shots on the walls as well. There was a large table in the center of the room with a big zipper portfolio laid on it, neatly stacked prints arranged around it. The walls were lined with cabinets that stored her equipment. She was trying to look busy at the table when Donnie's voice stopped her movements.

"Oh, no, you're not. You're as far from being cold and impersonal as it's possible for one person to be. This room looks more like you. This room and your house, that's you. Warm, vibrant and creative," he told her. The look of confusion in Angelique's eyes touched him to his heart and also made him get to the point. He wasn't here to torture her—quite the opposite. "Look, Angel, I'm going out of town. I'll be gone all week, but when I get back, I'd like to take you out. I think it's time we stopped ignoring this attraction and did something about it, don't you?"

Angelique was so surprised by his words, she couldn't answer at first. Then she said the first thing that came to her mind: a resounding no. "No, I don't. I don't think that's a good idea at all, Adonis."

He closed the gap between them in one step and put his left hand on her shoulder. With his right hand he tilted her chin up, then placed a soft, moist kiss on her lips. "I told you, I like the sound of my name on your lips. I like a lot of other things about you, too. And I think you like me, at least a little. Say you'll go out with me, just for dinner," he coaxed.

"I . . . I . . ." Angelique valiantly tried to remember why this was a bad idea. He was standing so close, the warmth of his body was igniting hers; his body chemistry was making his aftershave into an aphrodisiac and his lips felt wonderful, even for that short moment. Just as she was about to say no again, he touched his lips to her cheekbone, and the warmth spread over her like a blanket of passion.

"Say yes, Angel. Please say yes," he said softly.

"Yes," she said with a sigh. "Yes, I will."

After Donnie left the office, Angelique was ready to sit down for a long time and think about what had just happened. Despite all her efforts to stay in control, she was trembling. And today was just not the day for that, not when she had to go the museum to meet with the director. If it weren't for the fact that A.J. was coming with her, she'd have been a wreck.

He showed up to collect her a little bit earlier than they'd agreed on and she was truly glad to see him. She gave him a big hug and a kiss on the cheek, and then asked him why he was so early. "Not that I'm not glad to see you. I'm glad you're here," she said, inhaling his familiar scent. "You look very handsome. She's not going to pay me a bit of attention with you sitting there looking gorgeous."

He did look rakishly charming as always, this time in pleated black trousers, a black cable knit turtleneck and his long leather coat that made him look like a model. Although his long dreadlocks were gone as a result of the chemotherapy, he had a start on new ones in the form of a headful of black curls that spiraled every which way. He shrugged off the comment and concentrated on Angelique.

"I came early so I could see how nervous you are," he replied. He looked her over from head to toe and nodded approvingly. "You clean up nice. You look very uptown, just like a seasoned professional. Love the chopsticks."

"Thanks for the compliment. That's the second one I've gotten today. This is my serious-artist drag," she said with a short laugh. "Now let's just hope it impresses Miss Shabazz."

A.J. put his long, strong hands on her shoulders and gave her a little shake, quickly followed by another embrace. "Look, sweetie, I keep telling you you're the real deal. Your talent will speak for itself. Get your coat and your other goods and chattels and let's get going. You're going to knock her socks off," he promised her.

Angelique gave him a shaky smile of gratitude. "I just hope you're right."

In a short while, they were shown into Aneesah's sunny office at the museum. She met them at the door wearing a chic navy pantsuit with a beautiful Kente cloth throw over one shoulder. Her smooth brown face glowed and her shining black hair shone with good health; not a hair of her stylish, short coiffure was out of place. "Good morning! I'm so glad to meet you both," she said with a warm sincerity that immediately put Angelique at ease. She showed them to comfortable chairs and made pleasant small talk while offering coffee or tea. Soon it seemed A.J.'s prediction proved correct: she was completely impressed with everything she saw in Angelique's portfolio. After A.J. and Angelique set the mounted, matted pictures on the easels placed in the office for that purpose, Aneesah went into her own little world.

She was talking softly to herself and blotting moisture from her eyes, and then looked up with a huge smile. "I'm sorry, I don't usually go off like that, but I've never seen anything quite like this," she admitted. "I've seen some of your work in *Hour* magazine, and in *Elle*, but these are just incredible. Tell me again how you got started."

Angelique took a deep breath and looked at A.J., who raised one brow and gave her a nod of encouragement. "Well," she began, "my brother Clay was a photojournalist. That was his passion; it had been for as long as I can remember. He used to have a camera with him all the time. He took pictures of everything and he's the one who taught me how to use a camera. I used up roll after roll of film taking all kinds of terrible pictures." She laughed at the memory. "Clay was really patient with me, though. He traveled a lot, but whenever he was home he'd show me something new, how to set up a shot, how to use different cameras—he even showed me how to develop. I never really did anything with it until years later, though."

She paused for a moment and glanced at A.J. again. "My family's company, the Deveraux Group, has about twenty different magazines and about fifteen newspapers, as I'm sure you're aware. After I tried college, my brothers tried to find something for me to do in the company. I kind of went from place to place, from department, to department, wreaking havoc everywhere.

"I was the prototype of the spoiled little debutante. In fact, I was the gold standard of the Black American Princess, too cute to work and too rotten to stay in school. Luckily, my sister-in-law Vera had the compassion and foresight to put me with A.J." She looked at him again, this time giving him a huge smile that lit up the room.

"A.J. let me work as his assistant, and that's where my education in photography was continued. He taught me everything he knows about photography. Trust me when I tell you he's forgotten more than I'll ever know. He also taught me how to be a professional, how to respect my craft and the people with whom I associate. He taught me how to be an adult, basically. When he decided to leave fashion photography and make documentaries, I went with him and I took pictures of everything I saw. I met so many wonderful people and learned so much, I can never repay him. I owe everything to this man," she said passionately.

By now A.J. was looking a bit uncomfortable with this praise, and Aneesah was looking at him with distinct interest. He tried to deflect the plaudits by pointing out that Angelique's vision was totally her own. "Regardless of what she says, you can see her talent in the prints. She has a gift for capturing the essence of the moment and making a story come alive in a photograph, which is, of course, what art is all about."

Aneesah agreed wholeheartedly. "I completely concur. These African women are all so beautiful, but there's so much more than beauty in their faces. Were these all taken in one place?"

"Yes, they were, they were all from the same village. All

those women have either full-blown AIDS or they're HIV-positive," Angelique said quietly. "All those women have children, all of whom also have AIDS and HIV. And their husbands, who were infected by women working as prostitutes to support their families, infected each of them. This is a hard fact of life in many parts of Africa, unfortunately. I have pictures of the children, also, but I didn't know if you'd be interested in them."

Aneesah's face wore an unreadable expression and she was quiet for a long moment. "I don't know if you're aware of it, but I have an MFA in art history and my doctorate work is in cultural anthropology. What your pictures are depicting was a large part of my dissertation. I'd very much like to see those pictures. More importantly, I think that the public in general would like to see your pictures. I think they *need* to see your pictures. Like these pictures of women working; I'm in complete awe of them."

Angelique almost ducked her head at the praise, but caught herself in time. She was proud of the series of images of women at work. Like all her work, they were in black and white, developed on matte paper to better display the texture of the subject. She had shot women working as exotic dancers, showing them as they got dressed to perform, and as they dressed to leave work. Their stories were written across their faces like tattoos. She had taken shots of women working in fish canneries, in sweatshops, in diners, in institutional laundries, as well as female firefighters, basketball players and mechanics. There were women working in the small beauty salons that sprang up like weeds in every city, women cleaning floors and laying concrete. There was an amazing cross section of America depicted in her work.

"I want to call it *Working Girls,* but everything is so politically correct these days, I'm kind of hesitant," she admitted.

"You can call it anything you want. You know, your work reminds me of a combination of Gordon Parks, Moneta Sleet and Diane Arbus," Aneesah said as she continued to peruse the pictures. "These are the ones that made me cry," she added as she pushed a series of photographs across the desk. They were all of disabled adults, some with Down syndrome, others with different physical challenges. There was nothing sentimental or glamorized about the shots; they were just realistic depictions that gave the viewer another frame of reference for the subject. After another lingering look, Aneesah turned her full attention to A.J.

"You know, I'm quite familiar with your work as well. I think anyone who's ever picked up a fashion magazine is familiar with Alan Jay—you're one of the best-known fashion photographers in the world. But I also saw your film when it screened at the Detroit Institute of Arts. I was moved by it, completely in awe. And you're from Detroit?"

A.J. smiled and assured her that he was indeed from Detroit. "Born and raised in Hamtramck, graduated from Cass Tech."

Aneesah smiled in return. "So did I. Graduate from Cass Tech, I mean."

They looked at each other for a long moment, and then Aneesah collected herself and went back to the matter at hand.

"Angelique, what I'd like to do is have your work featured in a special exhibit. It's obviously too late for Black History Month since it's already February, but I'm thinking about April," she said, consulting a huge desk calendar. "Will that give you time enough to have prints ready for sale?" When Angelique looked surprised, Aneesah gave her a smile of encouragement. "This is going to be an extremely successful exhibit," she said warmly. "This is going to be the start of something huge for you. I'm very honored that we're going to be the first place to showcase your remarkable talent."

She looked at the pictures on her desk and on the two easels and sighed with satisfaction. "You know, you should be putting these into book form. What you need is an agent," she said firmly.

A.J. grinned widely and leaned toward Aneesah. "Thank

you so much for saying that. I've told her the same thing several times. I'm glad she heard it from an expert."

Angelique didn't say anything at all; she was too overwhelmed by the reaction to her work. Aneesah excused herself from the office for a moment to confer with her assistant. A.J. turned to Angelique and took her hand.

"Hey, kid, this is the part where you look happy. This is when the good times start to roll," he said gently.

Only someone who knew her as well as A.J. could have possibly understood when the single tear rolled down her cheek.

Chapter Ten

A.J. watched in amazement as Angelique finally sat back and made a noise of total contentment. The remains of a huge meal were on the table in front of them and she was utterly replete. "What I don't understand is where you put all that food," he said, shaking his head in wonder. "You eat more than I do and you know how I love to eat."

They were at one of Angelique's favorite places, La Shish, a restaurant that featured excellently prepared Middle Eastern cuisine in a beautifully serene atmosphere. They had gone to the one in Troy on Rochester Road; there were several of them in the suburban areas around Detroit. She had eaten her way through two bowls of Mediterranean salsa—a lovely combination of chopped tomatoes, capers and lemon juice with subtle seasonings—along with three baskets of fresh, warm, miniature pitas baked on the premises, plus a bowl of hummus, also made daily. She'd also consumed grape leaves stuffed with lamb and rice, tabbouleh and a salmon dish she hadn't tried before. And, as always, their incredible lemonade, which was homemade and more like a smoothie than the traditional thin drink. Her eyes were slightly glazed from the sheer enjoyment of her meal, but she did respond to his question.

"I have no idea where it goes," she admitted. "I eat like a horse and I never gain a pound. And I'm really trying to gain some weight—I want to look like a woman, not a stick."

A.J. laughed in her face. "If you were bigger, you'd want to be smaller. Just give it a rest, will you?"

Angelique made a face. "Men like to have something to hold on to. My brothers all say that nothing wants a bone but a dog. Those boys like *meat* on the bones. Look at Clay and Bennie. She was pretty slim when they got married but she's got a shape now, after five babies. And believe me, Clay is one happy man. Selena is nice and thick, Ceylon has always been healthy and Vera isn't thick but she's got a *body*, honey. Her figure can stop traffic, with those boobs and that booty; I've seen it happen. And since she's pregnant again, Marcus is about to lose his mind, he's so happy. And they're all tall, too. I'm like a skinny little kid next to my sisters-in-law. You know how you men are, ya'll want some hips and breasts and things to hold on to," she said, looking down at her undeniably slender thighs in disgust.

"Look, you've got bigger and better things to think about now, like your future. I told you, Angel, this is just the beginning. A lot of good things are going to start happening for you and you need to be ready for them. I think Aneesah is right, you need to get an agent, baby. You've got the potential to put together some beautiful books and you need to get on that."

Angelique didn't answer him at once; she busied herself looking around the restaurant, staring at the colorful photographs on the walls and the pretty beaded fringes that surrounded the light fixtures. Finally she spoke. "A.J., as poor as my reading and writing skills are, how am I supposed to write a book? I might be able to take pictures, but write a book? I don't think so."

A.J. grabbed Angelique's hand across the table. "Hey, now. We've had this conversation before, Angel. I don't know what it's going to take to convince you that you're brilliant, but you've got to believe in yourself. Dyslexia can't be the end of your world. I still think you'd benefit from some classes, some counseling, but I'm willing to take it one step at a time. As far as a book is concerned, don't sweat it, that's what editors are for. That's what ghostwriters are for, Angel. Do you think all those celebrities that write their memoirs and cookbooks and whatnot do it all themselves? Of course they don't, sweetie, they have professionals to help them. Don't let a bunch of 'what ifs' get in your way. You can do this, Angel. Trust me," he said firmly, squeezing her hand in his.

She did trust A.J., more than she would have believed possible. He knew her better than almost anyone; he knew her good points and her bad, he'd seen her at her best and at her worst and he knew all her secret fears. If there was anyone in the world that she trusted, it was A.J. So on the way back to the studio, she asked him a question she knew he would answer honestly.

"A.J., what does it mean when someone who doesn't like you kisses you?" She tried to look nonchalant while she posed the question but she couldn't make eye contact without giving herself away.

"What have you been up to, Angel?" He glanced over at her as he expertly maneuvered his ancient and venerable Peugeot through the expressway traffic.

She tried looking innocent, then gave up the fruitless attempt. "Okay, look. I'm the one who started it; I admit that freely and without reservation. I told you I kissed Adonis Cochran on New Year's Eve. I still don't know what came over me, but I grabbed him and kissed him. Then he didn't even speak to me on New Year's Day, which I figured meant that he really couldn't stand me, or something. We never have gotten along and it was pretty out there for me to be forcing him into a lip lock. Well, then the day of the Super Bowl party we had to leave the house on a semifake errand to give Lisette and Warren some time alone. We ended up at his house and that time *he* kissed *me*. And this morning, he came to my studio to tell me that he was going out of town and that he wanted to go out when he came back. And he kissed me again. So what does it all mean, A.J.?"

He listened to her recitation with a slight smile on his face, a smile that got bigger when she was finished. "It means that you two are attracted to each other and the desire to act on the attraction is mutual. So go out with him and have a good time. Nobody's saying you have to marry the guy, just have some fun," he said, reaching over and taking her hand. "You deserve to have a good time, Angel."

"I have plenty of fun, A.J., I really do. I don't need to date Adonis Cochran in order to enjoy life. Besides," she mumbled, "I'm not his type. I don't know why he wants to go out with me."

A.J. let go of her hand and quickly thumped her on the side of the head with his thumb and middle finger. "That's twice you've put yourself down today. One more time and I'll be forced to take steps," he threatened.

She gave an exaggerated "ouch" in mock pain. "I'm not putting myself down, I'm stating a fact. I'm *not* his type. Every woman I've ever seen him with is like that Aneesah Shabazz. He likes tall women, full-figured women, really smart women who can rearrange molecules and run museums and do open-heart surgery and things. He'd never be interested in someone like me, not for long." She narrowed her eyes for a moment in thought. "You know what? I'm pretty sure he used to date her a long time ago. I could be wrong, but I don't think so. Not that I'd really know. Before I moved up here I spent much of my time trying to avoid those Cochrans. They intimidated me half to death."

"Yeah, well, he'd better not be playing with you," A.J. growled. "Not if he wants to keep that pretty face of his. I think you're underestimating your unique and exceptional appeal once more, Angel. If he has any sense at all, he sees you for the beautiful, unusual, *exasperating* woman that you are and he wants to get to know you better. Go out with him and see what happens."

"I'm beautiful, unique and exceptional, huh? So why didn't

you fall for me, A.J.? You know I'm crazy about you," she said with a smile.

"And you know I'm too old for you," he said, not meeting her eyes. "So let's not go there again. And tell that Cochran if he tries any funny business, I'll be paying him a little visit." This time, though, A.J. wasn't smiling.

Donnie spent four days on the road, visiting some of the key stations in Michigan and taking a few important meetings with affiliates in Chicago and Ohio. He was justifiably proud of the strides Cochran Communications had made in the years since he had assumed the chairmanship of the company. What had been five small urban stations in the early days of his father had grown to fifteen stations when his sister Benita had started running things. Now the company had more than forty stations, ten of which were television stations. They were also fully partnered with the Deveraux Group in Contemporary Urban Issues, a twenty-four–hour news network that was the brainchild of Donnie and Marcus Deveraux. He'd made a true contribution to not only his family business, but to the communications industry as a whole. He had every reason to be relaxed and satisfied as he flew home in comfortable first-class accommodations from Chicago. Normally he would have snoozed during the flight, but this afternoon he found that he couldn't.

Right now his mind was full of thoughts he would have found totally unbelievable a few weeks ago. For some reason, he had Angelique Deveraux on the brain and he couldn't get rid of her. Not that he really wanted to, although he wasn't sure why. She certainly wasn't the kind of woman he normally went for, but he had an undeniable attraction to her and it was fruitless to deny it. She was funny, feisty and beautiful, although not in the way he always preferred. He smiled to himself as he recalled her slender frame and how delicate yet enticing she felt pressed against his body. And to top it all off, she kissed like nothing he'd ever imagined. Nothing in his most erotic experiences could have prepared him for the way her mouth responded to his. Leaning deeper into his seat, he felt the familiar stirring that came lately whenever he was around Angelique.

Whatever the attraction was, he was willing to explore it further, to see where it led the both of them. She wasn't immune to him, either, that much was certain. Try as she might to deny it, Donnie knew Angelique was interested in him, too. He wasn't vain or cocky when it came to women; on the contrary, he tried to always treat women with the utmost respect and admiration. And he had every intention of doing the same to Angelique as soon as he was back on the ground.

Donnie was in the best of spirits as he entered the lobby of the Cochran building from the elevator. He'd parked in the underground garage and could have taken the elevator directly to the executive floor, but he had a reason to stop on the ground level. Two reasons, actually: one was because he loved just looking at the building his brother had designed. Adam had taken an abandoned brick structure and turned it into a modern marvel, an imposing edifice that combined the best of the new while revering the old glamour of a bygone Detroit.

The ground level had an old-fashioned arcade consisting of a newsstand, a coffee bar, a florist, a barbershop, a gift shop and an old-fashioned apothecary complete with a soda fountain. There was never a vacancy for the leased areas and there was a waiting list for space that went on for years. The marble floors, the vaulted ceiling with the original light fixtures and the Diego Rivera murals that were rescued by Adam and restored by an expert crew hired by Alicia all lent an air of distinction that was unequaled in the city. The Cochran building was definitely a piece of prestigious real estate and another example of how Donnie had strengthened the company.

Donnie greeted several employees and acquaintances as he made his way across the lobby. His destination was the florist, where he purchased a spray of bird-of-paradise. Their exotic coloring and almost sculptural beauty made them the perfect choice in his mind. He was whistling softly as he crossed the lobby again and went down the hallway to the first-floor studio of ANGELIQUE DEVERAUX, FINE ART PHOTOGRAPHY, BY APPOINTMENT ONLY. He smiled as he looked at the neat brass letters in a deco-styled font outside her door, then frowned as he looked through the glass to see Angelique and a strange man—a strange man who was holding her in his arms and kissing her.

Angelique came out of the man's arms without a trace of embarrassment, even after she realized it was Donnie bearing down on her buzzer like a madman.

"Matt, this is the guy I was telling you about," she said as she went to the door to open it. "You're back," she said to Donnie. "When did you get back?"

Donnie entered the studio with the air of a lion stalking its prey. He didn't respond to Angelique's question at first, but simply looked at her. She waved her hand in front of his face to get his attention.

"Hello? Hello, are you in there? Are those for me or are you redecorating?" she asked, indicating the bouquet in his hand.

"They're for you," he said gruffly, thrusting the flowers at her like he was handing off a baton in a relay race or something equally unromantic.

Clearly pleased by the flowers, Angelique took them in her right hand and, with her left, reached for Mateo's hand. "Thanks, Donnie, that was very thoughtful of you. This," she beamed, turning to face Mateo, "is my best friend in the whole world, Mateo Antonio de Alfonso y Joaquin Santana. We haven't seen each other in a long, long time and he's come to visit," she said, still facing Mateo.

"Nice to meet you," Donnie said, although his face looked anything but happy to see the man. This Mateo was about six-one, slender but well muscled and very exotic-looking with curly black hair, tawny skin and long-lashed hazel eyes. He had a cleft in his squared chin, high cheekbones and a full, pouty mouth that looked like it had seen a lot of action. Donnie grew grim as he reflected that he had witnessed a little of that action himself.

Angelique took her hand away from Donnie's and turned to put the flowers on the low table. Indicating the sofa, she suggested they sit down. Mateo sat at one end and she took a chair across from him. Donnie continued to stand, his expression unchanged. He was trying not to let it show but suddenly his stomach was churning and his head was pounding. This was not the reception he'd envisioned, not by a long shot. He'd anticipated giving the flowers to Angelique, making plans for a romantic dinner and maybe getting another one of her remarkable kisses. Definitely one of those. Instead he walked in to find her wrapped up with someone he'd never seen or heard of before. It suddenly dawned on him that Angelique was talking; he'd been too put off to really listen before. "I'm sorry, Angel, I didn't hear you. What did you say?"

Still facing her friend, Angelique repeated what she'd said before, eliciting an odd response from Mateo, or Matt, as he was called. He gave Angelique a wicked grin and moved his fingers in the distinctive and unmistakable pattern of sign language. Angelique made a sound of disgust, and then signed back as she spoke to him. "That is so rude. What have I told you about that? No, he's not deaf, he's just tired, and that's why he didn't hear me. Now behave yourself."

She continued to talk to Donnie and signed while she was speaking to him. "Matt likes to think he's funny, you have to excuse him," she said, and shrieked as Matt playfully spanked her leg in retaliation. Signing rapidly, she said something that made Matt fall back on the sofa in laughter. She saw Donnie looking at the two of them and felt self-conscious for some reason.

"How was your trip? I hope it was successful," she said softly. "You really do look a little tired."

Donnie finally smiled at the concern in her voice. "Yes, it

was very successful, as a matter of fact. Listen, I don't want to take up your time, I see you're busy. How about if I call you later?"

"Sure, that would be fine." After a second she looked at him quizzically. "Umm, do you have my number?" she asked, still signing.

Matt signed something that was apparently hilarious, as Angelique's eyes widened and she burst out laughing. "He says *you* might not have my number but he has yours. I told you, he thinks he's funny."

In the elevator Donnie ground his teeth and thought he'd never met anyone less humorous in his life. He managed to get to his office without snapping anyone's head off, but his mood hadn't improved in the least. He took off his topcoat and tossed it on the chair across from his desk, walking over to the small walnut refrigerator in the corner of the office. He took out a cobalt-blue bottle of his favorite mineral water and opened it. Staring moodily out the window, he drank most of it without tasting a thing. Finally, he went to his desk and sat down, then picked up the phone and punched in a familiar number. After exchanging pleasantries, he got right to the point. "What are you doing after work? Okay, sure, I'll be there. Thanks, Warren, I'll see you then."

Chapter Eleven

A few hours later, Warren was in the kitchen of his big, still mostly unfurnished house in Farmington Hills preparing dinner. He was completely at home in the kitchen, as was evidenced by the expert way he was putting together what looked to be a savory meal for a cold night. He placed fresh basil leaves under the breast skin of a roasting chicken while Donnie watched him.

Warren looked at his friend and made note of his foul mood. "What's got you so down and out, man? I haven't seen you like this since you got your ring returned."

Donnie gave a half smile. "Technically, the ring wasn't returned since it was never accepted. I need to get rid of it, too. I keep forgetting to take it back to the jeweler," he reflected.

"Is that what's got you looking like ten miles of bad road? Just take the ring back to the store, end of story. And take it back fast—you're just asking for trouble having it lying around. Get rid of it," Warren said. He rubbed the inside of the chicken and the neck cavity with pesto and placed a lemon half in each opening, then covered the plump bird with olive oil and finished with a sprinkle of sea salt and a twist of the pepper mill. Warren glanced at the wall clock before slipping the prepared bird into the oven. "You want something to drink?"

"Yeah, sure. Anything," Donnie said. He was sitting on a tall stool by the work island in the middle of the kitchen, leaning on his elbows and looking pretty much like Warren's description. When Warren pushed a pilsner glass at him with some sort of red concoction in it, Donnie raised an eyebrow and looked at him questioningly.

"Drink it, it won't kill you," Warren said with amusement.

Donnie took a sip, and, sure enough, it was pleasant to the palate, slightly fizzy and tart with an underlying sweetness. "This is good, what is it?"

Warren looked a little sheepish. "It's pomegranate juice with lime-flavored Perrier," he admitted. Before Donnie could revile him for serving a sissy drink, Warren added that it was Lisette's favorite, which reminded Donnie of why he was so glum. Watching Warren prepare a perfect salad, he unburdened himself.

"Warren, I think I'm losing my mind," he told him. "I work too hard, I play too little, I'm tired and I'm in love with somebody I can't stand." He gave a short laugh. "Okay, I'm exaggerating. Of course I'm not in love with Angel, and I don't mean that I can't stand her but for some reason she's on my mind a lot. A whole lot. And today I almost went ballistic because she was hugged up with this guy she says is her best friend." He shook his head and told Warren the whole sorry tale, starting with his good-bye to Angelique and how he'd swept into her office bearing gifts, only to find her entwined with a tall, dark and handsome stranger. "Man, it was not my finest moment, believe me. I have no idea what made me so crazy but it was like I could feel all the molecules in my body rearranging themselves. I was . . . I was . . ." He groped around vainly for the right word while Warren poured red-wine vinegar into a mixing jar.

"The word you're looking for is 'jealous.' You were jealous, pure and simple, Cochran, and it's because you like Angelique more than you're willing to admit," he said wisely.

Donnie drank the rest of the pomegranate cocktail as he considered Warren's words. *Jealous? Me, jealous, of Angel and her little friend?* He tried to remember an occasion when he'd been jealous over a woman, especially one he hadn't actually dated. No, it couldn't be jealousy. "No, Warren, I don't think that's it. I think I was just caught off guard, that's all. I just wasn't expecting to see her with a guy."

Warren finished adding finely minced rosemary and freshly ground pepper to the jar with the vinegar and wiped his fingers on a damp towel. Picking up a bottle of olive oil, he looked at Donnie with a pitying smile. "Cochran, give it a rest. You like Angel; you like her a lot and you don't want to give it up to her. So go ahead, keep fighting it and make yourself miserable. But remember this, as long as you don't deal with your feelings, you're going to be miserable. Serves you right, too."

"Listen to Dr. Phil! When did you become an expert on relationships?" Donnie said in amusement.

Warren looked completely serious when he replied. "When I found Lisette. I'm not claiming to be an expert or anything, but I recognize the symptoms. It's all those years of medical training—I'm an excellent observer of human nature," he said, raising his glass cheerfully.

"So tell me this, Warren. What made you all of a sudden decide to ask Lisette out? I thought you weren't going to try to get close to her. I thought you had all these reservations and stuff. What changed your mind?"

Warren smiled, more to himself than to Donnie as he shook the salad dressing vigorously. Putting the jar into the refrigerator, he took out a bunch of asparagus and put it on the work island. "We were all spending a lot of time together, me and my little harem. If I went over to Angel's house, she'd have Lisette and Paris there. If we went to a movie, it was usually the whole group. Lisette was just so sweet and pretty, it wasn't like I could ignore her. You know what she looks like Cochran—she's a doll. And she has a wonderful personality besides. Well, the weekend of the auto show was what did it," he said as he picked up the asparagus and washed it thoroughly.

"We all piled in the SUV and went off to Cobo Hall and the girls kind of disappeared. After we got in there they scattered and it was just Lisette and me. She and I walked around, looking at the cars and talking, and then it happened." He stopped speaking for a moment while he broke the tough ends off the asparagus.

Donnie tapped on the oak countertop to remind Warren that he was still in the room. "Then what happened? Don't leave me hanging, man. You got any more of this?" he asked, holding up his empty glass.

"It's in the refrigerator. The juice is on the door and so is the Perrier. What happened was this: we were looking at a beautiful Bentley and the representative turns to Lisette and asks if she'd like to try the car out with her husband. She just smiled up at me and said yes and we got in the car," Warren said simply.

Donnie looked confused. "That's it? I don't get it," he said, frowning at the cute POM bottle that held the pomegranate juice. It looked like a glass snowman.

"It was the *way* she did it, Donnie. She didn't hesitate, she didn't say I wasn't her husband, she didn't say we were just friends, she just looked up at me like she was totally proud to be with me and we got in the car. She acted like being with me was the most natural thing in the world. That's when I knew that no matter what happened, I had to get to know her better. I had to take the chance. And when Angel and Paris decided to have their little matchmaking soiree, everything just fell into place and I've been a very happy man ever since."

The doorbell rang and Warren smiled broadly. "There's my honey now," he said with evident pleasure and he went to open the door for her. They entered the kitchen holding hands and cooing at each other like newlyweds. Lisette looked pleased to see Donnie and went over to give him a quick sisterly kiss on the cheek.

"It's nice to see you again, Donnie. How are you doing?" she asked.

Warren came up behind Lisette and wrapped his arms around her, bending down to give her a most unbrotherly kiss on the neck. "He's miserable because he doesn't have what we have, honey."

Lisette's tender heart melted at Warren's words. She turned around in his arms and put her hand on his face. "Don't make fun of him, sweetheart. You should be helping him like our friends helped us," she said with a gentle smile.

Donnie looked from Warren to Lisette in amazement. "So you set out to shanghai him and you admit it?" he said to Lisette. Staring at Warren, he went on, "And you knew they were matchmaking and you went along with it? This was okay with you?" he asked incredulously.

Warren and Lisette both laughed at Donnie's expression. "Cochran, man, I would have *paid* Angel to come up with this idea. Are you crazy? I was going to beg Lisette to go out with me anyway; they just made it easier, that's all."

Lisette looked up at Warren adoringly and said, "You never have to beg me for anything, Warren. I wanted to be with you, too. I always have."

Donnie correctly surmised that now would be a good time to leave. Refusing their repeated invitations to join them for dinner, he insisted on departing. Warren walked him to the door while Lisette set the table for two.

"Listen, buddy, I do have one piece of advice for you. Whatever you do, don't mess over Angelique. I'm not saying that you and she are going to end up in love like me and Lisette, but don't play with her, man. She's a very special person and she deserves better," he said meaningfully.

Donnie put on his suit jacket. "Warren, first of all, I'm not going to mess over anybody and I'm a little insulted that you'd suggest I would. And second of all, do you realize that you just said you were in love with Lisette?"

Warren held up his hands in supplication. "I'm sorry, I didn't mean to impugn your honor or anything, and I know you wouldn't deliberately hurt her or anyone else. But I've gotten very fond of her; she's like a little sister to me. And, yes, I did use the word 'love' in the same sentence as Lisette's name. She's also very special to me. Very, very special," he said with quiet assurance.

As he shrugged into his topcoat, Donnie gave Warren a look of grudging admiration and envy. "Well, I guess you have it all together, man. If you're happy, I'm happy."

Warren took pity on his friend. "You will be if you don't fight it," he advised. Donnie looked perplexed and Warren was happy to enlighten him. "I noticed that you've stopped called her Evilene and now you refer to her as Angel. When did that happen?"

Donnie didn't have an answer for Warren as he left the house and got into his cold car. While waiting for it to warm up, he asked himself the same question. *When* did *that happen?*

Lisette joined Warren in the living room just in time to see Donnie backing out of the wide driveway. She leaned into his side and breathed in his wonderful masculine scent as he wrapped his arms around her.

"Lisette, you know I've fallen in love with you, don't you?" he said softly.

Without hesitation she turned in his arms so that she was facing him. "I love you too, Warren. And because I love you so much, I have to tell you something and I hope you'll still be in love with me afterward," she said sadly.

Donnie was sequestered in his office, ostensibly looking over budget projections for the next quarter, but in reality he was doing what he'd been doing more and more of lately: he was thinking about Angelique. Over the past few days, Donnie had an opportunity to ask himself a great many more questions as he tried to make sense of his new feelings. Ever since the day he'd seen her in Matt's arms and he'd gotten the lecture from Warren, Donnie had been in turmoil. Part of the problem was that Angelique was just so inaccessible since Matt had come to town. Even though she was perfectly friendly to Donnie, she was also busy. They managed to have dinner together once, but even that wasn't what he'd hoped for since Paris and Matt also came along. They'd shared an excellent meal at Xochimilco in the trendy Mexican Town section of Detroit and then gone dancing together at Parabox, one of Angelique's favorite dance clubs. It was New Latin Generation night and she had danced all night with what seemed to be every man in the place—Donnie frowned as he recalled that part of the evening.

He didn't know why he hadn't remembered how well she danced, but she was out there putting everyone else to shame with her moves. The only other time he could remember Angelique dancing was at her brother Marcus's wedding, and to be honest, he'd been pretty busy meeting the flock of beautiful women who were in attendance. That night, though, Angelique had amazed him. She'd been wearing black leather pants and a red camisole with matching bolero-type cardigan in a bright red angora, and her hair had been curlier than usual. She was a graceful, sexy figure on the dance floor and she commanded every eye as she executed the intricate steps. What's more, Matt danced with her several times and they made an exquisite-looking couple, something else that irritated Donnie.

Donnie took a couple of calls while he continued to peruse the figures with the help of his laptop, but his mind kept going back to that night. Paris had also deserted him to dance but she eventually came back to the table and drank copious amounts of club soda with lime. She'd eyed him curiously and then asked the question he was dreading.

"So why aren't you out there dancing, Donnie?"

He'd tried not to cringe and surprised himself by answering her honestly instead of indulging in his usual nonanswer. "I hate to dance, Paris. I've always felt kind of gawky, to tell you the truth. When your head is as far from your feet as mine is, getting on a dance floor is just asking for trouble," he'd told her.

Her eyes had crinkled with laughter and he'd shrugged. "Besides, I was watching my brothers doing the Electric Slide or something one night and it was just scary, if you ask me. They looked like big ol' giraffes bobbing for water. From then on I decided to protect the public by restricting myself to slow-dancing only." He watched Matt and Angelique dance some more and asked Paris how Matt could dance so well if he couldn't hear the music.

"Angelique says if the music is really loud, he can feel the vibrations. And he wasn't born deaf, he lost his hearing gradually. I don't know if that makes a difference or not."

Snapping out of his reverie, Donnie suddenly looked at his watch and realized how late it was getting; on impulse he decided to take a walk around the office to clear his head. After rising from his desk and stretching, he took his suit coat from the closet and headed out. He really did try to stick to his plan—he strolled around the executive floor, chatting with a few key employees, and dropped in on the lower floor that held the radio station—but continued his "walk" only until he'd reached the elevator and gone down to the first floor. His footsteps were deliberate and purposeful; he went right to Angelique's studio. There was a computer-printed note on the door that puzzled him: it read *Closed for Wedding*. He stared at the note for a moment, then went to find Fanchon.

Fanchon Rencher was the highly efficient concierge of the building. She knew everything that went on within its environs and was quite fond of Angelique. If Angelique had taken the day off for a wedding, Fanchon would know.

He showed her the note and she immediately started smiling. "Oh, Mr. Cochran, you should have seen them," she said warmly. "Angelique was so excited she looked like a little girl. She and that handsome man just about ran out of here and all she had time to tell me was, 'We're eloping!' She said she'd be back next week."

Fanchon was startled by the look of utter fury on Donnie's face. "Is something wrong, Mr. Cochran?"

"Nothing to worry about, Fanchon, just something I have to check out for myself," he muttered as he turned away.

Angelique was in the middle of a happy dance when the pounding started at the front door. She looked up in surprise and went to see who could be making all the racket. Excusing herself from her guests, she went to the foyer with curiosity all over her face. The face she saw at the front door increased the curiosity.

"Adonis, why are you beating on my door like that? Have you finally gone all the way crazy?" she asked as she held the door open.

Donnie didn't answer as he burst through the door and stood over her like some kind of vengeful warlord. "What has all this been about, Angel? Have you just been playing with me because you could? All the time we've been talking on the phone, trying to get to know each other better, waiting for that so-called friend to leave town so we can spend some time, and you're *eloping?* What kind of game are you playing with me?" His anger and hurt were plain in his words, his tone of voice was several decibels louder than Angelique had ever heard.

"How did you hear about the wedding?" she asked innocently.

"Fanchon, that's how. I saw the note on your studio door and I asked her about it and she said you told her you were eloping," he snarled. "How do you think that made me feel?"

Confused, she looked up into his furious face. "I'm not

eloping with anybody. Who says I am? *Matt* is eloping, him and Nicole. Where'd you get the idea that I was eloping with anybody?"

By now Donnie became aware that there were other people present. Matt had entered the room and with him was a small, slender woman Donnie had never seen before. She had an exotic, startling beauty with golden brown skin and thick curly brown hair with golden highlights. She had green eyes and a big port-wine birthmark that spread over her right cheek like a starfish, marring her arresting features—or it should have; she was so pretty, it seemed like an enhancement of her beauty. She also seemed to have a good sense of humor as she was quite amused by the scene before her.

"So this is the great man, hmm? You're right, Angel, he's quite a beauty," she said mischievously. "Adonis is definitely the right name for this one." She was turned toward Matt as she spoke so he could read her lips. She also signed the words.

Donnie was taken aback as Angelique reached for his hand and led him into the center of the living room. "Adonis, this is Nicole, my other best friend. She and Matt are eloping. We're going to Las Vegas tonight for the wedding. Now do you understand?"

"You said, 'We're eloping,' " he said stubbornly. "You didn't say your *friends* were eloping."

"I did? Well, maybe I said it wrong, who knows. What I meant was that we're all going to Vegas to get hitched!" she ended with a happy yelp. She let go of Donnie's hand and continued the happy dance with Matt. "We're gettin' married, we're gettin' married!"

Nicole hadn't lost her smile; she walked over to Donnie and linked her arm through his. "And you're coming with us, too, Adonis. This is going to be the best weekend of your entire life."

Chapter Twelve

Angelique came awake slowly, very slowly, due no doubt to the pounding in her head. She was burning up; her head felt like a marching band was going through it and she was sure she was suffocating. She tried to move but her arms wouldn't cooperate—it was like she was restrained in some way. There was a low, rumbling noise like a machine vibrating in her ear, a steady sound that didn't help the considerable pain in her head at all. She thought it was night, but she wasn't sure. Maybe her eyes were closed. She tried to open them, and after several attempts was able to see a hint of light. Encouraged, she rested a few seconds, then opened her eyes wider. Suddenly things were clearer, but not much.

The noise that was causing her such discomfort was the gentle snoring of Adonis Cochran and the reason she wasn't able to move was because he had his arms locked around her. One of her arms was underneath his big body and the other one was around his waist and her face was buried in his chest. They were both fully dressed, thank God, but she had no idea where they were or how they'd gotten there. All she knew for sure was that her head was splitting open and she had to go to the bathroom right then and there or risk permanent disgrace. She had to get him off her and quickly.

Immediately, she started moving around to the best of her ability; she couldn't risk any sudden moves, due to the condition of her bladder.

"Wake up! Adonis, wake up, wake up, *wake up!* Let me out of this bed," she said croakily.

He finally stirred with a loud snort, abruptly turning over onto his back and releasing her. She sprang from the bed and stared around the room until she could discern a door that might lead to a bathroom. Dashing over, she whimpered in gratitude at finding a great big beautiful bathroom, which she used immediately. After taking care of the most pressing matter, she went over to the marble vanity and looked into the mirror, wincing at what she saw. Her hair was in total disarray, her makeup was nonexistent and her clothes . . . well, they didn't even merit discussion. She was a pure-d mess, no question about it. But why was she here and how had she ended up in a bed in a strange hotel with Adonis Cochran of all people? She needed some answers and soon.

Stumbling back into the bedroom, she made her way to the window and cruelly opened the draperies wide. The brilliant sun streamed through the windows and made her already sensitive eyes water. She groped her way back over to the bed and grabbed Donnie, none too gently. "Wake up! Adonis, wake up! Why are we here? What's going on?" she rasped out. Her voice was scratchy and her mouth had a horrible taste. On top of everything else, she was incredibly thirsty. Hitting Donnie in the knee a few times as she called his name, she returned to the bathroom where she found the toothbrush and toothpaste left there for the guests. She brushed her teeth three times with her head lowered against the pain. She managed to rinse her mouth out thoroughly and drank several tumblers of water. After a most unladylike belch she turned to go back to the bedroom and jumped as she found Donnie standing in the doorway of the bathroom, looking as bad as she did.

"What in the world happened here last night?" he asked, his eyes squinted against the bathroom lights.

"I was hoping you'd be able to tell me," she said with a frown.

"Well, I can't. And if you don't want to get to know me really, really well, real fast, you need to scoot," he suggested.

He didn't need to tell her twice as she was already out the door. While he was availing himself of the facilities, she took a look around the room, which was actually a suite. Besides the big bedroom with the king-size bed and the plush, luxurious bathroom, there was a living room where she took refuge to think. Her head was still pounding and she felt like she'd been beaten with several bags of wet sand. Other than that, she couldn't formulate a single logical explanation for how she and Donnie had wound up sleeping in each other's arms in a luxury hotel suite. She looked down at her rumpled, creased dress and the hose with a giant run in one leg and tried to understand her situation.

Donnie finally appeared in the living room. He'd apparently taken a shower, from the looks of his damp hair and the white terry-cloth robe he was wearing. He actually looked way better than she did, something that annoyed her to no end. He walked across the plush carpet and sat on the sofa that faced the one on which she was sitting. "Well, I feel a little better. I'd suggest a nice, long, hot shower for you, too. I called for the laundry service; they'll come get our clothes and have them back to us in two hours. I also ordered some room service and some Alka-Seltzer, just in case you feel as bad as I do," he said.

"My goodness, aren't you the efficient one," Angelique said haughtily, and wished she hadn't. First because there was no need to be rude, and second because talking made her head hurt even worse.

"Look, Angel, why don't you go take a shower and give me your clothes? We can eat breakfast and figure out what we're going to do, okay?" He spoke very nicely in an even, calming tone that for some reason set Angelique on full alert.

"Figure out what we're going to do about what?" she asked suspiciously.

"About this," he said, holding out a piece of paper.

Through her fog Angelique could make out only a few words, *Certificate of Marriage* and the names *Adonis Cochran* and *Angelique Deveraux*.

"Oh, holy crap," she muttered. "What have we done?"

In a couple of hours the pounding in her head had lessened and she actually felt better, something she would have believed impossible after Donnie revealed the marriage certificate. She had taken a long, long, hot shower, shampooing her hair and letting the hot water beat down on the back of her neck and her temples until some of the pressure was relieved. She'd actually been able to eat the breakfast Donnie had ordered, which surprised her. She'd come out of the bathroom wearing the other white terry-robe thoughtfully provided by the hotel, with her hair wrapped in a towel. Donnie wouldn't allow her to feel self-conscious; he'd escorted her to the living room where the room-service trolley awaited. He'd ordered scrambled eggs, bacon, sausage and biscuits with fresh sliced fruits and a huge pot of steaming, fragrant coffee. Best of all, there was a bowl of creamy-looking grits with a big pat of butter melting in the middle.

"Angel, if you eat something and take the Alka-Seltzer, I promise you'll feel better," he said as he filled her plate. Her eyes widened and she uttered the first words he'd heard her say since her reaction to the certificate.

"I can't eat all that," she protested.

He laughed and teased her. "I'll bet you can. I've seen you eat, remember?"

She did manage to eat quite a bit of the well-prepared food and felt a lot better after the pain reliever started taking effect. She finally felt well enough to look directly at Donnie, something she'd avoided since she went into the bathroom to shower.

"Thank you. I think I'm going to live now," she sighed. "Although I'm not sure I want to. Adonis, what does that certificate mean? We aren't really . . . We didn't . . ." She stopped and took another sip of coffee. Somehow she couldn't say the words.

"We aren't really married?" Donnie said quietly.

Angelique nodded her head. His next words made her crumple in her chair.

"I'm afraid we are, Angel. While you were taking a shower I made a few phone calls. First of all, we're at the Bellagio. We checked in late last night—well, early this morning, I should say. We *are* legally married; it's not some kind of weird joke. I called the wedding chapel where we did the deed and it's a legitimate marriage. As to why it happened, I'm still pretty fuzzy on that. I was hoping you remembered what we were up to last night."

Angelique's face went blank and she started to shake her head but the residual pain made her stop. "I don't remember anything about us getting married," she said. "All I remember is getting off the plane and going to some chapel with Matt and Nicole. I remember having to wait around forever because it was Valentine's Day. There were lots of people who wanted to get married and it took forever, I think. I remember . . ." She paused. "I *think* I remember them getting married." Her face puckered with the effort to recall the events of the previous night. "I think we picked out a dress for Nicole to wear because she didn't want to get married in jeans. And I definitely remember drinking a lot of champagne. Lots and lots of champagne, in fact."

"Do you remember what happened to Matt and Nicole? They're not staying here, I checked. At least, they're not registered under Matt's name or Nicole's."

His words penetrated the last of the fog that surrounded her. "They went on their honeymoon. They left—" she squinted with the effort of recall, "to catch this really early flight to some island someplace. They're going to be gone for a week and then they'll be back in D.C."

"In Washington, D.C.? Is that where they live?" Donnie asked.

Angelique attempted to nod again, then put her hands on her temples when that proved too painful. "Yes, they do. Matt is a professor at Gallaudet University; it's a college for the deaf and hearing-impaired. Nicole has a studio in Georgetown where she makes jewelry. Really beautiful jewelry," she said. Thinking about her friends made her smile in spite of everything. "They've been my best friends since high school. We were always together, the three of us. Whenever I'd get into trouble in Atlanta, I'd take off for D.C. until the heat was off." She laughed. "I don't know what I'd have done without them."

Donnie was drinking coffee while she made this recitation and he tried to listen to her every word, but for some reason he kept focusing on how cute she looked in the too-big robe with the towel wrapped around her head. She really was a beauty, sitting in the sunlight without a speck of makeup to disguise her natural prettiness. He should have been more upset about the situation, but was surprisingly relaxed and calm.

"Why are you so calm about this? You don't seem the least bit upset," she accused him. "You're acting like this is just nothing, like it's all a big joke."

What Angelique didn't know was that this was the real Donnie; he was always a cool head in a crisis. One of the reasons he'd been so successful in business was because he was clearheaded, logical and unflappable. His relationship with Angelique may have been out of his control, but when chaos reared its head, he was definitely the man to have on your side. Acknowledging her concerns with a nod, he set his cup down and reached for her hand across the table.

"I'm sorry, Angel, I don't want you to think that I think this is a joke or something. I guess you don't know me well enough to know how I roll, but this is just the way I handle things," he said with a squeeze of her hand. "But trust me, baby, I'm not trying to treat this like it's nothing. Here's the thing, Angel: we can get this annulled with no problem. We can do it here or we can wait until we get back to Detroit.

Nothing to it, we just say never mind, we were just kidding and it's like it never happened. We just go on with our lives and no one will have anything to say about it."

Instead of taking away her concerns, Donnie's words seemed to multiply them. She suddenly couldn't look him in the eye and excused herself. When Donnie came into the bedroom to find her, she was sitting in the middle of the bed looking lost. Alarmed by what he saw, Donnie joined her on the bed, sitting on the side.

"Angel, what is it? You should look relieved, baby—we can make this all go away," he said soothingly.

Angelique didn't answer at first, but then she looked at him with an expression so bleak it wrenched his heart. "I don't know if I can make you understand. If my family knew about this, they'd flip out, all of them. This is like the worst thing I've ever done and for me that's saying something. Nobody in my family has ever screwed up as much as I have and this is just the topper. I got drunk in Las Vegas and got married in some sleazy joint to somebody who can't stand me. That's just disgusting, Adonis, it really is," she said sadly. She was sitting Indian-style and suddenly leaned forward and put her elbows on her knees and her face in her hands.

Donnie watched her obvious misery for a moment before swinging his legs up onto the bed and pulling her into his arms. "Don't do that, Angel. It's not like you were in that sleazy joint by yourself, you know—I was there, too. And I was at least as drunk as you were, so I'm no paragon of virtue, either," he said comfortingly.

"Oh, don't be nice to me," Angelique said. "That just makes it worse because you're not like me. You're *good,* like that perfect family of yours and those perfect brothers of mine. Nobody's going to think any less of *you* because of this, but they're going to be on me like white on rice. And I can't blame them, honestly I can't. Crazy stuff follows me around, it always has."

By way of answer, he pulled her onto his lap and held her

closer. "Angel, nobody's going to find out about this," he told her fiercely. "And if they do, they'd better mind their own business if they know what's good for them. We're adults, we're not children. This is between you and me and nobody else, okay?"

Angelique was so enjoying the novelty of being comforted that she didn't say a word, she just leaned farther into his shoulder and sighed, a soft sound so poignantly sad it wrenched his heart.

"Now what is it, baby? Why do you sound so sad?"

"Because. Because nobody in my family or your family has ever made a mockery of marriage like this—it took me to really screw it up. Marriage is supposed to be sacred and forever and important, it's not supposed to be something that happens because you're too drunk to know what you're doing. I never really thought I'd get married, but now if I do I'll always know that it's not really my first marriage. I don't care what annulment means, this is still my first time getting married and look at what a mess it is. This is so typical of me," she said with a slight hiccup. "You don't even like me." She buried her head in his shoulder, making the turban fall off and her still-damp hair fall forward in disarray.

"That's not true, Angel," Donnie said softly. "Now that you're not biting my head off every two minutes, I like you just fine. And you like me, too. Admit it."

She laughed softly as he cuddled her and demanded that she confess her true feelings. "You think I'm cute and you want me, Angel, you know you do. Say it! Say you're crazy about me!" he said comically.

By now she was giggling at his foolishness and almost forgotten the fix they were in. She sat up straighter and looked him in the eye. Putting one hand on his shoulder and the other on his face, she smiled. "I like you a little bit, I think. You've been very sweet to me and I really appreciate it," she said nicely.

Donnie didn't pay her words any attention, he just kissed her, lightly and sweetly. Then the passion that was always just under the surface began its inexorable rise to the top. He increased the pressure on her lips and they parted to his seeking mouth, the warm sweetness of her tongue driving him into a minor frenzy of desire. The warmth of her body lit a flame in his and he forgot everything except the feel of her lithe body in his arms. Unconfined by clothing other than the terry robe, he could feel her lissome frame and it wasn't enough, it wasn't nearly enough. His big hand started sliding up her bare leg, pushing the fabric aside. A soft sound from her increased the desire; he was burning for her, a hot thirst that only she could quench.

A sudden knock on the door caused Angelique to come back to herself and she leaped off his lap with a look of horror on her face. She backed away from him and dashed into the bathroom without a word, leaving him to deal with the knocking. She leaned against the closed door of the bathroom, her heart pounding like a piston. What had she almost done? She'd almost succumbed to the unexpected, that's what.

Finally, she had enough strength to leave the solidity of the door and sit on the vanity bench by the marble counter. She took deep breaths to slow her heartbeat and eventually it worked. Adonis Cochran had been holding her, kissing her, seducing her wearing only a robe with nothing else on, and she'd loved every second of it. If she were to be honest, she knew that if the knock hadn't sounded at the door, she'd be in that big bed wrapped up in Adonis and not another thing. Her heartbeat had returned to normal and the heat that had consumed her had finally ebbed, but she wasn't ready to face Donnie. *Maybe I'll just stay in here the rest of my life—he'll never notice,* she thought glumly.

Donnie tapped on the bathroom door, calling her name as he did so. "Angel, baby, come on out. Our clothes are here and we can get dressed and leave. I didn't mean for it to go that far," he said sincerely. "I wasn't trying to put the moves on you, but you're so beautiful, I . . ." He stopped speaking and smiled because Angelique opened the bathroom door a crack and was looking at him with a carefully neutral expression. "Come on out. I won't bite you and we do need to talk, Angel."

As regal as a queen, she opened the door and walked past him without saying a word. She headed for the bed and veered away sharply, going into the living room where she took a seat on the sofa. Donnie followed her into the room, trying not to smile. He sat down in a large armchair adjacent to the sofa and began to speak. "I apologize for what happened, Angel, I really do. I was supposed to be making you feel better and I ended up groping you like a crazy man. That was inappropriate and it won't happen again," he said solemnly. "But in my defense I have to say that you're so sexy and sweet, it would've been impossible for me to not kiss you."

Angelique tried hard to keep her expression aloof and failed. She was so surprised and touched by Donnie's words that a glimmer of a smile crept across her face. She immediately tried to look stern again. "The thing is, Adonis, we can't let things like that happen. We've got to get this thing annulled as soon as possible before anyone finds out." A little of her former dismay was apparent in the look of sadness that flickered over her face.

Donnie leaned forward and took her hand again. "It'll be okay, Angel, I promise you it will. This is going to be quick, discreet and painless," he vowed.

Worry still nagged at Angelique. "Suppose it isn't? Suppose . . ."

Donnie took her other hand and held them both firmly. "Suppose we get dressed and get out of here? I'll take care of everything. You're my wife now, don't forget that. Nobody's going to mess with you, not if they want to live," he said with a comic ferocity that was only half in jest. It did the trick, though, as Angelique smiled and agreed to get dressed so they could go home.

*   *   *

In a short time they were ready to leave. Angelique made one puzzling discovery when she found her cell phone in two pieces in her purse. "What do you suppose happened to this?" she wondered. Staring at the cell phone, she had another thought. "Adonis, Paris was out of town this weekend at a conference. She's going to be back on Monday. What am I going to tell her?"

Donnie glanced at her and tried to hide his admiration for her beauty. Her cream-colored, silk jersey wrap dress was restored to its normal pristine condition and the taupe heels she wore with it accentuated her long, shapely legs. She was wearing new hose that had been procured by the desk downstairs and she looked nothing like the disheveled, disoriented woman who'd awakened that morning. Her hair had air-dried into a thick mass of waves, and even without makeup she was stunning. He realized he was about to be caught staring and cleared his throat. "Umm, what did you say?"

Angelique stopped rummaging in her purse and looked at her "husband," trying not to let his good looks send her into another tailspin. The cleaners had done a wonderful job on his deep brown suit and the ivory shirt he wore with it. He was tying his tie, a brown and gold patterned silk one, and he looked good enough to eat with a small spoon. It was her turn to act disinterested while she answered his question. "Paris is going to be home on Monday and I want to know what to tell her. You don't know her as well as I do, she's like a bloodhound. She'll figure out something is up as soon as she walks in the room," Angelique fretted.

"Don't worry about Paris, we can handle her. Can you give me a hand with this?" he asked, indicating the tie.

She gave him one of the few genuine smiles she'd been able to muster all day. "Yes, I can, my brothers taught me how. Sit down, you're too tall," she instructed. In seconds she'd tied the long length of rich silk into a neat and perfect Windsor knot, smoothing his collar as she finished. "Okay, you're all finished." Inside, she was on fire from the desire to kiss him again, but outwardly she was cool and collected.

After taking a last look around the suite, Mr. and Mrs. Cochran went downstairs to check out of the luxurious suite and head back to Detroit to straighten everything out. They waited for the elevator in silence, a silence tinged with the anxiety emanating from Angelique. Donnie looked down and gave her a smile that was meant to reassure her. "It's okay, Angel. I'll take care of everything," he said as he pushed the LOBBY button in the elevator. They rode down in the empty car without saying a word; when the doors opened, they emerged into the lobby. Donnie put his hand to the small of Angelique's back and started to guide her to the desk to check out.

A sudden flash of light made them both turn to face a group of reporters who had been lying in wait in the lobby.

"Turn this way, Mrs. Cochran!"

"Mr. Cochran, what made you two decide to elope?"

"What was your family's reaction to the sudden wedding?"

The questions were coming from all directions and microphones were stuck in their faces so rapidly that Angelique didn't have a moment to react. Donnie however was much quicker. Locking his arm around Angelique's slender waist, he held up his hand and spoke to the crowd like they were old friends. "Hold it, folks! We'll be issuing a statement later, but for right now I want to take my bride home so we can plan our honeymoon. If that's all right with you, of course," he said with an easy smile.

After a few more jocular comments, the reporters did indeed part their ranks to allow them through. In minutes Donnie had checked them out of the suite and they were in a cab headed to the airport. Angelique had been too stunned to speak; now she started to rage. "I can't believe you! Why were you acting like—"

Her words were cut off as Donnie silenced her the only way he could think of—by kissing her hard and fast.

When he felt her body relax, he pulled away to whisper in

her ear, "Wait until we're alone, Angel, unless you want our first fight to make it to the wire services, too."

She gave him a look of pure fury but did as he asked. She didn't say another word.

Chapter Thirteen

The next few weeks were what Angelique imagined hell to be like. Some intrepid paparazzi had seen her and Donnie emerging from the wedding chapel and taken a few shots that were released to the tabloids and wire services, and their fifteen minutes of fame was recorded for all and sundry to view. The thought of the resultant news reports was enough to turn her stomach. *Media Conglomerates Make Marital Merger* was written under one picture. *Beautiful Music for CEO and Bride* read another. There were dozens of them in every publication from *People* to *Jet* and in every single one was a picture of her and Donnie with their mouths plastered together like sweaty prom dates. Their plan to keep the nuptials a secret seemed naive to the point of insanity by now.

Even worse were the reactions of their respective families. The memory of the immediate repercussions gave Angelique shooting pains in the stomach. On the long and silent ride to the airport in Las Vegas, Donnie had taken the time to check his own cell phone and found it packed with messages from all his brothers, his father, her brothers, his sister and Warren. All the messages were variations on the same theme: what in the world were you thinking. Thanks to his quick, if ill-advised, thinking in the lobby of the Bellagio, it now seemed like this was a love match. An impetuous adventure by two people who were madly in love was how the press perceived it. A boneheaded damn-fool caper was how his brothers saw it. And what her brothers had to say didn't even bear repeating. In addition, there was the reaction of her mother and A.J.

Angelique was sitting on the broad windowsill of her new bedroom, the formerly unfurnished bedroom of Donnie's house. Her bedroom furniture had been moved from the house she'd shared with Paris and was now arranged in the room across from her husband's room. She didn't even have any boxes to unpack; in typical Angelique fashion, she'd gotten everything put away within forty-eight hours of being in the house. She wasn't alone in the room—Jordan and Pippen were lounging at her feet. The two dogs had attached themselves to her from the moment she moved in and never strayed far from her. If Donnie wanted to see his pets, he had to find Angelique because that's where they normally were, wherever she was in the house. And since she spent most of her time in the studio, at her old house or hiding in her bedroom, she didn't see much of Donnie, which was how she liked it.

She took a look around the room, and when she couldn't find one thing to rearrange or dust or hang up or put away, she walked over to the bed and sat down on the side of it. Her cream and gold damask bedclothes were out of place in the room with its burgundy, navy and dark green striped wallpaper. The walls needed to be stripped and the walls needed to be painted, maybe a soft cream with a rag patina added by hand, or a French vanilla with a luminous gold overlay. She thought about the other things that could be done to spruce up the room before she caught herself and realized that this room, like everything else in her life, was temporary. She wasn't a permanent part of Donnie's life any more than he was a permanent part of hers and in a little while they would go their separate ways. Jordan and Pippen sensed her sadness and came over to offer some cheer in the form of big wet kisses to her hands. She had to laugh and bent down to give them each a big hug.

"Do you want to go out? You want a walk? Okay, let's go," she said, rising from the bed. They went downstairs where Donnie was watching television. She tried to slip out the back door without saying anything, but Pippen was so excited about the prospect of going out that he grabbed his lead and trotted into the living room with it. Angelique watched him leave in dismay, hoping Donnie wouldn't take the cue. Unfortunately, he entered the kitchen with the lead in one hand and a heavy jacket in the other.

"Come on, boy, we'll get Jordan and go for a nice long walk, how about that?" he said as they entered the room. His eyes took in Angelique, wearing a jacket, hat and gloves and holding Jordan's lead in one hand and the ubiquitous pooper-scoop in the other. "Well. I guess we had the same idea. Do you mind if I come along?"

Angelique shrugged her shoulders to indicate assent. "Of course you can. They're your dogs, after all. Maybe you'd like to take both of them," she said, holding out the scooper.

Donnie's jaw tightened very slightly, but he just smiled. "No, I want to come with you. And I see you handing me that scooper. You think you're slick, don't you?" he said as he took it from her hand. "Let's go, guys." The four of them left the house and walked out into the damp cold.

They walked in silence for a couple of blocks until Donnie put his hand on Angelique's shoulder. "We've got to start talking to each other, Angel. I can only imagine how tough this is for you, but trying to ignore me isn't helping."

"I don't know what else to do," she said honestly. "When I wake up in the morning the first thing I wish for is that none of this ever happened but when I open my eyes, there's that ugly wallpaper and I know it's all true."

"Hey, the wallpaper was there when I moved in," Donnie said defensively. "And I wish I could make it all go away, but

I can't. I know that's what I told you would happen, but I was wrong and I apologize."

"Adonis, you don't have to keep apologizing. It wasn't your fault that we were seen; it wasn't your fault that the story got out. I'm not even mad at you about making it seem like we got married on purpose. Well, I'm not mad anymore," she amended.

Donnie grinned at her. "Are you sure? You were pretty hot for a while. You said you'd never forgive me for making you live a lie," he reminded her as he draped a long arm over her shoulders.

Angelique pushed against him playfully and gave him a small smile. "Don't remind me of that, please. I know I was being a drama queen, but I think I had good reason." Both of them fell silent as they each recalled the aftermath of the impromptu wedding.

As soon as she'd walked into the house on her return to Detroit, the phone started ringing and didn't stop. The first call was from her oldest brother, Clay. "Angel, we're sending the jet to pick you and Cochran up. We need to talk to both of you," he'd said in a dangerously calm voice. He seemed to be the spokesman for the brothers because she didn't hear from the rest of them. Her mother, however, had called right after she hung up with Clay and the memory of that conversation still made her stomach hurt.

"Angelique, I can't imagine why you would do something like this. To just run off into the night and get married without a word to anyone—what in the world have I done to make you behave like this? I know we haven't been as close as we should have been, but how could you let me find out from some television gossip that my only daughter is married? Why, Angel?"

Angelique shuddered at the memory and unconsciously pushed closer to Donnie, who still had his arm around her shoulder. They had indeed gotten on the TDG jet the next morning and flown to Atlanta to face her family. The scene with her mother was every bit as bad as she'd anticipated; she simply couldn't find the words to explain what had happened and just bore her mother's anger and pain in near silence. Lillian was the one person Angelique didn't want to disappoint and yet that was all she ever seemed to do. To her, Lillian was the personification of elegance and loveliness, a true gracious lady, and she deserved a better daughter than Angelique could ever be.

Without realizing it, she leaned her head against Donnie, who stopped walking and put both hands on her shoulders. "You're thinking about your mom again, aren't you?" She nodded without speaking. "Let's go home. It's pretty cold out, how about if I make you some soup?" She nodded again.

In a short time they were in the warm, bright kitchen while Donnie prepared what he referred to as his Soon to be World-Famous Hamburger Soup, which Angelique confessed sounded quite gross. "It sounds weird but it's really good. If it makes you feel any better, it's not my recipe; Tina, my sister-in-law, gave it to me."

While he started the preparations for the soup, he tried to imagine how Angelique was feeling. The trip to Atlanta hadn't been the epitome of a warm welcome home. As she had predicted, the consensus seemed to be that somehow she was responsible for the debacle. Benita didn't say it—she was completely neutral, albeit surprised. Angelique's other sisters-in-law, Selena, Vera, and Ceylon, were also careful not to place blame and, like Benita, were supportive of Angelique. The Deveraux men, however, were less supportive and more critical of the situation but in a manner that rubbed Donnie the wrong way. He recalled his conversation with her brothers Malcolm and Martin and could feel his jaw tighten up again.

"Donnie, of course I have no idea what happened between the two of you, but I assure you that getting it annulled shouldn't be a problem. I have to tell you that I'm really disappointed in my sister; I thought she'd outgrown these kinds of pranks," Malcolm had said in a weary tone of voice.

Before Donnie could say anything, Martin had spoken up with something about how irresponsibility had always been Angelique's middle name and he was sorry her foolishness had led to this. "She didn't even consider the fact that we're in business together and what it could have meant from a corporate standpoint," Martin observed. "I really thought she'd stopped this kind of acting out."

Back in the present, Donnie gave a particularly vicious chop to the onion he was preparing for the stockpot. Something about the way her family seemed to just assume she was somehow to blame irritated him in a way he'd not expected. He'd been terse to the point of being curt with her brothers and he wasted no time in letting them know that the decision to marry had been a mutual one and he wouldn't tolerate any criticism of his bride. He'd been equally cool with her mother and stepfather. He liked and respected all of these people, having known them from the time his sister first started dating Clay, but the very notion that someone could make Angelique uncomfortable by even a wrong look was something he wasn't having. Family relationships were on shaky ground in Atlanta, but they weren't much better in Detroit.

Opinions varied in his family but the only neutral vote was his brother Adam. Big Bennie was very fond of Angelique and referred to her as Babydoll, that "little spunky gal." For some reason they'd always gotten along like a house afire and he was rather pleased they were married. Andrew also was supportive, as he knew Angelique better than the other brothers. Alan and Andre, the legal counsel for Cochran Communications, were frankly livid. They had nothing against Angelique personally, they simply couldn't believe their brother would do something so foolhardy without so much as a prenuptial agreement.

"From a legal standpoint, this is like suicide, Donnie," Andre had railed. "Our companies are connected and you take this foolish step without considering what it could mean to us from a fiscal standpoint. That little girl could cause us untold grief when you divorce."

It was his casual use of the word *divorce* that had really rankled Donnie—the assumption that there was no way they could possibly stay together, that she was too fickle to maintain a relationship. It was all there in Andre's tone of voice. Donnie had wasted no time in letting his brothers know what time it was, that this was his business and had nothing to do with them and that if they even thought anything unkind about Angelique, they'd have him to answer to.

Considering the fact that he'd always been exceptionally close to his family, the new coolness governing them was galling, to say the least. Donnie was taking out his angst on the celery now, chopping it with a good deal more vigor than was called for. But his conversation with his brothers was still weighing on his mind, especially the part where Andre had reminded him that a mere two months ago he had proposed to another woman. "You were ready to marry Aneesah before Christmas and now you're married to Angelique Deveraux. I don't know what a shrink would have to say about this, but it doesn't sound to me like you know what you're doing, Donnie." Andre's smug tone had almost made Donnie lose his temper.

"Just leave Aneesah out of this, Andre, she has nothing whatsoever to do with any of this." Donnie's voice would have frightened anyone but an older brother; Andre had persisted with his questions.

"Does Angelique even know you were engaged to Aneesah?"

"No, she doesn't, and she doesn't need to know. The only people I told were my brothers and their wives. Pop doesn't even know I asked her. So as long as my brothers keep their mouths shut, it's a nonissue," he said with icy finality.

As the soup began to simmer and the fragrant aroma filled the kitchen, he looked at Angelique who had volunteered to make cornbread to complete the meal. She looked thinner than usual, and pale. He knew it was due to the stress she'd been under and the strain of her family's disapproval. Plus, she was in the midst of preparing for her exhibit and needed serenity more than anything. If he could have thought of another way to handle that mob of reporters at the hotel, he would have. But acting like a happy couple had been the quickest way to defuse the bomb of inaccurate media coverage, and it had worked. He also never wanted anyone to know the truth behind their wedding; he felt that would hurt Angelique even more. So they had decided to stay married for a while and think of some logical reason to part after all the hoopla and speculation had died down.

It wasn't a perfect plan by any means but it was the first thing he could come up with. What he wanted more than anything at this point was to protect Angelique from any kind of humiliation or shame. They'd both been a little crazy that night, no question, but why should she have to suffer for it? The gist of the story had finally come out when Matt and Nicole had returned from their island honeymoon. They had supplied the details the champagne had taken away. Nicole had called and Donnie and Angelique each got on an extension.

"You two started drinking champagne on the plane and you were both a little silly," Nicole reported. "And while we were doing all that waiting around, you drank some more. And some *more,*" she added gleefully. "And the more you drank, the happier you got and the more affectionate you got. You guys were holding hands and kissing and talking mush talk and after we got married you decided that you had to get married, too, and you did. It was really sweet; Matt and I were your witnesses. Then you decided to go to the Bellagio and we went off to the airport and didn't hear anything about it until we got back, but we didn't really pay it any attention because we were *there,* you know? We knew what went on so we weren't worried about it. Maybe we should have stopped you two, but you looked so happy."

Even though it was good to have some details supplied, it didn't answer the big question of how and when the inevitable divorce would occur. And it didn't answer the question that kept nagging at Donnie, the question of why there had to be a divorce at all. For a reason he couldn't explain, the very idea of divorcing Angelique was one he didn't want to contemplate. He wasn't ready to say why, but he knew he wanted to stay married.

Paris and Lisette looked at each other, then looked at Angelique, who definitely was not acting like herself. She was quiet and distracted and picking at her food. Since Lisette had made a fabulous meal, she was naturally concerned that her friend wasn't eating. "Angelique, what's the matter? Surely you can tell us, you know we'd understand, whatever it is," she said comfortingly.

Paris reached over and stroked her cousin's arm. "Look, Angelique, after you explained the whole situation with the so-called wedding, we kept it on the down low, didn't we? Even after those brothers of yours were raking me over the coals, I kept my mouth shut. That's between you and Donnie and nobody else needs to know. I know pretending to be in a real marriage is hard, and I know you must have some things to get off your chest, so tell us what's going on, sugar," she coaxed.

Angelique made a little face and tried to smile. "I'm sorry I've been such a pain. I just have a ton of stuff on my mind. The exhibit, for one thing, and my family for another. I think I broke my mother's heart, my stepfather is upset with me because I upset *her;* my brothers think I'm an idiot and I'm pretty sure I've permanently offended God by making a drunken mess of the marriage vows. The person I respect more than anyone, A.J., is so disgusted with me, we're barely speaking. Oh, and before I forget, I don't want to divorce my husband. Other than that, everything is just peachy," she said bitterly.

Lisette and Paris both lit up at that last piece of information. Lisette jumped up and removed the remains of dinner, chattering like a magpie as she did so. "Forget this stupid pasta, we can always nuke it later. This calls for dessert and right now. Paris, you get the plates and I'll get the gâteau and then we'll talk."

Soon the aroma of strong espresso was scenting the room and the women were sharing an intensely rich flourless chocolate cake with crème fraîche and raspberries. Confidences just seemed to flow when there was high quality chocolate at hand. Paris was naturally the first one to speak up.

"So you don't want to divorce Donnie even though that was the plan? You want this to be like a real marriage? When did you come to that conclusion?" she asked with ill-concealed curiosity.

Angelique sighed and looked at the morsel of cake on her fork before devouring it. This was the first thing that had tempted her appetite in days; chocolate had always been her weakness. "I don't know exactly when I realized I didn't want to let him go, but I can't pretend I don't care about him. He's been so sweet to me, so kind and caring and just . . . *sweet.* He made me soup one day, really good soup. He won't let my family say anything bad about me, or his family, either. And he doesn't act like it was all my fault. He says he's to blame, too. He hasn't yelled at me one time, and that includes when I was screaming at him after he told that pack of reporters we were married for real."

She shuddered slightly at the memory and ate the last bite of her cake. "May I have some more, please? This was wonderful."

Lisette served her the cake and asked what she meant about screaming at Donnie.

"Oh, girl, you should have seen me," she said, making an embarrassed face. "I went ballistic because he was acting all cool and suave like this was a real wedding, and he never said a word to me about what he was going to do—he just blurted it out at the hotel and I had to go along with it. And he did the same thing after we got home, he just told everybody that this was our business and to stay out of it. It was the best thing to do, I guess, but it was just driving me crazy that he could be so cool and tell all those lies without blinking an eye. So I went off on him. More than once, I might add, and he never yelled at me or told me I was being a spoiled brat, which I was." She sighed.

Paris and Lisette were completely captivated by this story and were both leaning forward on the milk-painted farmhouse kitchen table. Paris wanted more information. "So did you ever apologize?"

Angelique stopped with another bite of cake halfway to her mouth. "Of course I did, I'm not a heathen. At least, not anymore," she amended. "I apologized the next day and he was very nice about it. He even hugged me. . . ." Her voice trailed off and she remembered that morning in great detail, the fact that they'd been in the kitchen and that Donnie was still getting dressed and had on a wife-beater and an old flannel shirt he'd yet to button. The memory of his hard, flat stomach and the glimpse of the silky hair on his chest still made her heart beat erratically.

Paris, bless her nosy heart, zeroed right in on that expression. "You also realized that you're married to a big ol' sexy man, didn't you? You really *want* him, cousin, in every way. So why don't you get him?"

By now the second piece of cake was gone and Angelique stared unhappily at her plate. "I can't 'get' him, Paris. Just because he's being really sweet to me doesn't mean he wants me, too. And I've told you before, I'm not his type. I'm not a woman he'd ever go for, I'm just some pitiful child he feels sorry for right now. I'm stupid, I'm not crazy," she muttered.

By mutual agreement Paris and Lisette both gave her a playful smack on the back of the head. When she looked up in surprise, Lisette told her, "We said we would do that if you started being mean to yourself again. You have to be honest with him, you simply must. Besides, I don't think you know what you're talking about this time. Come with me, *cher,* I have something to show you."

Mystified, she and Paris followed Lisette into her second bedroom she had outfitted as a small, feminine study. She took out a manila folder and handed it to Angelique. "Look at that picture and tell me the man is indifferent to you! You can't do it, can you?"

Angelique opened the folder and there was a newspaper photograph of her and Donnie as they were leaving the Bellagio. Their coats were over their left arms in deference to the Nevada heat. Donnie's right arm was around her waist and he was looking down at her as though she was the most precious thing in his universe. Her face was turned toward his and they looked radiantly in love, even in the midst of the media ambush. Without realizing what she was doing, Angelique's fingers touched the image of Donnie's face. She looked more unhappy than ever.

Lisette looked shocked at the sadness in her friend's face. "What is it, Angel? Don't you see how much he cares for you?"

"No, I don't. Don't forget, I'm a photographer. And I know better than anyone that pictures *do* lie."

Lisette disagreed with her at once. "Angel, I've seen you together and you're not alone in your feelings. He cares for you, I can tell. If you want this marriage to be real, you have to make it so. Tell him how you feel. I finally told Warren I was the one who had caused his engagement to be broken and you know how afraid I was to do that."

This news caused Angelique to forget her own situation for a moment. "You're kidding. What did he say?" she demanded.

Smiling for all she was worth, Lisette told them. "He had just told me he loved me and I told him I loved him, too, but I had to tell him something. We sat down and I explained how angry I'd gotten when that wretched Tracy said those terrible things about him and I wanted him to know what kind of creature he was about to marry. I told him how I set the whole thing up, how I plotted and schemed. Then I shut up and I waited. I just knew he was going to be furious and I was waiting for him to say something terrible to me. Instead, he started laughing. He laughed and laughed, and when he could talk he told me he'd always suspected I'd done it on purpose and he'd always wanted to thank me for keeping him from the biggest mistake of his life. And the next day he bought me this, the sweet man," she cooed as she showed them a delicate gold chain with a sizable round diamond in the middle.

"So, telling the truth brought us even closer together. You should tell Donnie how you feel, Angel. What could you possibly lose?"

"Besides my sanity and what's left of my dignity? My heart, probably." She looked at her digital watch, which was buzzing. She'd set it to alarm because she had to leave early. "Look, thank you for dinner, it's my turn next. I hate to run, but I have an assignment. There's this wonderful black hockey player and I get to take pictures of him for *Sports Illustrated*—Jarome Iginla with the Calgary Flames. He's one of the best players in the NHL and quite handsome, too. A.J. is taking me to the Red Wings game tonight."

The three women went into the living room, where Lisette fetched Angelique's coat and purse. Paris gave her cousin a big hug and reminded her that it was always better to tell the truth. "I think you're going to get a better reaction that you know," she said.

Lisette concurred. "Tell him how you feel, Angel. That was the advice you gave me and see how well it worked out?"

Angelique looked from one dear friend to the other and threw up her hands in defeat. "I'll think about it, I really will," she promised.

A.J. arrived to collect her for the Red Wings game and she left, saying she'd call later. Paris looked at Lisette and predicted that her stubborn cousin wouldn't say a thing. "But that doesn't mean *I* won't. They don't call me Martha May matchmaker for nothing."

From the looks they were getting from the female patrons, Donnie, Warren and Adam were the best-looking men in Champps, a big sports-type bar in Farmington. It was a rare occasion when Adam took time off just to hang out, but tonight seemed to be a good time. Donnie was in the mood to talk and Warren and Adam were his best sounding boards.

They had finished their meals and were waiting for dessert. At least, Adam and Donnie were—Warren had sworn off all sweets. Donnie couldn't resist a crack.

"What's the matter, man, Lisette got you on a diet?" he asked with a grin.

"No, as a matter of fact she acts like she thinks I'm cute, which is real strange. I've never had a woman who didn't start trying to get me to lose a few pounds. Lisette never says anything about my weight or how much I eat," he said in a tone of wonder and gratitude. "But I need to lose some weight for *me*—you know what I mean. Lisette could have anybody in the world, I don't want her to think she has to be stuck with the fat doctor."

Donnie scoffed at Warren's concerns. "Warren, Lisette is crazy about you. You could gain fifty pounds and you'd still be her teddy bear, don't be stupid. What's your cholesterol? What's your blood sugar? What's your heart rate? Are you healthy? Because you've been thick ever since I met you. Look at your dad and mom, they're both big and both healthy. . . . Aww, look at me preachin' to the choir. You're the doctor—how's your health?"

"It's fine, thanks for asking," Warren said sardonically. "If you must know, this is a matter of vanity, not health. But speaking of health, what have you done to Angel? She's lost a lot of weight, man. I don't think she's too happy right now."

It came as a complete surprise to Donnie when Adam agreed with Warren. "Yeah, bro, what are you doing to my sister-in-law? She's supposed to be blooming right now and she looks wilted. If you can't take better care of her than that, you need to send her to me," he said, giving Donnie a hard look.

Donnie's arm moved abruptly and he knocked his water goblet over, spilling the contents onto the floor. Warren and

Adam looked at each other before looking back at Donnie, who was obviously furious.

"Look, I know Angel is unhappy and I'm doing everything I can to make it right," he said. "There's a lot going on you don't know about and I'd just as soon keep it that way; it's too personal. But no, she's not happy with the way the families reacted and I can't blame her. She's not happy about all the press coverage, and I wasn't either. She's trying really hard to make her exhibit perfect. Did you know she's donating all the proceeds to charity? There's a lot more to her than people realize. She's smart and funny and she's a good listener, she's a darned good cook and she's the most organized woman I've ever met in my life." He shook his head. "She's kind of frightening that way, as a matter of fact."

Warren had to pick at him a little. "So you went shopping without a list and look who you ended up with, Cochran."

Donnie looked blank for a moment until he realized what Warren was talking about. "Aww, don't go there, Warren. All those grocery lists and special qualifications, that was just a bunch of crap," he admitted.

Now it was Adam's turn to dig. "But you were ready to marry Aneesah just a few months ago. You were all messed up because she'd turned you down. Are you sure this isn't just some kind of rebound?"

Donnie looked disgusted for a second then answered his brother. "No, I'm not on the rebound from Aneesah. She and I had this same conversation, by the way, and it wasn't nice. She got all over me and I barely got away with my life. You know she's the one that's setting up Angel's exhibit at the museum, right? Well, that's another story anyway." He paused while the server removed the fallen glass and replaced it with a fresh one. After apologizing for his clumsiness, he waited until the server left and continued.

"This is how I know I'm not on the rebound. Listen, this is what happened," he began, and proceeded to tell them the whole story of the Las Vegas wedding. When he finished, it was hard to say who looked more astonished, his best friend or his normally unflappable brother. There was silence around the table for a moment, broken when Donnie added wryly, "I don't think I have to tell you that this is for your ears only."

Adam gave a short laugh that held no amusement. "So you got drunk, woke up married and you're planning on just getting a quiet divorce at some point in the future? *This* was your big plan? Man, I ought to bust you in your head! You should have been taking care of Angel and this is how you treat her? No wonder she's wasting away. This kind of pressure is too much for anybody and any fool can see she's special. She's creative and sensitive, you moron, and you've got her in a terrible position. She's lying to her friends and family, lying to the whole world and just waiting for the axe to drop. What's wrong with you, Adonis? Did we drop you on your head when you were little or something and I just don't remember it?"

Before Warren could start on him, Donnie held up a weary hand. His brothers only called him Adonis when they were truly angry about something. "Adam, you're not saying anything I haven't said to myself. But if it gives you any pleasure at all, you need to know that I don't want to divorce her. I want this to be a real marriage. I don't see how I'm going to let her go," he said quietly. "I've fallen in love."

Now it was Warren's turn to laugh, but it was a loud, hearty one full of real joy. "Well, it's about time you woke up, Cochran. So when do you plan to let your wife in on this?"

Donnie was saved from replying by the ringing of his cell phone. He pulled it out and saw Angelique's name on his caller ID. He smiled and answered in his best voice. "Hi, Angel. Where are you?"

"This is A.J. and we're in the emergency room. Angel had an accident."

Chapter Fourteen

Donnie stood motionless beside Angelique's bed. Her doctor had assured him it was just a concussion, and that she would be fine, but his heart hadn't stopped pounding since he got the phone call from A.J. It was a freak accident, that's all it was; she'd been hit in the head by a deflected hockey puck and knocked unconscious, then rushed to the hospital and subjected to every test known to man—but she would recover. She didn't look fine to him, she looked little and pale and helpless. *He* felt helpless, watching her sleep. If anything had happened to her . . . he went cold, absolutely cold at the thought. A nurse came in to take her vital signs and when she picked up Angelique's slender wrist to take her pulse, Angelique stirred.

Her eyelids fluttered and blinked open and she looked at him dazedly. Then her eyes widened and she stared at him for a long moment; she glanced at the nurse and looked around the room, her eyes coming back to rest on Donnie as she looked questioningly at him. Relief rushed through him like a warm flood as he saw her gaze becoming more alert. "Where am I?"

"You're in the hospital, Angel. You gave us quite a scare," he said. "A hockey puck went out of control and bounced off a pillar, then it bonked you in the head. You've been out for a few hours, but it seems to be a concussion, nothing more serious. You'll be able to go home tomorrow, you just need to get some rest tonight. A little pain reliever and you'll be fine," he assured her.

Angelique lay perfectly still during his words. She looked at the nurse, who was still performing her tasks. Then she looked back at Donnie and spoke again. "Are you my doctor?"

The nurse's eyes got big and she answered before Donnie could say a word. "*Doctor?* Honey, this is your *husband!*"

Angelique sat up straight in the bed, wincing a little a she did so. She had a pretty rugged headache, after all. But she smiled at the tall, very handsome man. "You're my husband? That's nice. What's your name?"

In a short while, the doctor was assuring Donnie that Angelique would be fine, that her temporary loss of memory wasn't unheard of and was far from permanent. "It's called retrograde amnesia and it can happen after a trauma to the head like the one your wife suffered tonight. It usually goes away in a few hours. We'll keep her here overnight and you can take her home in the morning."

"I don't want to stay here. I want to go home," Angelique said firmly. She was sitting up now and Donnie was sitting in a chair by the side of the bed. She had taken his hand earlier and showed no signs of letting go. She looked at him with her eyes full of entreaty and repeated her words. "I want to go home with you, right now." Turning to the doctor, she asked why she couldn't leave. "My husband can take care of me. Can't I leave now, please?"

Dr. Feinstein scratched his chin and looked at the determination on her face. "Well, it would be better if she was here so we could monitor her regularly," he began. Angelique's stony expression told anyone who knew her that this was only the calm before the storm. This was the point at which it was always better to compromise than risk a scene, and Donnie recognized the signs.

"Look, Dr. Feinstein, my brother is a physician and my best friend is also. My brother has privileges here, maybe you know him: Andrew Cochran."

The doctor's concern fell away from his face. "Of course, I know him. I think it should be fine. As long as you check her regularly and you're in contact with your brother, there shouldn't be a problem. I'm going to give you a list of symptoms and if she starts exhibiting any of them, bring her right back in. Actually, the sooner she's back in familiar surroundings, the sooner her memory will come back. I'll have the nurse bring in the information," he told them. After a little more conversation, he left Donnie and Angelique alone in the room.

She smiled at Donnie, a ravishing smile full of trust. "Well, I think I need to get dressed," she said, looking down at her dowdy hospital gown. She finally let go of his hand and pushed back the thin sheet and blanket to reveal long, shapely legs, bare up to the hips where the gown had twisted. "Are you going to help me?"

Donnie swallowed hard as he realized the full import of the act. "Why don't I get your clothes and the nurse and she can help you get dressed," he said quickly.

Fortunately for his sanity, Angelique agreed. "Okay. Don't forget to come back for me," she said cheerfully.

After he got her situated with her clothing, he went out into the hall to wait for her. He took a deep breath and leaned against the wall to steady his nerves. Whatever else it was, life with Angelique was never dull.

The doctor had warned Donnie that Angelique might be groggy and disoriented for a few hours and suggested he put her to bed and check her pupils every hour. Dr. Feinstein had obviously never dealt with someone like Angelique. She was animated all the way home and more interested in the falling snow than her temporary amnesia. "That looks so pretty! It looks like Christmas," she remarked at one point.

Donnie finally got her home and into bed, a feat much more complicated than he'd expected. First she had to play with the dogs. She may not have remembered them, but they were still her great champions and they preened and danced around and played with her to their hearts' content. She was absolutely delighted with Jordan and Pippen, and rather charmed by the house, which she insisted on touring. Donnie had to demand that she get into bed by threatening a quick return to the hospital. She looked crestfallen, but agreed. Then she complicated matters by asking why her clothes were in the guest room.

It hadn't occurred to Donnie that she would expect to sleep in the same bed with him, but since she had no recollection of their unorthodox marriage, she thought sharing a bed was perfectly normal. He stammered out something about them redecorating and reorganizing the closets and she seemed to accept it. It seemed a harmless fabrication until she went into the "guest room" and came back with a sheer pink confection in which to sleep.

He suggested that she find something warmer, as the Weather Channel was predicting a huge snowstorm for later that night. "It's going to get really cold, Angel. You need to have on more than that." *And I definitely need for you to be covered up.* They compromised with her in one of his old T-shirts, which fit her like a nightshirt. She climbed into bed and looked at him expectantly.

"Aren't you coming to bed?" she asked sweetly.

"In a little while. Remember I have to check on you every hour," he reminded her.

"Okay, well, I'll stay up with you, I'm not sleepy," she replied.

"But you need some sleep. Doesn't your head still hurt?"

She looked a little uncomfortable and admitted that yes, it did. "But I can't go to sleep unless you're here with me," she said doggedly. She looked so sweet he couldn't resist any longer and finally agreed to come to bed with her. He always slept in the nude so he had to dig around to find an old pair of shorts and a football jersey for himself; he didn't own a single pair of pajamas. He slipped under the sheets and was touched and surprised when Angelique slid over next to him like she'd been doing it for years. She cuddled into his side and gave a soft little sigh, then rose up on one elbow and studied Donnie's face carefully, leaned over and kissed him softly. "My husband," she murmured and lay down again with her arm around his waist. He returned the embrace, holding her close until she fell asleep.

It was the most tortuous night of Donnie's life. He was prepared somewhat for the interest his body took in hers, but not for its persistence. He was as hard as a rock and the fact that Angelique was extremely affectionate in her sleep was no help at all. She made soft little moans as she was sleeping and rolled over on him so many times, he wasn't getting any sleep at all. When she wasn't adjusting her body to his and twisting her hips against his huge erection, she was stroking him and sighing with what was undeniably desire. Having to wake her up every hour on the hour wasn't a picnic, either.

He kept the bedside light on low and had a flashlight next to it. He would gently stroke her face and call her name until her eyes opened. They were always warm and full of affection until the brilliant light violated her vision. He would then hold up his fingers and ask her how many she saw. After the four o'clock wakening, she smiled sleepily and spoke to him softly. "Sweetheart, may I see that for a minute?"

He handed her the flashlight, which she promptly threw across the room. "Put that thing in my face again and I'll show you a different finger. Cut it out!" she growled.

Donnie laughed in spite of everything. This was the Angel he knew and loved. She would be fine. *He* might not survive if she didn't keep her hands off him, but she was going to be fine. He drifted off to sleep only to wake up and find her lying completely on top of him without her T-shirt. He tried to slide her off his body but she pressed closer to him and opened her silken thighs a bit, the better to accommodate his body. Sheer panic set in, causing sweat to break out on his brow. This was temptation beyond temptation but he couldn't give in—it was wrong. How could he even think about making love to her in this condition? She didn't know who she was, who he really was; she didn't remember any of the circumstances surrounding their current relationship. His hands stroked the satiny smoothness of her long bare back and he finally had to roll her off him with more force than he would've liked. He had no choice: it was that or total surrender.

Incredibly, she didn't wake up, but turned over onto her back and treated him to his first look at her beautiful breasts, comely brown orbs that were lusher than he'd imagined. Her tempting brown nipples were big and erect, begging for his touch. His hands clenched and unclenched on the sheets and he finally threw the covers over her and got out of bed with great difficulty. He limped into the kitchen, stubbing his toes a couple of times as he tried to maneuver through the darkened rooms. Reaching his goal, the refrigerator, he made a makeshift ice pack out of a plastic bag and stifled a groan as he slapped it onto his aching member. His face contorted in pain as he looked down at the traitor and said, "Serves you right. Now maybe you'll calm down when I tell you to."

The next morning Angelique was in wonderful spirits. Despite the fact that she still had no recollection whatsoever of her life, she was surprisingly sanguine about it. She had someone who loved her and would take care of her and the doctor said her memory would be back anytime now. In the meantime, she lived in a nice house, she had two lovely dogs that apparently adored her and she had a big, beautiful man as her husband.

She sat up in bed, a bit dismayed to find that he'd gotten out of bed before her. She wanted nothing more than to roll over into his arms. Every time she touched him she was bathed in a blazing passion she wanted to explore. She looked around for the T-shirt she'd worn to bed and smiled when she found it tossed on the floor. She'd apparently taken it off during the night, and no wonder: it was hotter than Billy-be-damned in the house. Sliding the shirt over her head, she went in search of the bathroom to take care of a pressing need and brush her teeth thoroughly. She stared at the toothbrushes in the holder and realized she didn't know which one was hers. She liked the looks of the green one and took it, reasoning that it really didn't matter since she'd probably shared every bodily fluid possible with her husband. The thought gave her a delicious little shiver. She decided to take a shower, but first she wanted to find Donnie.

She walked down the hall and was accosted by Jordan and Pippen, who were very happy to see her as always. After petting them and telling them what clever boys they were, she ended up in the living room. There was Donnie, stretched out on the sofa and looking really uncomfortable, huddled under a knitted throw. She went over to him and kissed him under his ear. "Wake up, sweetheart. It's morning."

His eyes popped open and he smiled at her before wincing in discomfort.

"Why are you out here on the sofa, Donnie? I'll bet your back feels terrible. How about a hot shower to get the kinks out?"

He sat up slowly, due to his back's unnatural position. Swinging his legs down to the floor, he took a good look at Angelique. "You look awfully chipper. How's that head?"

She shrugged. "It still hurts a little. I seem to have a big bump on the side of my head, wanna see?" Before he could answer, she came and knelt in front of him and rested her arms on his bare thighs so he could examine her head. His long fingers probed her thick black hair and he did indeed find a sizable knot. While he was doing that, her warm palms were tracing circles on his thighs, creating a sensation that was difficult to ignore and impossible to deny. He pulled her up to sit on the sofa next to him. Praying for control, he suggested that Angelique take a shower, also. "The steam will make you feel better and I'll get you an ice pack for the head. I'm really good at making ice packs," he said with a grim smile.

"Well, why don't we shower together?" Angelique said seductively. "That way we can get nice and clean at the same time."

Trying to conceal his panic, Donnie insisted that she shower alone. "I'll fix us breakfast while you do that."

Angelique looked disappointed, but she was touched by his offer of breakfast. "That's very sweet of you, Donnie. You don't have to go to work today?"

Donnie couldn't help himself—he leaned over and kissed her on the temple. "I'm not going in today, baby. I don't want to leave you, for one thing, and nobody is going anywhere for another. Look out the window."

Angelique went to the living room window and pulled the draperies open to a winter wonderland. It had snowed about ten inches during the night and was still coming down in fat flakes. Her look of utter delight needed no exclamation; she just stood there and drank it in. Donnie looked at her and surrendered to the charming picture she made. He went to stand behind her and wrapped his arms around her. "It is kind of pretty out there, as long as I get to be in here," he said, nuzzling her neck.

Angelique turned around in his arms and hugged him. "With me?" she asked flirtatiously. "I'm glad to be here with you, too. By the way, what color is my toothbrush?"

He looked at her oddly and said, "It's purple, why do you ask?"

Chapter Fifteen

Donnie and Angelique were sitting in the living room with the draperies wide open, watching the snow. Things had been progressing quite smoothly, once the after-shower incident passed. He'd been in the kitchen trying to figure out what he could possibly fix for breakfast when he heard Angelique's voice behind him. "Donnie, where is the washing machine?" He'd turned around to see her standing in the kitchen, wearing hip-hugging white cotton panties with tiny pink pin dots and a tiny pink bow in the front. She was also wearing a very seductive half-cup bra made of the same fabric and a pair of thick white socks that should have looked totally out of place. Instead she looked incredibly sexy and adorable and he was extremely glad the refrigerator door was blocking his nether regions from her view.

"Put some clothes on!"

Angelique looked stunned for a second, then put her hand on her hip and stared at him. "If you didn't have the heat set on 'hell' I might be able to get dressed! This place is like an oven!" She tossed her hair back and flounced out of the kitchen, mumbling.

Donnie groaned and reached for more ice cubes. After his immediate reaction to seeing her beautiful body subsided, he went to the thermostat, turned it down and went to find his very angry wife. She had dressed in jeans and one of his old sweatshirts and gave him a hostile look.

"I'm sorry, baby. I didn't mean to yell at you. I turned the heat down. Since you're from Atlanta, I thought you might be cold, I guess."

Angelique looked more intrigued than angry. "I'm from Atlanta? How long have I lived here?"

"About eight months."

"Did I move up here by myself? Do I have a family in Atlanta?" she asked curiously.

Suddenly Donnie's heart turned over. Poor baby, she had no memory of anything about who she was and where she came from. "I'll make you a deal. You let me take a shower and get dressed and I'll tell you anything you want to know. How's that?"

She gave him a sly smile and stared at his long, strong legs and broad chest. "Well, if you just *have* to cover up that gorgeous body, I guess it's okay." She moved slowly toward him and licked her lips. "You don't have to get dressed on my account, though. You can wear a lot less if you want." By now she'd reached him and put her hands on his hips.

Donnie found the strength to put his hands on her shoulders and gently guide her backward out of the room. "Cut that out. You're not ready for what comes next."

"Because of a little bump on the head?" She pouted.

"Yes! Yes, that's right, because of your head. Give me fifteen minutes and I'll make you a breakfast you'll never forget and tell you anything you want to know," he promised.

When he finally emerged from the bedroom, he was attired similarly to Angelique in old baggy jeans, thick gray socks and a tattered Alpha sweatshirt. He walked down the hall and was stunned to smell something really appetizing coming from the kitchen. To his utter surprise and gratitude, he found Angelique putting crisp bacon on a layer of paper towels to drain. There was an aromatic smell of coffee mixed with the sweet smell of the maple-cured bacon. She then turned her attention to the thick slices of bread on the counter, dipping each one into an egg mixture to prepare it for French toast. The table was already set for two and the scene was one of total domestic tranquillity. The snow continued to rage, but inside it was like being in a fairy tale.

"Angel, what is all this? I told you I was going to fix breakfast."

"I know you did, but I wanted to surprise you. Why can I remember how to cook but I can't remember anything else? Isn't this weird?" She didn't seem very concerned, though, as she continued to work until the French toast was laid neatly on the grill.

After the excellent repast, they sat facing each other across the table. Jordan and Pippen had long since given up on getting a handout and were asleep in the laundry room. Angelique looked quizzically at Donnie. "I thought you said it was March."

Donnie confirmed that it was indeed March.

"I never knew it could snow this late in the year," Angelique said. She stared out the window, enthralled by what she saw. "It's so pretty!"

"That's because you grew up in Georgia, baby. If you grew up here like I did, you wouldn't think it was so cute. And you'd be used to it—it's not unusual for us to get a big dump of snow right before spring."

Angelique sipped the last of her coffee and looked at Donnie with a smile in her eyes. "Okay, I fed you. Now I'm going to clean up the kitchen and then you're going to tell me who I am."

Donnie insisted on cleaning the kitchen and further insisted that Angelique lie down while he did it. He made a fire for her in the living room and she curled up on the sofa, enjoying the fragrant fire and the feeling of being cared for. When she woke up she was cuddled up in Donnie's lap and he was asleep, with his long legs stretched out in front of him. She was warm and relaxed and perfectly content to stay where she was forever. There was something about being with this big, handsome man that eased all her fears and made her happy. She began to stroke his face softly, tracing his thick eyebrows, his high, defined cheekbones and his beautiful lips. His eyes opened slowly and locked on hers. They didn't speak; they just stared into each other's eyes. They were lost in each other, bound together in a long, timeless moment that spoke more loudly that any words could.

"How long have we been married?" Angelique whispered.

"Not very long. We got married on Valentine's Day," he answered. He didn't really want to talk, but he knew it was a better idea than the alternative, which was to take her into the bedroom and make love to her until she screamed his name without stopping.

"Did we have a big wedding? Was my family there? What *about* my family, anyway—do I have parents?"

Donnie settled her more comfortably in his arms and began talking. "We eloped. Got married in Vegas on Valentine's Day," he said in a soft voice. "You're from Atlanta. You have a mother named Lillian and a stepfather named Bill Williams. His nickname is Bump and he's a famous jazz musician. Your mother is very beautiful and very sweet and your stepfather is a card. He's one of the funniest men I ever met. He's also my sister's godfather; he's been a friend of our family for a long time. You have four brothers and all of them are older than you. Clay is the oldest, then Martin and Malcolm, who are identical twins. Marcus is the youngest. All your brothers are married and you have a bunch of nieces and nephews. You're the baby of the family and the only girl." He rubbed his cheek against her soft, fragrant hair.

"Four brothers," she said with wonder. "What happened to my father? Are he and my mother divorced?"

"No, baby, your father died when you were a little girl," he said gently. "My mother died when I was a baby, so that's something we have in common. I'm also the youngest in my family." He proceeded to give her the Cochran family history.

Angelique was fascinated by everything he told her. "How did we meet? Was it love at first sight?"

Donnie laughed and assured her that it was nothing of the kind. "We met years ago when your brother Clay started dating my sister Benita. Everyone calls her Bennie except for me and my brothers and her husband. Anyway, the first time I saw you I thought you were beautiful and you thought I was a jerk and that was about it. We never got along, especially after you sabotaged Benita's wedding shower," he said carelessly.

"After I *what?*" Angelique looked horrified and Donnie wished he'd never brought it up. "What did I do to her shower? Tell me, I need to know."

Hesitantly, Donnie told her that she had invited all of her brother's old girlfriends to the shower, instead of inviting real guests. "It was just a prank, Angel, and it turned out fine. Benita's so cool, she just made friends with everybody and it wasn't a bad thing, not at all."

Angelique wasn't buying it, though. "I don't care what you say, Donnie, that was a horrible thing to do. I must be a terrible person," she said quietly. "Your family must hate me."

"Angel, I'm sorry, I shouldn't have told you that. You may have tried to disrupt Benita's shower, but you more than made up for it when she and Clay were separated."

"They were separated? Why?" she asked, wiping away moisture from her eyes.

"It's another long story. When she was pregnant with their first child she had to go to California on business. While she was out there a drunk driver hit the car she was riding in. She was terribly injured and she lost the baby and she and Clay blamed themselves for it. They were so eaten up with guilt that they stayed away from each other for months until you got them back together," he told her.

"I did? So maybe I'm not so bad after all?" She sounded so humble and hesitant that she won Donnie's heart all over again.

"Baby, you're wonderful. My family loves you, especially my father. He calls you Babydoll and he thinks you're spunky. He always liked you, especially after the shower incident; he thought it was funny as hell because he wasn't too crazy about Benita marrying Clay."

Angelique's eyes got big when he related this. "Does he like Clay now? He's not still mad at him, is he?"

Donnie said no. "No, my dad respects Clay and, in his own way, he loves him. Benita is happy, which is all that matters to him. And she and Clay have some beautiful kids, so that makes him happy, too. My father used to be really possessive of Benita; she was his oldest and his only girl. Clay had to let him know what time it was and Pop had to deal with it."

He continued to hold her closely and nuzzle her cheek and neck as he spoke. "My nieces and nephews all love you. You're wonderful," he whispered and kissed her forehead, her cheeks and her chin.

"So I moved to Michigan about eight months ago. Why did I come here?" She sat up a little so she could better see his face. "Was it because I missed you so much and wanted to be with you?"

Donnie smiled at the eagerness in her voice. "Your cousin Paris Deveraux is doing an internship with our company because we're partnered and all our executives train with both companies. So she's up here now, and she's your roommate. And the man you were working for, Alan Jandrewski, moved back home to Detroit and you came with him."

Something about the way he said the name made Angelique ask if she and this man had been involved. "No," Donnie said emphatically. "You're just good friends."

The familiar yearning for her took over him once again, engulfing his body in fiery sensation. He wanted her so bad, it was a physical ache, but he forced himself to behave. They couldn't continue to hug and kiss like this if he was to keep the promise he made to himself not to touch her until her amnesia was gone. As if a brilliant idea had just occurred to him, he said, "Hey, we'd better call your cousin Paris and let her know what happened to you."

He gently placed her on the sofa and reached for the cordless phone on the coffee table. When he didn't get a dial tone, he raised an eyebrow. "I wonder if the lines are down. I'd better check." He left the room and came back shortly, reporting that all the phones were dead. "So it's cell phones or nothing."

Angelique nodded and patted the seat next to her on the sofa. "Well, so much for that. Come sit down and let's talk some more," she said in the seductive voice that was beginning to drive him nuts every time her heard it.

"Better idea: let's watch TV and find out what's happening with the storm." He picked up the remote and pointed it at the big flat-screen TV and tossed her the *TV Guide*.

"Let's watch a movie instead," Angelique said. "Something hot and sexy. I'll read the listings to you." She opened the book and started to read out loud. She read slowly and haltingly, hesitating over each syllable and stumbling like she couldn't see the words. She stopped and rubbed her hand across her eyes. "Wow. I must have hit my head harder than I thought."

Donnie was staring at her with concern in his eyes. "Well, the print's really small in that. Here, try this," he said, handing her an *Ebony* magazine.

She smiled her thanks and tossed the offending *Guide* aside. "This is better," she agreed and started reading again— with the same results. This time her face puckered in concern and she stared helplessly at Donnie. "I think I'm going to go lie down for a while. My eyes are really bothering me, I guess."

Donnie agreed that a nap would be the best thing and he waited until she disappeared down the hall. He picked up his cell phone and hit the speed dial for Paris's cell and was relieved when she answered.

"Paris? This is Donnie and I wanted you to know that Angelique had a little accident last night. No, no, she's fine, I think. She got bopped in the head with a hockey puck at Joe Louis Arena and she doesn't really remember anything but the doctor says that it's fairly normal in these cases. No, she's not freaking out, she's having a ball, actually. I just wanted to let you know what was going on."

After her chatty response, Donnie asked her the question that was uppermost in his mind. "Paris, Angel tried to read something out loud and it was . . . well, it was like she couldn't read very well. Do you know anything about that?"

Paris was silent for a long moment, a moment during which Donnie's anxiety built. Finally she started to speak.

"Okay, pal, it's time you knew this. Are you sitting down? If you aren't, get a seat, this'll take a minute." In a short time she'd told him everything he needed to know.

When Donnie got off the phone, he sat on the sofa and stared straight ahead, his eyes focused on nothing. He was still trying to process the information he'd been given. Paris had told him of Angelique's severe dyslexia and he was both humbled and amazed by what he'd heard. Some things were beginning to click into place like the cylinders in a combination lock; he was beginning to understand a lot more about his wife. Now he could understand why she'd had such a giant chip on her shoulder, why she'd been so angry so much of the time. Some of the things Paris told him had appalled him, like the part about Angelique being sent away to boarding school. Some things had amazed him, as he realized the extent of her ability to cope.

Paris had explained some of the things Angelique did to compensate for her reading ability. "Well, she's very good with numbers, for one thing. But, please, whatever you do, don't call her Rainman. That's what they used to call her in school and she doesn't think it's funny at all. She drives that Saab because it has OnStar, the system where your car talks to you. It gives her a lot more confidence driving because she knows she can call OnStar and get directions and roadside assistance and stuff. She has trouble with directions—that's why she wears the silver bracelet on one arm and the gold one on the other, to help her remember right and left." Her words left him stunned, but she had some advice for him, too.

"The thing is, Donnie, Angel is very intelligent, but deep down inside she really thinks she's stupid. Dyslexia means she learns differently—her mind just works differently. Just try to imagine how your life would be if you couldn't read very well. What kind of limitations would that put on you? But Angel always figures out a way to do something, she's very determined and creative. Just don't feel sorry for her or start treating her like she's helpless, because she's not. She's unique."

Donnie lost track of time as he thought about what Paris had told him. Angelique was truly one of a kind. His admiration for her grew even more profound as he considered the impact the dyslexia had on her life. Suddenly it dawned on him where he could get more information and he hit the speed dial for Warren's number.

Warren answered the phone, sounding like he really didn't want to be bothered. "What do you want, Cochran? I'm having a snow day with my sweetheart and it was very romantic until you called," he complained.

"Sorry about that, man." He rapidly explained about Angelique's bump on the head and his subsequent discovery that she was dyslexic. "I just need some more information about it, Warren. I feel really stupid but I don't know a whole lot about dyslexia."

Warren was not only a medical doctor, he was a Ph.D. and head of the department of neurolinguistics in the College of Medicine at Wayne State University. His department specialized in the branch of linguistics that studied the relationship between language and the various functions of the nervous system. Developing teaching methodologies for learning disabilities like dyslexia was a part of that. Warren listened to Donnie's concerns and told him he could get him some information. "As soon as the weather lets up we'll get together and talk. In the meantime, you be good to Angel. I told you she was special and this proves it."

"Thanks for the information, Warren. And don't worry about Angel and me. I know how special she is and I plan to let her know, too."

Warren pressed the END button on his cell phone and rejoined Lisette in her cozy kitchen. When he had attempted to leave the night before, she had insisted he stay, due to the terrible weather. And he had agreed as long as he stayed in her guest room, to her great disappointment. He stood in the doorway a moment and watched her work. She was making him a special dish her mother had taught her, a Senegalese dish called Chicken Yassa. She looked up from her work and gave him the radiant smile that never failed to make him melt inside.

"Hello, my darling. Have you come to watch me?"

He returned her smile and walked over to sit at the wooden table. "Honey, I never get tired of watching you, you know that. But I have to talk to you about something." He told her what Donnie had related to him over the phone and waited for her response.

"Oh, poor Angel. What a strange way for him to find out her deepest secret." She sighed. "I knew about her dyslexia; she told me about it not too long after we met. She was so afraid he wouldn't want her if he knew she was dyslexic. She really believes that it affects her intellect, not just her learning. I hope he has sense enough to treat her gently. If he were to make her feel bad because of this, I would . . . I would . . ."

Warren interrupted her tirade to assure her that Donnie

would do no such thing. "He told me last night, before her accident, that he loves her. He wants her happiness above anything, Lisette. He'll be good to her."

Lisette's eyes lit up and she left the counter and wrapped her arms around Warren's neck, then sat down in his lap. "Oh, that's wonderful." She sighed. "Now they can be as happy as we are."

"Maybe, but I don't see how," he replied as he bent his eager mouth to her willing lips.

When Angelique awoke, she felt odd. The pain in her head was almost gone and she felt refreshed, but curiously disoriented. For some reason she was feeling uneasy and strange and she couldn't figure out why. She looked around the room at the pictures she saw displayed and it suddenly hit her. She held up her left hand and stared at it. Everything was becoming clearer to her. She scooted up so her back was against the headboard and sat there deep in thought. That's the way Donnie found her when he came to see how she was doing. He sat down on the side of the bed and looked at her troubled face.

"Hey, there. You look deep in thought. What is it, Angel?"

She returned his look of concern with a bleak expression. "We're not really married, are we?"

Donnie almost fell off the bed. "What do you mean, we're not married? Of course we're married."

"I don't have a ring. There aren't any pictures of me anywhere in this room, much less anywhere in the house. And we haven't made love at all. We're newlyweds, so you say, but you never put your hands on me. I think you're lying to me."

Donnie moved from his position to sit closer to Angelique. He held his hand out to her and she placed hers in it in a gesture of trust. "I'm not lying to you, Angel. We really are married; I have the certificate if you'd like to see it. I don't have as many pictures of you as I should, but that's your fault," he teased her. "You only like to take pictures, you don't like to be in them. But I do have a picture of you." Reaching over to the small chest that served as a nightstand, he opened the top drawer and took out a framed photograph and handed it to her.

She made a soft sound of surprise as she looked at a picture of her in a fantastic tangerine-colored dress. She was smiling brilliantly and looked beautiful and happy, even to her own eye. "Where was this taken?"

"This was from your brother Marcus's wedding. You were the maid of honor," he told her. "And as for us not making love, baby, you've been in an accident. What kind of husband would I be if I was pawing all over you before you had a chance to recover?"

Angelique finally put the picture on the nightstand. She looked deeply into Donnie's eyes. "So it's not because you don't want to make love? Are you sure? I thought you just didn't think I was sexy or something."

Donnie laughed out loud and grabbed Angelique, pulling her into his embrace and rolling over so that she was on top of him. "You, not sexy? Oh, my God, I've been putting ice down my pants and taking cold showers and sleeping on the couch, anything I can think of to keep my hands off you. I've been going out of my mind from wanting you, baby."

Angelique felt better from hearing his heartfelt words, but she still had one question. "But where is my wedding ring? I don't have an engagement ring, either. Why is that, Donnie?"

Donnie hesitated only briefly. The things he'd just told her weren't whole truths, but they were more truth than fiction. He cared about her more than he thought possible and he just couldn't stand to have her look so bereft. Making himself another promise to make everything right as soon as possible, he sat up and gently set her aside so he could retrieve something else from the drawer by his bed. He took out a Tiffany box and handed it to Angelique. "It has to be sized, which is why you don't have it on. But here you are, my dear."

She opened the box to find an ornate wedding ring set in platinum with a huge center stone and an elaborate wrap-around band. "Wow. Put it on me, please," she said eagerly. He did as she asked and slid the ring on the proper finger, and, as he'd said, it was several sizes too big.

"See why it's still in the box? We'll get it fixed as soon as possible. Do you want to keep it on? You could put it on a chain or something."

Angelique shook her head and put the ring back in its box with no reluctance. "No, I can wait. It's beautiful, Donnie, thank you very much," she said but without the exuberance he would have expected. Just then Jordan and Pippen started barking like mad. Donnie laughed and said the snowplows must be out. "Let's go see what that racket is all about, it could just be their way of telling me they're hungry."

At the mention of food Angelique commented that she was hungry, too. "Can we have some soup?" she asked. "Some of that soup with hamburger."

Donnie was delighted. "I think you're starting to remember things. I made you hamburger soup not too long ago," he told her. "Do you remember anything else?"

"I'm not sure," she replied. "Who is Evie?"

Chapter Sixteen

The next morning Angelique awoke to the sounds of Detroit digging itself out of a record-breaking snowstorm. She was warm and comfortable, although a little bit unhappy that her husband wasn't in the bed with her. But on the other hand, it was probably better that he was gone. Angelique had suddenly remembered everything, every single detail of her life and their life together. It was just like Dr. Feinstein said: after a couple of days, her memory had returned. She should have been elated but she wasn't. She was both happy and sad, an odd reaction. She was happy because during the brief time that she'd had amnesia, Donnie had been so loving, just what she wanted from him. She was sad because she had no doubt that as soon as he knew her memory was back, they'd return to a farce of a marriage and she'd be sleeping in Siberia, aka the guest room, once again.

She didn't want to get out of bed, for fear of breaking the enchantment that had surrounded them. When she thought about what they'd done the night before, she had to wipe her eyes because the memory was so poignant and sweet. They'd had lunch and talked some more, then Donnie took the dogs out and Angelique had persuaded him to let her come out as well. He agreed that she could come in the backyard for a few minutes, only because she'd never seen so much snow in her life. He made sure she had on enough socks and sweaters and two thick scarves as well as a knit hat and two pairs of gloves with her warmest coat. "I can't move!" she complained.

He insisted that she needed all that gear and finally took her outside into the backyard. It was like being in a snow globe or being somehow transported to a Christmas card. Jordan and Pippen loved the snow and raced up and down with great enthusiasm. She and Donnie played like a couple of children until it got too cold even for Angelique. When they finally came in the house, they dried the dogs with old towels and Angelique made big cups of hot tea. It was one of the best afternoons she'd ever had.

After dinner that night, Angelique questioned Donnie about her photography. "What kind of pictures do I take?"

Donnie answered that by getting out her portfolio, which was stowed in the guest bedroom. He'd told her, "I have to confess, Angel, I've never looked in this, so this is all new to me, too." He'd unzipped the portfolio and they began looking at her photographs together. Donnie had been stunned as he'd seen the range of her work. They pored over the pictures together as Donnie told her she was having an exhibit at the African-American museum the following month.

"A whole exhibit? Me? Wow. Is my stuff good enough for that?" she'd asked him.

He'd answered that hers were the most profoundly moving works of photographic art he'd ever seen. "I'm totally humbled by your talent, Angel, I really am."

She had teased him by saying, "Bet you didn't think Evie could do this, huh?" He had confessed that Evie was his pet name for her, or it had been back when they didn't get along. She'd responded by saying something about SpongeBob and they ended up chasing each other through the house with the dogs joining in and the entire evening had been warm and funny and eventually romantic.

After things calmed down, Donnie had lit another fire and they sat on the sofa holding each other, talking very little.

They simply stared at each other and kissed once in a while, very softly. It was enough just to be in each other's arms, more than enough. When it was time for bed, Angelique suggested that she sleep in the guest room so as not to disturb him and he'd looked at her like she was crazy. "You're never sleeping anywhere but with me, Angel. Come on, let's go to bed." And they slept in each other's arms all night, blissfully at peace—until she woke up this morning and all her memories were back.

She squinted her eyes slightly and realized that she also remembered what had happened the night they got married! Even that had come back to her, but instead of being elated about it, she just wanted to make it all go away again. Because with her memory returned, she would have no chance of keeping her marriage. None whatsoever.

Her eyes were moist from unshed tears and her throat burned with the effort not to cry. Somehow she had to let Donnie know how she felt about him, let him know that she didn't want a divorce. But how? Subterfuge and lying weren't her strong points, which was why the whole fake marriage thing was wearing on her. She was used to being in hot water, it was a chronic condition when she was growing up. She could take whatever punishment was dealt out; she was quite stoic about it. But if she told Donnie the truth, that her memory was back and she was in love with him, how would he react?

She could hear him coming down the hall and smiled in spite of her angst. He was singing and making a lot of racket, even though he wasn't wearing boots. She considered pretending to be asleep but she wanted to see him too badly. He stuck his head in the door and gave her his most charming smile.

"Good morning, baby. I'm going out to clean out the driveway and the walk. I just wanted to let you know I'd be outside," he said.

"Good morning to you, too. What would you like for breakfast?"

"Whatever you feel like fixing. Don't go to too much trouble, you're supposed to be taking it easy, remember?"

She gave him a ravishing smile of her own. "I'm fine. I really am. You be careful out there."

By the time Donnie had cleared a path to the garage door, retrieved the snowblower and cleaned off the driveway, the sidewalks, the front and back steps and the back stoop, Angelique was all ready. She'd had a nice long bubble bath and was scented and lotioned and dressed in an outfit that wasn't blatantly sexy, but eye-catching all the same: jeans with a scanty little rose-pink sweater with a deep V in the front and back. She wasn't wearing any jewelry because if her plan worked, it would only get in the way. She'd made a wonderful breakfast consisting of salmon croquettes, grits, and biscuits, and she had the eggs whipped and ready to go into the skillet to be scrambled. She'd sectioned two grapefruits and put them in some nice little glass bowls and set the table attractively. Now all she needed was her husband to come in the back door. He did, covered in snow and looking exhausted.

"Do you want breakfast first or a shower?" she asked.

"If I was a gentleman I'd say a shower, but I'm starving, so how about some food?" he replied with a sheepish grin.

"Wash your hands and have a seat," she invited. "It's all ready except for the eggs."

After devouring the breakfast he couldn't stop praising, Donnie went to take a shower. He wasn't thrilled with the idea of another cold shower, but he couldn't be in the same room with her without wanting her. She looked so sexy in that sweater, he wanted to forget breakfast and drag her into the shower with him. He could picture her wearing bubbles and nothing else, a seductive smile on her face waiting for his hands to bring her to fulfillment. He groaned aloud as he realized that it was precisely this kind of thinking that got him into trouble. Turning the cold tap up high, he gave himself an arctic blast of water before getting out of the shower, then took a towel off the warmer and wrapped it around his waist before heading into the bedroom.

He was shocked to find the fireplace lit and Angelique sitting in the middle of the bed. She looked at him with a shy smile and said, "I need to talk to you about something, Adonis."

"Sure, Angel, what is it?" He was on his way to the closet when he realized what Angelique had called him. "You called me Adonis. You remembered! Your memory is back." He sounded slightly dazed.

"Yes, it is. I remember everything, Adonis. And what I have to tell you is this. I want . . . I want you . . ." she said in a voice so soft he could barely hear her.

He couldn't stand looking at her another moment. He came over to the bed and sat down so that he was propped up on the pile of pillows with his long legs extended, then held his arms out to her. She went into them willingly. He held her for a long moment, loving the feel of her body next to his, the softness of her sweater teasing the bare skin of his chest. He tipped her head back and kissed her eyes, her cheeks, and her tempting neck. Pulling her even closer, he began to speak in a voice full of passion aching to be fulfilled.

"Let me tell you what I want, Angel. I want to be a real husband to you, in every sense of the word. I want to be the last face you see at night, and the first one you see in the morning. I want to be with you for as long as we both live, until death do us part. I want to make you laugh, I want to comfort you when you cry, I want to be your friend, your lover and the one you turn to for shelter in the storm. I want you, my Angel. Just you. I love you, Angelique Clarissa Deveraux Cochran, and if you can find it in your heart to forgive me for being an idiot, I'd like to start right now. Can you love me, Angel? Can you look past all my imperfections, all my stupidity and my selfishness and trust me to be the man you need me to be?"

Angelique was trembling from emotion and tears were running freely down her face. Donnie kissed them all away with a smile. "Hey, you don't shed tears, you cause them, remember? Don't cry, baby. I'm going to tell you a secret. I can't stand to see you unhappy. It makes my heart break in a million pieces when you do that," he whispered.

"But I'm not sad, I'm happy," she told him. "Do you really love me?"

"Absolutely. Even though you used my toothbrush, I love you. Even if you start calling me SpongeBob again, I love you. I love you, my Angel."

Her eyes closed and he cupped her face in his big, warm hands to bestow the first real kiss of their marriage. Their lips touched in a delirium of desire that was all encompassing. They parted their mouths at the same time, to give and receive the passion that had been building for so long. Donnie began an exploration of her mouth with his tongue, licking and caressing with her as a willing accomplice. The moans of pleasure that filled the room expressed their joy at becoming one. They broke apart long enough to divest Angelique of her clothing and take the towel off Donnie.

At last they were in each other's arms with nothing between them. With the heavy draperies drawn, the fire was the only light in the room. It bathed them in a golden light that served to echo the fire in their hearts. Donnie reached into the nightstand to retrieve a condom. "We have plenty of time to make babies. This is just us, Angel. Just you and me and all the love I have for you," he told her as he rolled the condom onto his now-massive erection. "Now come here and let me love you."

He positioned her on top of him and they lay there, barely breathing as they learned the feel of each other. He kissed her again and again, stroking her body over and over, loving the feeling of her silky skin. He kissed her neck and her shoulders and she tightened her grip on his shoulders, sighing in ecstasy as he unleashed feelings she didn't know she could have. He rolled over so that their positions were reversed and he was lying on top of her as her hips began to move in the ageless dance of mating. He slid his hands down her body and held her in place. "Not yet, Angel, not yet," he groaned. He kissed her collarbone and licked her down to her beguiling breasts he had desired for so long.

He captured a nipple in his mouth and kissed it as thoroughly as he'd kissed her mouth, tenderly at first, then increasing the pressure until she screamed his name. After treating both breasts to this sweet torture he began to take her body to higher levels of abandon, using his tongue to explore her stomach, her navel and her sensitive inner thighs. She wept out loud, crying his name helplessly as his seeking mouth finally found what it yearned for, the most feminine, intimate part of her that yielded up its sweet nectar as he pleasured her beyond imagination. Waves of startling excitement washed over her as he worked his magic; she felt like she was exploding into a comet of unending bliss.

Just when she thought she couldn't stand any more sensation, he finally relented and kissed his way back up to her waiting lips and repeated the pulsating rhythm as their mouths sought more and more of each other. When they finally stopped, she couldn't speak, she was so spent from the release to which he'd brought her. "Adonis . . . oh, Adonis, I've never done that before." She sighed.

"Did you like it?" he asked as he waited for the wild pounding of his heart to subside.

"I loved it. It was beautiful," she whispered.

"You're beautiful. And I've never done that before, either, so we're even," he said quietly.

She looked at him skeptically and he confessed. "There was never anybody I wanted to get to know *that* well, if you know what I mean. I always said that was for my wife on our wedding night. And that's you, and this is it, our wedding night."

Touched to her heart, Angelique pointed out that it was

still daytime. "Well, then, we'll just have to do this until it gets dark," he growled. "Come here, baby, we have work to do."

This time she would not be denied; she forced him onto his back and straddled his body with hers. He held her hips as she looked down at him, her face a picture of innocent sexuality. "Are you ready for this, Angel?" By way of answer she moved her body and adjusted her hips so that the broad tip of his erection was positioned against her opening. "Yes, Adonis. Yes, yes, *yes!*" Her head went back and she slid down onto his massive hardness, crying out loud as he filled her. He held her firmly as they established a pace that brought them both the pleasure they wanted to give each other. She leaned forward, clutching his broad shoulders and felt herself lowered onto the bed as he turned her onto her back. He didn't stop the pumping, rhythmic motion that was bringing her back to the peak of frenzied ecstasy she had just ascended; she matched his every move until they were both bathed in sweat and screaming each other's name.

Hours later they were still wrapped in each other's arms. They had gotten up a few times to feed the dogs and let them out, to get something to eat and to shower together twice, but for the most part they were content to make love over and over until the shadows lengthened and the day began to fade into dusk. They also talked, making plans for their future and continuing the process of getting to know each other. They were feeding each other grapes in the middle of the big bed when Angelique gave him a sideways glance.

"You know about it, don't you?" she asked. At his inquiring look, she elaborated. "You know my big secret about being dyslexic, don't you? You had to figure it out when I was trying to read to you yesterday."

Donnie looked at her for a long moment and the love he felt for her was plainly written on his face. "I didn't know at first. I thought it was because your concussion was worse than we realized. I called Paris to get some answers," he admitted.

Angelique nodded. "But you didn't treat me like I was deficient, you treated me like a woman. Your woman," she said softly.

"You *are* my woman, just like I belong to you now. I'm yours, my Angel." He leaned over and kissed her.

They were both naked in the middle of the bedclothes, which had been rumpled so badly that Angelique insisted on changing them. Donnie had teased her about her fetish for cleanliness and she had blithely ignored him as they tucked in fresh crisp linens. She was admiring his body in the firelight; the desire to explore it was building once again. But before they got to that point, she had to finish telling him what was in her heart.

"When I woke up this morning and all the pieces fit back together, I was scared. I was so afraid that you wouldn't want me, that you were just humoring me and feeling sorry for the little special-ed child. I even thought about not telling you that the amnesia was gone. I wanted everything to just stay the way it was, but I also wanted it to last forever. So I had to tell you the truth." She stopped to take a big grape from his fingers, looking like a golden nymph as she did so.

"I had to believe that since you heard me stammering and stumbling over those words and you didn't treat me any differently that maybe, just maybe you could start to care for me. And you do." She smiled at him, a radiant smile full of adoration that made him fall in love with her all over again.

He took the bowl of grapes from between them and set them out of the way. Grasping her hands, he guided her to lie down on his chest while he covered both of them with the sheet. He kissed her forehead and her lips, and held her to his heart while he talked. "Angel, you are the most fascinating, incredible woman it's ever been my privilege to know. You have so many wonderful facets, I'm never going to know all there is to know about you. You're everything any man could ever want and I plan to spend every day of the rest of our lives making you happy, just so you know."

She ran her hand over the hard muscles of his broad chest, enjoying the smooth warmth. "I love you, Adonis. You're everything I always wanted and never thought I'd have," she said drowsily.

She was almost asleep on his shoulder when she remembered what she hadn't told him. "I remember our wedding, Adonis. I remember getting married."

"That's wonderful, baby, tell me about it tomorrow." He yawned and in minutes they were both sound asleep.

Chapter Seventeen

Lisette couldn't stop smiling as she looked at Donnie and Angelique across the table. She and Warren were dining with the newlyweds at Sweet Georgia Brown, a posh restaurant in Greektown. And Donnie and Angelique were acting like newlyweds, to her delight. They were warm and affectionate with each other, holding hands and unable to keep their eyes off each other.

"My, my, my! What a difference a snowstorm makes," she teased. "Look at you two, you look like you invented love."

Donnie kissed Angelique's dimples and smiled. "Don't forget the hockey puck," he reminded her. "I owe a special debt of gratitude to the Red Wings and the Calgary Flames."

Angelique laughed and squeezed her husband's hand. Then her smile got dreamy and she looked at Lisette. "And I think he did invent love. Being married to him is the most wonderful thing in the world. Better than chocolate." She sighed.

"My goodness," Lisette said, awed. "If I didn't have my Warren, I'd be terribly jealous right now." She put her hand on Warren's arm and smiled at him adoringly. He looked at her with his heart in his eyes and gave her a brief kiss on the lips that spoke volumes.

The two women excused themselves from the table to visit the facilities and their men rose as they left the table. Donnie watched every movement of Angelique's body as she walked away and Warren had to give him grief about it. "Look at you, Cochran! A few months ago you were ready to marry someone else and now you can't let her out of your sight. You're one lucky son-of-a-gun, you know that, don't you?"

Donnie fervently agreed. "Yes, I do. I feel blessed in the extreme. I have the pleasure of being with the most exciting, the most beautiful woman in the world and she loves me. Love is a beautiful thing, Warren; you tried to tell me and I wasn't hearing it. You were right and I was totally wrong."

Warren got serious for a moment, asking Donnie if Angelique knew that he'd proposed to someone else not two months before they got married. Donnie also got serious. "No, I haven't told her that. You know she's working with Aneesah to get the exhibit set up at the museum, right?" At Warren's look of horror, Donnie hastened to reassure him. "No, it's not bad, not at all. They get along well and she knows that I used to date Aneesah. Aneesah called me after the news got out about the wedding and gave me a hard time." He laughed. "She talked about me like a dog and reminded me that she'd warned me this would happen. That love was something that sneaked up on you and took over when you least expected it."

He smiled at the memory of their conversation. "But she also said she would make sure that nobody knew that I had proposed to her. She said that was between us and it would stay that way."

"Like I said, Cochran: a lucky son-of-a-gun. . . . Where are those women? I still haven't figured out what they do in there," he complained.

"I told you, they talk about us. So now it's your turn,

Warren. I've led the way, when are you going to make an honest woman of your Lisette?" Surprisingly, Warren didn't have his usual snappy comeback. He looked away from Donnie and finished his wine in one gulp, signaling their server for more.

Meanwhile, Lisette and Angelique were back where their friendship started, in the ladies' room. "Marriage really agrees with you, Angel. You look even more beautiful than before. Donnie must be an extremely romantic man," Lisette said enviously.

"Oh, Lisette, he's wonderful. We drive in to work together most of the time and we have lunch together as often as we can. He brings me breakfast in bed on Saturdays and we cook for each other during the week. We go to church together on Sundays and then we spend the rest of the day together just doing nothing. He's the best friend and support in the world. And he's so romantic!" She fanned a hand in front of her face to indicate extreme heat. "I'm so happy I could cry. But you know what that's like—you and Warren are in love."

Lisette looked crestfallen and Angelique was alarmed at how quickly her friend's face had changed. "What's the matter, Lisette?"

"Warren doesn't want me," she said sadly. "He's sweet to me and attentive and all of that, but he's a perfect gentleman. He's never tried to, you know, make love to me. And when I try to get really amorous, he manages to push me away. He treats me like a pretty little doll, but there's no real passion. I don't know what to do, Angel, I really don't."

Angelique was appalled for her friend's sake. "I don't know much, but I do know that Warren loves you like crazy. You have to get to the bottom of this and the only way I know how is to level with him. You've got to talk it out. Maybe he just wants to wait until you're married, have you thought about that?"

"Well, if that's the case, why doesn't he propose? Warren

is so sexy, such a big, handsome teddy bear, if I don't get with him soon I'm going to drug him and tie him down!" She looked determined enough to do it, too.

"Ooh, don't hurt poor Warren, girl! I'm sure there's a happy medium in there somewhere. In Warren's defense, though, isn't it nice to be with someone who likes you for you and not what he can get from you?"

Lisette looked shamefaced and agreed. "I should be smacked, I know. I have a wonderful man who treats me like a lady and I'm complaining because I want to jump his bones. I'm a wench, I really am."

"No, you're just in love. Now let's get back out there before they forget who we are," she said.

Lisette scoffed. "As if that handsome Donnie could ever forget his beloved wife."

"And Warren could never forget you. Open communication, Lisette, that's the only answer."

The day of the exhibit opening finally came, and with it a cases of nerves Angelique wasn't anticipating. She was hot one minute and cold the next, her head hurt and she couldn't keep anything down. She was totally miserable and all the comfort Donnie had to offer didn't help. At present he was holding her in his lap and rubbing her arms and back while he nuzzled her neck.

"Look, sweetness, I'm going to get you some Vernor's and crushed ice. It'll help settle your stomach. Maybe you can get some crackers down, too," he suggested.

Angelique started to nod her head, then stopped as it made her dizzy. "Do we have any gingersnaps?" she asked. Her favorite snack lately was Vernor's ginger ale and the hard, crunchy, ginger-flavored cookies. The thought of the combination made Donnie gag, but she'd been so nervous about the exhibit, he indulged her every whim.

"I'll see. In the meantime, you lay here on the sofa and get some rest. It's going to be fine, baby. We both walked through last night and it looks perfect. It's an amazing display, Angel. You have every reason to be proud of it."

"And every reason to be terrified, Adonis. My whole family is coming up here for this and I don't want to disappoint them. I want them to be proud of me," she admitted.

"Angel, how could they not be proud of you? You're so talented, it's actually frightening. You make your subjects look so real, it's like you could reach into the picture and touch them. They're astounding photographs, Angel. And if it means anything, I'm so proud of you, I could burst. You, my queen, are an extraordinary woman," he said as he gave her a wet, tickling kiss right in her dimple. "Now, you sit here and I'll be right back with your ginger ale."

Her eyes moistened in gratitude for his loving attentiveness. "You're too sweet to me," she murmured.

He held her for one more moment, and whispered, "It's not possible to be too sweet to you. I love you, my Angel."

A couple of hours before the opening, Angelique was walking through the carefully displayed pictures, looking in vain to find something wrong or out of place.

"You're wasting your time, Angel. It's perfect. Just like you."

Angelique turned to find A.J. standing behind her with a smile on his face. She opened her arms for his hug and he enfolded her in his arms and held her tightly.

"I'm so glad you're here. How'd you know I'd be a nervous wreck?"

"Because I know you, Angel. How've you been? How's that husband of yours treating you?"

They hadn't seen each other since the night of the Red Wings game. After calling Donnie from the hospital to let him know about her accident, A.J. naturally waited with her until her husband arrived. He and Donnie had exchanged words that would have led to a fistfight had not the hospital personnel intervened. There was no love lost between the two men. Donnie knew a predator when he saw one and he was sure A.J.'s feelings were more than brotherly. And A.J. was equally sure that Donnie wasn't capable of giving Angelique the unconditional love she deserved.

Angelique gave A.J. a beautiful smile and turned around in a circle in front of him. "See for yourself! How do I look?"

A.J. had to admit that she looked radiantly happy and totally fulfilled. She was wearing off-white in the form of a slim-fitting, silk, jersey wrap tunic and wide-legged pants. She had on a pair of incredible gold earrings made of interlocking flat circles that hung almost to her shoulders. They were a gift from Donnie and accentuated her graceful neck, drawing attention to her sculpted collarbones. Her hair was arranged in a sophisticated chignon that gave her the look of a young Lena Horne. She looked absolutely beautiful and A.J. told her so.

"I have to tell you, Angel, you look great. Just remember, if he makes you unhappy in any way, any way at all, I'm here for you." He spoke with such sincerity that Angelique blinked her eyes. She was about to say something when Paris interrupted her.

"Girl, you have got to see this! Come on, Angel, hurry up!"

She and A.J. followed her to the front of the museum where they could see the street. Three ultralong black limousines had pulled up in front and the doors opened to let out the Deveraux men. As Clay, then Malcolm and Martin and Marcus emerged from the various cars, even Paris had to draw in her breath.

"Ooh-ooh-*wee,* if they weren't my cousins I'd be having some issues, girl," she said as she watched the tall, powerful and very handsome men assist their beloved wives and children.

"Yeah, yeah, yeah. It's a lot more impressive when they're not coming after you," she said, rubbing her temple with her forefinger. She went out on the sidewalk to start greeting her family, leaving A.J. and Paris looking after her. At least A.J. was looking at Angelique. Paris was watching A.J. and, being Paris, said what was on her mind.

"You love her, don't you?"

A.J. honored her perception by not pretending he didn't know what she meant. He looked at Paris with a bittersweet smile. "That's supposed to be my secret. No one was supposed to know."

Paris's tender heart broke at the look on his face. "So why didn't you ever tell her? I don't think it was because of the age thing, was it?"

A.J. smiled again. "Angel always said you were the most perceptive person she knew. It was because I was waiting for her to grow into herself. I didn't want to try to have a relationship with her because she needed to have some independence, to have some success on her own. She needed to prove to herself that she could take care of herself and have a career of her own, not just bask in someone else's shadow. And my wish for her came true. Just not in the way I expected," he said ruefully.

Paris put her hand on his arm and gave him a gentle squeeze. "I don't know what to say, A.J."

"Say that you won't hesitate, like I did. Say that when you have a chance at love, you'll take it and run with it. Don't lose your chance at love, Paris. It's too rare and too special to be wasted."

By now the Deverauxes were pouring in the door with greetings and hugs and kisses. The older children were there; the nanny who traveled with them when the whole family went on the road was caring for the babies at the hotel. The exception was Martin and Ceylon's little girl, Elizabeth, who was not about to be left with the babies. She was being carried in a pair of strong arms until she was handed over to Paris.

"Well, hello, sweetheart, how are you? And how's your daddy?" she cooed, looking up at the man who'd put Elizabeth in her arms. "Martin, how are things . . ." Her words died a natural death as Paris looked into the smiling eyes of Titus Argonne, the only man in the world who left her speechless.

Angelique was still on the sidewalk, hugging her brothers and sisters-in-law, when Donnie pulled up in his Jaguar. He sprinted to where Angelique was standing and took off his topcoat. "Angel, what in the world are you doing out here with no coat on? Sweetheart, it's way too cold for you," he said, wrapping his coat around her shoulders. Keeping his arms around her, he finally seemed to realize that her family was there, too.

"Oh, hey, how's everybody doing? Come on in, y'all, it's freezing out here." He escorted Angelique into the building and held the door for the rest of the attendees from Atlanta. He was so attentive, he completely missed the looks that passed between certain members of the family.

Angelique, in the meantime, was beginning to feel like a much-cherished doll being passed from hand to hand. First her mother and Bump had to hug her and fuss over her.

"Angel, you're absolutely blooming, baby. I've never seen you looking so wonderful. Are you happy, honey?" Her mother's concern was evident in her intense expression.

"Mama, if I was any happier, I'd have to be twins. I'm absolutely wonderful," she assured her.

Bump looked her over carefully; he took his role as her stepfather very seriously and the two of them were quite close. "Well, I'm sorry I didn't get to give you away, but I must say that marriage agrees with you. Lookin' good, Shorty!" Angelique hugged him tightly and smiled up at him through happy tears.

"Don't make me cry, my mascara will go everywhere." She sniffed. "I've been so nervous about this, I've been a wreck."

Clay was next; he hugged her tightly and smiled down at her from his towering height. "Angel, these are magnificent. I keep remembering a cute little girl with pigtails who followed me all over with her little camera, and now look what you've become. You're an exceptionally talented and beautiful woman and I'm proud of you, baby."

Those sentiments were repeated over and over as Angelique was passed from one brother to another. There were also hugs and greetings from all her sisters-in-law on both sides of the family, and Donnie's brothers. Last of all, she was greeted with enthusiastic hugs from Miss Martha and Big Benny before finally landing back with her husband.

The private part of the showing was over; it was time for the exhibit to open. Donnie looked down at her and pronounced her perfect. Kissing her on the temple, he whispered something in her ear, something that made her smile. As the doors opened, she was standing with her very proud husband on one side and the museum director, Aneesah Shabazz, on the other.

The rest of the evening went by in a blur for Angelique. Matt and Nicole couldn't attend the opening, but they sent a huge green plant and a promise to visit during the Christmas holidays. Everyone seemed to be having a wonderful time and the pictures received great acclaim. But the best part of the evening for Angelique was the warm words of praise and pride from every member of her family—although the fact that she had put something over on Paris was a close second. She'd known Titus Argonne was coming to Detroit to discuss corporate security with Donnie, she just neglected to tell Paris.

"You could have told me he was coming!" Paris whispered.

"Would you believe me if I said I didn't know?" Angelique asked innocently.

"No!"

"Well, you'd better smile, sweetie, because he's headed this way." Angelique could swear she heard Paris's heart beating from where she stood.

* * *

The next few days were as exciting as anything Angelique could remember. Her family stayed for two days after the exhibit and there was constant activity, what with dining out and visiting and just plain catching up with each other. The biggest thing, aside from the excellent reviews and the loving response of her family, was the bridal shower her sisters-in-law had for her. The party was held at Bennie's father's house in Palmer Park, a huge old brick house with lots of room for all the women and the veritable horde of children.

Angelique wept when she saw all her favorite women gathered in one place, especially when she thought about the shower she'd sabotaged so many years ago. She hugged Bennie tightly and wouldn't let her go. "I was such a little wench, Bennie! How could you ever forgive me?"

Bennie's eyes filled with tears, too. "Aww, sweetie, I loved your brother with all my heart, I couldn't help but love his family, too. And I saw you as an unhappy young woman who needed something more in her life. Besides, you got me my man back," she teased her. "Now come on and enjoy this shower. There's a cake in there that looks like it fell out of heaven and I want some."

Lillian and Martha were hostessing the affair with plenty of assistance from the Deveraux and Cochran wives. Paris also was in attendance, of course, as were Lisette and a few women from Cochran Communications. Bump and Big Benny looked in for a moment but made their escape early as neither one could handle much of the high-spirited chatter. Big Benny did take a few minutes to spend some time with his newest daughter-in-law, however.

They were in the solarium off the library of the big house, sitting next to each other on the settee. Big Benny hadn't changed much over the years: he was still the same towering, white-haired titan he'd been when Angelique's brother married his only daughter years before. He'd suffered a very slight stroke the same year Bennie had her tragic accident, but showed no effects of it. His gait, speech, and demeanor were all that of a much younger man, primarily because his wife watched him like a hawk. She had to—otherwise he would have lived on a very rich diet washed down with bourbon. He liked his creature comforts and he liked his newest daughter-in-law, too.

"Babydoll, you did us proud, you know that," he told her. "I always knew you were as smart as a whip. I'm glad Adonis had sense enough to marry you. He needed somebody like you, somebody with some spunk and fire to her. You two are gonna have some pretty babies." He gave her a one-armed hug and a sly grin.

Angelique gently pounded his knee with her fist. "Not for a while, Mr. C! We just got married!"

"So what? I need a grandbaby," he said, trying to sound forlorn.

Angelique laughed. "Mr. C, you already have thirteen."

"Unlucky number. That's why I need another one. You and Adonis need to get busy. And for God's sake, quit calling me Mr. C. Call me Daddy," he said grumpily. "I can't be a Mister if you're married to my son and gonna give me some grandbabies. I was always partial to the number fifteen."

Angelique was still dazed from this conversation when she rejoined the women, who were still eating the delicious cream-filled cake and chatting volubly. There was an array of lingerie and perfume and personal items spread all over the living room and they were still oohing and ahhing over the delightful surprises. Suddenly Lillian and Martha got everyone's attention.

They both stood up and said something no one had yet approached. Lillian began by saying how elated she was that her only daughter had found such happiness. "I can see that you're in a wonderful place now, Angel, and I couldn't be happier. But Martha and I think it's time you started thinking about a reception, at least. The only other two who ran off to get married were Selena and Malcolm and even they finally let me have some kind of celebration. So what we want to know is . . ." She turned to her coconspirator, Martha, who took over.

"When do we get to have a reception for you two? We want to celebrate your love and commitment with a lovely celebration. So you two need to pick a date," she said firmly.

Angelique was stunned. She'd never considered anything of the sort and had no idea what to say, other than to thank them and say she would talk to Adonis that very evening. All the women cheered and began planning, discussing whether summer or fall would be the best time, whether it should be in Atlanta or Detroit. Angelique suddenly felt exhausted and had to excuse herself. She emerged from the powder room to find Selena waiting for her with a smile on her face.

"Not feeling too good, hmm? Well, don't worry, it doesn't last long. The important thing is to get good care and as soon as possible," she said wisely. "Here's another little something for you; I didn't think it was wise to give it to you in front of everyone." She handed her an oblong box, prettily wrapped in pink paper with a white bow. Inside were an early pregnancy test and a silver rattle.

Angelique stared at Selena in total shock. Selena, one of the top OB-GYN doctors in Georgia, gave her a hug and a smile. "It's going to be fine, Angel. I doubt anybody else has guessed, but you take that test as soon as possible. I've been delivering babies for a long time and I just have a sixth sense about it. Congratulations, mommy!"

Part Two

Chapter Eighteen

"Adonis! Honey, come look at this," Angelique cried. She was standing in the bedroom and the excitement in her voice was unmistakable. Donnie put down the morning paper and came into the bedroom to find his very sexy wife standing in front of the full-length standing mirror wearing a brilliant smile and nothing else. She was cupping her bosom and looking elated.

"Baby, come see this! I have boobies, real boobies," she said happily.

Donnie laughed gently at her, coming up behind her and caressing her breasts with his big hands. He squeezed them gently and smoothed his warm palms over their exquisite softness, but very gently, because they had a tendency to be tender.

"Angel, you always had real breasts. I should know, they're one of my favorite parts of your amazing body." Breathing a little harder, he continued to caress each one, burying his face in her neck.

"Of course I had them before, but look how much bigger they are. They're bigger and rounder and they look much better, don't you think? I love being pregnant." She sighed.

Donnie couldn't answer—he was too occupied with stroking his wife. His hands moved from her breasts down to her stomach, where he caressed her smooth belly that was just beginning to really show. He braced his legs wide apart as he slid his questing fingers down lower, to stroke the curly hairs that shielded her femininity. Finally he was able to speak. "I love you being pregnant, baby. You get more beautiful every day and more desirable. I want you so bad I can't stand it," he admitted. "Every time I look at you I get weak in the knees."

Angelique leaned forward a little so that her bare bottom was positioned on his manhood. "Yes, but you get strong everywhere else," she purred. She undulated her hips so that there was no mistaking her intention. "I think you have on way too many clothes, baby."

In deference to the blazingly hot August weather, Donnie was wearing only a pair of loose-fitting cargo shorts that he got rid of quickly. He embraced Angelique and they kissed long and passionately as he slid his hands down her body. Anchoring his hands on her hips, he picked her up while she wrapped her legs around him and he entered her from this standing position. The rhythm was quickly established and their unending desire to please each other led them to a trembling completion. Bathed in perspiration and needing more, Donnie walked over to the bed with her still locked around his waist. They lay down to begin a second trip to paradise.

Still intimately joined, he began moving inside her while their mouths sought each other in a hot, prolonged kiss. All too soon, Angelique was quivering on the brink of release. She gasped and screamed Donnie's name over and over and he joined her in a deep, pulsating orgasm that left them both shaken and satisfied.

He chuckled. "We're not going to be able to do this when your mother is here. A little loud loving in the afternoon is fine when we're alone, but I don't want to shock my favorite mother-in-law," he drawled as he licked the beads of perspiration from his wife's neck.

Angelique returned the favor by running her tongue

along his collarbone, then sighing as she savored the salty essence of his skin. "I'll try to behave, beloved, but I can't promise anything. I don't know what it is about being pregnant, but I seem to be insatiable these days. I can't resist you," she whispered and kissed him on the mouth.

After Angelique had discovered that Selena was absolutely correct and she was pregnant, she had become despondent instead of excited. She couldn't bring herself to tell even her beloved husband because she didn't know how he would react. She kept remembering his words the first time they made love, that there was plenty of time for babies and that this was just for them. She alternated between being frightened and being elated and the resultant stress exacerbated her morning sickness to the point that Donnie was frantic. Upon finding her losing yet another meal, he insisted on taking her to the hospital. Finally, she had to tell him. She made him sit down and she told him, as quietly as possible, that she was pregnant. She had closed her eyes to avoid seeing his expression and opened them to find him kneeling in front of her with tears running down his face.

"Angel. My Angel, why didn't you tell me? When did you find out? When are you due? Is that a good chair for you to be in? Come here, come with me," he said, scooping her up in his arms. He took her into the living room and sat down with her on the sofa.

"Baby, you've made me so happy, I can't see straight. I'm going to be a daddy, Angel! And you're going to be a mommy, the best mommy in the world. I love you, Angel. I'm so happy you're my wife. You make me happy every day of my life. I can never show you how much I love you," he murmured into her neck. He'd finally realized that she wasn't speaking and asked what was wrong. "Umm, baby? You can jump in here anytime."

Now it was time for Angel to start weeping, big silent tears that heartbreakingly ran down her cheeks.

"Oh, baby, what's the matter? Why are you crying?" Donnie asked.

"Adonis, I'm not going to make a good mother, I'm going to be a terrible mother. I won't be able to read our baby bedtime stories. Suppose I do something bad with their medicine or their baby food because I read it wrong? And besides," she sniffed, "dyslexia is genetic. Suppose I pass it on to our children? I don't want our babies to take after me, Adonis, I really don't."

The first thing Donnie did was rock her and comfort her until the tears stopped. Then he reassured her. "Honey, I know plenty of Ph.D.s that I wouldn't trust with a stray cat, much less a child. There's more to being a good mother than reading bedtime stories. You're so creative, you'd paint them bedtime stories and act them out—don't even worry about that. And if you want to, only if you want to, there are some things we can do to help with the dyslexia. I didn't say anything before because I didn't want you to think I was trying to fix you or make you over. I'm not trying to do that. I was lucky enough to find the perfect woman for me the first time out, and you don't need fixing. And as for them taking after you, who better?" He smiled at her and hugged her closely. "You have no idea how wonderful you are, you really don't. You sit here for a minute and I'm going to show you something. Be right back."

He left the room and returned with a thick photo album and proceeded to show her pictures of himself as an adorable little boy, a terribly gawky preteen and, finally, an adolescent who personified the concept of "pizza face." Angelique gasped when she saw the pictures; they looked nothing like her handsome husband.

"Oh, my God! My poor Adonis, that looks really bad," she sympathized. The pictures truly didn't resemble Donnie in any way. His face and neck were covered with cystic acne, big, fierce, red pustules that made his face lumpy and totally unappealing.

"I was the most miserable child you ever saw, Angel. My skin broke out when I was twelve and it didn't clear up until I was nineteen. Benita never stopped looking for something to cure my acne and she finally found a good dermatologist and a formula that really worked. I think that's why I worked so hard in school, because I had to feel good about something in my life. The acne was on my back and my chest as well, by the way. It was a terrible time in my life. So don't hope that our babies take after me, they might end up with that horrible skin."

Angelique was shaking her head in amazement. "This is so sad and so ironic. I was always considered to be a very pretty child, but dumb as a post. I heard one of my teachers use those very words once. People seem to think that children can't hear or something because they never hesitate to say whatever they want in front of them. I hated being pretty," she confessed. "I thought that if I were plain or really ugly, people would be nicer to me, they wouldn't be so hateful. They always thought I should be able to do things that I couldn't do and it gave them pleasure to see me fail. They were never as hard on the average-looking children." Suddenly she blushed bright red. "I'm sorry, that sounds so conceited, doesn't it?"

"No, it sounds like you didn't have very good teachers, certainly not very compassionate ones. But there are all kinds of ways to learn better reading skills now, and there are some counseling places that specialize in that kind of thing. If you want to go, we'll go. It's up to you, Angel. But right now you have to tell me two things. Tell me when our baby is coming, and please, oh, please, God, tell me you're happy about it."

Angelique hugged him tightly and showed him her deep dimples in a wide smile. "I'm very, very happy, my husband. I'm going to have your baby! And I'm going to give him to you for Christmas, how does that sound?"

The months passed quickly, and soon it was August and Angelique was a very busy, as well as a very happy, expectant mother. She did agree to go to a center that would help improve her cognitive skills and one of the things she and Donnie learned to do was side-by-side reading, where they sat next to each other and read aloud from the same book. After a month or so of this her reading skills improved tremendously, and so did her interest in books. Donnie brought her some she thought were the most wonderful in the world—novels by Pearl Cleage—and she was utterly captivated by them. *What Looks Like Crazy on an Ordinary Day, I Wish I Had A Red Dress,* and *Some Things I Never Thought I'd Do* all served to take her to a new level of interest as well as skill; she wanted to read more and more. Soon she started taking great pleasure in getting books that not only had lyrical phrases but hot love scenes in an effort to reward Donnie for taking the time to read with her. They became well acquainted with authors Francis Ray, Leslie Esdaile, Bette Ford and Beverly Jenkins. Donnie was particularly fond of Jenkins's historical novels, while Angelique's favorite was Janice Sims, who wrote exceptional contemporary novels.

Now paper and hardback books were everywhere in the house, not just the audio books she had utilized so effectively before. She was extremely proud of herself and eternally grateful to her understanding husband. The only thing that would have made her life complete was the one thing she wouldn't ask him for: a ring. The platinum one from Tiffany was still in a drawer and she made no effort to get it sized because she hated it. It was big and gaudy and not to her taste at all, but she was so pleased that he'd bought it for her after their debacle of a wedding in Vegas, she couldn't bring herself to say anything. What she wanted was something simple and pretty in yellow gold, but she felt it would be ungrateful to ask for another.

She also wanted a real wedding, but she wasn't about to bring that up, either. She just couldn't see spending all that money when they were already married. So it wasn't the wedding of her dreams—at least she could remember it now, and frankly it wasn't as sordid as she'd feared, it just wasn't what she thought of when she thought of a wedding. It was nothing like the wedding of Lisette and Warren, that's for sure. They were getting married that Saturday and her mother was coming in on Sunday, so Angelique had plenty to do without worrying about rings she didn't need or weddings she shouldn't have. Her life was good and she had no complaints.

As was usual at any gathering, Paris, Angelique and Lisette were the last three remaining. This time it was appropriate because the occasion was the bridesmaids' luncheon, which was traditional before a wedding. Lisette had treated her four bridesmaids and maid of honor to a lunch she prepared herself at her home. She would soon be leaving the house forever, as she would be moving to Farmington Hills with Warren. Her sister Miriam, the maid of honor, had to leave as she had a date with a man she was quite serious about. Warren's sister Valorie had to depart due to babysitter concerns, as did the other bridesmaid. So it was just the three of them sitting around in the partially packed house, talking. They were finishing off the last of the nonalcoholic pomegranate Bellinis Lisette had made while they talked about the changes the year had brought.

"I met Warren for the second time in January, and here it is August and we're getting married. Of course, I had to chase him down like a dog and beg him, but it worked," she said with a laugh.

Paris stared curiously at Lisette. She had been out of town for several long stretches and missed some crucial developments in the Lisette and Warren romance.

"What are you talking about? Ever since he met you Warren has been knocked off his feet; what do you mean you had to beg him? And is there any more of that fruit salad?"

Lisette went off and came back with the bowl of fruit salad and three big spoons. She shrugged as she handed out the spoons. "May as well eliminate the middle man, you know we're going to eat it all. Now, my dear Paris, the thing is that my Warren was being a perfect gentleman. A true gentleman—he took me out, wined me and dined me and he never put his hands on me," she said indignantly. "Oh, he would kiss me until I couldn't remember my own name, but he never acted interested in anything else. I couldn't figure out what was wrong because he always told me how much he loved me. And I love him, too, too much to not find out why he didn't want to make love to me." She stopped to scoop up some fresh pineapple from the now-communal bowl and went on.

"Well, I'm bold, but not *that* bold, so I had a hard time figuring out how to approach him. And then everything sort of became clear one day. We were invited to a party given by a dear friend of mine. I was very pleased about the invitation because Clinton was my very first sweetheart and we had stayed friends for years, even though he lived in Texas. Now he's moved back to Michigan and he was throwing a party and Warren didn't really want to go, but he didn't want me to be unhappy, so we went. And when he met Clinton, the look on his face was simply priceless." She laughed.

"Clinton is about six feet tall and he has reddish-brown hair, light skin and lots of freckles. And he's a big man, actually bigger than Warren, in fact. Warren was too polite to react, but on the way home he had all kinds of questions for me like how old I was when I dated Clinton, how long we went together, if Clinton had a weight problem then. . . . That's when it dawned on me. Warren is somehow self-conscious about his body. He seemed to think of me as some kind of little porcelain doll and he didn't want to get undressed in front of me. I didn't know whether to laugh or to cry, so I yelled."

Angelique's eyes filled with merriment and she said, "You went to the Evilene School for Mean Divas, did you? Shame on you!"

Lisette didn't look one bit ashamed as she finished the story. "I was just furious with him. It was as if he thought I was too shallow to appreciate a big, handsome man like him," she said with a flash of remembered anger. "What did he think I meant when I said I loved him? Where was all this leading to if I didn't find him sexually attractive? Oh, I went off on him for old and new, I really did. Of course we had to make up after that, and we made up and made up and finally it began to sink in that I find him irresistible in all ways. We were almost there when he discovered that I'm a virgin. Well, honey, he jumped off that bed like it was on fire and the whole argument started over again. He refused to touch me because I hadn't been touched."

Paris stopped fishing for mango pieces to interject. "Wow, that's what you call a deal breaker. So what did you do?"

"I got a chair and stood on it so I could yell in his face. It was terrible, I sounded worse than Pepé Le Pew, I was crying and yelling and talking broken English and the bottom line was if he didn't plan to marry me, he'd better get out of my house, out of my life and leave me the hell alone because I loved him too much to play games and I was through with being frustrated. Now you have to understand that I was wearing a sheer pink push-up bra and a matching thong and nothing else. I was quite a sight, I assure you."

"Ooh, Lisette! No, you didn't, girl! What happened then?"

"He put his shirt on, zipped up his pants and left. I called my sister Miriam and talked to her half the night; I was sobbing the whole time, of course. And the next day he came to my door with a dozen orchids, a bottle of Moët et Chandon, a huge box of Godiva chocolates and this," she said merrily, waving her two-karat ring with the perfect blue-white oval diamond. *"Et* voilà, here we are about to be married. Although he is *still* a perfect gentleman," she said ruefully. "He's making me wait for our wedding night."

Paris looked particularly impressed with Lisette's story, something that didn't escape Angelique's notice.

"I see those wheels turning over there," Angelique said. "I hope you're taking notes. You're going to be back in

Atlanta full time pretty soon and you won't have that as an excuse. Titus Argonne's agency is based in Atlanta, and from what I could see at the exhibit, he's quite interested in you, too. So when are you gonna bust a move?"

"I hate it when you talk slang, you do it so poorly," Paris said haughtily. Then she sighed deeply. "I have no idea what makes me so tongue-tied in front of that man. Although this time it was much, much worse. He asked my about my work with Cochran Communications and I started babbling like Bubba from *Forrest Gump*. 'We got big radio stations and little radio stations and we got medium-sized radio stations and we got stations in Michigan and we got stations in Chicago. . . .' It was horrible. And the worst part was I couldn't stop," she moaned.

Angelique's eyes twinkled in sympathy. "Tell Lisette what happened next," she suggested.

Paris took the last slice of peach out of the bowl with her fingers and ate it moodily. She mumbled something Lisette had to ask her to repeat. "I was babbling like a maniac and he was standing there looking at me with this really nice expression on his face and all of a sudden he leaned over and kissed me. Not a big juicy kiss, just a nice little peck. And then I could talk like a normal person," she said in wonder.

"Well, it seems as though he knows what he's doing," Lisette said with a laugh. She rose to clear the table of the empty fruit bowl. "What is it about this man that perplexes you so? Is he very handsome?"

Paris groaned and clutched her heart, raising her other hand in mute testimony. "Girl, girl, girl. He's about six-five and his skin is a little bit lighter than Angel's. He has these high cheekbones, and his eyes are a funny color. Sometimes they look blue, sometimes gray. His hair is somewhere between light brown and dark gold, he's clean-shaven, broad shoulders, really good butt . . . Yeah, he's pretty handsome." She sighed.

Lisette cleared her throat and waved her left hand with its sparkling bounty under Paris's nose. "Being shy gets you nowhere, my dear. Being bold, now that's another story. Do what you have to do, but get it done. I have spoken!" All three women burst out laughing.

Paris and Angelique watched carefully as Lisette's dress was lowered over her head. She had chosen a simple, elegant confection of white silk georgette, off the shoulder with elegant reembroidered Belgian lace around the deep neckline and the cap sleeves. She was going to wear a delicate wreath of gardenias in her hair in lieu of a veil and she was far and away the most collected person in the room. Her mother, Amyanah, was shedding happy tears as she attempted to put the wreath on her daughter's head and Miriam was fussing over the bridesmaids.

Warren's mother, Pauline, was also teary-eyed from sheer happiness. She was so relieved that her son hadn't married the harlot Tracy, and so pleased with Lisette as a daughter-in-law, that she couldn't contain herself. Janice Bowden, a friend of Lisette's and her final bridesmaid, also worked at the design salon with Lisette and was a raving beauty. It was hard to believe she had four children. After Paris and Angelique exclaimed over how well she'd kept her figure, Janice smiled and confessed that while she had four children, she'd only given birth to one.

"I adopted my three oldest long before I met my husband Curt," she explained. "And before I had my baby I was as skinny as a rail. Thank goodness I got a little meat on my bones now. I can't wait to have another." All five attendants were wearing soft, pale green, tea-length dresses in silk chiffon. The lone flower girl was Justine, Valorie's adorable three-year-old daughter. She was wearing a beautiful green frock with a white lace bodice and puffy organza sleeves and was being very well behaved. Miriam's current woe was that Angelique was showing a lot more cleavage than she had at the last fitting.

Angelique shrugged as she looked at herself in the ballet-style gown with the thin spaghetti straps. "Sorry about that, Miriam, but this is the baby's doing," she said cheerfully. "Remember, we'll have those chiffon stoles on in the church, that'll help cover me. And nobody's going to be looking at me anyway. This is Lisette's day and all eyes will be on her."

Lisette did indeed look like a vision in her gown with the flowers in her hair. The gown set off her petite figure perfectly and her expression of loving serenity made her even more beautiful. Angelique was busy snapping pictures of all the preparations for the ceremony, even though Lisette insisted on her being in the wedding party—she didn't want her acting as photographer; A.J. agreed to do that for the couple, just because they were Angelique's friends.

The women were almost ready to form their processional. Amyanah gathered all the women together for a final prayer before the ceremony began. Every eye had a tear when it was finished except for Warren's irrepressible sister, Valorie.

"For the love of Mike, this is a wedding, people. This is a happy occasion so get with the program—waterproof mascara is only going to take us so far," she said with loving exasperation. "We all look fabulous. Lisette, you look like a dream, and mamas, y'all need to get to steppin' because it's almost time to begin."

In a few moments the women had lined up for the processional. Armand, Lisette's tall, handsome father, was ready to escort his daughter down the aisle to the man who had waited a lifetime for her. The church was fragrant with the scent of gardenias, freesia, and roses, as well as the earthy smell of the ferns used abundantly in the decorations. Angelique had to fight for control; she wanted to weep as she entered the church and was escorted down the aisle by Adam Cochran. Donnie was already at the altar, as he was Warren's best man. When all the bridesmaids were assembled, the doors to the church closed as the processional for the bride began. The doors opened suddenly and Lisette floated in on the arm of her father, looking so luminous with love for Warren that she almost didn't look real.

Donnie completely missed the part where Lisette entered the church—he was totally focused on his wife and couldn't see anything else. She looked incredible with the afternoon sun slanting through the stained-glass windows, bathing her in an opalescent sheen. The sheer chiffon scarf draped over the front of her gown and loosely held in the back with a gardenia was identical to the other bridesmaids', but it looked very sexy on her. Her incipient motherhood made her more than lovely to Donnie; she was the personification of all that was woman.

With a sudden spark of recognition, he remembered the night he and Angelique had taken their vows in a gaudy little wedding chapel. He remembered everything, as if something had just knocked him into another sensibility and all the memory came flooding back. They deserved, no, *she* deserved to have a beautiful wedding with all their family and friends in attendance. Right then and there he decided that no matter what it took, he and his Angel were going to have a real ceremony, and soon.

Chapter Nineteen

Lisette and Warren entered the elevator and rode up to the bridal suite in complete silence, due mostly to the fact that they were kissing madly the whole time. They were spending their wedding night at the Athenaeum, the ultraposh hotel in Greektown. They would be taking a flight to Hawaii the next morning where they would have a long and leisurely honeymoon. When they reached their floor, Warren swept Lisette into his arms without breaking the kiss. He carried her to the door of their suite and they crossed the threshold into their married life.

Warren gently set Lisette on her feet and took both her hands in his. "Hello, Mrs. Alexander," he murmured.

"Hello to you, Mr. Alexander," she returned. "Have I told you how happy I am that you married me?"

"It was my pleasure entirely, Lisette. I love you more than I thought it was possible to love anyone," he said softly.

Lisette stood on her tiptoes to receive his kiss and smiled with tender love after it was over. "Then show me, my love. Show me how much you love me. I'll be back in a very few minutes." She pulled out of his embrace and blew him a kiss before going into the suite's master bathroom where her things had been placed earlier. Before Warren could go into the other bathroom, she was back with a sheepish smile.

"Can you undo this for me? I forgot that I had an army of women helping me into it."

Warren was happy to oblige in undoing the row of tiny lace-covered buttons. When the buttons were undone, the low cut strapless bustier she wore under the gown was revealed. Warren stroked her velvety back and was chastised by his bride.

"Oh, no, you don't! You made me wait forever for this night and now you have to wait for me." She turned around and pulled him down by his tie to kiss him. "But not very long. You'd better be ready for me, my love." And she disappeared back into the bathroom, leaving her love-addled husband alone.

He recovered nicely, though, and went to take a quick shower and don the opulent-looking silk jacquard robe Lisette had purchased for him. It was a rich creamy French vanilla color that looked wonderful against his dark brown skin.

Earlier, Valorie had come up to the suite and added a few special touches. There were expensive candles scented with gardenia, a stand with an ice bucket in which a bottle of Moët et Chandon chilled, two Baccarat crystal flutes, a basket of fruit, cheese and chocolates and an array of romantic CDs. The bed had been turned down and there were pink rose petals and white gardenia petals strewn across the bed.

Warren lit the candles in the bedroom as well as the ones in the living room. He put on a Kevin Mahogany CD and was about to uncork the champagne when a soft noise drew his attention to the bedroom. Lisette was standing in the doorway wearing an outfit that made him bless the day he had asked Angelique to go to that auction. It was a very short gown made of silk organza with lace cups and very thin straps. A lace thong was visible through the nearly transparent fabric and she was also wearing a short matching robe. On her small feet she wore a pair of high-heeled satin mules with a silk flower on the toe. One of the gardenias from her wreath was nestled in her hair, right above her ear. She looked incredible: sexy yet innocent and totally in love. He held out his hand to her and she came to him at once, floating across the room like a goddess.

He sat down on the chaise longue and pulled Lisette into his lap, where they kissed for several long minutes before either of them said anything. "Lisette. My Lisette," he said softly. "Is this real or another one of those dreams I've been having about you?"

By way of an answer she took his handsome face in both hands and pulled him down to kiss him softly, gently and thoroughly. "This is as real as it gets, Warren. I've been waiting for you my whole life; I don't want to wait any longer," she breathed.

He offered her a glass of champagne, which she refused. "Not right now. Right now, I want my husband," she said with a wealth of meaning in the simple words. Warren stood up with her in his arms and said, "As always, Lisette, your wish is my command." He carried her off to the bedroom to begin their lifetime of love.

Donnie was looking at his wife with his heart in his eyes. They were in the kitchen of their home eating a midnight repast that consisted of scrambled eggs, grits, toast and grilled ham. Angelique had found that one of the best ways to avoid · rning sickness was to eat when the baby said it was hungry, which was why they were eating such incongruent food at such a late hour. Lisette and Warren's wedding reception had ended earlier but they had opted not to attend any of the after-parties; they just wanted to go home.

Angelique had changed out of her gown and was wearing a cute sundress with little flowers all over it; she often wore it around the house. Donnie had also shed his tuxedo and was wearing a pair of drawstring pants and an old T-shirt. They talked about the wedding and how happy Lisette and Warren had been.

"It was so beautiful." Angelique sighed. "It was the wedding she dreamed of ever since she was a little girl. She was so happy."

"Warren was so happy he couldn't stand himself." Donnie laughed. "He's so in love with Lisette, he was crying when she walked down the aisle. You hear about stuff like that and you think it would be embarrassing, but it was nice. It was very appropriate for him, he holds nothing back from her."

Angelique nodded in agreement and began to clear the table in her usual frenzy to put things back in order. Donnie took her wrist and stopped her. "You sit down, baby. I'll take care of this. You do too much around here as it is. Mrs. Montez feels like you don't want her here," he said, referring to their weekly housekeeper.

"I had no idea," Angelique said sadly. "I'll try to do better. And Mrs. Montez should just wait until the baby comes, there'll be plenty to keep her busy."

She continued to sit at the kitchen table, deep in thought. Donnie watched her for a moment before he rejoined her. Taking one of her long, slender hands in his, he leaned forward to get her attention. "Angel, I have to tell you something. I finally remembered it, all of it. Our wedding, I mean. When I was standing at the altar today watching you, it all came to me out of the blue."

Angelique's eyes grew huge. They had never talked about it before. Even though Angelique's memory of the Las Vegas nuptials had come back to her after her amnesia went away, they had never discussed it. But now that they both had a recollection, it seemed right. Donnie continued to hold her hand and led her through the dining room into the living room were there was soft music playing and a couple of her favorite candles were lit. A provocative fig fragrance drifted through the room and seemed to personify the late summer.

They sat on the sofa—rather, Donnie sat and Angelique sat in his lap with her legs elevated. She laid her head on his shoulder and he began to speak.

"It started when we were on the plane going to Vegas. You were sitting with Matt and I was sitting with Nicole, who never shuts up, by the way. She talked and talked and told me all about you, about what you were like in school, what kind of friend you were, how wonderful you were and I had to agree with her because I knew it was true. I could look across the aisle where you were sound asleep and all I could think about was how pretty you looked, how much fun you were, how I looked forward to seeing you every day. When I came back to Detroit after being out on the road, all I wanted to do was see you, make you laugh, kiss you." He kissed her then, a soft one on her forehead.

"When I saw you all hugged up with Matt, I wanted to break his skull. I really did, I'm not proud of it, but I did. And on the plane, wow, you just looked so sweet and adorable, I couldn't think of anything else but the possibility of not being with you. The flight attendant started bringing around drinks and you woke up and we all had champagne. We started drinking toasts to Matt and Nicole and I drank a toast to you, then another one . . . I was pretty mellow when we got off the plane. When we got to the chapel, Matt and I kept drinking champagne while we waited for you and Nicole to find a dress. Well, I should say that I kept drinking, Matt kept pouring.

"While they were getting married, I kept looking at you and I knew I wanted to be the man you married. I didn't want to get on another plane and fly back here without making you mine. I kissed you and said that I wanted to take care of you forever. You kissed me back and said that we should take care of each other. I kissed you again and said you had to be mine, that no one else could have you. You kissed me back and said you wanted me, too. And we kept kissing, right there in the chapel and the justice of the peace said the next wedding had canceled and he had an opening if we wanted it. And we both said yes—yes, we wanted to be married right then and there, and we were. We weren't sloppy falling-down drunk. We were pretty merry, but we weren't passing out or anything.

"We held hands and he said the vows and we kissed some more and we were really happy because we knew it was meant to be. It sounds corny and ridiculous, but that's the way it happened, or the way I remember it. It wasn't sordid at all, Angel, but it wasn't right."

Angelique froze in his arms. His recollection mirrored hers, except for the part about her being asleep on the plane. She hadn't been asleep—she was wishing she were on her way to her own wedding with Donnie. And now he was saying that it wasn't right.

His arms tightened around her and he kept talking in his low, deep voice. "It wasn't right because we should have had a beautiful ceremony like Warren and Lisette. We should have had flowers and candlelight and music and all of our nieces as flower girls. Your family should have been there, and mine, and everybody should have seen how happy we are to be together. That's what should have happened, Angel, and that's what could have happened, but I couldn't wait. I wasn't man enough to wait until we got home and court you like you deserve. So I'm asking for a second chance, Angel. I want you to marry me all over again in front of God and everybody. Please say you will, say that you forgive me for not controlling myself and that you'll allow me to make it up to you."

Angelique relaxed again in his embrace. She stroked his forearms with their coating of silky hair, and said, so softly that he could barely hear her, "Yes, I will, Adonis. But not right away—after the baby comes. We'll have a real cere-mony and everyone we love will be there and it will be beau-tiful and meaningful. And I love you very much for thinking of it. You're a wonderful husband," she murmured and turned her face up for his kiss.

"That's because I have a wonderful wife. I love you,

Angel," he said before kissing her beloved face. "But I think you need to get into bed now, because your mom's flight comes in early tomorrow. Are you excited about her coming?"

Angelique yawned and said that she was. "I've never had her come visit before. I hope we have a good time," she replied and then fell asleep on her husband's shoulder. He continued to hold her for a long time before taking her to bed, just loving the fact that she was in his arms.

Lillian wasn't quite sure what to expect when she came to stay with Angelique and Donnie, but it wasn't what she got. Their house was immaculately clean, and this was before the housekeeper's visit on Tuesday. Angelique had cautioned her about Jordan and Pippen, but dogs, even big ones, didn't bother her. "Didn't I tell you that we're now the proud owners of two black Pomeranians? Bill was so crazy about those little dogs of Vera's that he went out and got two little ladies. He named them Ella and Sarah and he takes them everywhere. I think he plans on taking them to the gold course next," she said, shaking her head.

In any case, Jordan and Pippen had won her heart by giving her winning smiles and holding up paws to shake when she got to the house. They were being perfect gentlemen and the fact that Angelique had taken them to the groomer also helped. Their coats gleamed like every other surface in the house. Lillian had to admire the way the house looked, especially the room they were fixing up as a nursery. Angelique showed her the wallpaper that had come out of the room; she'd kept a piece of the hideous burgundy stripes as a memento. Now the room was all peach and aqua and yellow, soft pastel shades that made it look fresh and pretty. Angelique's bedroom furniture was going to be put into storage and they were going shopping for baby furniture soon.

Angelique kept Lillian busy for the first few days, taking

her to see the Cochran building and her studio, touring the new developments in downtown Detroit, shopping at the Somerset Town Center, lunching at La Shish and P.F. Chang's, visiting Renee and Andrew and Big Benny and Martha; she practically ran her mother's legs off. She was checking off things like a travel agent with an itinerary.

The two women were now in the dining room, where they'd been looking at books of baby furniture.

"Tomorrow I thought we could go to Windsor, Mama. Prices are lower there because of the exchange rate. And they have some great prices in the duty-free shop. That's the best place to get perfume and things like that," Angelique reported.

Lillian finally threw up her hands. "My goodness, Angel, we don't need to go to another place. Let's just stay home and talk tomorrow," she said firmly. "I come up here to see my only daughter and I get Superwoman instead." She laughed. "I want to know how you're doing, my love. I want to go shopping for my grandchild, not for me. I want to talk about your wedding, even though it's not until next Valentine's Day. I just want to sit and relax with you, is that okay?"

"It's fine with me, Mama. Are you sure you're comfortable in your room? Do you need anything?" she asked anxiously.

Lillian assured her that she was fine. There had been fresh flowers in the room, a basket of current magazines and several novels and another basket with towels and toiletries. In addition there was a small television with a copy of *TV Guide* on top of it.

"My goodness, no! I don't need anything, dear. You and Donnie have spoiled me shamelessly. In fact, I'm making breakfast tomorrow so you can get some rest. Expectant mothers need as much rest as they can get, you know." She smiled at her only daughter and said truthfully, "I'm so looking forward to being a grandmother. This is so exciting, Angel."

"Mama, you have thirteen grandchildren already and another on the way, or did you forget that Vera is also expecting?"

"Fourteen is a boring number, we need number fifteen. Besides, my daughter is having her very first child—that makes it a miraculous event," her mother said fondly. "And sixteen has always been my lucky number," she added with thinly veiled meaning.

The next morning Donnie was surprised to find his mother-in-law in the kitchen when he got up to make Angelique's herbal tea. He liked to get the water on so that when she arose she could have it right away. Instead, Lillian was bustling around the kitchen, making what looked to be an elaborate Southern feast. He was struck, as always, by her startling resemblance to Nancy Wilson, with her deep, rich coloring and the distinctive blaze of white hair in the front.

"Good morning, Lillian. Something smells wonderful."

"Good morning to you, Donnie, there's coffee already made," she said in a cheerful voice.

"Thanks, but I'm not drinking coffee right now. Angel can't have it so I drink herbal tea with her. I was just about to put the kettle on for the tea," he explained.

"Oh." Lillian was nonplussed that she hadn't thought of that herself, but she rallied quickly. "Well, I'm making her favorite breakfast, cheese grits, sausage, scrambled eggs and fresh biscuits," she said proudly. She noticed a flicker on Donnie's face and asked if there was a problem.

"Well," Donnie said reluctantly, "she really can't tolerate too much grease right now. Sausage would really upset her stomach. She can handle a little ham, if it's really lean. And for some reason she can't stand butter right now—just the thought of it makes her sick. So she's been eating a lot of dry toast. She usually has fruit, dry toast and oatmeal with no butter. The thing is, she'll eat anything you give her, so you have to kinda watch what you put on her plate."

Lillian looked slightly chagrined as she looked up at her handsome son-in-law. "My goodness, I should have thought of that," she admitted. "I've been so busy trying to prove that I'm a good mother that I didn't even ask if she had a restricted diet."

She sat down at the kitchen table, looking so crestfallen that Donnie sat down with her. She looked at him with a hint of tears in her eyes and confessed her fears. "I don't think I've been a very good mother to Angelique," she said quietly. "I've never known her as well as I should; we weren't as close as a mother and daughter should be. I always felt like I failed her as a mother, that I should have been able to get through to her, to communicate with her better. But I never could." Her sadness was so evident that Donnie felt compelled to give her an awkward hug.

"Lillian, you have to know how much Angel admires you. She adores you, she thinks you're the most perfect woman in the world. All she ever wanted to do was be like you, that's what she told me. More than once, I might add. Despite what you think, you were a wonderful role model for her and you are the person she respects more than anyone else," he told her.

"I don't see how, Donnie. I just wasn't there for her when she needed me," Lillian said sadly. Her smooth brown face puckered in distress. "When Angelique's father died, I went a little bit crazy. I don't think anyone knew how much his death affected me. I was pregnant, you see, and I lost the baby. It just seemed like the last straw, him dying the way he did and then me losing our baby, the last piece of him I would ever have." She took a long, shuddering sigh and stopped for a moment to compose herself.

"Poor Clay, he drove himself crazy trying to keep everything hushed up over the way his father died. It really wasn't necessary; I knew what his father was like. I knew he had a roving eye, I knew that he had women in different places, so when he died in that hotel room in California, it wasn't as big a shock to me as Clay believed it would be. I should have told him then, but I was too numb, too wrapped up in myself. I'm very ashamed of how I conducted myself back then.

I should have been stronger, been less selfish, especially when it came to my baby, my only little girl. By the time I was ready to act like a mature woman again, her brothers had taken over and she was an angry, confused little girl. I don't think she's ever gotten over it." She sniffed. "I think I need a tissue."

Donnie obliged by handing her a fistful of paper towels. He flushed at the look of amusement on Lillian's face. "I'm sorry, Lillian, let me get you some real tissue," he said apologetically.

Lillian waved her hand as thought it was of no importance. "Oh, don't worry, this is fine. You're a very sweet young man, aren't you? You have good looks, good manners, and a good head on your shoulders, and you love my daughter. I was prepared to not like having you as a son-in-law. I had no idea what made you two go gallivanting off to Las Vegas, of all places, but I was prepared to be very angry with you. And I liked you, I always did. I liked all of Benita's family, you're lovely people. But I didn't think you were what my baby deserved."

She reached over to touch his arm. "I was wrong. Very, very wrong. You love my daughter with all your heart; I can see it every time you look at her, every time you touch her. When you came galloping down the street to give her your coat because you thought she might be cold, I knew. That Vegas wedding may not have been my choice for my child, but she couldn't have chosen a better man."

Wiping away the rest of her tears, she stood up with her usual aplomb. "Now that I've made a total fool of myself, I need to make a breakfast my child can actually eat."

"Umm, Lillian, I don't have any restrictions, so I'll be more than happy to take care of this delicious repast," Donnie said innocently.

They laughed and hugged each other tightly, a hug that lasted until they realized that Angelique was standing in the doorway watching.

"So where's this breakfast, Mama? I'm starving," was all she said.

Chapter Twenty

The oppressive heat of summer began to fade away and the cool of fall was comforting to Angelique. She had decided that she was just hot-blooded by nature, because she found that she thrived on the cooler temperatures of Michigan. She and Donnie had been to Atlanta to visit her family and the damp heat had made her quite miserable. She had enjoyed being with her mother and her brothers but it was a relief when she could come back to lower temperatures. Everything seemed to annoy her, especially the heat. Her sisters-in-law tried to tell her that part of her sensitivity was due to her pregnancy, but she didn't believe it.

"None of you acted like this," she said sadly. "I'm very happy and blessed to be having this baby and I should be in a good mood all the time, like you were," she protested.

Vera laughed out loud at that. "Oh, sweetie, nobody's in a good mood for nine months. As thrilled as I was to be pregnant, as happy as I was to be giving birth to Marcus's baby, there were times when I was a total shrew, believe me. Girl, I gave your poor brother hell, just ask him if you don't believe me."

Selena confirmed what Vera told her. "Honey, your hormones are running amok right now. Nobody expects you to be little Mary Sunshine the whole nine months. With the last baby, I made poor Malcolm sleep in the guest room because I couldn't stand the sound of his breathing," she said with a laugh. "Of course, I was extra, extra sweet to him after the baby came and I'm still making it up to him, but I was a mean heifer."

Now in the cool breezes of October, Angelique still had trouble believing that her serene, sophisticated sisters-in-law were as petty and horrible as she was. There were days when everything seemed to irritate her from the way Donnie chewed to the way he walked. Jordan and Pippen escaped her wrath only because they were so adorable. They seemed to sense that something wonderful was happening to their mistress and they were always extra gentle with her.

Andrew, Donnie's oldest brother, also recognized her angst for what it was. "Sweetie, don't be so hard on yourself. No one can control these things, it's just part of being pregnant, part of your body getting ready to bring forth another life. That's an awesome power, a huge responsibility. You can't control your hormones. I'll tell you a secret: my wife put a gun in my back after she delivered the triplets and said I was never getting in a bed with her again."

They were at Renee and Andrew's house for dinner, and she and Andrew were chatting on the big deck that extended off the back of the Indian Village house. Angelique's eyes were enormous when Andrew made his confession, but Renee heard him as she was bringing out vegetables on skewers to grill.

"It was a blow-dryer, not a gun, as he is well aware. But at that point in time I meant every word. Sex with him was the last thing on my mind, giving *me* three babies at once. Of course," she said with a smile, "I got over it." She gave her handsome husband a big kiss and went back into the house.

In spite of Angelique's mood swings and general hyper-sensitivity, Donnie was being the most attentive and caring husband he could be. He took an interest in every aspect of the birth, attended every doctor's appointment with her, went to Lamaze classes with eager anticipation and did everything he could to make her comfortable. That night after they got home from Renee and Andrew's, he ran a bubble bath for her and not only scrubbed her back, but when she emerged from the bathroom had her lie down on the bed on top of a big fluffy bath sheet.

"I have a surprise for you," he crooned.

"What is it?" she asked sleepily. Those long bubble baths always made her sleepy.

"Something you'll like. Something we'll both like, baby."

Suddenly her body was treated to a warm gush of sensation and his long, clever fingers were massaging her growing belly. He rubbed her gently and lovingly, talking to her as he did. "I love this belly. I love it. I love you for giving me this baby, Angel. This will help you relax and it will also keep that pretty belly from getting too many stretch marks," he said softly. "Not that I care, I think they're sexy. It makes a woman look like a real woman, in my opinion."

Angelique sighed with pleasure and the sighs turned into moans as he continued his massage to include her entire body, even her ultrasensitive breasts. Somehow, even though they were tender and easily irritated, Donnie always knew just how to touch them. They were so sensitive by this point in her pregnancy that the feel of the warm oil and his big hands caressing her brought her near orgasm in minutes. "Adonis . . . Adonis," she whispered.

He continued to caress her, bringing his hands down her sides to stroke her hips and down her outer thighs and kissing her velvety inner thighs. "Adonis," she cried with more urgency.

"I'm right here, my love, what is it?"

She opened her eyes to glare at him. "You know what it is, don't tease me!"

He wiped his hands on the towels, smiling down at her. He removed his shirt, then stood up to take off the rest of his clothing. "I'd never do that, my Angel." He lay down next to her and rose up on one elbow so he could continue to stroke her. "Kiss me, sweetheart."

She was more than happy to oblige; she loved the feel of his lips. They were kissing wildly and sweetly and his questing hand went farther than the rounded belly he found so enticing. He explored the silky hair and went lower, finding her wet and waiting for him.

"Open for me, sweetheart," he whispered, but his words were unnecessary as her response to his touch was immediate and passionate. She was shaking with desire, trembling on the brink of fulfillment and she was incredibly beautiful to Donnie. He loved watching her come to completion, loved the way her expressions changed as he brought her higher and higher to peak after peak of ecstasy. Her long lashes lifted and she stared deeply into his eyes as the waves of pleasure washed over her, as his fingers delved into her womanhood and brought her even more pleasure. She kept their eyes locked as long as she could but the sensation was too much and her eyes squeezed shut as she called his name over and over. He relented, but only as long as it took for him to enter her body; in minutes they were throbbing as one, lost in the delirium of their bliss.

When they could resume normal speech, Donnie raised an eyebrow and smiled down at his supremely satisfied wife. "I may have to keep you pregnant from now on if this is the response I get."

She stretched and smiled back, a sweet and sexy smile that only he could elicit from her lips. "I may have to let you. I think we might need another bath, Adonis. And this time, I'll scrub your back."

"That sounds like a plan," he agreed.

"But first, let's try something else." And in a little while it was his turn to cry her name aloud.

* * *

The Halloween decorations had just been taken down and Angelique was thinking about Christmas. She was looking forward to the holiday with an anticipation she hadn't felt since she was a young girl. In less than two months she would be holding her baby in her arms, she would be able to see the joy on her husband's face and be able to bask in his love. She felt the joy of the impending holiday more fiercely after her doctor confirmed that her due date was December twenty-fifth. She felt like a Madonna, more closely connected to her family and her spirituality. She wanted to truly celebrate the holiday this year in a big way. And she reminded Donnie of this often.

"When can we get our tree? I want a live tree, I want a really big one that'll smell up the whole house," she told him.

Donnie laughed affectionately at her enthusiasm. "Angel, we can get anything you want, you know that. But can't we wait until Thanksgiving at least? Do you know what a live tree does if you get it too early? It dries out, that's what it does. I'll be sweeping up needles until the Fourth of July."

They were getting dressed to go to church and she was enjoying the sight of her man doing a reverse striptease as he put on his crisp shirt, then his pleated midnight-navy slacks. He tucked the shirt in and zipped the pants, then realized he had an audience.

"Quit looking at me like that, you know where it ends up," he scolded.

"I'm behaving, honestly I am," she said playfully. "I just like to look at you, is that so wrong?"

She was sitting on the side of the bed struggling with her panty hose. "I truly hate these things. These are inventions of the devil, they really are." That task completed, she rose with difficulty and sat down again, heavily. Rubbing her tummy, she asked Donnie to hand her the dress she'd selected. "The navy-blue one with the white collar and cuffs, please."

After donning the dress, she made it to the bathroom to

brush her hair and use the facilities. By now Donnie was also ready, completely attired in his dashing suit and looking very elegant. He had thoughtfully brought her shoes, which he would slip on her feet in the living room.

"I feel like Cinderella when you do that," she said dreamily.

He grinned. "That must make me a prince."

"You're my king," she corrected him. "Can we have two trees? One in the living room and one in the dining room. Maybe one in the game room, too," she said thoughtfully.

"You are obsessed with Christmas," he said with a grin. "Yes, we can have as many trees as you want. We can have one in our room, in the baby's room; the dogs can have one, for all I care. We'd better get going if we're going to be on time."

"We can put doggy treats on their tree," she said happily. "They have to celebrate, too, you know."

Her due date added to the family speculation about the baby's name. She and Donnie made up a series of ridiculous baby names with which to tease the family. "Crayon if it's a boy, and Crayola if it's a girl," they'd say. Or, Vernor for a boy and Ginger Ale for a girl. The worst was Livernois for a boy and Dequindre for a girl. Nobody believed that they would really name their child after a city street, but with those two, one never knew. After church everyone converged on Big Benny and Martha's home for brunch and the speculation continued.

Donnie and Angelique smiled widely when asked if they'd picked a name yet. "Yes, we're calling it Jingle if it's a boy and Belle if it's a girl," they chorused.

Later, when Angelique was in the kitchen helping Martha prepare brunch, Martha commented on Angelique's demeanor. "You know something, dear, I think you're a lot happier," she said gently. "Not that you exuded misery or anything, but you just seem more content, more relaxed. It's so nice to see you like this."

Angelique was a great fan of Martha Cochran. Martha

was still trim and graceful and had a quiet charm that had served her well in all her years of arranging tours at her successful travel agency. She'd finally sold the agency, but her innate grace was just a part of her nature. She had silvery hair cut into a fashionable short bob and her dark brown skin simply glowed. Angelique couldn't resist giving the older woman a hug. Martha had always been very kind to her, even before she moved to Detroit. And Martha was dead on the money: ever since her mother's visit, she had been much more at peace with herself.

She and Lillian had had a long talk during her visit, a talk that ironed out a lot of misunderstandings. The morning Donnie and Lillian had their heart-to-heart, Angelique had overheard much of their conversation. After Donnie left for the office, she and Lillian had lingered in the kitchen over coffee and Angelique's inevitable herbal tea. After a few moments of comfortable silence, Angelique told her mother that she'd overheard the conversation.

"I wasn't deliberately eavesdropping, I couldn't help it," she said apologetically. "But I don't want you to think you were a bad mother, Mama. I wasn't a very good daughter."

Lillian's eyes had filled with tears and she contradicted her. "How can you say that, Angel? I'm your mother, darling, it's my job to understand you and nurture you."

"Even if I made that impossible? Come on, Mama, you know I was a difficult child. I was spoiled rotten and I was angry all the time. I was like a little wild animal and you know it."

"I know no such thing. When you were a baby, Angelique, you were the sweetest little thing in the world. You were very spirited and lively, but you were also uncommonly sweet. You were one of those babies who was always smiling and easygoing, such a joy to care for! You loved taking baths and you let me dress you in the girliest little dresses, and put bows in your hair. I could change your clothes three times a day and you didn't protest. The only thing you hated was being confined. I found that out when I put up a baby gate.

You went wild, Angel, you screamed the house down until I removed it. It was the same thing with a playpen, you just couldn't abide it. If I put you down and told to you sit there, you would. You'd be right there when I came back. But if I tried to restrain you in any way, ooh, girl it was *on,*" she said wryly.

Angelique was fascinated by this account. "But, Mama, after I started school and my grades were so bad, I got so angry at everyone. I was mad at my teacher, mad at the counselor, mad at you, I think I was mad at Daddy for dying, too. I was so miserable and so hostile, how could you have loved a creature like that?"

Lillian slammed her hand down on the table. "I could have tried harder, Angelique! I should have been more understanding, I should have kept you at home instead of sending you to that school, I should have done more to let you know that you were my heart, my little girl and no matter what it took I was going to make it better," she cried, her voice full of self-recrimination.

Angelique was crying now and they hugged each other tightly. "Mama, look at us, we look like a family on one of those tell-all talk shows." Her attempt at humor seemed to work, as both women laughed nervously. "You did the best you could, and I know in my heart that you did. That's why I was able to change my life, change the way I was living. You made that possible because you took me to church every Sunday and I learned about God and forgiveness. I always knew that if I asked God to forgive me and make me a better person, He would. And when A.J. got sick, that's what I did," she said simply.

"What do you mean, dearest?"

"When A.J. got that brain tumor, I thought my world was over. You have no idea how much I loved him and how much I needed him in my life. I don't mean I loved him like a boyfriend, although I did have a huge crush on him for a while. I mean, he taught me so much about photography and about life that I thought I would die if he didn't get well. He was too good a person to die. I prayed every day, every hour that if God would spare A.J., I would change. I told Him I'd be a better person, a less selfish person if He would just spare A.J. And He did, so I had to keep my promise."

She took a last sip of the tea that was now stone cold, but she didn't seem to notice. "Mama, when I went traveling with A.J., it was the most humbling experience I've ever had. I couldn't even conceive of the kind of poverty that exists in some parts of the world. The diseases, the famine—it was incredible. I had taken my entire existence for granted and it made me so ashamed. That's why I eat everything that's on my plate, no matter if I like it or not, because I at least have enough to eat. I can turn on the water and it comes out clean and fit to drink; there are lots of places where that doesn't happen. Even in this country, Mama. But what am I telling you this for? You've always been active in charities. And so am I, now," she said proudly.

Lillian was amazed by what her daughter was telling her. For the first time in a long time, she felt connected to her youngest child and the woman she had become. There would always be a part of her that regretted the years they weren't close, but she would make sure that this closeness would remain for the rest of their lives.

The rest of her visit was a great deal of fun. Instead of running from mall to restaurant to gallery, they took it easy and relaxed together, watching Angelique's collection of old movie musicals. It was something they'd done when Angelique was quite small and Lillian was amazed that she remembered and still liked the same movies.

"I have a lot to learn about you, my dear, and I'm looking forward to every bit of it," Lillian said before she left.

When Donnie and Angelique took her to the airport, it was with genuine regret. Donnie had to pry them apart to get Lillian on the plane.

"Lillian, I promise we'll be down in a couple of weeks. I can see that we'll be spending a lot of time in Atlanta," he said as he hugged her. Altogether it was a memorable and wonderful time in Angelique's life, a time she would always treasure.

So when she agreed with Martha that she was a lot happier now, she was telling the truth. A better relationship with her mother, a truly happy marriage and a beautiful baby . . . she couldn't ask for anything more. And Christmas was coming. A year ago she'd been wondering if she'd ever be happy again and now she knew what true happiness was.

Before Thanksgiving had arrived, Angelique was in a Christmas frenzy. To Donnie's loving amusement, she had set up a holiday timetable that included dates for volunteering at a soup kitchen and a convalescent home, dates for decorating the house inside and out and the exact date all their Christmas cards would be sent out. She had taken what she called a family portrait, consisting of her and Donnie posing with Jordan and Pippen, both of whom were wearing big red bows on their collars. She made sure that her burgeoning belly was well displayed, too. She was still thrilled about being pregnant, even though it was getting a little stressful.

Sleeping on her stomach was completely out of the question, but sleeping on her back was no easier. She had to sleep propped up on so many pillows, it was like she was sitting up. And she found herself getting crankier as the days went on. There were days when she would cry at the drop of a hat. Just seeing a sentimental holiday commercial could set her off. There were other times when something like not being able to see her feet would make her so frustrated, she would end up throwing a shoe. The day she went out of the house with one brown shoe and one black one was memorable indeed.

In balance, though, life was good. She wasn't going into the studio every day now, as she was taking very few assignments. But on the occasions that she went in to work, she was thrilled with the traditional holiday look of the lobby and arcade. With the classic restoration of the building, it reminded her of an old-fashioned movie musical set. There were Christmas carols playing and tasteful decorations, enough to satisfy even her desire for festivity.

Donnie delighted in indulging her every holiday whim and began putting up the outdoor lights early just to please her. They went shopping for Christmas decorations one weekend, and, thanks to her persistence, scoured all of southeastern Michigan for beautiful baubles.

One day she and Paris even ended up going to Frankenmuth, a German town near Saginaw that was home to Bronner's, known as the Christmas Wonderland. They'd gone to Saginaw one Tuesday afternoon for their regular hair appointments with Danny Watley, one of Vera's dearest friends and the owner of the Hair Gallery in Saginaw; it was a sign of his skill that both women went to see him once a month to keep their hair glowing. They would do their own shampoo and sets but no one was allowed to do anything serious to their hair except Danny.

On the drive up to Saginaw, Angelique had sung along with the Christmas music she insisted on playing, to Paris's amusement. She was happy to tease her cousin about it, too.

"Angel, remember last Christmas when you were so blue and lonely? Now look at you. You're a happily married lady, soon to be a mommy and you've got enough holiday spirit for ten people. I'm so happy for you," she said.

Angelique smiled a huge and blissful smile and rubbed her firm, hard tummy with both hands. "I'm very happy for me, too. For me, for Adonis, for my family, for everything. It's unbelievable, isn't it?"

The hour-and-a-half drive to Saginaw was over quickly and they pulled into the parking lot of the Hair Gallery. Tuesdays were Danny's light days and the lot wasn't crowded. Angelique walked into the salon employing the little-pregnant-lady waddle so often seen in the last stages of pregnancy.

Danny's eyes got big when he saw Angelique. "Look at you, you look like an olive with a toothpick stuck through it," he exclaimed when he saw her big pregnant belly.

Angelique smiled and embraced the tall handsome man and paid no attention to his teasing. She knew Danny well enough not to take him seriously. He eyed her speculatively as Paris hung their coats up in the back of the immaculately clean shop.

"When did you say you're due?"

"Christmas Day," she said proudly.

He shook his head. "You'll never make it to Christmas," he predicted. Years of working, with women, plus being exposed to the gestations of his many cousins, made Danny uniquely qualified to speculate. "That baby is coming out before December twenty-fifth." He looked at Angelique front, side and back and shook his head again. "You'll never make it all the way to term."

Neesha, a cousin of Danny's who managed the salon, emerged from the shampoo room to hear his prediction. "Pay him no attention," she said airily. "He sounds like he knows what he's talking about, doesn't he? Well, he doesn't. As a baby predictor he's a good hairstylist," she said, then squealed as Danny grabbed her and gave her noogies. She rubbed her head as she sat down at the desk. "Seriously, Angel, just ignore him. He knows nothing about it, he's just guessing."

Angelique didn't comment; she was busy getting her box of gingersnaps and a carton of fat-free Lactaid milk out of her tote bag. "Anybody want some?" she asked, waving the two items.

In a few minutes, Danny had her situated at the shampoo bowl, where she settled into the chair and sighed with relief. When he asked what she'd been up to lately, she smiled.

"Getting the nursery ready for the baby, of course, and getting the house decorated for Christmas. I haven't been this excited about Christmas coming since I was a little girl, Danny. It's like all the joy and magic of the season have come back to me," she said happily. "I'm driving my poor husband crazy, but I can't stop buying Christmas decorations. And all I put in the CD player now is Christmas music."

Donnie was totally sympathetic. He loved the holiday, too, and always pulled out all the stops. "Have you been to Bronner's?" he asked. "You've got to go there, you'll love it."

He explained about the store and then said, "Frankenmuth is only about twenty minutes away, and I don't have any more appointments today, would you like to run over there?"

Paris and Angelique had been awed and fascinated by the gigantic store full of the most exquisite decorations either woman had ever seen. Danny stayed with Angelique as they walked the store. "Ooh, Danny, look at that!" she exclaimed, pointing at a nearby display.

Danny suddenly grabbed her hand and stared at it. "I'm too busy looking at *this*. When is that man going to get you a ring? You've been walking around with a bare hand long enough, don't you think?"

Angelique blushed to the roots of her hair—her shining, perfectly styled hair, thanks to Danny. "He already did," she confessed. "It's sitting at home in the little Tiffany box because it's too big. And I never took it to have it sized because I don't like it. The stone looks like a headlight and it's platinum. It's just not me."

Danny looked disgusted. "Girl, I ought to beat you. Your husband buys you a beautiful platinum wedding ring and you're too cute to wear it because the stone is too big? You should be ashamed of yourself. Have I taught you nothing about fine jewelry and the need to have as much as possible?"

Angelique had glanced at her ringless hand, and she had felt shame. Even before she had declared her love for him, Donnie was committed enough to buy her a big beautiful ring and she was too picky to wear it. "You're right, Danny. I think I need to do something about that."

Chapter Twenty-One

Danny's words stayed with Angelique over the next few days. He was right: she was being ungrateful about Donnie's gift. Maybe the rings weren't to her taste, but the fact that he'd gone out and purchased them after their Vegas wedding made them special. And the fact that he never nagged her about them or even mentioned them in any way made him special. She went from feeling ungrateful to ashamed of her behavior, and said this to Lisette when she made a lunch date with her.

"I'm taking that ring to Tiffany's today to arrange to have it sized to my finger. Lisette, I can't believe that I've gone this long without doing anything about the ring. I'm so ashamed of myself."

Lisette comforted her by reminding her that she'd had a lot to deal with over the past few months. "Give yourself a break, sweetie. I think it's completely understandable. I'll be glad to go with you, though. Where shall we go for lunch?"

They had lunch at the California Pizza Kitchen before going to the Somerset Collection across the road from Somerset Mall. Lisette had the car valet-parked so Angelique wouldn't have to walk too far in her very pregnant condition and the two women went into the mall and found the Tiffany & Co. store.

Lisette sighed in happiness. "I hate to admit it, but I love this store. Everything looks better in a Tiffany box." She laughed.

"I hate to disagree, but this thing is just not me. If it were a classic Tiffany setting in plain yellow gold, maybe, but this looks like he bought it for another woman," she exclaimed.

Lisette had to agree. "But remember, Angel, he didn't know you nearly as well as he does now. You have to give him points for trying, though. It is a magnificent ring, it's just not *your* ring."

Their salesperson was very accommodating and helpful. She had Angelique sitting on a tall stool so she wouldn't put too much strain on her back. When Angelique was comfortable, the woman examined the ring. "We were wondering when you were going to bring this in for sizing, ma'am. It's been exactly one year since it was purchased. Mr. Cochran didn't want to have it engraved until it was properly sized," she said warmly.

Angelique laughed and said there must be a mistake about the date. "My husband didn't buy this ring until February of this year," she explained. "We were married on Valentine's Day and he got them after the wedding. We eloped."

"No, I think you may be mistaken. He purchased this ring in November of last year. He even left the names he wanted engraved on the rings, Aneesah and Donnie. And you're Aneesah, correct?"

"No. No, that's not correct at all," Angelique said faintly. Without another word, she rose from the stool and left the store without looking back.

Warren came home to find a very upset wife waiting for him. "What's the matter, baby? I can see something's upset you, what is it?"

Lisette went into his comforting arms and allowed him to hold her and stroke away some of her concern. "Oh, Warren, this has been the most horrible day!" She explained to him about going to Tiffany's with Angelique to have the ring sized and Angelique's discovery that, despite what he'd told her, Donnie had bought the ring for another woman.

"Warren, if you could have seen her face, it would have broken your heart. She turned around and walked out of the store in a daze; she left her purse, the ring, and me. I had to grab everything and go out to find her—she was just sitting next to a fountain, looking like her heart was broken. Why on earth would he do something like that, Warren? Why did he lie to her about that ring? And how could he pretend to be in love with Angel when he was ready to marry someone else not two months before they got married? What kind of man is he?"

"A stupid one, I'm afraid. He's not a bad man, honey, but he did handle this badly," Warren said sadly. "He never intended to hurt Angelique, and I know for a fact that he truly loves her, but he made a horrible mistake. I knew this was going to blow up in his face one day."

Lisette drew away from her husband as though he were a total stranger. "Are you telling me you knew about this? You knew he was involved with another woman?"

Warren held up his hands in supplication. "Hey, don't shoot the messenger! Come on, honey, let's sit down while I explain this to you." He led Lisette into their living room, which was now fully and beautifully furnished, thanks to his wife. He sat down in the big armchair she had purchased solely with his comfort in mind. Taking her onto his lap, he held her closely and breathed in her fragrance for a few moments. Then he looked around the room and took a deep breath.

"Every time I come home, Lisette, I think about how lucky I am to have you. My life was pretty meaningless before you came into it and I thank God every day that we have each other. You made my house a home and you made my life complete. And believe it or now, Angel did the same thing for Donnie."

Lisette was mellowing until he mentioned the name of the enemy. She pouted and crossed her arms tightly.

"Honey, listen to me. Donnie and Aneesah were college sweethearts. They dated for a few years before she decided to go to California for her graduate studies. When she moved back to Michigan last fall, she and Donnie started dating again and he decided to ask her to marry him. She turned him down flat because she knew he wasn't in love with her. She told him that he was in love with the idea of her and it ticked her off to no end.

"She was right, though, because I will admit that he had this laundry-list approach to matrimony," Warren said.

Lisette looked puzzled and she asked him what he meant. "A laundry list—you know. She has to be this tall, this old, this size, this degree, this, that, the other thing. He was more interested in finding a type of woman than finding the right woman. She told him so, I told him so, his brother told him so and we were all correct. When he connected, I mean *really* connected with Angel, it was perfect. He is really in love with her, Lisette, I mean in love for the first and only time in his life.

"That is so ironic and sad, Warren. When Angelique first started acknowledging that she was interested in Donnie, she said it would never work out, that he would never be interested in her because she wasn't his type. She didn't think she was smart enough or accomplished enough for him and it seems she was right."

"No, no, honey, you're wrong. He really does love her. He adores her, that's for real. Whenever I'm around him it takes him about thirty seconds to start talking about his Angel. He thinks she's the most incredible woman in the world. He talks about her constantly and brags on her to anyone who'll listen. All he does is think about ways to make her happy. He's truly in love, Lisette."

"But Warren, the ring! How could he have deceived her like that?"

Warren shook his head and held up a hand. "When she had that temporary memory loss, she noticed she didn't have a wedding ring and she told him he was making it all up; she was really upset and scared. And genius boy whipped out this ring I told him to return—I told him that more than once," he muttered. "He takes it out and says, 'Don't cry, sweetie, here's your ring.' I told him he would come to rue the day he did that, and, unfortunately, I was once again right."

He held his wife and they kissed a few times, sweet reassuring kisses meant to take away the pain they felt for their friends. "How is Angel doing? It's not good for her to be upset right now. Is she at home by herself?"

A tear-clogged but resigned voice answered him. "No, Warren, I'm here," Angelique said wearily. "And I'm not going back to that house. It's not my home anymore."

Despite Warren and Lisette's protests, Angelique insisted on leaving their home. She had called A.J. from the guest bedroom and he was on his way to pick her up. "I need to be by myself for a while, to decide what to do next. I can't go back to that house. I never want to see him again," she said in a voice so full of pain it was hard for Lisette to hear.

Lisette jumped from Warren's lap and went to her friend. "Oh, Angel, please don't do anything rash. At least talk to him, let him tell his side of the story," she entreated.

Angelique went from sad and listless to coldly furious in seconds. "I already know his side of the story. I was just some kind of play toy for his amusement," she said savagely. "He must have gotten some good laughs out of me, fooling me into thinking he wanted me to be his wife when I was just a last-minute substitute for Miss Perfect, Aneesah Shabazz. He let me go to that museum every week, working with her and thinking she was a friend and all the time she was the woman he wanted! He must have been trying to get back at her for some reason. I don't know why he did it, I don't care why he did it, but I'm through with it," she said fiercely.

Just then the doorbell rang and Lisette went to answer it. She led A.J. into the living room and Angelique fell into his arms. "Take me away from here, A.J., please."

A.J. looked at Warren and Lisette and his confusion was obvious, but so were his feelings for Angelique. "Come on, Angel, let's go. You need to lie down, you shouldn't be upset like this in your condition." He took the coat Lisette handed to him and put it on Angelique. Nodding to Lisette and Warren, he led her out the door to his waiting car.

Warren stood beside Lisette in the doorway and watched them leave. "I don't know if we should have let her go with him. Donnie's not going to like this at all," he mused.

Lisette's eyes flashed and, as always when she was upset, her French accent popped out. "I could not possibly care less what Adonis thinks," she snapped, the word *thinks* coming out as "theenks." "He made his own bed, now he can lie in it!" With a disgusted "Hmmph," she flounced into the bedroom and closed the door.

Warren thought about what his wife had said, factored in his long friendship with Donnie, multiplied it by his feelings for Angelique and calculated the risk, then took out his cell phone and hit SPEED DIAL. "Cochran, we need to talk, brother."

"What's up, Warren? By the way, you haven't seen my wife, have you? She was having lunch with Lisette today and she's not home yet. Her car is here, but she's not. Have you talked to Lisette today?"

"Yes, Donnie, I have. They went to lunch today at Somerset, and then they went shopping. Seems that Angel was tired of walking around with a naked hand and she was feeling guilty because she really didn't like the ring you bought her. So she took it to Tiffany's to have it sized because she was tired of not wearing your ring, and she was ashamed of herself for being so picky. Care to hazard a guess as to what happened next?"

Donnie dropped the phone in his panic and quickly picked it up again. "Oh, man, they didn't tell her when I bought it, did they?"

Warren took no satisfaction in the frantic sound of his friend's voice. "They told her a lot more than that. They told her the names you had planned to have inscribed on it."

"Where is she now, Warren?"

Warren ignored the question. "You should have seen her, Cochran. I've never seen anyone as hurt in my life. It was worse than telling a little child there's no Santa Claus."

"Where is my wife, Warren?"

"She's not here. Lisette brought her here and had her lie down for a while. She called someone to pick her up."

Donnie's relief was apparent. "Oh, great, she called Paris. I'll call over there and go get her. I know she's mad and hurt, but I can explain everything to her," he said, speaking rapidly and with more assurance.

"She didn't call Paris. She called A.J. and he came and got her. She left not too long ago. She says she's never going back to that house again."

Donnie's short-lived relief vanished. A towering rage took its place. "She went where? With who? Man, how could you let her go anywhere with him? Why didn't you keep her with you, Warren?"

"Why didn't you take that stupid ring back when I told you to? Why didn't you tell her the truth? She shouldn't have found out like this, Donnie. I let her leave with A.J. because she's a grown woman, and she knew what she wanted to do. She doesn't need any more stress right now. In her advanced state of pregnancy, she needs to be as tranquil as possible and if being with him makes her happy, so be it. Remember, she's my friend, too, and I care about her." Realizing that he was being rough on Donnie, he added, "I thought you needed to know, that's why I'm calling you. Lisette is going to have my hide when she knows what I did, she's pretty hot with you right now."

"Thanks, I guess," he said, the words rich with unspoken feelings. "Look, I gotta go, Warren, I'll talk to you later."

"Wait a minute! What are you getting ready to do? Don't do anything stupid, Cochran. You need to cool off before you do something you'll regret," Warren cautioned.

"I've already done something I'll regret for the rest of my life: I hurt my wife. Now I'm going to bring her home."

Chapter Twenty-Two

A.J. was trying hard not to let his level of concern show. Angelique really didn't look well. Her normally glowing skin was clammy and pasty and she seemed a bit winded. Her eyes were red and she was obviously struggling to hold back the tears. They were in his loft apartment in Harbortown where he'd brought her after they left Farmington Hills. Normally she liked to sit next to the windows on the long, wide bench he'd made. She could sit and watch the river below for hours; she loved the relaxing effect it had. Now she was curled up in the corner of his long sofa, looking lost. Nefertiti, his cat, seemed to sense her distress and lay by her feet. She was a lap cat only if invited, and she had impeccable manners.

Angelique looked at the cat's pretty, anxious face and patted the cushion next to her. "Come on, baby, come keep me company," she crooned and Nefertiti immediately jumped on the sofa and snuggled up to her. "A.J., she's so beautiful. I want her."

"I'll get you one for Christmas," he promised. "Now, talk to me, baby. Tell me what happened to get you so upset. You shouldn't be getting all worked up like this. It's not good for you and it's definitely not good for the little one."

Tears sprang to her eyes and she swiped them away, but not quickly enough. A.J. pulled a huge leather ottoman in front of her and sat down on it so that he could hold her hands. "Come on, baby, talk to me," he entreated.

Angelique took a long, shuddering breath and began to explain how she and Lisette went to Tiffany's to get the ring sized and what she'd found out. "So there I am, looking like Boo-Boo the fool, thinking that these rings were bought for me when he bought them for another woman. And that woman was that Aneesah Shabazz, of all people. I thought she liked me, I thought she was becoming a friend and here she was laughing at me behind my back all this time. How could he treat me like that, A.J.? Why did he have to lie to me?" She took another long, tearful breath and tried valiantly to stop the tears that were overflowing.

A.J. couldn't take it anymore. He stood up and scooped Angelique and the very surprised Nefertiti into his arms and settled down on the sofa with them. "I know it hurts, baby, but you can't cry like this. You can't let yourself get this upset, sweetheart. You have to think about the baby. I don't know why he did what he did, Angel. Men aren't the brightest creatures in the universe. They make mistakes and lots of them. I'm not going to try to figure it out or justify it—that's up to him. I just want you to be okay. Please stop crying, baby," he pleaded.

Nefertiti added her sentiments by giving a soft "meow" and licking Angelique's hand while she stared at her anxiously. "See, you're getting Nefertiti all upset. She has a very delicate constitution, you know. She's sensitive, just like you."

Angelique surprised herself by laughing. It was a soft and weak laugh, to be sure, but she did stop crying. A sudden pounding on A.J.'s big double doors made both Angelique and the cat jump. A.J. set the two gently to the side and went to see who was beating on his door like a fool.

When he saw the grim face of Donnie through his peephole, A.J. set his jaw decisively. He opened the door at once and stepped outside, closing it behind him. "What do you want, Cochran?"

Donnie was in no mood for fun and games. "I'm here for my wife, Jandrewski, what do you think I want?"

"I'm not sure what you want. You've got a phenomenal woman, a woman far better than anything you deserve, and you treat her like trash. You drag her to the sin pit of the Western world for a sleazy little farce of a marriage, you impregnate her and you don't bother to tell her she's not your first choice for marriage, that she was a drunken mistake. And the lies just kept on coming, didn't they? You let her think you cared about her, that you bought her a wedding ring, but no, that wasn't true, was it? That was something you bought for the other woman, the one who had sense enough to tell you to hit the bricks.

"And best of all, you kept this all to yourself while your innocent wife was *working* with your would-be fiancée. How do you think she's feeling right about now, Cochran? Are you proud of yourself? Happy with what you've accomplished? Because you've just about destroyed her, I want you to know that."

Rage was dripping off A.J. like sweat from a prizefighter. He was pacing back and forth and every so often punctuated a remark by poking Donnie in the chest. Donnie had had enough and grabbed the man's hand. A.J. wasn't quite as tall as Donnie, but he was muscular and had enough adrenalin pumping to do some serious harm. None of that mattered to Donnie, though.

"Look, man, I just want my wife. Where is she? I need to take her home; we need to talk about this. This is none of your damned business anyway. Now get the hell out of my way, I need to see my wife!"

"You don't deserve her, Cochran. You're not fit to wipe her boots. She needs to be loved, Cochran, she needs to be with someone who's going to give her the love and understanding and support she needs," snarled A.J.

Understanding broke over Donnie in a flash. His face lit

up in a feral smile that held no hint of humor whatsoever. "You're in love with her, aren't you? I knew there was something more to this so-called friendship. You want my wife, don't you? Well, I got news for you, pal, she's mine and she's going to stay mine," he said viciously.

"Like hell she is, not when you treat her like garbage." A.J. suddenly stopped talking and grabbed the lapels of Donnie's topcoat with his left hand and landed a right hook with the other. After his initial shock, Donnie immediately retaliated and they were embroiled in a full-out fistfight until Angelique's faint voice from the doorway made them stop.

"A.J., A.J., I'm bleeding . . . help me."

The next few hours were hellish. The only thing Donnie could relate it to was when his beloved only sister had been in the accident that caused the loss of her first child. This was even more agonizing because this was his wife, the person he loved more than anyone else. After rushing her to the hospital, he was forced to wait around with A.J., who had followed them and showed no signs of leaving. The doctor had come out to speak to them once, but the rest of the time had been spent waiting for lab results, waiting for consults, just waiting.

He had to call Warren and Lisette and let them know what was going on, as well as Paris. He was hesitant to call her mother just yet; he wanted to wait until they were sure of her condition. But he did call Renee and Andrew. Andrew surprised him by coming right over to the hospital. He gave Donnie a brief hug and said, "What's the point of being a doctor if I can't use my clout once in a while?" Then he disappeared into the restricted area and left Donnie alone with A.J. once again.

A.J. was the first to speak. "I probably owe you an apology, Cochran, but I don't want to give it to you. I can't sit here and pretend I like you, or act like the way you've treated Angel is okay with me. But for some reason you mean everything to her, and what matters to her, matters to me. She would want me to apologize. I *can* say that I regret my behavior; I'm not a violent person by nature."

Donnie raised his eyebrow and smiled to himself. He'd never heard a more ungracious apology, but he had to respect the man's honesty. "No, you're not violent, except when it comes to my wife," he said dryly. "I shouldn't have goaded you. I always kind of knew how you feel about her. You're not the only one who regrets their behavior."

Adam emerged from the elevators and looked at the two men separated by a distance of two chairs, each with an icepack, one on Donnie's left eye and one on A.J.'s right. Adam shook his head in disgust. "You two are pathetic. How's Angel doing?"

Donnie moved the icepack from his left eye and touched the now-swollen skin. "She's sleeping, they gave her a sedative. I haven't been able to see her yet. How did you find out she was here?"

Before he could answer, the elevator doors opened again and Alan and Andre stepped out, wearing identical expressions of concern. "Renee told us Angel was in the hospital. How is she?" Adam said.

A.J. took the sudden onslaught of Cochrans as a cue to leave. "Tell Angel I'll be in touch. Call me if anything happens," he said as he removed the icepack from his right eye and tossed it in the trash receptacle. Nodding to the men, he got on the elevator.

Impatiently, Alan turned to Donnie. "How is she? What are the doctors saying?"

Donnie repeated what he'd been told. "Andrew is talking to the doctor now. I don't know when they'll let me see her. I'm not going to lie, I'm scared—scared to death. If something happens to her, I have no idea what I'll do. And if something happens to our baby, she just won't be able to handle it. I know she won't. She wants this baby more than anything," he said, his agony evident in every word.

"Not more than she wants you, Donnie," Alan said quietly.

Andre agreed. "We should have said something before, but time just gets away from you. We were pretty salty when you all got married, but even we can tell that you two are really in love."

"Yeah, even the two 'romantically deficient' Cochrans can see the real thing," Alan said wryly.

"Who are you calling romantically deficient?" Andre said indignantly.

"I'm just repeating what your wife told my wife. And my wife agreed and said I was the same way," Alan said glumly. "Anyway, a fool can see that you two belong together. She'll be fine, Donnie, she has to be."

Donnie thanked his brothers for their unexpected support and stood up to begin walking around in circles again. Just then, Angelique's physician came out of the restricted area with Andrew. His words were an immense relief to Donnie.

"Your wife and the baby are doing just fine. She needs to be on bed rest for the next few weeks, right up until she delivers. It looks like she has toxemia, also known as preeclampsia. It's a condition that's marked by high blood pressure, sometimes edema in the legs and ankles, and can lead to seizures. She must be kept quiet and still and I mean no stress whatsoever. None—you understand?" Donnie nodded numbly. "Your wife is young and very healthy, and there's no reason she won't be able to carry this baby successfully but it's going to take a lot of tender loving care to make that happen."

"It's not a problem, doctor. Whatever she needs, I'll see to it that she has it. Can I see her now?"

"For a few minutes, then I'm going to put her into a room. She needs to stay here for a couple of days until she's stabilized."

Donnie approached the bed with his heart in his throat. He was probably the last person on earth she wanted to see, but he had to see her, he had to make sure she was really all right. The bed was propped so that she was in an upright position and her eyes were closed. He brushed a lock of hair away from her face and was gratified when her eyes opened. He was stunned when she held out her hand to him.

"Adonis, I'm scared," she whispered. "I can't lose our baby, I can't. I'm so scared."

Donnie leaned over the side rail of the bed and stroked her face. "Don't be afraid, Angel. God's not going to let you lose our baby. I'm going to take care of you, Angel, don't worry about anything. Nothing, you hear me? I'm here for you, baby." He kissed her forehead and her cheeks, and wiped away her tears with his thumb. "It's going to be fine, my Angel. Just fine."

Chapter Twenty-Three

Angelique was ready to go home. The two days she'd been in the hospital were absolute torture, even though everyone was as kind as could be. She had brief visits from Big Benny and Martha, Lisette and Warren and her sisters-in-law. Renee's visit was especially comforting to her. Renee just hugged her and held her and let her talk. Afterward, she reassured Angelique that everything would be fine.

"The girls remember you in their prayers every night and they can't wait for their Auntie Angel to go home and get better. They're really looking forward to a new cousin. Honey, you have the collective prayers of this entire family and your family, too. And don't forget that my family in Cleveland is praying for you, too. You're going to be fine. And so is your marriage," she predicted. "This is a bump in a very long road, sweetie. You two have what it takes for the long haul, trust me."

Donnie certainly acted the role of devoted husband to the hilt. He was with her in the hospital every possible moment and insisted on spending the nights with her even though the reclining chair in the room was horrifically uncomfortable for him. She was glad he did, though. As much as she didn't want to admit it under the circumstances, she needed him;

she needed his strength and comfort. When she woke up and he was by her side, it made her feel cherished. She deliberately put the ring and all it implied out of her mind—this was too important. The baby was all that mattered, not she or Donnie or the stupid ring. Even the lies he'd told her meant nothing.

The nurse came in and *tsked* at Angelique. "Now, Mrs. Cochran, you know you've got to eat more than that if you want to go home."

Angelique nodded but made no promises. The hospital food made her gag, despite her vow to always eat anything she was given. There might be famine in the world, but right now she couldn't see how the diminished appetite of one pregnant lady could make that much difference. She glanced at the wall clock. Donnie had gone home to shower and change and darned if she wasn't counting the minutes before he got back. She tried to be grumpy about her vigil, but found she lacked the energy. She finally drifted off to sleep. Later, a delightful aroma and the sound of her husband's voice awakened her.

"Hello, baby. Do you think you could handle some stuffed grape leaves from La Shish? And a salmon pie?" There stood Donnie, with a bag from La Shish and a carton of Edy's apple cinnamon sorbet. Her heart just melted.

When she was in the throes of morning sickness, there were very few things that would stay down. Donnie discovered that sorbet was one of those things. One morning he'd brought her a carton of Edy's boysenberry sorbet and held out a spoonful to her. She'd swallowed the icy, slightly tart sorbet and felt better almost at once. It soothed her throat and made her thrashing stomach calm down. In short order she had polished off the entire carton and had no remorse over it. From then on he'd kept the freezer full of Edy's in wonderful flavors: mango, lemon, strawberry, blueberry. A particular favorite was the apple cinnamon, and to see him standing there with it brought back all the love and caring he'd shown her throughout her pregnancy.

He pulled her bedside tray over to her, adjusted it for her comfort and pulled out her La Shish feast. The salmon pie was like a turnover made of flaky pastry and filled with a fresh and very tasty flaked salmon filling. It was one of her favorite things on the menu and he'd remembered it. He'd also brought her a fistful of the little blue mints in La Shish wrappers because he knew she loved them, too. She got a little teary-eyed as he arranged her lunch.

"What's wrong, my Angel? Do you want something else? I'll get you anything you want," he said anxiously.

She sniffed. "Why are you being so nice to me?"

He smiled and leaned over to kiss her. "Because I love you and our baby more than anyone in the world," he whispered. "Come on, sweetie, eat this before your sorbet melts."

The best news of the day came later when her doctor released her to go home. Yes, she had to be on bed rest and she had to be very careful to stay calm and quiet, but she was going home. Donnie went to take care of the paperwork related to her release. He said he'd be back shortly; he wanted to make sure everything was attended to properly regarding her transport home.

While he was gone, she had another visitor. A.J. came in bearing flowers and a very soft stuffed cat that bore a strong resemblance to Nefertiti. She was so glad to see him, she threw out her arms for a hug. "A.J., it's so good to see you! I never got to thank you for the other night when you came to get me. I'm sorry I had to drag you into it. And your eye looks suspiciously like someone else's I know. I'm not going to ask how that happened," she said with dry humor.

A.J. shrugged and said, "A difference of sociopolitical ideologies, nothing more. How are you feeling, Angel?"

"A little nervous, a little scared, very ready to go home. I'm going to do everything in my power to have a healthy baby, A.J. If that means I have to spend the next month in bed, then that's what I'm going to do," she said fervently.

"I have absolute faith in you, Angel. You told me that under no circumstances was I to consider dying and here I am, healthy as a horse. Now I'm claiming good health for you and little Dequindre or Livernois." He grinned. "You're going to be fine, baby. If you need me, I'm only a phone call away, okay?"

"Okay," she agreed and smiled as he took both her hands and kissed her soundly on the forehead.

After A.J. left, the nurse's aide came in to get her dressed. She was almost ready when Donnie came back to the room. In a few minutes he had all her belongings tucked into a tote bag and the nurses had helped her into a wheelchair. She was holding the flowers from A.J. and the little cat. The ride downstairs took only moments and soon she was outside, enjoying the brisk cold wind. It was her first fresh air since the disastrous night when she'd been admitted and she closed her eyes and took deep, cleansing breaths. She opened her eyes to find a huge limousine parked in front of her instead of the Jag she was expecting.

"What's this?"

"This is your ride home, darling. I want you to be comfortable," Donnie told her as he lifted her into the spacious back seat. He got in after her and made sure she wouldn't feel a single bump on the way home.

After a short and very smooth ride, they were home. Donnie opened the door and came back to the limo for her, sweeping her into his arms once again. To her surprise the exterior of the house was completely decorated, right down to the wreath on the door, and all the lights were on, even though it was daylight. It was a very sweet gesture on Donnie's part, so sweet that Angelique buried her face in his shoulder to hide her happy tears.

"Are you crying? Stop that, Angel, it's supposed to make you happy," he said.

"I *am* happy, can't you tell the difference?"

As soon as they were in the house, she looked around for her boys. "Jordan, Pippen! Come here, guys, where are you?" she called.

"Umm, they're at Adam's loft," Donnie said sheepishly.

"I thought they'd get on your nerves or something. You need quiet, Angel."

"Then you'd better get them as soon as possible," she said as he gently deposited her on the bed. "This is their home and they belong here."

Donnie helped her into a comfortable gown and showed her the things he'd done to make the room nicer for her. There was a small flat-screen, plasma television with a DVD player and cable and a bedside table like the one in the hospital. All her flowers, even the ones from A.J. were arranged around the room. A mini stereo system was within her reach along with a pretty cloisonné bell. She smiled when she saw it.

"And what is this for?"

"Anything you need, anytime you need it," he assured her.

"You're going to spoil me," she whispered.

"That's the idea, baby, now why don't you go to sleep for a while?"

And sitting up against the barrage of pillows he'd arranged, she did just that.

Despite being comforted and cosseted at every turn, Angelique had moments of sadness. This was supposed to be her Christmas of joy and nothing was turning out the way she planned. It certainly wasn't for lack of trying on Donnie's part. He did everything he could to make her happy. The evening she came home from the hospital, she awoke to find her boys standing quietly by the bed, their tails wagging and their eyes alight with joy.

"Oh, there you are! How are my fellas doing? Did you miss me? I missed you," she cooed.

They were perfectly behaved, lying down near the dresser so she could see them. She was allowed to walk to the bathroom only, and one of them would accompany her down the hall and wait for her.

Donnie went into the office only three days a week, and

told her he would be off from Thanksgiving through the New Year. When she protested that he was spending too much time away from work, he scoffed.

"Baby, we're in the computer age. I can access anything I need right here. And since you turned that empty bedroom into a nice office, I have the perfect place to work. Besides, I have several assistants to whom I pay very large salaries. If they can't keep the place running, we need to rethink their contracts."

Lillian would not be denied, of course, and she came up to spend a couple of weeks with her daughter. It might have been easier on Donnie if he'd withheld certain information, but he'd learned his lesson about that. He picked Lillian up from the airport, and on the long ride from Romulus, where the airport was located, told Lillian the sad story of the ring and how Angelique had found out that he'd proposed to another woman before they married. Lillian, to her credit, listened to every word carefully.

"My goodness. You really made a mess of things, didn't you, son?" Lillian looked at him thoughtfully. "If I'd heard this story from someone else, or if I'd heard it before my last visit, I have to tell you, I wouldn't be sitting in this car. I'd be at home with my child and I'd probably be interviewing hit men. You can find lots of things on the Internet these days," she said dryly.

"I'm not going to make you feel worse than you do, I'm sure that you've had lots of people more than happy to do that for you. I know that you're aware that you did a rather stupid thing, something that truly hurt the person you love the most. I also know you won't do anything like that again. That's no small thing, you know, to make a horrible mistake and learn from it. The thing is, Donnie, Angelique is a very sensitive person. 'I'm sorry' isn't nearly enough to make this up to her. She needs to feel completely secure in your love for her. I believe that you love her and I believe you are devoted to her happiness. But you've got to make her believe that again and it's not going to be easy. How are you going to regain her trust and make her believe in your love again?"

Donnie was so overcome with gratitude for his mother-in-law's forgiveness, he took her hand and kissed it. "Well, I do have an idea about that, Lillian. Tell me what you think about this." For the rest of the ride home, he explained what he had planned.

Donnie was vigilant about not leaving Angelique alone. When he had to go out, Martha was there to sit with her, or Renee, or Paris or Lisette. Somehow they worked it so that she always had company and someone to make sure all her needs were met. The day Donnie left early to pick up Lillian, Big Benny was "the designated sitter," as Angelique referred to her loving companions. He came into the bedroom while she was looking through pictures. One of her favorite holiday movies, *White Christmas,* was playing on DVD, and she was singing along with one of the tunes as she looked over her work.

They embraced and he made himself comfortable in the big overstuffed armchair. They chatted about this and that, and she started showing him the photos.

"Babydoll, I've never seen anything like the way you take pictures. It's like you reach into a person a pull out a little bit of them in each shot," he said appreciatively.

She showed him some commission work and a lot of family pictures she'd taken just for fun. "Look at this one of Marty and Malcolm. They're growing like weeds, aren't they?"

Benny chuckled as he looked at his grandsons. "And they're pistols, too. When Benita tells me the things they get up to, it's hard to believe," he said.

"Oh, believe it, Daddy. Those two are like a SWAT team. And the bad thing is, they're so darned cute. Nobody wants to believe they're as incorrigible as they are until they do something really wild."

"Must be a twin thing," he said sagely. "Benita and Andrew were hellions, and so were Alan and Andre."

Angelique grinned and said, "Well, these little ladies won't be, they're just too sweet." She handed him a picture of Bennie and Clay's youngest children, the twin girls named Isabella (called Bella), and Katerina (called Kate). "Aren't they beautiful?"

Benny smiled lovingly and agreed that his grandchildren were exceptionally lovely. She handed him more candid shots and looked up to find him staring at a particular picture with a strained expression. "Daddy, what is it?"

The alarm in her voice made him look up slowly. "I'm sorry, Babydoll. I didn't mean to scare you. I wanted to know where you got this picture from." He handed the picture to her and she looked at it anxiously.

"He was over at the house one day and I took it. That's a good friend of Bennie's. His name is John Flores and he's the therapist who helped Bennie after her accident. They've stayed in touch all this time and they see each other every once in a while. He was working at Emory University in Atlanta for a while. Don't you think he favors Adam?"

Benny took his time answering. He took the photo from Angelique's fingers and looked at it for a long time. "Yes, he does favor Adam quite a bit. And I know why he does. Do you want to hear a story? It's not very long, but it's very interesting," he said quietly. "I don't want to upset you or anything—maybe I should wait until later, until you're feeling better."

"Oh, no, you don't! You'd better tell me right this minute. I hate it when somebody starts a story and won't tell it." Angelique looked as curious as a child.

"All right, Babydoll. I'm from a small town in Michigan called Idlewild . . ." he began.

The story took almost an hour to tell, and when he was finished, Angelique's eyes were huge. A lot of questions had been answered, but there were even more raised. Before she could unleash the barrage of inquiries boiling inside her, noise from the front of the house let them know Donnie and Lillian had come home.

Benny smiled at Angelique. "We'll talk later," he said with a conspiratorial wink.

It was wonderful having her mother there, even though it made for close quarters. The baby's room had been completed and the only extra bed in the house was now the convertible sofa in the office. She and Donnie still shared a bed, something she wouldn't have believed possible. Her fear of losing the baby had pushed everything else out of her mind and she needed the comfort and safety of his arms. From the first night she came home from the hospital, they'd shared a bed and she wouldn't have it any other way. Sleeping in her strange upright position was much easier when she was curled into Donnie's strong arms. He would hold her until she went to sleep and, unbeknownst to her, would continue to hold her all night.

Lillian's presence made a festive Thanksgiving possible, although it wasn't the one she'd expected. The plan was for everyone to go to the annual Thanksgiving parade held in Detroit. Some of the men were going to the Detroit Lions game, but for the most part everyone would have dinner at Renee and Andrew's house. That was out of the question for Angelique. It was still fun, though. Lillian made a big, old-fashioned dinner with the traditional turkey, cornbread dressing, squash, green beans, spinach salad, and cranberry-orange relish. There was also a ham and sweet potatoes, plus homemade rolls and cornbread muffins. And there was company, too. Paris was there all day helping her aunt Lillian prepare the feast. Everyone stopped by on their way to the parade, so she got to have little visits with her in-laws.

Donnie had bought her a small chaise longue that was cleverly made like a long armchair. It was incredibly comfortable to sit on; Angelique's back was supported and her legs were able to stretch out in front of her. After her confinement, it was going into the baby's room.

When Renee showed up with her four little girls, they

stood on either side of the chaise and rubbed Angelique's tummy, talking to their new cousin. Alan's wife, Tina, brought her family, which included her daughter Lillian. Lillian had insisted that Clay's mother was her grandma from the first time they met. She'd been calling her "Grandma" since she was three years old and nothing had changed. She and the older woman had a special relationship, partially because they shared the same name, and they were delighted to see each other.

Martha and Big Benny stayed for dinner and there was a stream of company all day, including Lisette and Warren. Lisette had softened in her attitude toward Donnie, at least to the point of being cordial if not effusive. Adam and Alicia Fuentes also stopped by for a brief visit. It was a warm and homey day, even though it wasn't what she'd expected for her first Thanksgiving as a married woman. But she was grateful for the day she'd had. It was wonderful—the baby was well and her husband rarely left her side. It was a day to give thanks, indeed.

The next day was a little different. Donnie helped her into a nice bubble bath and he even bathed her. He was supposed to just wash her back, as usual, but ended up doing most of the bathing. He wrapped her up in warm towels and took her back to the bedroom, where there was a nice new maternity outfit on the bed, nice black knit pants and a cheerful red top with a Christmas design.

"How cute! What's the occasion?" she asked.

"Nothing in particular. Your mom just thought you might like something festive to wear," he told her.

She got lotioned and scented with Cashmere Mist and put on her new outfit, which also included some cute little black velvet flats with Christmas trees on the toes. She was smiling at the shoes when Donnie came back to take her to the living room.

"Donnie, look at these! My mother is so thoughtful," she said happily.

"Yes, she is," Donnie agreed. "Now come with me, my Angel." He picked her up and carried her into the living room, where she was stunned by what she saw. There were all her friends, all her favorite people, trimming a huge tree that scented the house with its lovely pine fragrance. Lisette and Warren, Paris, all of Donnie's nieces and nephews, and, best of all, Matt and Nicole, too, as well as her dearly loved stepfather, Bump. Neesha, who did party planning and weddings as a sideline, was busily directing everyone, and the room was taking on a festive air that was intoxicating. Even Danny was there, tacking greenery across the fireplace.

There was a table set up with piles of presents wrapped in baby paper on it. On cue, instead of screaming "Surprise," Prescott and Drew, Donnie's nephews, unrolled a banner that read *Welcome to Your Baby Shower.*

Angelique was totally blown away. The effort that had gone into this, the love and the ingenuity it had taken made her teary-eyed. She was amazed that so many people cared about her. It wasn't a loud or boisterous celebration, given her need to stay tranquil, but it was a lot of fun just the same. Her Deveraux sisters-in-law had come through handsomely, sending expensive and beautifully wrapped presents, which Bump brought with him on the plane. She got so many beautiful and thoughtful gifts, including really practical things like cases of diapers and baby wipes, she couldn't contain her emotion.

She was trying to thank everyone and stem the tide of happy tears. "This is the most thoughtful thing I've ever heard of," she sobbed happily. "You are the most loving people in the whole world."

Danny informed her that it was all her husband's doing. "He's the one who dragged us all out of our beds at the crack of dawn. I'm still trying to digest yesterday's dinner," he said with a smile. "Donnie is just extremely persuasive."

At that point Donnie got everyone's attention. "I have something I'd like to say to my wife, and I want you all to be witnesses," he said. "I did something truly stupid not too long ago. Actually, 'stupid' isn't the best word—criminally ignorant and cruel is more like it. I've been trying to think of a way to make it up to her, since she was kind enough to allow me a chance to stay in her life."

Angelique wanted to be embarrassed, but she couldn't—Donnie was looking at her with such love and tenderness, she couldn't look away from him, couldn't feel any shame.

"I want you all to know that I'm a very, very fortunate man. I have the privilege of being married to the most incredible woman in the world. She's beautiful, she's brilliant and talented and she's funny, compassionate and kind. She is the most fascinating woman I've ever known, and she can do anything. Anything she decides to do, she does and she does it in a way that's totally unique, totally her. She's tough, she's resilient and she doesn't take any mess, so don't ever try to put one over on her, she'll see right through it," he said with a wry smile.

"She makes every day a delight, and I won't live long enough to have a boring day with her. Every moment I get to spend with her is a treasure beyond price. That's why I want to marry her all over again on our anniversary. Next Valentine's Day, I want her to be my bride all over again, but this time I want her to wear *this* ring, the ring that my father put on my mother's hand when he took her in marriage. Will you do that for me, my Angel? Will you do me the honor of becoming my wife once more?"

He knelt beside the chaise and opened the box. Angelique's eyes lit up: this was just what she had in mind for a ring. It was yellow gold and there was a nice round one-karat diamond in a simple Tiffany setting with smaller stones on the matching band. It was simple and old-fashioned and just beautiful. She wanted to reach for the small box, but something stopped her.

Donnie knew true panic as he looked at her face. "Angel, won't you accept this from me?" he asked again.

Angelique finally spoke. "No."

Everyone gasped, which made her wave her hand impatiently. "Oh, no, of course I mean yes, yes, of course yes, just not right this second, if you don't mind. We have something to do right now, honey. My water just broke."

Chapter Twenty-Four

"Come on, baby," Donnie said encouragingly. "We're almost there, Angel. You're doing so well, sweetheart, you can do this."

He was at the head of the narrow delivery-room bed, holding both of Angelique's hands. It had been a long and difficult labor, and he was trying not to let his anxiety show. Angelique wanted to have a natural childbirth, but he was ready to tell them to do a cesarean—whatever it took to have it over with.

Her hair was covered in one of those horrid paper caps and she was bathed in sweat, her face red from exertion— but to Donnie she'd never looked lovelier. He kissed her temple and put his forehead against hers. "You can do this, my Angel. Just one more push, baby, one more."

Suddenly her face contorted into a mask of determination and a shout was heard from the doctor. "Beautiful! Here she is . . . oh, Mom and Dad, you have a beautiful little girl!"

Lusty cries filled the delivery room and a huge sigh of relief issued from Angelique. Donnie's eyes flooded with tears and he kissed Angelique's forehead and cheeks, thanking her over and over again.

"Dad, would you like to cut the cord?"

That task completed, the baby was whisked away for a moment to make sure her breathing passages were clear and to quickly weigh her and wipe some of the mucus from her tiny face. Then she was placed into Angelique's trembling arms.

"Adonis, look! Look at her, isn't she wonderful? Isn't she the most beautiful baby you've ever seen? Hello, sweetheart. I'm your mommy," she crooned. The baby opened her eyes and stared into Angelique's face for a long moment. "That's right, darling. I'm your mommy. I'm going to take good care of you, sweetie. And this is your daddy. Oh, Adonis, isn't she amazing?"

Donnie could barely speak through his tears of sheer gratitude and love. "She's perfect, Angel. Just perfect. Thank you, baby, thank you so, so much."

The delivery-room staff allowed Angelique a few more moments to bond with her daughter, who continued to look into her mother's face. Then they had to take her away to make her pretty for her public. They also had to get Angelique into recovery and then to her room.

"Daddy, you can go to the waiting room now and make the big announcement. She'll be in her room in about an hour," a nurse said.

Donnie could hardly stand to let Angelique out of his sight, but he kissed her forehead and her hands and said he would see her soon. "I love you, my Angel. You made me so happy, I can't express it. I love you."

He left the birthing area and stripped off the paper gown, the hat and the shoe covers and threw them away. He was still shaking and all he had to do was watch. It was incredible what women had to go through to give birth. He was awed, humbled and very, very grateful that she had trusted him and loved him enough to give him a child. He leaned back against the cool, hard wall and said several prayers of thanksgiving. Finally he went through the automatic doors to the waiting area, where their family was anxiously awaiting word of the delivery.

"She's here. Our baby is a beautiful, absolutely adorable little girl. She's fine and her mommy is the most wonderful woman in the world," Donnie said proudly. His father was there, and Martha, Lillian and Bump, Lisette and Warren, Paris, Renee and Andrew; almost everyone who loved Angelique was there. Donnie was overwhelmed with love and support. He could feel the tears running down his cheeks but he didn't care. He was so grateful, so thrilled and so very thankful, he couldn't have cared less that he was crying in front of everyone. After hugs and kisses and congratulations all around, he made an announcement.

"The baby will be in the nursery soon for everyone who wants to see the prettiest little girl in the world. In the meantime, I'm going to go see her mother and tell her again how much I love her."

Angelique was sitting up in bed, looking tired but radiant. As exhausting as her labor had been, nothing could compare to at last being a real mother. The nurse handed the baby to Donnie, who stared down at the little girl who'd already won his heart. Angelique held out her arms and Donnie placed the baby into them. "Here she is, my Angel. I know I'm a little biased here, but this is the most beautiful child I've ever seen in my life. Look at her, Angel, look at what we made."

Angelique sighed with joy as she looked at their baby. "Adonis, she really is pretty, isn't she? It's not just because we love her so much, she's really adorable," she said in awe. And they had indeed produced a captivating little girl with a headful of silky black hair and long eyelashes. When she made little faces, a tiny set of dimples could be seen, as well as the prettiest little rosebud mouth. It was time for her first feeding and Angelique eagerly prepared to breast-feed her. With the nurse's assistance, the baby was soon sucking away contentedly and Angelique was the picture of maternal bliss.

Her hair was caught up in a ponytail, she wore not a speck of makeup or a hint of jewelry, yet his wife was incandescent in her beauty. "Adonis, get that little camera out of my bag," Angelique instructed. We have to have a picture of this." She never took her eyes off the baby as she spoke. In a few minutes, when the baby had taken her fill, she was about to fall asleep when Angelique deftly placed her on her shoulder and stroked her tiny back until a nice burp was heard.

"My goodness, you're a clever girl, aren't you?" Angelique praised her. She was reluctant to relinquish the baby to the nurse, but she did.

"We have to put this little beauty in the nursery so your family can see her. And you need some sleep, Mommy— having a baby is no small thing," the nurse said with a smile. "I should know, I have four of them."

Angelique smiled tiredly at her husband. "You need to go home and get some sleep, too, sweetheart. This was a big day for both of us," she said sleepily.

"I know, but I don't want to leave you," he admitted. "I want to stay here with you. I never want to leave you again." He nuzzled her neck.

Suddenly she paled and her face became covered in a fine sheen of perspiration. "Adonis . . . I don't feel so well."

It was like a scene from a medical-emergency show on television. Donnie rang for the nurse. When the charge nurse saw Angelique's pallor and labored breathing, she quickly flipped back the blanket and sheet that covered Angelique and revealed a pool of blood on the pad underneath her. She pulled the emergency cord that would place a STAT page.

"Mr. Cochran, I need to ask you to leave, we've got to get your wife back into surgery," she said urgently.

He had no time to react as the highly skilled personnel rushed Angelique from the room. He followed the cart out the door and was again rebuffed by a capable nurse.

"Mr. Cochran, it will be fine. They're trained to give your wife the best possible care and they'll have her fixed up and in recovery in no time. Have faith, Mr. Cochran, it will be fine."

Donnie collapsed in the only chair in the room and leaned

forward with his hands covering his face. Adam entered the room to find him that way.

"Donnie, what happened? Where's Angelique?"

"She's back in surgery. She started bleeding and they had to take her back in. Adam, if she doesn't make it, I don't know what I'll do. This is wrong, Adam, it's just wrong. She wanted our baby so much and she worked so hard, this can't be happening, it can't be."

Adam grasped his brother's shoulder and told him not to worry. "It's going to be fine, Donnie, she's young and healthy, she's got to be fine. Come on, let's find the family, they're down at the nursery drooling over my niece. Let's go, Donnie," he urged, "you need to be with family right now."

In a relatively short time, Donnie was in the surgical waiting area surrounded by his family. They had all prayed together and were just waiting to hear about Angelique's condition. Finally, the doctor came to speak to Donnie. He took him into a private area to give him the news.

"You wife is going to be just fine, Mr. Cochran. We were able to stop the bleeding, which was a result of the toxemia. She will be able to have more children, too—I don't want you to think this means she'll be barren, or that's she's too delicate for more babies. She'll probably be better off with cesareans from now on, but we can talk about that at length once she's fully recovered. In the meantime, you look like you could use a hot shower and a shave. Why don't you go home for a while, she'll be in recovery for another hour or so before she comes back to her room," he said. "Besides, I don't think you need to worry about her being alone—you have the most devoted family I've ever seen and I've been doing this for a long time. I'll be in to see her later today."

Donnie shook the doctor's hand and returned gratefully to the family. "She's going to be fine," he said with a shaky smile, "just fine."

* * *

Lisette entered the bedroom, looking fantastic as she always did to her husband. She was wearing a red, silk, charmeuse chemise and a matching robe and she was carrying a carafe of wine and one wineglass. Humming softly, she set the carafe and the glass on the round table on her side of the bed and smiled at Warren as she removed the robe and laid it neatly across her vanity chair. He returned the smile, although he questioned the single glass.

"Don't I get any? Or are you going to make me drink out of the bottle?" he asked.

She didn't answer him at first, she merely sat on the edge of the bed and removed her little red backless slippers. Then she slid under the covers and nestled closed to his side. "We're going to share a glass, darling. That's much more romantic, don't you think? So much has gone on lately, I think we need to relax and be grateful for all our good fortune. Angel has had her beautiful baby and she and Donnie have straightened out all their difficulties. And we have each other, which is to me the most wonderful thing in the world."

"I think you're right, honey." He reached for her and for a few moments there was nothing but the sounds two passionate lovers make when kissing.

Lisette sighed with satisfaction as she stroked Warren's big, broad chest, covered with silky black hair. "You are so sexy it drives me mad," she whispered. "I think about you all day. When we're together like this it makes me so very happy, my love. I'm so glad you're mine."

"When you talk like that it drives me crazy, Lisette," he growled as he deftly removed the slinky gown from her pliant body. "You can get anything you want from me, you know that, don't you?"

She purred with satisfaction as she turned in his arms to straddle his powerful thighs. "Anything I want? That's good to know, darling, because there is something I want. I'll tell you what I want next Christmas, Warren. I want to give *you* something precious, because I love you. I want to have your baby, a strong sturdy little boy with your beautiful smile, your strength and your spirit. May I have that gift?"

Just before he consumed her with passion, Warren managed to say, "If that's what you want, honey, that's what I want to give you. I love you, Lisette."

Like everything else that involved Donnie and Angelique, the baby's homecoming was unique. Donnie had procured another limousine to bring the two most important people in his life home without incident. He carried them into the house as though they were made of the finest crystal. While Lillian held her newest grandchild, Donnie got Angelique settled on her chaise. Angelique smiled at her handsome, devoted husband and stroked his cheek.

"You've got to stop doing this, Adonis. I can walk, you know, and I'm not on any kind of restriction. I just have to take it easy for a couple of days and then I'm good to go," she said fondly.

Donnie took her hand in his and kissed her fingers while he looked deeply into her eyes. "Just so you understand, I'm going to be taking care of you and Lily Rose for the rest of my life, so get used to it. I'm not going to smother you, but you have to allow me to indulge you. You must grant me this, my Angel."

Lillian still couldn't get over the thrill of holding her daughter's child. When Donnie and Angelique had finally revealed the baby's name, there were tears from both sides of the family. They named her Lillian Rose Bennett Cochran, after both their mothers. Angelique's mother and Donnie's late mother shared the same first name, and Bennett was Lillian Cochran's maiden name. They called her Lily Rose, and it was a perfectly appropriate name, for she was a true beauty.

"I think it's time for this little one to eat," Lillian said gaily as she brought the baby to Angelique.

Angelique quickly prepared to nurse her and took her in the crook of her arm. She smiled down at her innocent bundle of joy and reveled in the sharp tug that always preceded a good feeding. She had no idea that anything could be as fulfilling as breast-feeding, and she made a mental note to let Lisette, Paris, and Nicole know it was the only way to go.

"While you're feeding the baby, I'm going to get you some lunch, dear," Lillian said as she left the room.

Donnie built a fire and made sure it was drawing properly before coming to join his wife and daughter. There was a big ottoman nearby and he sat down on it, smiling as he listened to the song his wife was singing to Lily Rose. With all the decorations lit and the scent of the pine filling the house, the fire crackling and a light snow falling, she was softly singing, "Have Yourself a Merry Little Christmas" to her newborn daughter. Angelique reached out for Donnie and smiled when he leaned over and kissed her. She stroked the side of his face and suddenly grabbed his earlobe.

"Just remember, darling, if you ever tell me another lie, I won't be responsible for what happens. If you think I was mean when I was Evilene, just try telling me another whopper like the ring story."

Donnie laughed at the determination on her face. They had discussed the disastrous ring fiasco and Donnie had apologized profusely and sincerely. He'd also returned the ring and purchased an astounding peridot necklace and earrings for Angelique, as well as a pearl starter necklace for Lily Rose.

He gently removed her hand from his ear and kissed her fingers. "I'll never tell you anything that isn't true again, my Angel. You mean far too much to me. And besides that, I'm too afraid of you to try it."

It was Angelique's turn to laugh fondly at her husband. She held up her left hand and admired her ring again. "Adonis, this has been a very big year. This time last year I couldn't remember why Christmas was so wonderful. I felt all alone, unhappy, just lost. Now I have my beautiful baby, my beautiful husband, and I remember why Christmas is the season of miracles. I've had more than my share of miracles this year, and more happiness than I deserve. I love you so much, Adonis, it's going to take a lifetime to show you."

They leaned toward each other for a gentle, tender kiss.

"I love you, my Angel. You're my miracle, you and Lily Rose. And this is a lifetime I look forward to sharing with you. Thank you for loving me, baby."

"The pleasure is all mine, for always."

Epilogue

The house was filled with the sounds and smells of the holiday. Christmas carols were drifting from the stereo, the game room was filled with assorted Cochran nieces and nephews, Jordan and Pippen were snoozing in front of the fire and there were friends and family all around. Angelique had never felt so content in her life. Everyone had come to have brunch with the new family, and, despite her mother's protest, she had felt energetic enough to help with the preparations.

"But, Mama, I have to start doing more and moving around more or I'll never have my energy back," Angelique pointed out. "You can't be up here forever. I've got to get back on my feet completely."

"Just don't rush it, Angelique. There's no hurry—you're not in a race, you know."

"I know, Mama, but I'm going to tell you a secret: I want to start working on our Christmas present. I still can't believe it, you know."

In an act that continued to stun both her and Donnie, Big Benny had given them his gift over their Christmas Eve dinner. He presented them with the deed to the house in Palmer

Park and announced that he and Martha were moving into a condo.

"Are you kidding, Daddy?" had been Angelique's response to the gift.

Benny's eyes had twinkled at her and he assured her that he was not. "We want to scale down our lifestyle and we want to keep the house in the family. And this house is getting a little crowded for you."

They had reiterated this idea when they came over after church for Christmas brunch.

"We just don't want the upkeep of a big house anymore. This will be so much better for the both of us; we'll be able to travel more and just relax without having to maintain that gigantic place," Martha told her.

"You children need a bigger place and I never wanted that house to leave the family. It's yours with my blessing," Benny said as he cuddled Lily Rose. "This is a magnificent baby. She gets prettier every time I see her." She rewarded him with a tiny grimace that could have been a smile—or a little gas.

After Angelique was finally shooed out of the kitchen permanently, she went to shower and change into something festive in which to greet their guests. Donnie was on the bed, lying on his back with his arms crossed behind his head.

She smiled. "There you are. I've been missing you," she whispered as she cuddled up next to him.

"I can't have that, my darling. How are you feeling?"

"Perfect. Absolutely perfect. How are you feeling?"

Donnie sat up and braced himself against the headboard, bringing Angelique with him so that his body supported her. "I'm feeling very humble, Angel. I'm feeling grateful for my wife, my baby, my family and my friends. And I'm thinking about A.J., too," he admitted.

Angelique understood completely. A.J. had come over early on Christmas Eve to visit Angelique and bring her and the baby presents. The best gift of all was the portrait he'd taken of Donnie, Angelique, and Lily Rose. A week or so be-

fore Christmas he'd brought over a professional backdrop
for their session. They dressed in off-white so that at last
Lillian would have her complete set of family pictures. A.J.
had had a difficult time posing them, as Donnie kept looking
at Angelique instead of the camera. But he promised them
they would have something beautiful and memorable and
that's just what he gave them. The baby was wide awake, her
big eyes staring curiously into the lens. Angelique was leaning against Donnie with her eyes slightly closed and Donnie
was kissing her temple, oblivious to any onlookers. They
looked serenely and supremely happy and in love.

A.J. had given the portrait to Angelique and watched in
satisfaction as her cheeks flushed pink and her eyes flooded
with tears.

"All I ever wanted was for you to be happy, Angel. I think
I got my wish. You're an exceptional woman, one of a kind.
And that's a remarkable baby you made, she's just what I
would have expected of you. Be happy always, Angel." He'd
kissed her on the forehead and left shortly afterward.

Angelique was still in awe of his generous gift. "That was
a wonderful thing he did for us, wasn't it? A.J. has meant so
much to me, I'm glad you two have started to get along. He's
my best friend, Adonis, I'd hate to lose him."

"You never will on my account, Angel. He's a good man.
We'll be friends one day, I'm sure," he promised.

They were quiet for a few minutes, enjoying their closeness. Angelique finally broke into their reverie with a confession. "I have to tell you something. I've been mousing
around for the past few days and it suddenly dawned on me
that your dad wanted me to tell you this, or he wouldn't have
told me. He knows I'm not going to keep any secrets from
you."

Donnie raised an eyebrow and grinned. "That sounds like
Pop all right. So what is it you have to tell me?"

Angelique related the story Big Benny had told her on the
day he'd sat with her. When she finished, Donnie looked as
dazed as she had.

"So what are we supposed to do now?" she asked.

"I don't think we have a choice, Angel. But we're not doing anything until after the wedding. Once we get back from our honeymoon, we'll start on it then." He looked at her with great love and tenderness.

"Until then," he smiled and picked up the remote for the CD player, "let's just have a merry Christmas, my Angel."

With a flick of his thumb, the room was filled with the sound of her most beloved songs and she relaxed in the arms of her most beloved husband. "Merry Christmas to you, too, Adonis. This is just the beginning of a lifetime of them, you know."

His eyes filled with love for her as he agreed. "A lifetime of love."

To my readers

I continue to be overwhelmed by the loyal support from my readers. Your kind letters and cards mean so much, especially this past winter when I was recovering from surgery. Your thoughtful comments and insights make me feel that my work has made a difference to you. I am touched and humbled by your response to my writing.

I hope everyone experiences a renewal of faith and hope this holiday season the way Angelique did. She was a wonderful character to write, rich and complex. A lot of you have been asking what was going to become of the headstrong young woman. I hope you're pleased with how she turned out.

Thank you again for your readership and your support of my efforts. I look forward to sharing more stories of love with you.

Please check out my web site: www.melanieschuster.com.

Stay blessed!

Melanie
I Chronicles 4:10
MelanieAuthor@aol.com
P.O. Box 5176
Saginaw, Michigan 48603

About the Author

Melanie Woods Schuster currently lives in Saginaw, Michigan, where she works in sales for the largest telecommunications company in the state. She attended Ohio University. Her occupations indicate her interests in life; Melanie has worked as a costume designer, a makeup artist, an admissions counselor at a private college and has worked in marketing. She also is an artist, a calligrapher, and she makes jewelry and designs clothing. Writing has always been her true passion, however, and she looks forward to creating more compelling stories of love and passion in the years to come.

BOOK YOUR PLACE ON OUR WEBSITE AND MAKE THE ARABESQUE ROMANCE CONNECTION!

We've created a customized website just for our very special Arabesque readers, where you can get the inside scoop on everything that's going on with Arabesque romance novels.

When you come online, you'll have the exciting opportunity to:

- View covers of upcoming books

- Learn about our future publishing schedule (listed by publication month and author)

- Find out when your favorite authors will be visiting a city near you

- Search for and order backlist books

- Check out author bios and background information

- Send e-mail to your favorite authors

- Join us in weekly chats with authors, readers and other guests

- Get writing guidelines

- AND MUCH MORE!

Visit our website at
http://www.arabesquebooks.com